REVIEWS

This is the most engaging Science Fiction I have read for a long time. The heros overcome threat after threat and just when you think they can relax and put their feet up, there is a bigger problem to solve!   TJ

Amazing story, excitement from beginning to end. Enjoyed reading it. I recommend it.   H.P

This book really had me all the way through to the end. Likeable and realistic characters - good and hate-able bad guys.   D.R.

I thought this book was pretty action packed. Hilarious situations mixed in with desperate ones. Had you either laughing or worried about what would happen next. I'd recommend reading it.   L.G.

I read this one before the first book. Loved the story and pace, so I had to read Ruby Lake. No boring moments. Funny stuff in this book. Had me laughing - when I wasn't on the edge of my seat.   B.B.

Thought the book was a hard-core Sci-Fi story. Really enjoyed it. It was true Science Fiction with plot twists and much adventure. Funny thing, it even had romance in it. Can't wait for the next book.   L.B.

I want a dog like Bo! She was one of my favorite characters. Great story. Kept me interested all the way through. I would recommend this book to any Sci-Fi fans or anyone who just wants a good, entertaining story. R.M.

RUBY RIDGE

By
Ron Howson

For the paranoid: this is a work of fiction. Names, characters, businesses,
places, events and incidents are either the products of the author's
imagination or used in a fictitious manner. Any resemblance to actual
persons, living or dead, real or imagined, or actual events or locales is
purely coincidental, but we know who you are.

Cover design and editing:
Thomas J. Mason
thomasjmason@att.net

ISBN: 978-0-9909371-3-5

TABLE OF CONTENTS

Chapter One

They arrived as they thought they would, with one major exception: they arrived in the midst of a blazing battle. The Quantum tunneling was instant. No sooner had Jason pulled the trigger, sending a 30.06 round hurtling toward Dr. Bradley's head, and the bay door of the commandeered Invader transporter had closed back on Earth, than they arrived at the Invaders' Home Planet.

Jason and his army were met by the Armada, promised them back on Earth, engaging the Invader defenses – three defense satellites in high orbit over the planet. The ships were from the coalition of races facing extinction at the hands of these monsters. It was just sooner than Jason had expected. While the Armada was already engaging the planetary defenses, space stations, satellites, moon bases, Jason and his forces arrived.

The Invaders stuck to their formula on any invasion. They would come in and bombard the planet, take out all major cities on their first pass, then the secondary cities on the next, and then the outlying populations. The ineffective space-based defenses, satellites, air defense, and any other minor annoyances like ships would be destroyed before they launched their shuttles and landed on the planet surface.

It was their formula, one that was unchanged in every video of every invasion watched back on Earth of civilization after civilization being demolished, race after race being exterminated, and world after world being conquered. Back in the War Room on Earth, it was decided that this would be the most likely formula of attack the Invaders would be prepared to stop, which is why the strategy for saving the Human race would be different.

There is another thing that would make it different. The humans knew a secret. It was possibly the singularly most guarded secret in the known universe; the universe known by man as well as every other race engaged in battle today and every other race that fell into extinction at the hands of the Invaders. It was the secret of their power source that Jason Brand had solved that had brought the Invaders' ship they were using back to life after over a century of floating dead in space.

It was the secret that no other race had been able to discover. They would use that secret today in the hope that by the time the Invaders had found out that their secret was out, it would be too late. A secret is only good when it is a secret. A secret is a liability if you think it is still a secret when it is not. It can be exploited and used against you.

That is what Admiral Harding was going to do today in this battle. He would exploit that, and when the Invaders had discovered that their secret was no more, it would hopefully be too late. Jason had done the unthinkable, the unimaginable, and the inconceivable: he found the secret.

There is nothing like a space battle. That was the discussion before they left; that you cannot compare it to any other kind of battle, but the closest thing to it would be a naval battle. Back on Earth in the War Room, that was the reasoning behind appointing Admiral Harding to head the counterattack on the Invaders.

The strategies considered were all good and were all sound, but his view on it made the most sense and had the most likelihood of success. Treat the low orbit as the surface of the ocean. Everything above it would be treated like enemy aircraft while everything below would be like submarines and mines. Everything on the same plane would be another ship. He had a good tactic for handling the immediate defenses, and a good strategy to carry out the overall occupation.

The one thing that was imperative, the one thing the success of it would all depend on, was finding and disabling the Quantum Relays and Quantum Capacitors that powered the Invaders' weapons before they launched more transports and before others were recalled from different planets. Every minute spent with those functioning would mean millions of people dying on Earth as the cities were bombarded.

What the Humans had on their side was surprise; their own secret. Before the Invaders realized the secret, they had to find and disable the Invaders' power source. It wouldn't be hard to find. In fact, it would be simple to find. It would be the most fortified and protected item on their planet.

But first, while the Invaders still thought the commandeered transport was theirs, and while they still thought it would be filled with their own, come to the rescue of their Home Planet under attack, the Humans in their captured ship had to disable the Invaders' defenses. In a blink, they appeared in the midst of flying space debris and ships shattered by the Invader weapons and defenses.

The attack was concentrated now on a station above the low orbit where the commandeered transport had arrived. Back on Earth, Jason had just stepped into the landing bay as the ship vanished from sight. Eric had just pulled the shuttle through the doors and he had come out with Jason's dog, Bo, and a handful of runners.

They arrived before Jason even took his first step toward the bridge, when he heard Admiral Harding issuing orders over his head set. "Evasive maneuvers," Harding called out, and the sixteen-mile-long transport started dodging the dead ships. "Get me a view of that station," he commanded.

The transport, just one of which had sent entire races to their death, was now theirs. Normally powered by the Invaders' sun, Jason had unlocked the secret of its power. He had devised a way to power it with Earths' own sun, and placed his own Quantum Relay back on Earth to send power timelessly across space.

"I want to see that landing bay," the Admiral began issuing orders, loading more shuttles, and preparing for a desperate battle for the survival of mankind.

Jason instantly knew what he was talking about. They had seen them back in Earths' library. They watched failed attack after failed attack against them. They were deadly and merciless. He also knew that if the Humans attacked it with the transport, the invaders would know their secret; they would know they had come.

There was a loaded shuttle waiting for him to jump into that would take them to the station. They would enter that station with marines, fighting their way to the control room, and they would disable the Quantum Capacitor and leave it dead.

But there was a problem. The Armada was not supposed to be here. It was too soon; too fast; too early, and the only ones who knew that it was the Humans in this transport right now, were the Humans. The Armada may not harm the transport, and the Armada may not be able to destroy the station, but it would obliterate a single shuttle.

"Dr. Hilliard!" Jason yelled, as he was rushing to the shuttle, "Can you get hold of that Ambassador and tell them there is a single shuttle heading toward the station? Tell them not to fire at it," and without waiting for an answer, he boarded the shuttle and jumped to the helm.

Eric stood next to him as he brought it out of the bay and headed toward the space station. "You guys back there, grab some of those invader weapons; I think we'll be needing them," and headed it directly toward what looked to be a landing area, adding. "And get your air on."

It took only a second or two before they came under fire and Jason had to dodge the craft around a piece of broken ship to block the shots. There were six members of the armada now engaging the station - the only six that were left. He could get behind the ship with the broken hull and block three of them from view as he approached, but the other three would still have direct line of sight and fire.

That being his best bet for survival, he sped toward it, dodging fire as he went. As he got closer, he was blocked from the view of all six ships. There were still survivors in the dead ship. He was close enough now that he could see them through the portals. He got up closer. "They look almost human," he said, "and I don't think the Armada will fire on survivors."

The back of the ship was nearly torn apart from the rest and he could see bodies floating dead around the opening. He pulled in as close as he could and maneuvered the shuttle between the two pieces where there was a corridor with a sealed off entry leading to the bridge. He maneuvered his shuttle to it and opened the back with a warning to his crew.

"Alright," Dr. Hilliard came through the headset. "I was able to get through to the Ambassador and everyone's been notified to steer clear of you. You're good to go, Jason."

"Go and get those people off this ship. It's going to break apart and burn up in the atmosphere," Jason called to the Marines in the back.

Six of them jumped up and banged their guns against the door leading to the bridge. It opened and several of the inhabitants came out with weapons drawn, ready to fight off an Invader boarding party. The Marines just pointed to the back of the shuttle and they all started piling in on top of everybody else.

When they were packed in like sardines, Jason pulled the shuttle around and gave the dead ship a shove toward the station and then pulled the shuttle back. As the derelict approached the station, he would be obscured from the station until it would fire on the approaching hulk to keep it from colliding. That is when he would pull around and enter the station, hidden amongst the chunks of alien craft.

It worked as planned and he dodged the flying debris once more and entered the landing bay on the station. There was only one other shuttle in the bay, and seeing Invader guards at the airlock, he turned the shuttle sideways and landed to the far side of it, hiding the shuttle doors and allowing the Marines to disembark undetected. "You guys get ready," he ordered, "I'm about to drop the door. On one! Three. Two," and the door was dropped.

The Marines took up position inside the landing bay, preparing to charge forward once they took out the guards. It was all about stealth now and killing them before they knew they had been boarded and before an alert could be sent.

The two guards, after watching the shuttle land, became curious as they waited for their comrades to come out and started to approach the craft. The marines crept in between the two shuttles and waited. As the guards made it past their shuttle and headed to Jason's, they moved forward and dropped them, quickly and silently.

Next, they set charges and blasted the airlock, sending Invaders flying out to the vacuum of space, their lungs pulled through their throats and into their mouths and their eyes dangling out of their heads from the instant vacuum.

Jason was up and charging toward the entrance, the Marines, Gizmo, and Eric right behind him. Their mission: Shut down communications to the surface, get that Quantum Capacitor, and shut down the station. The new arrivals rescued from the destroyed ship ran up behind the Marines to join the battle.

Straight away, they were held at the entrance by small arms fire. Small arms fire from the Invaders that is, which was not small at all. Jason looked around, every minute meaning another city on Earth destroyed. "Eric. Get at the shuttle helm and get ready to fire one down this hallway when I tell you," he yelled.

Eric raced back into the shuttle and turned it toward the door while Jason cleared a path for the shot. "Ready?" Eric asked.

"Now," Jason yelled. The shot went through the station and out the other side and they all charged in. "Gizmo, let's hope that shot killed their communication. Now where's that damned capacitor?"

The lights were still on, so he knew the shot hadn't hit the power source. The Marines piled forward and took up positions. The power on meant that the Armada was still being destroyed. He wanted their firepower when they went down to the surface. He needed it.

The corridors went off in four directions from the main room they were in and the Marines split into teams for room clearing down each. Gizmo, smart man that he is, remarked that the Capacitor would most likely be on a different level than the landing bay in case of an accident in the shuttle bay.

Jason turned and looked at the rescued Newcomers and decided to see what they could do. He took a handful of them down a corridor with him to clear some rooms while he assessed their training and capabilities.

The first room, Jason and Gizmo went in before them, slicing the pie as they approached the fatal funnel, the door way, checking from the center to the corners around the entry and moving toward the back. "Clear", Gizmo yelled out while the Newcomers watched looking back and forth at each other.

The next room, Jason motioned to what he assumed was the leader of the Newcomers. Four of them took up positions, two on either side of the entrance. Two went down and cleared to the corners, but two of them lifted off the deck and flew into the air, covering from above as they all moved toward the rear.

"Shit. I want to do that," Jason said.

"Me too," Gizmo replied. "Must be those things they have on their uniforms. I was wondering what they were. Some kind of anti gravity device, I guess. I like it."

"Think they've done this before? Looks like they might know what they're doing," Jason commented.

"Anti gravity? I think they know better than us. But let's not let 'em know it," Gizmo replied as they watched.

The Newcomers encountered two invaders toward the back of the room behind some equipment and all four opened up on them and put them down. Jason and Gizmo were in firing before the first one hit the ground. They ran to where they fell and looked around to see what they were doing and what they were working on, hoping they were working with the capacitor. They quickly surveyed the room and started toward the exit with the Newcomers in tow.

"That room just cost us two cities back on Earth. We have to find that capacitor," Jason was saying as he picked up the pace to a sprint toward the next entrance.

The Newcomers sensed the urgency and flew past Jason and Gizmo who were now crouched and preparing to enter. They went right into action, two up, two down, and straight to the back of the room while four more piled in behind them. Four more would guard the hallway going in each direction, sixteen in total.

Seeing that there was nothing there, Jason and Gizmo turned and darted toward the next entrance. The leader was soon to catch up and gave Jason a little tug on his shoulder and wagged a finger in the air, as if to give a warning not to get ahead of the team.

"They're right," he said to Gizmo. "We have to work with them. They're good. We can't gum up their routine."

The leader spoke into his helmet, looked at Jason and Gizmo, and began issuing orders. They watched the others gather closer around them, then, sixteen more of the Newcomers were sprinting toward them. The leader pointed and issued orders and eight each were assigned to Jason and Gizmo, surrounding them on front, back, and sides.

"What the..." Gizmo was saying as four of the Newcomers motioned to the leader to come and look. Then they motioned for Jason and Gizmo.

It was a shaft going to another level, much like an elevator shaft without the elevator. Four of them jumped in, followed by another four. Then the leader started with the other eight. They all landed and moved forward with their weapons high and ready. Two of the Newcomers grabbed Jason by the shoulders, and two more grabbed Gizmo and they floated down the shaft behind them.

Before they landed, the others had dropped down in front and started moving forward. They were surrounded again following the Newcomers, being herded by them. The first sixteen had taken up positions behind some cabinets and were crouched. Jason and Gizmo were brought to take cover behind some equipment and a hand signal was given.

Instantly the room exploded into action and before Jason or Gizmo could get their weapon trained on something, they were tackled by the Newcomers. They could hear the weapons firing and they could tell they were impacting. They fought to get up, but there were four each on them, and four more each standing nearby.

"Damn it, Gizmo. What the hell is this?" Jason yelled. But all he could hear from Gizmo was muffled sounds of struggling.

Jason managed to get some movement of one of his arms and tossed one of them off, then another. He had a leg free now and kicked one off against the cabinet. He was able to get up as four more charged toward him. He threw two of them and was about to kick at the third when he saw what they were doing; they were covering Gizmo, protecting him. It's what they were doing. They were covering them with their own bodies.

A shot came by the head of one of the Newcomers and Jason grabbed him and pulled him toward a piece of machinery and crouched. He looked around and grabbed his weapon off the ground. The other Newcomers saw that he was safe and that he was not about to allow himself to be protected; he was not there to be protected; he was a warrior like them. He looked over at a man on top of Gizmo and whacked on his helmet with a motion of his thumb to get off.

They all complied and let them go. "Piece of...assholes. What the hell was that?" Gizmo protested holding his weapon in front of him in a threatening manner.

Jason could see Gizmo was furious, and the worst thing to happen right now would be to lose focus and react. They need cool heads. Earth was being destroyed and they couldn't afford to make mistakes.

"They thought you were a defenseless civilian, Giz," Jason tried to make light of it all. "Guess they thought you might need protectin'."

"They're going to need the protecting. I'll kick their alien asses," he snorted.

A few more shots came whizzing by their heads and they began to focus again. Jason poked his head around the corner to see where the others were and to get an idea of what was shooting at them.

"Looks like they got themselves pinned down," he said to Gizmo. "Think they might need our help?"

Gizmo poked his head around the corner to look and snickered. "No way. They got themselves stuck. Amateurs."

Jason looked around the corner again and saw what they were up against. Six well placed positions near the back of the room, about eighteen feet high on a catwalk. There was a clear field between the Invaders and where the Newcomers were pinned down; a killing field.

He waited for a moment to see what they would do. He watched them set up and take their shots and then crouch back down as they took fire over and over. That was it. They were pinned. They couldn't move forward and they couldn't retreat.

Jason sat for a few seconds, thinking that about a dozen more cities back on Earth had just been destroyed. He looked at the sixteen men who had apparently been assigned to protect them. He could not speak to them, but he could give signs they would understand.

He sent four to each side of the room. He had eight ready to go high on his count. They spoke amongst each other and the leader. They would all fire and force the invaders heads down while eight of them went high unnoticed.

"Gizmo. When they duck, I can still see a bit of a couple of them, what about you?" Jason asked.

"I can see the ass-end of one and a bit of another," he said.

"Well, I'm gonna use my 30.06 on them when they duck. I'm gonna shoot any part of them that sticks out. You do the same with your 308. It might not hurt them, but it'll sure scare the alien crap out of them. It'll keep their heads down," Jason said.

He pulled the Savage 111 off his back and took the caps off the scope. Gizmo grabbed his Bushmaster and did the same. The Newcomers close by all bent forward to see these new weapons. Jason held his hand in the air with three fingers up. The leader was watching the countdown. He dropped one finger and watched them all ready their weapons. He dropped the second as they braced for action. He dropped the third and they all fired at once sending the Invaders behind their covers.

Jason motioned to the eight to get up on the ceiling and move toward the front while he and Gizmo took aim. Jason fired and hit. Gizmo did the same. The Invaders screamed. He aimed at another and shot, then another and another. He had them pinned. Gizmo fired more rapidly with his semi-automatic, but his aim was good and he made them scream with each shot.

By the time Jason dropped his first magazine and slammed another in, the men on the ceiling had reached their positions and started firing down on the Invaders. That's when they all charged forward. The Invaders, seeing they had been outmaneuvered, tried to move position, but by that time the newcomers on the ground had them in their sights and they opened fire.

The remaining battle lasted less than a minute and the Invaders were dead. Jason and Gizmo were racing toward the back of the room before the Newcomers had even noticed they had moved. This had to be the room. It was too well protected. They fought too hard. It must be the one with the Quantum Capacitor.

They were climbing onto some equipment and leaping to the catwalk when the leader ordered their protection again. Jason saw them coming toward them and held up his hand. This time, they kept their distance. Jason and Gizmo frantically raced along the catwalk, checking equipment, looking for anything resembling the Quantum Capacitors they had seen on the Invader transport.

Six dead invaders on the catwalk and sixteen men to guard Jason and Gizmo were too many and they were getting in the way. Gizmo had to move a couple of them to get at some machinery. Every minute meant another city on Earth. They had to go.

Jason, trying to look into a piece of equipment with one of the men standing in the way, bent to look on one side, then the other. Then he grabbed the man and shoved him hard out of the way, and he took a step toward the leader of the Newcomers, clearly aggravated, with arms raised, and they were all pulled back.

At last, Jason saw it. "Giz. Check it. Before we do anything, we have to get rid of these guys. Nobody knows what these things are except a few of us humans. I don't know them well enough yet to let them in on our little secret."

"Agreed. Let's get them out of here and grab that thing. What's the plan?" he asked.

Jason was on the headset talking to Eric. "Eric. I think we got it. I'm gonna pull it off line. All the shields and weapons should go down. You have to tell the armada to stop firing at this station. I'll do a countdown."

"The Admiral has communication set up with the rest of the Armada. Just say when," Eric told him.

"How we going to get them out of here?" Jason mused.

"Just tell them to go. Seems like they do what you want. Think about it. We figured out the Capacitor and Relays. We're pretty important people. We are the most important people...maybe in the universe to them. Their survival, their entire race could depend on us," Gizmo said.

Jason walked toward the men on the catwalk and began motioning with his arms for them all to get off. They were soon standing down below looking up at the catwalk. Gizmo was hidden from view behind the protective cover the Invaders had used. Jason walked over and opened his satchel and told him to pull it on his count.

He got Eric on the headset again and counted down from five. Gizmo pulled it and the station went dead. Jason grabbed a rail and the Quantum Capacitor was secured. There were now no lights and no gravity. This was something they were not used to handling. Before they could figure out what to do, four men grabbed them again and brought them down to the Newcomer's leader.

Jason and Gizmo switched their helmet lights on and floated there for a moment. "Okay, that's about a hundred cities gone. Let's go," Jason said as he clumsily tried to move toward the shaft. Making swimming motions and trying to push off from equipment, they both managed nothing more than to launch themselves somersaulting clumsily through the chamber. They were grabbed once again and whisked away by the Newcomers.

"Eric. Call everyone back and let's get to the next station. We know where they keep the Capacitors now, so it'll be a lot faster," Jason called out.

The Newcomer leader dispatched their crew above to go through the satellite and grab any humans floating about. Jason and Gizmo were pulled up the shaft where sixteen other Newcomers had been stationed. "Dang. I guess we are important," Gizmo said.

"The other stations are down too," Eric came over the headset. "When you pulled that Capacitor, it must have been relaying to the other two at the same time."

"Oh, yah, that makes sense. Okay. That is terrific news. We are on our way. How did the rest of our guys do? They all okay?" Jason asked.

"Minor resistance. Nothing to protect in those other areas. They did good and they are all heading back." Then Eric asked, "How about you guys?"

"We are fine. We did good. They did good, these new guys. They are used to this space stuff. I think we should talk them into training us. Actually, Eric, we have to do that," Jason told him.

They were all packed into the shuttle like sardines again and shooting toward the transport. The Admiral had ordered most of the shuttles out to scout the surface for the main Quantum Capacitor and

Relay as soon as word got to him that the stations were down. It had to be knocked out. With the stations out of commission, the Armada could concentrate on finding it.

Every minute that went by meant millions of humans being killed. As soon as they found the main Capacitor and Relay and took it out of commission, the Invader transports, shuttles, and weapons they were using against Earth would be powerless. The Admiral ordered a sweep of the planet and the transport was descending toward the surface as Eric pulled the shuttle into the bay.

Chapter Two

The Marines piled out and began to organize into their units. The Newcomers did the same. Several dozen shuttles were sent on rescue missions as soon as the Invader Space Stations were shut down. There were ships of all kinds with broken hulls and dead engines. There were life boats and pods floating in every direction.

The shuttles started to pull in and unload the traumatized survivors. All of them were in a state of shock, not just from the battle and being blown out of the ether, but by being inside the ship they all feared and hated so much; the hi-jacked Invader Transport.

Jason and Gizmo watched as a shuttle pulled in filled with more Newcomers and watched them greet each other with slaps on the arms and shoulders and backs, and even some hugs. "They are so human-like," Jason thought.

He walked up to what he had all along assumed was the leader and remembering that they had atmosphere now that the Capacitor had been active, he pulled his helmet off as he walked up. The leader, watching him approach, began to do the same, unlatching it in the back and bending forward to take it off, and when it was off, Jason stopped dead in his tracks and stared at the most beautiful woman he had ever seen.

She had jet black hair and the bluest eyes imaginable. He walked up to her and smiled, and she smiled back, an amazing and warm smile that made him melt on the spot. He reached out his hand to shake and introduce himself and she looked at it quizzically. Then she held hers out and Jason shook it.

She looked around at the rest of her crew, and they all chuckled at the strange act. Bo came running and barking toward Jason and the Newcomers prepared to draw their weapons, until they saw Jason open up his arms and Bo jumping up and licking him.

Just then, the Admiral came over the radio. "Jason. The cat is definitely out of the bag. They know we are not them and they are about to man their ships. We've spotted forty of these transporters on the ground. You better get up here."

Jason and Gizmo sprinted toward the helm. "Wow. What a babe. She is gorgeous," Gizmo said as they ran. "And she thinks you're doing Bo."

"They look human. Wait. What?" Jason asked.

13

"Yah. That's right. Should have seen the look on her face when Bo showed up. Yup, she definitely thinks you're doing your dog," and he laughed. "I don't think they know what a dog is. Aliens, you know. You should have seen that look."

"Colonel Brand, I think we found the main Quantum Relay," the admiral started speaking as they walked in. "The Armada, what's left of it, has been informed of the location and they are going to begin targeting it. I'm betting the defenses will be a lot stronger than their space defenses."

"I'm sure it will be well defended. How long till we can see it?" Jason asked.

"Just a few minutes. But a worse problem, worse for the moment, is the forty transports sitting waiting to be launched. They get those off the ground and we are dead. That's what we're headed for right now," the Admiral pointed at a Dome. "That's where we figure the main relay is. Over there, just a few points off starboard are the transports. And see those lines. Those are what are what will carry the Invaders to their ships. Those are train lines of a sort."

The dome was created by a shield rising miles off the planet surface. Inside the dome was the base they would need to enter.

"Admiral. If we can launch our shuttles and take out the train lines, I can take a shuttle full of men and we can pull the capacitors out of every one of those Transporters. Then, they will be ours. Maybe we can use them. Send them back to Earth," Jason said.

"That is the plan. Deny them access to their ships and to their weapons, but you say you want to use them?" the Admiral thought for a moment. "Actually, you're right. We need to do that. Do you have a plan?"

"I do, Admiral. But Security is essential. We don't know these aliens. We don't want anyone else to have access to this power. We don't know who to trust just yet. We have one of these capacitors from the station. Nobody but us has seen them. Gizmo and I that is," Jason patted the satchel.

"And there is another thing," Gizmo said. "We don't believe these Invaders had the capacity to build this equipment. I don't think they had the intelligence. So someone else is most likely behind all this."

"Alright. So what do you want to do?" the Admiral asked.

"I want to take a shuttle with our own men, no aliens, all human. I want to get in the shuttle and show them what they are looking for on the way, then drop ten off in each transporter. That is, if they are not occupied. If invaders are in them, we'll have to fight our way into each one.

"But judging from the Stations we just took out and the small amount of resistance we encountered, I think their arrogance and dependence on their technology will be their downfall. I mean, they only had six Invaders guarding their entire Space Defense Capacitor and Relay. Maybe had a dozen more throughout the station.

"I'm betting they don't have anyone in those machines. They were just a little too sure of themselves. So I want our men to go in and take the Quantum Capacitors out, and we need to secure them, not let any other person or alien see them. Eric, Gizmo and I can do that while you see what it takes to bring that dome down," Jason said.

"Alright. We'll get some birds up and take out those train lines. Slow 'em down until you are done. Keep them off you until you have them all shut down. Colonel, we can't let even one of those transporters get air born." With that, the Admiral started arranging the men he would send and laying out the Operational Security.

Chapter Three

It took less than a minute, but it seemed like forever to Jason when millions of people are being killed on Earth. He watched the Admiral calmly and methodically going about his duties, issuing his orders, and making the necessary arrangements, and Jason had to admire his composure. It was this composure that would get the job done faster than if they were rattled and hectic. There was no panic.

In two hours back on Earth, the destruction of every city would be complete and the Invaders would begin landing shuttles to go in for the final slaughter and mop-up of any remaining life. They had been at the alien planet now for thirty-five minutes. Most of the major Earth cities would now be gone.

Jason and Gizmo raced back to the shuttle bay where the men for the mission had already been assembled and were entering the shuttle. Bo was bouncing along beside them, happy to be on another adventure. The alien Ambassador was near the shuttle entrance along with various alien species. It looked like they were having a heated discussion.

Jason, not wanting to waste another minute, went right past them and stepped into the shuttle. He turned and saw that the Newcomers were about to follow inside and he held up his hands to stop them.

The Ambassador stepped forward. "Mr. Brand. They insist that they come along to protect you. You and Mr. Gizmo are far too important for these sorts of adventures. The futures of all these races may depend on your knowledge and your skills. Please allow them to come to protect you."

"Bo," Jason called. "Guard."

Bo stepped forward and faced the throng with teeth bared and let out a deep and threatening growl. Then she let out a quick bark and they all stepped back at the sight of the vicious monster, none of them knowing the capabilities of such a beast, but knowing it must be fierce enough to challenge them all at once. "This is my protection," he said, as he closed the shuttle door.

On the way down to the Invader Transporters, Jason and Gizmo pulled out the Quantum Capacitor they had taken from the Space Station and explained where to find it on the ship, assuming they were all built the same. They all took a good look at it and passed it around between themselves with only a few questions.

"The most important thing is that no other being see it. So you grab it, and you secure it. We don't want anyone, or anything, or any other species or race to get their hands on this thing. It is too much power. We don't know them and we don't know who or what to trust. I think you all understand our position, right?" He asked. After they all nodded, he added, "The next most important thing, and perhaps even the most important thing of all is this: Did any of you bring an MRE? I am freaking starving."

Jason and Gizmo stood under a shower of Meals Ready to Eat that were tossed at them while Bo barked with excitement. After the packages had all landed, they kicked at a few of them with their feet and grabbed what looked good. Jason grabbed one for Bo as well, and they took their seats.

The MREs were getting nice and toasty as they started circling for a good look into the back of the transporters. Jason was watching as he fed Bo some chicken and he ate something with meat, he was pretty sure of it. But it was hot and had the calories he needed.

He had long since resigned himself to the fact that food in the Military is to eat, not to taste, and while he might enjoy a gourmet meal back at home, if there are any restaurants left, these MREs will serve their purpose: to load him up with the calories he needs to keep him fighting.

"Have you seen them? The enemy?" one of the men sitting beside him asked.

"Seen 'em. Tried to reason with 'em. Killed 'em," Gizmo answered.

"So what are they like?" he asked.

"They are big and they are powerful," Jason turned to the man and spoke loud enough for everyone to hear. "You don't want to get within reach of one. Best do your killin' from a distance. They're not slow either. But they are ugly. They are mean. They take out entire civilizations; kill every person and animal on a planet, without a thought of it being wrong. No conscience at all."

The shuttle was pulling around to land and let the first ten men out. Jason and Gizmo stood up and raised their weapons toward the shuttle door. "So you see one in there, you put it down. They won't surrender, they won't negotiate, and they won't do anything but kill you."

The shuttle pulled to the back of the transporter and ten men bounced out. Jason was with the first group. Gizmo would go with the next group followed by Eric.

"There's power on. There are a few lights on inside this one. That means the targets are here," Jason spoke into his helmet.

The Admiral came through his helmet, "Roger that. We're targeting the rail lines. They are heading your way, so you get in there and get the job done. We've been hitting them hard and they keep coming."

"Seventeen million of them fit in one of these transporters. Enough to take over and inhabit a planet. Forty transporters that we know of, sitting on the ground right here. That is a lot of Invaders." Jason was saying as he entered the shuttle bay of the sitting transport.

"Six hundred and eighty million, just to fill those ships. Who knows how many in that dome and around the planet. We have help from what's left of the Armada. Glad for that." The Admiral broke off for a moment and returned. "The Armada is useless against their defenses and is getting slaughtered by the dome, so I am assigning them to keep the invaders off you. We are headed to the dome. We'll see what kind of damage we can do.

"Jason. We just got word from the Ambassador. The Invaders are starting to break off their attack on a couple of their planets. I guess word is out. Those transporters will be heading here."

Jason did the math. "It'll take them an hour each, maybe more to get their ground forces back to the shuttles and loaded into the transporters. Then they'll be on top of us. We have to get that relay, Admiral. I'm pretty sure it's inside that dome."

"You double time it, Colonel. Get yourself back here." Jason could hear explosions through the helmet and explosions nearing his location. The Admiral clicked off, not waiting for a response.

The entire mission heard the conversation and all four hundred were moving with even more purpose now. Jason ran through his transport and grabbed the Capacitor without incident, and the transport went dead. He and his ten men bolted out the landing bay and ran to the next transport where Gizmo and his crew were.

They entered the craft and approached the engine room where he saw the men crouched with weapons pointed into a corridor and took up positions.

"What is it?" Jason asked.

"Not sure. Something moved," Gizmo replied.

Word started coming of team after team reaching their target and grabbing their Capacitors. The arrogance of power would be the Invaders downfall. There was not one Invader guarding a transport, not even a janitor.

Jason, Gizmo, and the team stayed still, watching and listening. A few lights were still on, so they hadn't gotten to the target yet. "Giz. You guys stay here. We'll grab the Capacitor and let's get out of here," Jason said.

19

A minute later, the ship went dark and the shuttle reported they were on their way to retrieve them. Capacitor secured, they all started toward the shuttle bay door. They turned their lamps on and were sprinting to the rear when Bo began to growl and her hair stood on end.

The teams kept moving, but Jason and Gizmo spun their weapons and froze, panning back and forth with their lights. "What is it girl?" Jason asked. He looked in the direction she was pointing. She kept growling, ears up and staring into the darkness. Something was there. Bo is never wrong.

Jason looked toward the back of the ship and saw the men silhouetted in the entrance. They were about to come back in when Jason gave hand signals. They broke into two groups and went to each side of the entrance and took cover.

Bo was growling and snarling louder and louder, but they still couldn't see anything. They continued to pan their lights and began moving slowly toward the exit, stepping cautiously backwards. Bo snapped at something, but they couldn't tell what it was. They couldn't see it, yet it was right there, close enough for Bo to snap at.

He considered the options. He knew Gizmo would be doing the same. They had the capacitor, but whatever was in there could have another. It was doubtful, but any chance of that had to be eliminated. They could not allow the launch of another transport, not even one. At the same time, in the brief moment of thinking about it, more cities back on Earth were disappearing.

Jason and Gizmo came to the same conclusion and were about to start firing into the darkness when they heard a voice. "You are Jason Brand."

It was more of a statement than a question.

"Yes," he replied, looking in the direction of the voice, not seeing anything.

"I am Braz. You are right Jason Brand. These beings did not make these machines. There is another apparatus at work. You are right to hide what you call the Capacitors."

"Where are you?" Gizmo asked.

"I'm here. I'm hard to see. But I'm here. It's how we lived through our own invasion, some of us. I just wanted to tell you that you are right to hide this technology. We will speak again, but time is not on your side. You should go. Bring down the dome, if you are able, before the Transporters begin returning. I will contact you again. Don't let anyone pressure you into giving away the secret of the Quantum Capacitors and Relays."

"Well, what about you? It looks like you know about it," Jason said.

"I do know about it. I know much about it now. I know almost everything you know. Even though we have seen them and even when we have been on the ship when they were functioning, we were unable to get it to work. You did it. But I trust myself and my race. After watching you, I believe I could trust you as well. It was you who put it all together. We couldn't figure it out. You did. I don't see you using it the way the Invaders did. But, as I said, there is something more sinister at work," Braz told him.

"Alright. So how will we contact you? How will we know when you are around?" Jason asked.

"Your beast will know." Bo was now sitting beside Jason without concern. "We used to have similar beasts before the invasion. They did not survive. They are missed. I have to go. You should go. My presence here must remain secret. I will contact you later," Braz said. "Hurry."

Bo stood up as if to follow Braz. Jason recognized her response as being the same as when one of her dog friends left, almost wanting to follow, a little disappointed at him leaving and Jason took note of the reaction. "You know, she is a better judge of character than I am."

Gizmo gave Bo a pat on the head. "I know. I've met some of your girlfriends."

They were on the shuttle heading back to the Transport and watched the men holding their prizes, turning them over and over and looking at the Capacitors. A special landing area had been arranged, out of sight of everyone, cordoned off, and well guarded.

"You know," Gizmo said. "It's true about how important we are. We have to watch ourselves. But there is someone we are forgetting. He may be way more important than we are, in the long run anyway. That's the kid. Cody. You know that, right?"

"You're probably right. I've been kind of thinking about that. I have been half assed planning something. Just haven't had time to put any real thought to it. I think we have to send him back home soon, but I've had him working on something, him and Hilliard. I sure hope they are done, because then we can fire up some of those transports we just disabled and use them," Jason said. "Hopefully, before the Invaders start arriving to kick our asses."

Chapter Four

They had been at the Invader planet now for about an hour and a half. Jason calculated that the transporters would likely have been on the final pass over Earth, after having destroyed all the major cities on its first pass, all the secondary cities on the second, and was probably mid the third pass, the little villages and towns and such.

Possibly ninety percent of the human race could have just been exterminated, depending on how quickly the Invaders had gotten out the alert that their home planet was at risk. Maybe more, maybe less. But they sent two transports to Earth this time. The bombardment would have already taken place. They most likely had already sent in the Invaders to the surface. If word did get out, they would have to load back up into the transports and return home. That would buy them a little more time.

But whatever was left of Earth, it would not last if they did not get into that dome and shut it down. The invaders would arrive back home. They would kill off the Armada in a matter of minutes. They would go back to Earth, and they would destroy it.

That would make it their third attempt at Earth. The first failed due to luck. But this second one, they sent two transports because of the first failure. The only living humans may be the ones deep in the bunkers and in the mountains like Ruby Ridge. The third attack, if it happens, well, Jason didn't want to think of that. It was up to him to stop it.

Bo had her attention up in the corner of the shuttle. Every now and then she would make a little squealing sound. Jason looked and could almost see something. It probably wasn't Braz, but it was one of them. It stayed there, out of the way and unnoticed.

It seemed that Jason and Gizmo were still being protected. He decided that maybe he wouldn't place themselves at so much risk. Too much was dependent on them. But so far, what they had done, they had to do themselves.

They jumped out of the shuttle and started toward the bridge and were met by the Newcomers along with a crowd of various alien species. As he walked by them, the Newcomer leader reached out and held his arm and walked with him.

The crowd followed until he was about to walk into the bridge. He stopped and turned and looked at them. The Ambassador was there and told him they were all just relieved that he, his beast, and Gizmo were alright.

"We're famous," Gizmo said.

"Blow me," Jason replied.

"You *are* famous," the leader said.

Jason stopped and looked at her, "You can speak. I mean English."

"Yes I..."

She was cut off by the Admiral calling them over. "You have to be more careful. We can't let you out and get into danger and get yourselves killed," he barked at them.

"We're fine, Admiral. So far, everything we did, we had to be there Admiral," Gizmo said.

"I don't care so much about you. It's these damn aliens won't stop complaining. Won't leave me alone," he said with a chuckle. "Take a look. We've called the Armada off the dome. They weren't doing anything but getting themselves blown up. We have them clearing out the Invaders outside the dome from behind any hills or cover they can find.

"There are still a lot of them heading toward the transports. They've wiped out, god, who knows. So many millions. The Invaders don't seem to care. They're mindless. They just keep coming.

"Watch this," he told them, and ordered the ship to fire on the dome. A charge went out and washed over it without harm, sending up a cloud of dust behind it. Then he ordered them to fire right at the base of the dome. A blast of rock flew into the air, again without phasing the dome.

They had unloaded some artillery which was firing on it as well. Nothing was penetrating or harming it. The dome would fire on the transport, and it would rumble and wash through it as well. They were in a stalemate.

Invaders would run out of the dome and go right through the shield unharmed and fire on the artillery positions and retreat back through the shield. While they were outside, they could be targeted and shot with both the human and the Invader weapons.

The Invaders seemed to have no plan for this event. It had apparently never been imagined by them that it would happen. Jason watched for a moment and then suggested to the Admiral that he turn the Transporter around. It was time to let out the army of Evil Walkers.

"It appears that the make-up of their bodies, the DNA, or something about them allows the Invaders to pass through the shield at will. The Walkers were made of the same DNA," Jason told him.

"Let me get with Hilliard and Cody and get prepared before you open the rear hatch to let them out. I would tell your men on the ground to watch out as well. I don't know how well behaved these Walkers will be," and Jason left with Gizmo and Eric, the Newcomer holding his arm once again.

"So, you were saying something about speaking English," Jason said to her.

"Yes. I learned it," she said.

"That was fast. How did you do that?" he asked.

"Well. The Ambassador has a translator. It's actually an implant. Not painful or anything," she told him. "You know, your language was actually easy. You could learn ours very quickly. It is based on similar vocables, sounds of the surroundings, animals and birds. It would be easy. Especially for you."

They entered the lab that Cody and Dr. Hilliard had set up. There were electronics placed along every table space. Dials and transmitters were buzzing and pinging. Cody had a helmet on and Hilliard was watching a video of reactions on the Walkers. In the middle of the table was the pod they had found in the cave back on Earth.

Jason picked it up and looked at the Newcomer. "We will have to talk about this translator sometime later."

"Of course," she said. "Looking forward to it."

Jason wondered if the translator also had manners programmed into it. But that is another subject and for another time. Right now, they had to get into that dome.

"Cody. Dr. Hilliard," he said. "How is it coming?"

"I think we pretty much have it set. If you want, we can test it right now," Hilliard told him.

"We'll test it on the fly. We have to unleash them now," he said.

Cody took the helmet off and came over to him. "I think it's fine. You want me to put it on or you?"

"You better do it, Cody. I have no experience with it. What about this pod. Will it get through the shield?" Jason asked.

"I think it will. This is where it is from. Other than a few parts inside that we put there, it emulates the same wave that the shield seems to put out," Hilliard said.

"So could you make a suit with the same wave and get us through that shield?" Gizmo asked.

"You are not going! I won't let you," the Newcomer protested. "You have to stop putting yourself in danger. Other people can do that."

Everyone stopped and looked at her. "Who is that?" Cody asked as if she were deaf.

"This is…you know, I don't know," Jason said. "What is your name anyway?"

"I am Deri," she said.

25

"Gentlemen, I'd like you to meet Deri. We met up on the station. Hell of a fighter," Jason said.

"Pleased to meet you," Cody and Hilliard said as they walked up to shake hands. Deri looked at them and remembered the ritual. She stuck her hand forward and allowed it to be shaken, smiling embarrassedly.

"So what about the suit?" Jason asked again. "Can you make one that will get us through that shield?"

"Well. Sure. Given enough time. But I don't think we have that time, do we?" Hilliard replied.

"Right. Okay. So let's go," Gizmo said, grabbing the pod and putting it under his arm the same way he held it coming out of the cave back on Earth. "Have you figured out a way to launch it yet?"

"Of course," Hilliard said. "That was easy."

They raced to the rear of the ship. It had been positioned so the Walkers would have a straight shot running at the structure under the shield. There was an opening that the Invaders were coming in and out and Jason wanted the pod launched right inside it. They could then set the frequency and the Walkers would charge toward the pod and enter the structure.

Jason looked over to the left of the transport about a hundred yards from the dome where some men had been fighting. There was a mass of dead invaders that had tried to charge. A man was standing on top of the pile as the remainder of the charge was being put down.

He had just run out of ammo and picked up a metal shard and rammed it through the eye of a charging Invader. Then he ran over to a wounded soldier and grabbed his weapon from him and finished off the rest before pulling the man to safety.

"Let's do it," Jason said.

Hilliard had the set up there in place on the fantail. It was an air delivery system and setting the air pressure would determine the distance the pod would be launched. "Okay. I calculated the trajectory based on this planet's gravity and air density. Stand back," he said.

A loud swoosh came from the end of the barrel and the pod sailed directly into the entrance. "Admiral, you can drop the gate," Jason called.

The gate lowered and the Walkers charged at the structure following the pod. Jason looked at Cody and nodded. He put on the helmet and looked toward the Walkers. A horde of Invaders rushed from the opening to meet the Walkers in battle. They were armed and were able to kill several hundred Walkers before they were overwhelmed. The Walkers tore them apart and continued to rush to the entrance.

The opening was not large enough for all of them and they began to pile up on each other like ants. Some were still able to enter, just not as fast as Jason had hoped. They needed to go in as an overwhelming force. If they were met with weapons right inside, they would create a dam of dead Walkers and not be able to clear out the structure.

"Dr. Hilliard!" Jason yelled.

"I'm trying! I'm trying!" Hilliard yelled back.

He was turning the frequency back and forth, trying to get the Walkers to run from the pod, and then charge back toward it in hopes of clearing the jam. It began to work. They ran away and cleared a path to the entrance. When he changed the frequency again, they all charged back in. This time the structure swallowed the entire swarm of Walkers.

They waited on the tail of the transport, listening to howls and weapons firing. "We should have sent a camera in with them," Hilliard said.

"Right," Gizmo said. "I'd like to see someone try to duct tape a camera to one of those Walkers."

Jason looked over to the left again to see the same man he had just watched setting mortar rounds on another approaching herd of Invaders. Several more men had joined to reinforce the position. He took up a .50 cal., and was unloading it on another charge, the pile of dead Invaders growing in the seconds that passed since he last looked.

He was firing on a charge and letting out his battle cry on his left, while he was about to be over-run on his right by another. Just when Jason expected them to be on him, the Invaders were sent flying by explosions. He had set proximity and pressure mines that took out the charge. When they went off, the man simply got on one knee and put his head a little lower, never letting up on the trigger.

A shuttle flew through the shield and landed. Invaders began piling out with weapons firing, rushing into the structure. "Shit. They're here already," Gizmo said.

Admiral Harding came over the head set, "The first transport just arrived and they are starting to unload their shuttles. One of the Armada was able to get on top of their transport with their ship and drive it into the ground with their engines, but not before they got some shuttles out."

Another shuttle pulled in through the shield and more invaders rushed out. "Bring the Walkers back out," Jason told Hilliard as the Invaders started firing into the back of the transport.

Hilliard turned the switch and they began to come out. A few at first and they were mowed down by the Invaders. Then more, and soon the Invaders were again overwhelmed and torn apart by the Walkers. Pieces of shredded flesh and Invader body parts landed up on the fantail where Jason was standing.

He looked around and saw some packages in a storage container. He took out two small packages and threw the first one at the shield. It vaporized as soon as it hit. Then he wrapped the next package in a piece of Invader flesh and threw that. The package went through and landed safely inside the shield.

"There are our suits," Jason said. "We'll skin a few of these bastards and get in there. If the transports are starting to show up already, we are going to be in bad shape really fast. Admiral, you watching this?"

"I'm watching. I'm sending out a party to retrieve some dead Invaders. How many people do you want to send in?"

"I think after the Walkers are done, thirty or forty should do it," and he turned back to Dr. Hilliard. "Send them back inside. We'll see if they can actually clear the place out."

Again the walkers raced into the entrance and vanished. More shooting was heard, more howling and growling. As the Walkers went deeper into the structure, the sounds were more and more muffled until they couldn't hear anything.

Jason looked over at the man to the left who was still engaged in battle. "You see this guy, Giz? He's a dang maniac; a one man army." They both watched him empty the .50 cal. and start pulling out grenades and lobbing them. As soon as he ran out of them, he pushed the pile of dead Invaders and set up another .50 cal. and started blasting away with it.

Jason's attention was drawn back to the Walkers. They waited and listened for noise from inside the structure. Nothing.

"I'll call them out again, and then send them back for another charge," Hilliard said. He turned the switch and in a minute they began pouring out through the entrance. Then he reversed it and sent them back in. There was shooting again, but not as much and that soon died down.

A moment went by while they waited and listened. "Should I call them back and do it again?" Dr. Hilliard asked.

"Maybe it's time to just call them back. Maybe we should just get in there now," Jason said.

"I'm ready. Let's do it," Gizmo said.

"Wait," said the Newcomer, "Now there is no reason for you to go in there and put yourself at risk. You know that. We can do that, my people, or you can send your own people. Just you two – you shouldn't go. It isn't needed."

"She's right," the admiral said. "No reason another team can't go in. You sit this one out."

Chapter Five

The Walkers were starting to come out of the structure and rush to the back of the transporter when another Invader shuttle flew through the shield. The hatch opened and the Invaders began to pile out and fire on the Walkers.

Almost half of the Walkers had made it into the transporter when the dome began filling with a green haze. Both the Invaders and the Walkers that were inside it fell dead as gas was released from the structure on all sides. They watched as everything inside the dome fell lifeless.

"Admiral. I guess that was their last line of defense when they get overrun. Gas everything and wait for more transporters to show up. So they did have a plan. Kill everything. They not only don't care about killing any other race, they don't seem to care too much for their own kind either," Jason said.

"Looks like. So this gas…Colonel, we have to get in there anyway," the Admiral said.

They all watched while the gas continued to fill the dome and drift down into the entrance. Nothing was alive inside the shield. The gas continued to fill the area until they could see it coming out of the entrance as well, mingling with the green heavy mix of poison on the outside.

"Yup. I guess their plan was to kill everything and wait for the transporters to show up and take the dome back over. It has to dissipate for that to happen. I don't recall any bio-suits in the Invader inventory, do you Dr. Hilliard?" Jason asked.

"No. Certainly not. So it will either dissipate, or something else or someone else will likely arrive and retake the dome," the doctor replied. "Scary thought; who or what else may be coming. But someone would most likely, no, most definitely be coming to re-take that dome and re-occupy that structure. On that we can be certain."

"Admiral. What kind of bio-suits did we bring? Do you have any idea?" Jason asked.

"Just looking it over now." The Admiral was silent for a moment, and then came back on. "Looks like we scrambled with a few dozen of them. But in our haste, I don't think we brought anyone that's ever used them. We're still checking."

"Looks like it's you and me again, Jason," Gizmo said. "You bring your suit?"

"Never leave home without it. Right?" he replied.

"We can get people into the suits and keep them back of us maybe, have some stay behind and pull them out if they get in trouble. We just have to do it, go in and get this thing off line," Jason said.

"What? What about us?" Deri asked. "We have experience with deadly atmospheres. It's part of what you would call 'Boot Camp' for us."

"Sure. We train everyone for gas too. Our guys can handle it," Jason said. "We'll be fine."

"So, you trained for combat in a containment suit? Zero gravity, you could run into that in there. Fighting alien races? Really? How much of that have you done? Jason and Gizmo, you are the two most stubborn people I've met. Brave, but stubborn. Is your entire race like you?" she asked.

"Colonel Brand," the Admiral said. "You two take her and her crew. The shuttle is pulling in now with the dead Invaders. They have been skinning them in-flight. Put a volunteer in one and make sure he can get through that shield first. Don't test it yourselves. That's an order."

"Yes, sir," Jason replied, and that ended the argument before it started.

One of the newcomers volunteered to test the suit. They had their own uniforms on that were already designed as their own containment suit. He pulled the Invader skin over his suit and closed it up as best he could and walked through the shield, turned around and waved everyone to come through.

Jason and Gizmo got into their HAZWOPPER gear once again. It was more than a little clumsy putting on the Invader skin over the bulky suit. The Hazardous Waste Operations and Emergency Response equipment from back on Earth seemed ridiculous compared to the Newcomers easy fitting uniforms.

"Ready to go?" Jason asked.

"Let's go, times a burnin," Gizmo replied.

"We're set too," Deri said.

The radios, calibrated now so they could all speak, they stepped out and through the shield into the murky green fluorescent gas and stood there a moment. Nobody dropped dead and nobody coughed and sputtered. Jason and Gizmo quickly peeled the dead Invader hide off and began their clumsy sprint for the entrance, taking position on either side.

Chapter Six

Almost two hours had gone by since they had arrived. If word had gotten to the Invaders back on Earth, they would be almost done loading back into the transporters and would be arriving any time. Hopefully, the General held them up and denied them easy access to their shuttles.

Jason, Gizmo, Eric and the Admiral knew that counting on that would be a mistake. They couldn't depend on the result of any fight except their own. The General back on Earth knew it too. He knew that the Human Army he sent to the Invaders planet could be wiped out as soon as it entered orbit and Jason knew that there was little hope for Earth against the Invader weaponry.

The standard operating procedure was to assume you are the last of mankind and you are fighting for its survival, whether you were on Earth or the Invader planet. Assume that you are it, the rest of mankind had likely been exterminated, and there would be no rescue.

They kneeled by the entrance while the newcomers formed up behind them. It was dark inside, and one of the newcomers tossed a light, a kind of flare they used, and lit up the area.

Jason glanced back at the fighting maniac and saw him take out another nest, still bellowing his battle cry and setting up some more mortar rounds before turning back to the entrance, and he and Gizmo entered the structure.

It had yellowish walls formed in smooth spirals winding up toward a ceiling with holes leading to the next level. There were dead bodies all around. Dead Walkers. Dead Invaders. Some in piles, some strewn about and torn apart.

Ahead, there was a pile of dead about twenty feet high. Jason walked toward it and saw that the Walkers had charged an automatic turret, eventually tearing it down off the ceiling.

"Turrets," he said. "Careful."

They went deeper inside where the pile of bodies was so high, that they had to pull some of them down to continue. He looked over the top and saw what created the dam of dead Walkers. There were two turrets pointed in their direction. As soon as he poked his head over the top, they focused and began firing, sending chunks of Walkers and Invaders flying all around them.

"Admiral," Jason called. "Admiral." Not getting a response, he realized the dome had blocked the signal.

31

"I'll be right back," Jason said and ran back to the entrance. "Admiral?" he called again.

"Colonel?" he replied.

"You see that guy off about a hundred yards from the stern. Big guy. Been there fighting this whole time? Looks like Army? He was just about to send up some mortars," he asked.

"Yes, Colonel. What about him?" he asked.

"Well. I'd really like it if he lived. I have plans for him," Jason said.

The turrets stopped firing after no movement had been detected. Two of the newcomers were signaled by Deri. They came up, reached into their pouches and each pulled out an item. They set a dial and lifted it up over the pile of dead, and the items flew weightless toward the turrets, exploding and knocking them both out.

"Deri. Tell your men, I don't know if all the Walkers got out. If there are some in there and were blocked by this pile here, don't think they are the good guys. Kill them as fast as you can," Jason told her. "They are worse than the Invaders."

She relayed this to her crew, and then she asked, "What are those things?"

Jason and Gizmo were crawling over the top and about to enter the next section of the structure. "Monsters," was all he said.

Chapter Seven

Private Dent was again about to run out of ammo. He had one foot on top of the head of an Invader while he fired the last few shots, still letting out his battle cry. He reached down and grabbed another weapon which was empty and tossed it. He looked around for a weapon, any weapon.

The only thing he could see was the metal shard he had used earlier. He grabbed it and held it up and yelled, "Damn you ugly bastards, come and get it," as one charged at him. He planted one end of the spear on the back of a dead Invader and skewered the attacking Invader with the other.

He turned to look for another weapon as a dozen or more Invaders were climbing up the pile of dead he had created. He was about to be overrun when explosions erupted all around and in front of him, throwing pieces of dead Invader in all directions.

Before the pieces had even landed, dozens of the Newcomers had positioned themselves all around him placing fire and taking out what remained of the charge. Two tanks rolled up and MRAPs began unloading personnel and equipment.

"Break time, Private," a man called to him as he walked up followed by thirty men. "Private, go over there and take a breather," pointing to an MRAP.

"Yes sir, Lieutenant." He walked to the rear of the, reached in and grabbed some ammo and reloaded, and flopped down, exhausted. One of the Newcomers gave him some water and watched him drink before he noticed that he had no idea who they were. He looked at their uniform and asked, "What are you? Is that Air Force, or... what is that?"

The Lieutenant walked over and told him to get on his feet. "Private. You are to go with these men, right now."

The Newcomers reached for his weapon. Private Dent looked at the Lieutenant for reassurance who nodded at him. Once they had his weapon, they took him by the shoulders, and like they had with Jason and Gizmo, they were airborne and carrying Dent with them, kicking and yelling curses at them all the way.

It took only seconds for him to be delivered to the landing bay where Colonel Eric Runningsprings was waiting for him. "Private. You've been assigned to us. Follow me. You'll be meeting with the rest shortly."

By the rest, he meant Jason and Gizmo, provided they lived. For now, he was going down to the deck with Cody and Dr. Hilliard. He had been handed his weapon back once he was on the deck. Eric looked at it and said, "You got Invader goo on your rifle. Got a little up close and personal, did ya?"

"A little, Sir. Seems they wanted to get a real close look at it. I let 'em," Dent said. "They're big."

"We got something bigger. Did you see them? They went into the dome," Eric said.

"I got a quick look. Was a little busy, but I got a quick look. You know, I really need to stock up. I pretty much used everything I had, grenades, ammo. Got a little bit back there when the MRAPs showed up. But if you want me to do anything, I have a better idea of what I'll be needing now. Nearly had to pull my knife there before those guys showed up," Dent said.

"Well, whatever you need, grab it now," Eric told him.

Private Dent loaded up. He was a walking armory by the time he was done. Eric was surprised he could carry that much weight, but he held it all as they went to the tail of the transport where Cody and Dr. Hilliard were waiting.

Dent was introduced and hands were shaken. He looked at the video feed of the Walkers in the hold. He looked over Hilliard's equipment. Then he went to the fan tail and looked to see where he had just come from. They were still charging that position, but the Invaders were now far outnumbered and out gunned.

He knew they were coming from an area some hundred and fifty yards away from where he had been under siege. But down there, he couldn't see it. He studied the area for a while. He looked around the transport and dropped everything he was carrying.

Dent walked back over to the edge again and studied the area once more. Then he walked back and picked up an RPG, aimed it, and fired at what everyone who watched him thought was nothing. But when the blast hit, it knocked them back. The people on the ground that were not already behind cover were thrown to the ground.

The transport rumbled and shook as a pillar of smoke rose into the atmosphere and the area went silent. They watched the people on the ground get up and take positions again.

"What was that?" Eric asked.

"Don't know. But it was sure something wasn't it. It's where I thought those maggots were coming from. Guess I was right," Dent replied.

"Guess they won't be coming from there anymore either," Eric said.

The Admiral was on the headset asking what the explosion was. Eric told him what he knew and the Admiral said he was sending some Intelligence Officers down to take a look. There may be more of them located around the dome.

Dent sat down and looked around at the dome. He grabbed some water and was about to take a drink when his canteen dropped to his lap and he fell dead asleep from exhaustion. Eric let him, and when the Intelligence Officers arrived, he told them what they needed to know and pointed out the location of the blast.

When Dent woke back up, they had already left to check out the area around the explosion. He stood up and watched them approach the blast area and surround it with men. It was only a few minutes of sleep, and other than feeling like his face was covered in some invisible slime, he felt recharged.

It was a bunker, they reported. There was nothing left alive in it, but it must have been well stocked and defended before Dent blew it up. They started on a hunt for any other bunkers outside the shield around the dome.

"Good work soldier. Those would have been big trouble for us later," Eric complemented. "So, a private, eh? You'll have to explain that one to me. I saw your work down there. Seems like you've been around this block before."

"Yes sir. Been around it a time or two," Dent said. "Thought I was done for down there that time."

Chapter Eight

Jason was over the pile of dead bodies and about to enter a large hall. He scanned the expanse as well as he could before stepping into the open. There were dead Walkers and a handful of dead Invaders strewn around.

"I don't like it," Gizmo whispered.

"Me either," Jason said. "Looks like a good place to set up a defense." He crept out to look around a side wall and came back and looked at Gizmo. "I really don't like it," and took another look.

"What do you think of this? See up there, those holes like we saw back in the entrance. I think we can go up and come across. If there is an ambush or defense set up, we can maybe flank their locations from up there. Maybe take them out from up there." He turned around and called, "Deri?"

She had been listening and was already talking to some of her people. A dozen of them pulled back and crawled over the pile of bodies again to see if they could come around and drop through the ceiling.

"I think if it were me, I might expect that," Jason said. "I might expect someone to do that if I were overrun. Maybe set a trap for them. Tell them to expect that."

"They heard you. Remember, the translator? You haven't had time, I know. But later, you can get the translator. That is if you like," she said looking in through the opening to the large hall.

"These walls were molded, it looks like. Maybe from an old destroyed city that was here." Jason looked around the corner again and said, "Well, this place ain't agonna clear issef, is it Giz? Better get to goin' before those transports start arriving by the dozen."

"Wait. Aren't you going to make sure it's safe first?" Deri asked.

"Safe? You mean there is something safe around here? What, you mean not go in because it might be dangerous? Maybe weren't invited? I think we have to at least draw fire if there is anything there," Jason said. "Your guys up top yet?"

"Just getting there. Jason, let some of my guys go first. They can draw fire. They have the gravity outfits. You can't move like they do. And that foolish outfit you two are wearing. How can you maneuver? When we get back, I'll get you something decent to wear." She said.

"You'd better check with Bo first, Deri," Gizmo said as he gave Jason a little jab with his elbow. "She can get pretty nasty."

Deri was setting up the formation for getting through the room. But that got her attention. "Who is Bo? Is that your beast?"

"Let's go," Jason said. "People are dying."

He was about to enter, but Deri and her newcomers passed him, two to the left, two to the right, two up and to the left, two up and to the right. They kept coming until they had all entered this way except for a handful to cover the flank and cover fire if they needed to get out.

Jason leaned against a column and looked over at Gizmo. "How are we going to find this? This structure is huge. Any thoughts?"

"Just clear the place, and when we hit heavy resistance, that's where it is. Problem is that it could take us days to find it. This place is miles high. Who knows how deep," he said.

Jason watched the newcomers proceed through the room. He expected to see the ones that dropped behind and went up through the holes at the entrance to drop down any time. "So, I know you've been thinking about it, but these weapons these Invaders have. What do you think?"

"I have been thinking about it. I figured you would be too. I think maybe…" Gizmo was cut off by the sound of weapons fire.

They both stretched to get a good angle at where it was coming from. "Did you see it?" Jason asked.

"No," Gizmo replied. "I think it came from back toward that, well, they have no corners, but over there," he said pointing.

"Deri. Are you alright?" Jason asked.

"We're fine. We found a nest of Invaders with masks," she said. "The unit up top should be coming through any time."

They listened for more contact, and it came. It came from up top. From the sound of it, they had met some heavy resistance.

"Yup. Just like I thought. They were waiting for them," Jason said. "You know, Giz, when they fire those weapons, it's not like they blow things up. Not really. And it's not like they remove mass. It looks to me more like all the particles, all the atoms disassociate. What do you think it would take to make every molecule lose or reverse its magnetic field and come apart like that?"

"Must be something bonehead simple, since these guys are boneheads. Then again, if it's so bonehead simple, why didn't all these aliens think about it and figure it out?" Gizmo mused.

"We've been working on it since we first ran into these monsters," Deri cut in. "Nobody has figured it out yet. Not in any civilization."

The firing and explosions continued both on their level and the one up above.

"You know, I bet that's what they made this place out of. They just paste it back together, you know, all the disassociated particles. Once we kill these bastards, let's take some samples," Jason said.

"Are you getting tired of waiting, Jason? Cuz I'm really getting tired of waiting. Plus, I forgot to take a leak before we left," Gizmo said.

"Hate when that happens. Especially with these suits." Jason tried to see where Deri ended up. "Deri, how's it going?"

"We're okay. Jason, we're okay, but the guys up top, well, they're pinned down," and she added with a little embarrassment, "And, well, we're kind of stuck too."

"You know, I have an idea," Jason said. "When we get back, let's get with the kid and Hilliard and see what they think."

The firing flared up again with more explosions up at the top.

"Hilliard is a smart guy, huh," Gizmo said. "And Cody, brilliant."

"Maybe we should go and see what is giving Deri so much trouble. Good thing they came along to protect us, right?" Jason said.

"That is joking, isn't it? You just did what you call 'poking fun at us' didn't you?" She asked.

"Believe me; we think you guys are the best. So, are the Invaders pinned down as well?" Jason asked.

"Yes. We can't move, but neither can they," she said.

"Well, I'm going to come in. When I say, you start firing and keep them pinned. But you are okay, right? You're not in danger unless you move?" Jason asked.

"Right," Deri answered.

"Okay. We are coming in on three." Jason poked at Gizmo and pointed at an opening across the room. He nodded and Gizmo nodded back. "One, two, three!"

Another explosion of gun fire opened up. Gizmo and Jason scooted across the room to the opening. There was another elevator shaft without the elevator, just like in the space station where they found the capacitor. They looked down and Gizmo said, "You don't think it's that easy, do you?"

"Let's see." He looked around at the newcomers that Deri had assigned to them for protection and said, "We need to go down there."

Chapter Nine

The Newcomers grabbed them by the shoulders again, and after the first four went down, the rest jumped and brought Jason and Gizmo with them. They landed with their guns raised and ready to take fire, but there was none.

Jason saw some equipment and ran to it for cover. Gizmo found a similar spot a short way from him, and the newcomers lined up on either side of them.

Another group of Newcomers showed up. "Your Admiral told us to tell you they are here. Six transports just arrived. Whatever it is you're going to do, now is the time to do it. He said this Armada won't last ten minutes."

"You go and tell him 'Roger that, Admiral'," Jason said. "Deri, you just keep them pinned down up there."

He turned to one of the newcomers and said, "I want you to take four of your guys and get up high and move toward the back. We'll start moving forward as soon as you start. We are out of time, so let's get going."

Jason and Gizmo stood up as the team lifted into the air. They started moving forward, ducking behind cover as they pressed toward the back.

"What the hell?" Gizmo said. "It can't be this easy."

"You know, they hardly had any guards on the station. Six. I don't think most of them even know what is in here. They keep their population ignorant," Jason said. "And they might have even pulled their guards to fight the Walkers up top. Here's hoping."

They were running now toward the rear. "Look, the catwalk," Gizmo yelled.

"It can't be this easy, can it?" Jason said.

One of the Newcomers came back with another message from the Admiral. "They are taking fire and will have to move into low orbit, Jason. The Admiral told me to tell you."

"Go tell him 'Roger that, Admiral'," and kept moving toward the catwalk.

He grabbed one of the newcomers and told him to take him up to the catwalk. Jason and Gizmo were at once grabbed and flown to the landing. There wasn't an Invader in sight.

"That way," Jason yelled and pointed.

Gizmo darted in that direction while Jason went the opposite way. Gizmo reached the Quantum Capacitor and called to Jason. As fast as he could run in his suit, he came over.

They looked at each other and looked at the staring Newcomers. Still not wanting them to see the Capacitor, Jason ordered them again off the catwalk and onto the floor. They stood looking up at them while Gizmo was well hidden behind a protective shield taking out the Capacitor. He pulled it and the structure went dead and the lights went out.

"Admiral. The dome. Is the shield gone?" Jason yelled.

Still not getting any radio reception, they stood in total darkness and listened to crashing explosions from the outside. The entire structure shook at one point. Jason and Gizmo turned their lamps on and yelled down for the newcomers to get them the hell out of there.

They were being lifted up the shaft with the noise of battle getting louder as they approached the next level. Firing continued from Deri and her crew, but it didn't sound like any Invader weapons were being fired. If he were successful, all Invader weapons went dead when the capacitor was pulled.

"Admiral," Jason called again. "Is the shield off?"

Jason saw Deri and her team standing now, firing on the Invaders that once had her pinned. The Invader weapons were indeed dead. Hopefully, that meant the shield was down. The team from above was dropping down into the large hall. Invaders were howling as they made a final mad charge at the Newcomers and were cut down.

There was a moment of silence and then the Newcomers broke out in cheers. Deri ran over and grabbed Jason and squeezed him through his suit. "You did it, didn't you?" she shrieked. "You did it!"

"I'm not sure. I haven't heard from the outside yet," he told her. "I vote we go and take a look. Then, we get to a safe spot. A defensible spot. But first, let's find that pod that Cody and Hilliard shot in here. I didn't see it when we came in. Did you, Gizmo?"

"No. It could be under the pile of bodies," he answered. "But let's get going before we run out of air."

Chapter Ten

They crawled over the bodies again and began searching for the pod that Dr. Hilliard launched through the door. Jason walked toward the outside entrance and tried to judge where it might have landed. While he was there, he could see the gas, still being pumped out around the structure.

It was the failsafe put in place in the event the structure was overrun. It would kill everything inside and out except for that handful of guards wearing masks. Later, when the returning Invaders arrived, they could move back in, fire everything back up, and the only problem they would have is disposing of the dead bodies.

That prospect of having the Invaders moving back in to take the structure back was gnawing at him now. He tried to get an idea of what was going on outside the structure. The transport they came in had gone and the armada was nowhere in sight.

The gas was still pouring out, but it did look like the shield was down and wind was now drifting the greenish poison across the front and away from the dome. The gas was heavier than the atmosphere, so Jason and Gizmo agreed they might be able to get up high to get fresh air if they had to.

He turned around and saw the Newcomers pulling the Invader and Walker corpses from the heap. "Gizmo," he called. Gizmo came over and he looked at his air gauge. "Almost time to be concerned?"

"I agree," he turned to look at the men moving the bodies and spotted the pod. He ran and picked it up and yelled, "Got it," and returned with it under his arm.

"Admiral?" Jason called into his headset, still getting no answer.

"What do you say we get outside and maybe upwind from this gas?" Gizmo suggested.

The Admiral finally cracked over the headset, "We're about fifteen minutes out, Jason. You and Gizmo. You did it, men. Congratulations. The shield is down. The dome is defenseless. The transports went dead. Some of them got on the ground and are heading your way. We are clearing them out, bombarding them now."

"That's good news, Admiral. Any word about Earth?" Jason asked.

"Nothing. We don't know if the transports that arrived here...well, we don't know where they're from," he replied.

"Roger that Admiral. We are running out of air here. We will find a place where there is no gas," he said.

"Roger. Out," the admiral replied.

Chapter Eleven

Jason and Gizmo checked upwind to make sure it was clear. The most obvious direction for them to go would be upwind, out of the gas. It was whipping around the structure, and that would be the direction they would go.

Deri called her men around. They moved forward in their own formation. Some high, some low. They came to a pillar and stopped and called to Deri. Deri called Jason and Gizmo over. Around the pillar they saw an approaching army of Invaders in a full charge toward the structure.

Jason whipped out his rifle and scanned across them. "It must be an entire transport of them, emptied out and on their way," he said. He caught a glimpse of one who was standing on a mound and directing the monsters.

In his hand was a capacitor, and he stood on the top of a hidden bunker where gas masks were being issued out to the rest of his force. This was their plan, and he was coming to power up the Quantum Relay. Jason got on his knee and rocked back and took aim. He couldn't kill the thing, but he fired on the capacitor, causing it to explode and send purple flames of hydrogen up the Invader's arm.

Deri pointed to their left and said, "Look."

There was another charging army. He searched to see if one of them was directing the charge. There was, and in his hand was another capacitor. This Invader had watched as Jason shot and blew up the last one, looked over and saw Jason drawing a bead on him, and before a shot could be fired, he leaped off his mound.

Jason swept the entire area. There were three more charges running full bore, grabbing masks, with only one thing in mind: Get a Capacitor in there and get the Relay started again. Every transport that went dead would have that one thing in mind. Get the power back on. Get their weapons working and kill the enemy. Them.

"We made a mistake, Gizmo. We have to blow the relay equipment. They are coming to turn it back on. Deri. Explosives?" he asked.

"Some," she said.

"Give me eight men and all the explosives you have. You stay here and hold them off as best you can. At least slow them down. Gizmo and I will be right back," Jason said.

They were running as fast as their suits would allow them back into the structure. Jason and Gizmo got to the pile of bodies and dived head first over it and rolled onto the other side.

As he got up Jason yelled into the headset, "Admiral! We have a little situation here."

Inside the structure, again, he was getting no signal. He had no time to turn back. The charge would reach them within another minute or two. He had to blow up the equipment.

Chapter Twelve

They ran to the shaft and didn't wait for the newcomers to grab them, they both started to leap. The newcomers had to grab them on the way down. Once they landed, they bolted to the rear. Two of the newcomers had already been through this twice, and directed the others to grab them up and fly them to the catwalk.

Once there, they got to the relay equipment and planted the explosives and jumped down as it went off.

"Wouldn't you have a backup if your entire race depended on it?" He asked Gizmo.

"Yup. Where?" he asked as he ran toward a wall with an opening. "I'll check this way."

Jason ran in the other direction toward another opening. "Hey Gizmo. The wiring, or whatever that stuff is they are using. Plumbing. Wouldn't it be either straight up or straight down, or, right behind the other relay?"

"That's how I'd do it. Let's see if we can get at it in either direction. Looks like this winds around toward the back," he said as he looked around the corner. "How about yours?"

"Yup. Meet you in the middle," he said as they both disappeared into the corridor.

They could hear gunfire up above. Up there, there were thirty two people, including Deri, holding off millions.

Jason and Gizmo ran through the corridor toward each other and met in the middle. There, they saw an entrance and they bounced through it, freezing at the sight. There was equipment everywhere; machines, controls, parts - Invader parts.

"This has to be it," Gizmo said.

Both he and Jason slowed down and started looking at what was in there. This was a treasure chest of parts. Everything they didn't know about their technology, they could reverse engineer from here. All their secrets would be known. Schematics. Drawings. Instructions. And parts, lots of parts. They were all there.

"God I hate to do this," Jason said.

"No choice," Gizmo answered. "We have to. If only we had a little more time."

"You're gonna have to leave that capacitor here too, and blow that up, you know, in case we get killed. Can't let them have it," Jason said as he patted the sack Gizmo had it stashed in.

They could hear Deri now through the headset. "They must have been pushed back inside," Jason said. "Deri, how you holding up?"

"About to be overrun. Nice knowing you Jason. Thank you for everything," she said.

"Don't give up yet, girl. You only give up when you're dead, and I'm not sure about that anymore either. We're about to set more charges. As soon as you hear them go off, you go up through those holes in the ceiling. Go all the way to the top. We'll meet you up there," he yelled.

They set every charge they had in that room. When it went off, it would take out everything in it along with the walls on either side. Once it was set, they ran toward the catwalk again. Gizmo was still carrying the pod. Jason grabbed it and rolled it under the catwalk.

"If we ever get out of this, we can send them a little present," he said, thinking the Invaders would be working frantically down there to repair the relays, and, if all else failed, they could send in the walkers. They would rush to where the pod was.

"Okay let's go," he said, and they let off the charges.

Deri's position was quickly overrun. She pulled her people back and lifted up into the Swiss cheese holes the Invaders had throughout their ceilings. The Invaders came pouring in and Jason, Gizmo, and the eight men were cut off with the Invaders heading straight to where they were.

"Back to the corridor!" he yelled.

As they ran back into the corridor, they saw where the explosion had blown holes through the walls in every direction. Jason ran to the parts room with the rest coming behind him. Through the settling dust, he spotted a hole to another corridor behind the parts room and they crawled into it. It seemed to run in a straight line out from under the structure. Cut off now, they had no choice. They ran.

"My air," Gizmo called.

"Me too. Me too," Jason replied. "Deri. What's your situation?"

There was no answer. He looked at one of her men who looked back at him with that intent expression; that mix of confused emotions, contained rage, revenge, and sadness you get when you've just lost someone in battle.

They kept running. They could hear the Invaders entering the room with the catwalk, and they could hear the anguished howls at seeing the relay destroyed. Then they could hear them coming around into the parts room and more howls and screaming were let out.

The radio crackled. They could hear it, but they couldn't make out what was said. They kept running until they heard Invaders behind them catching up. They stopped and spun, taking aim and unloading their weapons, dropping eight of them.

They were up and running again with more Invaders following. They could hear the angry noises as they passed their dead Invader comrades. The radio crackled again.

"Deri! Is that you?" Jason yelled. There was still no answer.

They stopped again and fired on another group. There were more of them this time, and more were not far behind. They turned and ran again.

Jason was thinking of dropping his 30.06. He couldn't use it against them, and it was four pounds of extra weight. Gizmo had tossed his Bushmaster already.

The radio crackled again. This time they heard it. It was the admiral. "We're pulling up to the structure now. You are surrounded by Invaders. Keep your heads down, we are firing on them."

"We must be outside the structure. We're getting signal from them. Maybe that's why we couldn't get Deri. The radio won't make it through some of these walls," Gizmo said.

"Admiral. We are heading underground in an angle, approximately twenty degrees from the entrance. Being pursued. We have no idea where this tunnel goes, but it is our only option," Jason yelled.

"Roger that," the Admiral paused. "We have cleared outside the entrance of enemies. Your friend Dent knows where you are headed, he said. Eric and he are loading a shuttle. Keep heading in the same direction."

"Who the hell is Dent?" Jason asked Gizmo.

"No idea," Gizmo said, running out of breath. "Really, I didn't think you had any friends. Imagine that. Oh, and by the way. We are both gonna be dead in another couple of minutes unless we get air. Then how is your friend gonna feel?"

They stopped and spun again to shoot the approaching Invaders. Jason and Gizmo stayed down on one knee, panting, struggling for air, and looked at the pile of dead bodies as the newcomers got up and prepared to continue running.

They looked up at the newcomers for a moment, then looked past them toward the end of the tunnel they were in, both knowing they had no air to make it, and they both knew if they took off their suits, the poison would kill them. Then they looked back at each other.

"You guys get going," Jason told the Newcomers. "Don't stop and don't look back. We're gonna do something."

They started running and Jason and Gizmo watched briefly, then turned and walked slowly toward the pile of dead bodies. Each step was treated as if it were the most precious moment they had. Jason was amazed at the heightened perception he had knowing he was most likely going to die right then. He could feel every step, the pressure on his soles, the feeling of his suit against his skin.

He could see the light from his suit bounce off the walls. He could hear their footsteps as they walked; their breathing, and the fast pace of the Newcomers fading away down the corridor. Things he would never notice before, things that were insignificant, things that were taken for granted were now amplified and filled every sense.

Everything all at once was amplified the same as everything else, and they both drank it in, enjoying every miniscule perception and awareness as if to fill a vast emptiness, treating each step like it was the rest of their lives.

"Well. It's been good Pal," Jason said.

"Me too. Real good. Always thought I'd eat it in this suit. But I thought it would be in Iraq or something," Gizmo said.

They dropped down and each rested their weapon on a dead Invader and readied themselves for the next bunch to charge up the corridor. They both looked behind them to see the newcomers beginning to slow down and look back at them.

They waved them on and yelled, "Go! Go!"

"Nope. We're not in Iraq, Giz. Where the hell are we anyway? This dump must have a name." Jason looked down the corridor at the new charging herd. "Getting hard to breath. How about you?"

"Yup. Can you believe they actually left us?" Gizmo joked.

"Yah, really. What kind of protectors are they?" Jason said as he readied his weapon. "Ready?"

"Sure am."

"Make 'em bleed, Pal. Make 'em bleed," Jason said as they started firing.

They had a little difficulty aiming as they ran out of air. Their focus was off. But the weapons they had didn't require the best of aim. They brought most of them down, and the ones remaining were injured. Then they fired again and finished them off.

They stopped and breathed hard from the lack of oxygen. Another charge was coming down the corridor at them.

"So," Gizmo said, out of breath. "There was this twenty one year old virgin."

"Okay. A twenty one year old virgin," Jason repeated. "Another fantasy story."

They both heard an explosion at the other end of the hall, but could not turn around to look. Their vision was getting blurred. Jason squinted and got ready to fire.

"You'll... have... to finish... the... story... later," Jason said and they both started to fire.

When they were finished, they rolled over with their backs against a dead Invader. Jason could have sworn he saw something coming at him, but he couldn't lift his weapon. Gizmo had already blacked out.

Chapter Thirteen

"I'm not made in China," Dr. Bradley said to himself, back on Earth, staring into the mirror. "I'm not, dammit. It's ridiculous. I've never even been to China."

He held up his hand to the mirror and read the words that had been melted into his skin, thinking how unfair it all was. "MADE IN CHINA", is what it clearly read. Then he turned his hand toward himself and saw that it read backwards.

He grappled with the concept for a moment. "How did it do that backwards like that? Now what are people going to think? If someone saw this, they would see it in reverse. They wouldn't know what it really said. It could say anything. Maybe they won't know.

"ANIHC NI EDAM, is what they would see. Something about cheese is what they could think. That cheese from Holland, Edam; those balls of cheese covered in red wax. Yes. The big cheese. That's me."

Bradley thought about how it all happened. It was so fast that he didn't have time, until now, to even go over it in his mind. That man. That horrible man ruined everything. Jason Brand. It was him and that other guy, Gidget, or something like that. "What a stupid name," he thought. "Well, they're dead now, for sure. I hope it was painful."

He pictured how it happened: the shuttle blowing a hole through the blast doors; his creations, the Evil Walkers, running through to the transport; all the activity of the military loading equipment. People frantically running back and forth, and then, that's when that man, that Jason Brand, shot at him and nearly shattered the glass around his observation deck.

The crack from the shot startled him and made him fumble the control in his hand. That's when the transport took off. As he was reaching for the control, the transport sent out an electromagnetic pulse that shorted it, burning into his hand the Made In China markings that he is now having to suffer.

"How much more can I stand?" He wondered. "It's just not fair. Well. They are gone now and good riddance to them. They are dead for sure by now. I hope it was painful." He turned his attention back to the new markings on his hand.

It is no good trying to hide it. Everyone could easily see it if they looked. It's worse trying to hide it. He held his hand up as if to hail somebody and saw what it would look like doing that to the mirror.

"Wait," he thought to himself. "That isn't bad," and did it again. "It reminds me of someone; someone important," and he did it again, thrusting his hand toward the mirror with the palm open.

"Yes it is someone important; another man who nearly conquered the world. Hitler!" He wrestled with the concept of the mirror and the image, "If I'm looking at it from my viewpoint, it is backwards. But in the mirror, it is frontwards. But if someone is walking toward me, they would be backward. So they would see it like..." It was too much for him and too confusing for a man with so much on his mind.

He did have so much on his mind, too. They were important things. He was in the middle of taking over the world, and his plan was in full play. He rubbed his head trying to gather his thoughts and looked down at his hands and wondered, "Have I ever been to China? Maybe this scar is going to be a good thing."

Then he did a couple more thrusts toward the mirror. "Yes. Someone important. And people should think I am important. And I am important. The most important person on Earth. I created a being better than man himself," and momentarily dropped into sadness as he thought of them being loaded onto the transporter.

"But there are so many other bases. They will survive. They will populate the Earth, and I will be their creator. Me," and he again thrust his hand toward the mirror. "Yes. Very important."

He sat and thought about the gas being released across the world into the underground bunkers, turning the remainder of the human race into madmen. "Zombies, that moron called them. That Gadget, or whatever his name is. Zombies indeed. Silly name calling is all that is. I hope his death was exceedingly painful; him and that horrible man, Jason Brand."

All was going according to plan, except that this base, the one he was in, the gas did not release. The electronics had melted from the electromagnetic pulse of the transporter. Magnets in the valves were instantly demagnetized. Now, he would have to come up with a separate plan for this base.

He would somehow have to get some of his creatures into the base and overrun it. "They would not stand a chance, these humans," he thought to himself. "They may think they are victorious now, but they are fools."

"FOOLS!" he yelled.

The door opened and two guards walked in. They looked around the room and one of them asked, "Everything alright?"

Bradley stood up and thrust his hand out, giving his new salute, and said, "Yes. Everything is perfect," being sure they were looking at the imprint on his hand.

The two stood for a brief moment and looked at each other in bewilderment and walked back out.

He contemplated their reaction and, in the end, decided that it was acceptable. It threw them off, made them uneasy. It would add some mystery to their perception of his importance and his brilliance. But he would have to be careful with his outbursts. He wouldn't want people to think he is crazy.

"Am I crazy?" he thought. "Have I lost my mind? No."

It was his daily ritual, trying to decide whether he had lost his mind or not. It was one of his first thoughts after he woke up, providing he slept at all, and it would be a discussion he would have with himself several times throughout the day.

Dr. Bradley went over his plan again in his mind. He went over how he created the Walkers. How he devised a method to make them aggressive. How he planned to turn the gas on the remaining captured population and drive them mad. It was brilliant.

"No," he decided. "I am not insane. Crazy people do not have the luxury of thinking they might be crazy. Therefore, how could I be crazy? I would not even think it if I were crazy. It is in the book. So it is written, so it must be. The fact that I wonder if I might be only proves that I am not. That is the undisputable science of it."

He continued to ponder the logic of his actions. The Invaders wanted to take over the planet. Catskill Pharmaceuticals wanted to rule the population with their drugs. Everyone wants to rule the world. Every country wanted to rule the world. The financiers want to rule the world. There are the communists, the capitalists, the religions. Everyone wants to rule the world.

He would do it. He would rule the world. It is not crazy. It is strategy. They have their strategy and he has his, and so far, he is winning. After all, why should he have less right to rule the world than they?

It is he that made all the genetic advancement that made the Walkers possible. It was he that concocted the drug to make the Walkers into the killers they are. It was he that was defeating the Invaders. Why shouldn't it be he who rules the world?

He looked into the mirror and started having visions of himself, standing in the sun on a hill, his arms outstretched, and below him, millions upon millions of Walkers, his creations, and he would be victorious.

Bradley heard a noise outside his door. The guards were talking with someone. Why shouldn't he have guards? He is, after all, the most important man in the world. It's about time they recognized it and gave him some protection.

"I am too important. The work I am doing is too important. It is very, very important," he thought, and then again losing control he yelled out, "Very Important!"

Again the door opened and the two guards walked in. He could see more of them outside now, and felt, finally, somewhat acknowledged for his stature.

"I have very important work to do," Dr. Bradley told them.

"You certainly do," the guard said. "The General is waiting for you. Would you come with us, please?"

As he was escorted down the hall, it never registered to Bradley that the guns the men were carrying were trained on him the entire time. When they met with another person or group coming down the corridor, Bradley would thrust his arm out in greeting, proudly displaying his new markings to them.

The reaction he received thrilled him. They would invariably stop in their tracks and look at him in silence as he walked by. Finally, he was getting the respect he felt he deserved.

The General was in the briefing room going over last minute details of the attack and the withdrawal of the Invaders. "We don't know the outcome of Admiral Harding's attack on the Invader home planet, but we do have some degree of certainty that Colonels Brand and Crozley were successful in some way. The only proof we have of that is that the Invaders broke off their attack and, we assume, retreated to defend their home planet.

"Minimally, they posed enough of a threat to them that they pulled out. Whether Brand and Gizmo were able to disable their power source or not is just not known, and until we find out, we must assume that the Invaders will return with an even greater force. There is no contact with any other bases or forces on Earth at this time. So the priority now is to regroup and set up new defenses with whatever resources we have left.

"Recon will begin immediately starting with the nearest bases and air strips, National Guard Armories; whatever we can salvage. In the meanwhile, we are working on getting any form of communications back up.

"At the same time, we have no elected officials on this base. We are dividing our recon to scout and find whoever they can. Until we do find some elected official, as much as I dislike the idea, we are under Martial Law, under the military.

"If the worst has happened, if our Government Hierarchy has been destroyed, we will hold elections amongst the survivors and form a civilian Government, as soon as possible. Until then, it's Martial Law and the Military is the Government, and according to laws passed by Congress, this new Constitution and Bill of Rights is now in force."

The General looked around and asked, "Any questions?" and after a couple of seconds said, "Good. You all have your assignments. Let's get the people safe and get our defenses back up. Dismissed!"

The room quickly emptied and one of Bradley's guards stepped inside. "General. The prisoner. Dr. Bradley, sir."

"Bradley," the General growled in disgust. He could be the first execution under the new Constitution, depending on how he answered the General's questions. "Bring him in."

Bradley was guided through the door, an MP on either side, and positioned in front of the General.

"Bradley. You are going to have to convince me of something here and now. You are going to have to convince me not to take you outside and put a bullet in your head," and he stood up and looked directly into his mad eyes and said, "And believe me, Bradley, that isn't going to be easy."

Dr. Bradley stood up taller and gave him his new salute. In his twisted mind, he knew what the General really meant. He meant that he knew how valuable Bradley was. He knew how brilliant he was. He knew that Bradley had a plan, and that it was working.

Bradley knew that the General really wanted to rule the world himself and that Bradley was a threat to his plans. "I know what you want, and I won't give it to you."

"Take him out and shoot him," the General said.

The men eagerly grabbed him and started marching him out the door when he yelled back, "But I will share!"

"Wait," the General ordered, motioning with his finger to bring him back. "What do you mean?"

"I mean I'm willing to share," Bradley said, thinking he would give him a small island or something.

"I want to know about the Walkers. Where did you really get that cloning; that splitting the DNA technology?" he demanded.

"I developed it," he answered.

"Alright. Take him out and shoot him," the General said again.

"Wait. Alright. Okay, so maybe not every part. I had help. I had some input," he said.

"Input from where?" the General asked.

"Just minor input. Just suggestions, really. Actually, not even. More like…"

"From where?" the general cut him off with a growl.

"Well. I worked with Catskill. So, of course there were groups we were part of developing different things," Bradley answered.

"So you got it from Catskill. Bradley. I'm not going to keep asking. Who in Catskill Pharmaceuticals did you get it from?" he demanded.

"It was me. I figured it out. Me," Bradley protested. "There was only input from a group at a compound in New York."

"Where in New York?" the General asked.

"The Catskill mountains. There was a compound there. In the mountains," Bradley answered.

The General looked at him again in disgust. It was all he could do to hold himself back from jumping across the desk and killing him with his bare hands. He would like nothing better than to put this man to death. But Bradley may have information of value still so the General restrained himself.

Instead he had the guards take him out into the corridor and hold him while he gave his aide instructions. "I want him interrogated. We have no Geneva Convention rules. We probably don't even have a Geneva because of him. I want him aggressively interrogated. There are no rules and there will be no humanitarian issues, no trials, nothing. So don't hold back. I want to know every detail of who was involved and where. If he dies in the process, it will save us a bullet."

Bradley was soon unceremoniously shackled. A bag was pulled over his head and he was marched away.

Chapter Fourteen

Jason woke up with an oxygen mask on and tried to bolt up straight. He was being held down, floating through the air, carried by Newcomers. He looked over and saw Gizmo coming to. They were still in the corridor filled with poison, and were restrained from pulling the mask off.

"Deri!" he yelled at the people carrying him. "Did you get her out?"

They could not make out what he was saying and he continued to float backward through the corridor. He turned to see where he was being taken, and recognized that he was near the end where he had sent the newcomers before losing consciousness.

The corridor had been blown through. This, he thought in his dizzied state, must have been the explosion he had heard. They carried him through the rubble until he saw Eric standing without a mask.

He ripped his mask off and wiggled loose from the newcomers. Gizmo was having the same reaction and they both were set uneasily on their feet.

"Eric. Deri was in there with her people. Did you get them out?" he asked.

"No. We just blasted through this bunker. Dent figured these out," he said.

"We have to get her. There are thirty-two people trapped in there. They are going up. We can blast in and come down from the top, work our way down until we get them," he yelled.

"Alright. Alright. You just sit down and enjoy the ride. We'll get up there and do that in the shuttle," Eric said. "You and Gizmo have been out for a couple of minutes. Why don't you put the mask back on and get some more oxygen. Dent and I will go in."

"Who the hell is Dent?" Jason asked.

"Oh. Dent. Yah, that's your friend. Remember?" Gizmo said.

They were soon in the shuttle lifting off and heading for the top of the structure. "Dent figured out those bunkers. That's how we found you," Eric said.

Jason laid back still catching his breath and looking around. "Admiral. Admiral!" he yelled when he realized he was in the open and had clear signal.

"Colonel. Welcome back," he answered.

"We have to release the Walkers into the structure again. We dropped the pod down where they might be trying to get the relay back up. We blew up what we could, but no time to search the entire structure," he said. "We can't risk them getting some relay back up."

"Roger that, Colonel. It'll take a few minutes to get in position," the Admiral said.

"Giz. The Walkers will go in there and mess the Invaders up good. But they'll also chase them up through those holes, up towards Deri. The Invaders will have to stop and defend themselves, but Deri and her people will be trapped," he said.

Gizmo looked at him, still wearing his mask and said, "So he went to his friend on his twenty first birthday and was all depressed because he was still a virgin."

"Oh, yah. The story. Welcome back, by the way," Jason said.

"So, Jason. I want what the Newcomers were wearing. Not that crap that ran out of air," Gizmo said.

Jason began to feel better and took off his mask. As the shuttle rose into the air nearing the top, Gizmo took his off. They both looked around for weapons.

"What are we going to breath?" Jason said. "We're out of air. Eric, did you bring some more?"

"No," Eric told him. "We'll have to send in the Newcomers if there is gas up at the top. I can see some drift out the bottom still."

"Look. You shoot that top off. The gas is heavier than the atmosphere. It'll start dropping. It'll act like a suction and pull air down into it and blow out the bottom. We can let the newcomers down first, when they give us the all clear, we can go in without masks," Gizmo said.

"Good thinking, Pal," Jason said. "Glad to have you back," and he slapped him on the arm.

"Admiral. Did you hear that? You are going to get a blast of poison gas right up your fantail," Jason said.

"We'll shut the windows, Colonel. Thanks for the heads up. As soon as the gas is vented, we'll release the Walkers. Out," the Admiral answered.

Jason stood up, he was a little woozy at first, but found his feet. Gizmo was standing now and looking around.

"Explosives, Explosives. Remember to bring more Explosives, Jason," he said.

"No joke," he said. "And what's with that radio? Sometimes works - sometimes not. We have to tell her we're coming and where to meet us. Eric, can you poke a little hole in that thing first. Just a small one. We don't want to blow them up if they made it up to the top already."

The doors to the cockpit slid open and Jason and Gizmo watched a large man walk to the back, pick up an RPG and stick it out the side. He pulled the trigger and blew a hole in the side of the structure almost at the top and walked back up to the front. Gizmo and Jason looked at each other and chuckled.

"Problem solved," Gizmo said.

"Yup. Better to get it done before ya get to thinking about it too much.'' Jason said.

"One of you guys fly over and stick your head in and see if you can see them. You have your air on, right?" Jason asked the newcomers.

Two of the newcomers jumped up ready to go. "Alright, alright, you can both go," he said and they jumped out and went straight to the hole.

"And Gizmo. You know what happens when you get to thinking about it too much?" Jason asked.

"Well, I suppose if you get to thinking about it too much, then you get to talking about it too much," he said as he walked over to look at the two newcomers poke their heads in the hole they just made.

The two men looked in and flew back over and told them they were not at the top yet. Eric pulled the shuttle back and blasted the top off. They could hear a "swoosh" of air being pulled down into it and looked down at the ground where dust was flying as the gas blasted out the bottom of the structure from its own weight.

They watched as the dust settled and the flow lost its force.

"And you know what happens once you get to talking about it too much?" Jason asked.

"Well, I suppose you might bring up new stuff and have to start thinking about it all over again," Gizmo was becoming exhausted. He patted himself on the shoulders, motioning for the newcomers to grab him and take him across and wondered if they may have taken a breath of the gas while they were out.

Jason and Gizmo were flown across and began the decent into the Invader structure. As soon as they were in, they lost contact with the outside, but were now in contact with Deri and her crew.

"Deri. It's Jason. You still with us?" he called.

"We're trapped. We are being forced up. We'll be at the top pretty soon. Then we'll be trapped. There's too many of them," she yelled.

"We're up top. We're coming down to meet you. Move up as fast as you can," he yelled back. Then he grabbed one of the newcomers. "You go to the top. You have to get messages from the ship and relay them to us and from us to them."

"Deri. We blew the top off the structure. Just make your way to the top and we'll get out of here. The shuttle is waiting." Jason looked at the newcomer at the top and yelled, "Tell them to release the Walkers."

"Here they come," called the newcomer after a minute passed.

They could hear the screeches and screaming and howling from below. The Walkers rampaged into the structure and began attacking anything that moved. Although they would ultimately head in the direction of the pod, if they came into contact with any moving or living thing, they would chase it down and attack it.

They could hear the calamity as it moved up from floor to floor. The Walkers were doing exactly what they were designed to do; kill Invaders. At first the Invaders stopped to try to counter the attack. Then they surged toward the top of the structure in an effort to get distance and organize a defense.

They could do neither and ended up in screeching panic. The ones nearer the top could not see what the ones below were running from, they just knew they were trying to get away from something and began climbing in terror.

Below, the Walkers that went toward the pod did the same thing. They charged toward the pod, killing and ripping apart, until the Invaders were being forced out the bottom bunker where Jason and Gizmo had just been dragged.

"Just fly up here, Deri! Don't bother fighting them. Just get up here!" Jason yelled.

"I'm coming. I can see light. I'm coming," she yelled back.

Two newcomers floated down to meet her and put down some suppressive fire. As soon as they made it back up, Jason and Gizmo started dropping grenades down the holes that ran throughout the structure.

The newcomers grabbed Jason and Gizmo on the way up and they went straight to the Shuttle. They turned to see Invaders bubbling up through the open top and falling over the edge until all that was coming up were the Walkers. Some would stop and look over the edge, while others, in their mad desire to kill, jumped and chased the Invaders down to the ground and died on impact.

After a few minutes, the Walkers turned back down toward the calling pod.

"Let's seal up that bunker," Jason called to Eric. "Keep 'em all in there."

Eric pulled the shuttle around and the big man came walking back again, picked up a launcher, pointed it out the side doors and fired, blasting the bunker shut. Then he put it back down and strolled back to the front, again without a word.

Jason and Gizmo watched him walk all the way in both directions and then looked at each other.

"And you know what happens after you start to thinkin' and talkin' too much about something?" Gizmo asked.

"Well. You might get to sittin' down and thinkin' some more," Jason said.

"And then, once you done all that thinkin' and all that talkin', and then talkin' and thinkin' some more, there just ain't no time left for a'doin'. And then where would you be?" Gizmo said.

"What are you two talking about?" Deri asked.

"Oh. Just the tail end of a conversation. So. Welcome back. You made it," Jason said.

"Colonel Brand," Admiral Harding came through. "Once you're cleared through medical, get back here for a debrief."

Eric switched channels so that he could speak to Jason and Gizmo. "Good work guys. That wasn't easy, I know it. You pulled it off. You guys…you're really something."

"Thanks Eric," they both said.

"Listen. When was the last time you two slept?" he asked.

They both looked at each other and thought about it. "Weren't we just sleeping? Does being unconscious count? I guess really, you mean a nap or actually slept, because we napped yesterday, or was that the day before? Maybe…the day before that?" Gizmo was trying to figure it out as he spoke.

"I think Eric is trying to tell us we need to sleep," Jason said.

"Yah. You're getting goofy. I don't mind, but let's not get too goofy," Eric said. "There is a huge meeting on the transport. Diplomats from all over are arriving to see you two. I mean from all over the universe. Different Galaxies, different species. I saw some of them. Crazy. I don't think you realize what you two have accomplished. How many species faced extinction?"

Gizmo and Jason looked in despair at each other. Sitting in a room full of people was not Jason's idea of a good time. Especially these people. Mini bureaucrats. He was tired. He was dirty. After all this, it was the last thing he wanted to do.

"Right," Jason said.

"Right. Got it Eric," Gizmo added.

Chapter Fifteen

They flew to the transport looking at the activity going on outside. The Seabees had already erected some buildings and helicopter pads. Apaches were landing. They were working on an air strip. Radar had been set up and tanks and artillery were being positioned.

They flew into the bay and were greeted by Bo, Cody and Dr. Hilliard. Jason sat for a moment and paid some attention to Bo while Cody and Hilliard filled him in on their progress.

Admiral Harding walked up and they all snapped to attention. Harding set them at ease and congratulated them on their successful mission.

"Any word yet from Earth?" Jason asked.

"No. Not a word. But that doesn't mean anything other than they haven't gotten word out. No way to do it," he answered. "Colonel Brand, Colonel Crozley, there are some folks waiting to meet you. You'd better get cleaned up. I'll see you in fifteen minutes in the meeting hall we've set up. These are your yeomen. They'll show you to your uniforms."

He walked off and the yeomen came forward to show them the way. Soon they had been cleaned and shaven and were putting on clean clothes, dress uniforms.

"You look better," a voice came.

Jason looked around and didn't see anyone. "Braz. Is that you?"

"It is, Jason Brand. Excuse the intrusion. I haven't been able to speak to you. You have been quite busy," he said.

"No problem, Braz. I have a meeting I guess I have to go to. Maybe after that we could sit down and talk," Jason said.

"I believe it would be better if we meet tomorrow. After you get some rest. But it is the meeting I wished to speak to you about, as well as give you my congratulations for the job you have done," Braz told him.

"What about the meeting?" Jason asked.

"It is important that you do not agree to anything in this meeting. Because you have defeated the Invaders, because the entire civilized universe will soon know you by name, you will have tremendous power. You are perhaps the wealthiest and most powerful being known. Since you conquered them, almost entirely yourself, by Universal Law, you now own whatever they owned, including the inhabitants," he said.

"Wow. That's…that's some news," Jason said.

"You will be pressured to share the Invader technology. You will be told you must do it, for their protection. You will be pressured because you do not know the law and how much power you have now. I think you should wait before you make any decisions or make any agreements," Braz warned him.

"Alright. I'll just tell them I will consider it or think about it or give them my decisions later," Jason paused a moment. "What about the Admiral? Why isn't he the guy who owns it all?"

"He did not figure it all out. You did. You went in and you personally conquered them. You and your beast are famous. Your friend Gizmo is famous. Stories are already being told about you three," Braz continued. "But I just wanted to tell you, what you say in there will be very important and will make ripples throughout the universe. And again, congratulations, and thank you. I will speak with you after you have rested," and he left.

Jason got up and left the room and was met by Gizmo in the hallway. Bo was following close beside him. He stood and took a deep breath. "Ready?" he asked.

"Ready," Gizmo answered.

Chapter Sixteen

They were lead by the yeomen to the meeting hall that was set up. It was sparsely decorated, and species from all around the universe were there waiting. They were met at the door and announced as if they were royalty. Even Bo was announced.

The gathering made every kind of noise imaginable. Some clapped; some made noises through various body parts. But all were enthralled and humbled by the presence of Jason Brand and his beast, Bo, and Gizmo. Some knelt. Some bowed. Whatever it was that was their custom to show respect, they did it.

They were lead to the back of the room and Jason was seated at the head of the table with Gizmo and Bo beside him on either side. A chair was there for Bo as well, which Jason told her to jump into.

The assembled dignitaries were all taken aback by the instant compliance of his famous beast. They had heard how she had defended him from a rushing horde of wild Invaders attempting to board the shuttle. It was in fact the embellished story of when he had her growl earlier that day to keep the newcomers out. But it had grown and now she was both feared and respected.

The fact that Jason had his beast with him at this meeting was itself a show of power and strength that did not go unnoticed. The dignitaries closest to her were very careful not to offend. They would look back and forth, first at Jason, and then at her. Bo sat patiently and obediently without much notice of the strangers, her head higher than Jason and most dignitaries sitting in their chairs.

The Admiral was in full dress uniform at the other end of the table watching. He was also taken aback, but it was by the welcome that Jason had received and recognized the respect he was being shown. He would be certain to show that same respect and not undermine it.

Deri was at the table watching every move. Braz had entered unnoticed and was in the corner near the entrance. Jason recognized him by a glimmer of light and Bo gave notice as well.

After the room quieted down, the Admiral stood. He looked at the Ambassador to be sure that the translator would function, and the ambassador nodded.

"Welcome all of you and thank you for coming. The people of Earth welcome you to our family. Today, you have come a great distance to see and speak to three great and respected beings, Jason Brand, Jerry Crozley, and Jason's beast, Bo," he began motioning in their direction.

The room again exploded into applause. Jason and Gizmo rose and did a half turn and bow toward everyone to acknowledge their presence. After the room quieted down a little, the Admiral started again.

"Civilization after civilization, galaxy after galaxy has suffered at the hands of the Invaders. Entire species, entire races, countless numbers of them have gone extinct at the hands of these monsters. Some you knew and miss. Some you didn't. But those who are gone, we will never know. That, my friends, is the greatest loss. But today, on this great day, we, together, celebrate our freedom."

Again, the room went into an explosion of applause.

The Admiral was watching the end of the table. Gizmo was beginning to nod off and Jason's eyes were getting heavy. Jason had Bo jump onto the floor after she became too excited over all the noise, scaring the nearby visitors. He was petting her head as she laid it on his lap.

No, sitting in a room full of people was never Jason's idea of a good time. Especially these people. Mini bureaucrats. They are all over the place on Earth. They were, at least, all over the place when he left, and here are even more; from all over the universe. They all want power, and what power they have now, they use it to collect even more.

Appointed or hired, but never elected, they are the hall monitors of their worlds. You can't escape them, these hall monitors. As the pleas for the Invader technology began, these were his last thoughts as he dropped dead asleep from exhaustion.

As Gizmo started to snore, one of the dignitaries commented that he had heard of some species doing this; that it was a form of meditation and a rejuvenation period. None had ever witnessed it besides Deri and Braz.

Admiral Harding, having heard the discussion through the translator stood and announced that they had heard their requests and that they would now meditate on it, adding that the meeting would continue the next day.

As the room emptied, some of the visitors tried to come around the back of the table to pay respects, but Bo stood and snarled as they approached Jason, causing them to go around the other direction.

In the hallway, Deri was surrounded. "You must talk to him. You know these humans more than any of us. You fought beside them. You have gained their trust," one of them was saying.

"We feel the weapons should be shared with all. So we can all be safe. We all need to protect ourselves, you and your people included," one was saying who had skin as dark and shiny as obsidian, wearing a glimmering grey robe.

Another with a greenish tint spoke, "And how do you know the Humans can be trusted to safeguard these weapons. We don't know them. As far as we know, they are still barbaric. They use nuclear weapons still."

Deri stood surrounded, listening to the reasoning they all voiced. Not knowing how her own planet had faired, she was considered as much an Ambassador as any of them. Finally, she agreed she would speak to Jason about it after he had finished his meditation.

Chapter Seventeen

A room had been set up for both Jason and Gizmo by the newcomers. Bo had one, but refused it and chose instead to sleep on the floor beside Jason. The next day, Deri brought new uniforms for Jason and Gizmo.

It was identical in appearance to the uniform he had worn at the reception, except it had installed in it the oxygen and anti-gravity devices. There was also a version of the combat uniforms with added equipment she planned to familiarize him with.

As she approached his room, she was again surrounded by the dignitaries pleading that she do their bidding and convince Jason to release the Invader technology and make it available to all. She left them waiting nervously at the end of the hallway and knocked on Jason's door.

"Come in," he said, and she disappeared into the room.

A few minutes later, Jason opened the door and Bo appeared with a command from Jason to guard, and there she sat, dutifully at the door. The dignitaries watched and waited. They began to hear noises from inside the room and looked at each other in bewilderment.

A few of them mustered the courage to approach the door to listen, and Bo growled and snapped, driving them back to the corner. Then they heard a moan. Then they heard screaming. Then there was more screaming, much louder. As it continued, it got louder and louder until the throng turned and ran in terror at the torture they all thought she must be receiving for making this request on their behalf.

Chapter Eighteen

More Ambassadors and dignitaries were arriving, so the meeting was put off until then next day, giving all an opportunity to be received and shower what gifts they had on the three heroes. Now, word was spreading about Deri and her unfortunate encounter with Jason and worry was spreading throughout the transporter about the short temper and swift meting out of justice of the famous Jason Brand.

Jason and Deri met with Gizmo in the galley to go over the uniform upgrades. She was demonstrating how to use the collar for either vacuum of space or poisons. "You just pull it up like this," she said, showing him to do it. "If you find yourself in space or in a poison atmosphere like yesterday, you just pull it over your head and it seals itself. Your helmets will just fit on top."

"Could have used that yesterday in the dome," Gizmo said.

"That was such a clumsy outfit you were using. But I suppose it did its job. Apart from almost killing you from lack of oxygen, that is," she said.

"This can be used in space, can it?" Jason asked.

"Yes. We use it in space. It will keep you alive. It won't protect you from impacts, so you put the helmet over it and you press it here..," and she showed them the spot. "Then it will withdraw back into the collar. Make sure you are in an atmosphere when you do it."

They were about to sit and enjoy a break when a yeoman came running up. "The admiral wants you in the reception room to eat with the guests, but before that, he wants you at the bridge. You have to get into your dress uniform. Right now. I mean, the Admiral says 'Right now.' Colonels."

"Oh, boy," Gizmo said.

"We made some of the same defenses and additions on your dress uniforms," Deri explained to Gizmo.

"So Deri. I guess I'll see you in the reception area. Are you going to dress up?" and Jason reached around her waist and pulled her closer. "I mean you are kind of the de-facto Ambassador. I'd kind of like to see you dressed up."

"I suppose I should. After all, I guess I am the ranking member here, I mean for us," she said. "I'll see you in the great room then."

Jason was in his quarters looking over his new uniform and checking out Deri's additions to it. He pressed on a patch and watched the clothing rise and float in the air when Braz spoke, giving him a start. "Jason Brand. I have something to show you."

"Well. Can it wait? I have a meeting to go to."

"It should be done right away. It is very important," he said.

"Alright. How long will it take?" Jason asked.

"No more than a few of your minutes to see it, about another ten to get there," Braz said.

The yeoman was banging on his door and Jason opened it. "Sir," he said. "The Admiral is getting furious."

"Just hang on," Jason told him, and closed the door.

"Braz. I have all these people waiting for me. And the Admiral wants to see me right away. Are you sure it can't wait?" he asked.

"No. It is much more important than any of that. Much more," Braz replied. "It is about spies and your security and involves Cody and your Doctor Hilliard."

Hearing that, Jason frantically pulled his battle uniform back on and was about to bolt down to Cody and Hilliard's lab when he realized he had communications built into his uniform that he could now communicate with anyone any time he wanted. "Admiral," he said, and the channel was opened.

He waited a few seconds before the Admiral came on. "Colonel. What's the hold up?"

"Admiral, we have a security issue. Can you hold this meeting off for a while longer?" Jason asked.

"What kind of security issue. Do you need a detail?" he asked, and ordered a security detail to Jason and Gizmo without waiting for an answer.

"I'm with a representative now, he is about to fill me in," Jason said.

"Which one? From where?" the Admiral asked.

"He has been with us for a while. I don't think anyone else has met him and he wanted to keep it that way. I guess it's time you met him, though," he said. "Can you hold them off for a while longer?"

Braz and Jason were soon on their way to the laboratory Cody and Jason had set up on another level. They were escorted by their security details, stopping any non-human they met along the route, and forcing them to turn and go in the other direction. Braz had made himself somewhat visible for the detail after they had bumped into him several times and nearly opened fire in surprise.

Cody and Hilliard were busy working when they entered. This was the place that made the transporter work and ensured their only connection to Earth. They were working on a project that Jason had given them earlier and were almost finished when Jason walked in.

"Gentlemen. I'd like you to meet someone," he said.

They looked around a little confused before they noticed his shape and stared at Braz.

"Amazing," Hilliard said.

"What are you?" asked Cody. "That is so cool. Is that something you are wearing or is it your natural...I guess, skin?"

Braz became even more visible for them. He held his finger up to his lips and the room went silent. "Nobody except a very few know that I am here and it is best that we keep it that way, for now at least. Please don't use my name when we speak in this room."

"Dr. Hilliard. Excuse my intrusion, but it was necessary and you will see why. I have been examining some of your recordings and there is one of importance that I would like to show you."

Braz walked over to Dr. Hilliard's laptop and punched a few keys and a video started playing. It was the one that Hilliard had shown Jason earlier. It was the Ambassador meeting Dr. Hilliard on the transport back above Earth.

They all gathered around and watched the delighted Hilliard speak with the Ambassador on his mission across the universe to find a defense against the Invaders.

"I've seen this," Jason said.

"Me too. Hell, I was there," Hilliard exclaimed.

"Watch," Braz said as the video played. "It's coming up. Right...here."

They all leaned toward the small screen and watched the Ambassador place a nearly invisible patch onto the table. The patch seemed to melt into the surface, making it entirely invisible.

Jason tensed as he recalled the conversation he had when Hilliard first showed him the video. Jason was angry and wanted to know how he knew the invasion was coming. Hilliard had explained that, although the Ambassador and their people could not tap into the Invader communications, they were very good at eavesdropping.

"Bastards!" Gizmo exclaimed. "Bastards."

Again, Braz held his finger up to his lips. He pulled out a device and walked over to the table they had been working at and waved it over the surface. The device lit up and Braz pulled a blade, scraping it over the area. Another patch peeled up and Braz held it for everyone to see.

He again put his finger to his lips and walked over to the video and pointed at the table on the screen. They all knew what he was saying. Any conversations in that room were now known by the Ambassador and whoever else was listening. This is where they had conversations about the Relays, about the Quantum Communicators. It was where Jason had explained his theory to Hilliard. It was where they had formulated some of their plans.

It was also clear to Jason and Gizmo now how the Armada had arrived before their transport and had almost been destroyed. They had known all along what progress they had made. Some of the planning was back on Earth, and some was in the transport, and he was trying to piece together what parts of the planning were done where.

Jason paced the floor as Braz stood to the side wondering what he was doing. Everyone in the room was silent. Jason started walking among the projects Cody and Dr. Hilliard had been working on, inspecting every part.

"Admiral," Jason announced into his uniform. "We have a situation. We have to meet."

"Alright. Get up here," the Admiral told him.

"Can't meet there, Sir. I'll arrange a location and call in a few minutes," and Jason clicked off and then clicked on again and said "Eric."

"Jason!" Eric came on the radio. "Wait till you see this. You are gonna be amazed."

"Eric. We have an OpSec issue. No more comm. Meet me at the fan tail. And bring that big guy I asked you guys to pull out," Jason told him.

"You mean Dent? He's right here. We'll be right down," Eric said.

"Oh. So that's who Dent is. Yah, bring him," and then Jason looked at Braz and asked, "You mind bringing that device and coming along?"

Chapter Nineteen

They met on the fantail. Jason left half of the security detail at the Laboratory with instructions not to speak and use hand signals only. Two vehicles were readied as Jason stood with Bo on the edge of the deck looking through his scope into an empty space on the Invader planet.

When the Admiral appeared, they all loaded into the vehicles and drove off. Once they were in the empty spot Jason had chosen, they stopped and got out.

"Well. Might as well get to it," Jason said, and began stripping off his clothes.

Gizmo, Hilliard and Cody followed suit as Dent and the Admiral watched dumbfounded.

"Dent. Admiral," Jason said, inviting them to do the same.

They looked at each other and started peeling off their clothes as Jason called Bo over and took her collar off. Once they were all down to their skivvies, Jason picked up the laptop and started walking away from the vehicles while the others followed.

When they were a good distance away, they stopped and the Admiral said, "So tell me why I'm standing on an alien planet in my underwear."

Jason flipped the laptop around to show him the video and stopped. "Um. Before I show you this, Admiral, let me introduce you to someone. This is Braz."

Dent and the Admiral looked around in surprise when they caught a glimpse of him. The Admiral reached out his hand and touched him, as if to make sure he was solid and really there.

"Braz has been with us the whole time. He is the one who brought this to our attention," and he flipped the video on showing the listening device being planted.

"I have found several of these throughout your transport," Braz told him. "I was not trying to spy on you, but I was trying to see who was spying. So excuse me if I had not made myself known to you."

"How many of you are here?" the Admiral asked.

"There are three of us. One each has now been assigned to watch over Jason and Gizmo, and there is myself. We too have been trying to unlock the Invader secret of their power. Jason has done it, with the help of Cody and Dr. Hilliard, and of course Gizmo and Jason's beast, Bo.

"We were close, but the last parts of it, Jason found it, and now I feel that this secret should be guarded," Braz said.

"So you know how it works, then?" the Admiral asked.

"Again, Admiral. Please excuse the intrusion. It was not our intention to spy on you. It is our nature to look and observe. We have no desire and no designs for this equipment except for our own defense.

"Now that you and your people have it and have all but defeated the Invaders, I see no use for it at all, except to guard it. I have watched your Jason Brand and Gizmo. I believe it is in the proper hands, although we would welcome having it, I am making no claims or demands," Braz told him.

As Braz answered questions from Admiral Harding, Jason had tables and chairs unloaded from the vehicles and set up. He had their clothes brought and placed on the tables, and while the Admiral spoke with Braz, he used the device he brought to scan the items.

Three listening devices were uncovered; one on the Admiral's clothes, one was on Jason's scope, and one that angered Jason the most was on the collar he was about to put back onto Bo.

They all sat down while the questioning continued until Jason cut in and said, "Earth is now in danger again."

This jarred the group into paying attention. "They know that we have our relay there. If they get there and find it, they can take it."

"Where is it?" the Admiral asked.

"I don't know. I intentionally don't know. None of us know. It was in case we were caught and interrogated. Not even the General wanted to know," Jason explained. "The only person here who knows is Eric."

They all turned to him and looked. After a moment of uncomfortable silence, Eric spoke. "Admiral. This was the plan. Nobody knows. Just me. I picked out the safest place I could. I dropped the equipment and some people there and they are guarding it. Too small a group to be noticed. Too remote to be seen."

"So, you're not going to say," the Admiral said.

"No, Sir. I'm not going to say," Eric responded.

"Good," he said. "That was the General's plan and you're following orders."

"But what if you got killed?" Dent asked.

"What if?" Eric said. "Then they would be hidden and the Earth would be destroyed. It's not like we, any of us, had any really high expectations that we were going to survive this. Neither would the people on Earth survive. It's almost a miracle that we've done this much."

"Not so much a miracle," Braz responded. "I watched you. Each of you. It was hard work and bravery. Quite admirable. But I will say, some of the decisions you made were, how should I put it, impossibly fortunate."

Jason was looking through his scope at a mountain range while he was listening. There was a small green spot up high, away from the Invader's destruction, and he saw what he thought might be a stream running through it.

"Eric and his spirits," Jason said. "Right, Eric? Your ancestors?" But before anyone could respond he said, "And that brings us to the subject that is now pressing; Earth. We have to get back and defend it."

"Right," Gizmo said. "Whoever has been listening and planting those patches has to know that the relay is there. They'll go after it."

"Another thing we must consider," Braz said. "A subject Mr. Jason and I have previously discussed is that these Invaders could not have made this equipment. They have neither the intelligence nor the dexterity to make it."

"This is a scary thought," Cody jumped in. "So who made it? Do you have any ideas Mr. Braz?"

"None," he said.

"But," Jason said, "I expect we will be finding out shortly. I expect them to be visiting, if they haven't already. Mostly, I expect them to come at the Earth. Attack it. Attack us here as well."

The Admiral stood up, "Alright. Let's get these aliens off our ship and get back to Earth and defend it."

"Wait," Jason said. "The General and I expected something like this. I've had Cody and Dr. Hilliard set up two different capacitors. We can send two transports back to Earth. Keep one here. Split our forces and send half with them.

"We'll send all the relays for the other thirty-eight remaining transports with Cody. Once they are there, Cody can send one of the ships back with enough re-programmed relays that will work that we can send them all to Earth, if we need."

"In the meanwhile, I think we should change ships. Who knows how many of those patches are there," the Admiral said. "Braz. Can we make more of these devices to sweep the other ships?"

Braz surprised everyone by calling over one of his people who none had seen up until then. He gave instructions to go and work with the Admiral and Human scientists making the devices and to help sweep an empty transport they could transfer to.

Jason stood up and said, "Dent, I'd like to introduce you to someone. This person is going to be the most important person on Earth. He just may be the most important human that has ever lived. I wanted you, I asked for you, for one reason; to defend him; to make sure he lives. Mr. Dent, this is Cody."

Dent stood and looked back and forth at Cody and Jason and said, "Good to meet you, Cody."

The kid was flustered and embarrassed. "Good to meet you as well, Mr. Dent," then looked at Jason and asked, "But how do you figure? You are more important than me. You and Gizmo. You figured it all out, not me."

"Not without your ideas, we didn't. And what you are going to do back on Earth makes you by far the most important. Dent, you will be going to Earth with Eric and Cody. Dr. Hilliard will be staying here with us. We will give you a small force so you don't draw attention; a couple hundred men and plenty of weapons.

"Cody, as soon as you get there, you have to get those capacitors loaded up and get communication up. You will be placed in that secret location that only Eric knows. It will be your job, Dent, to make sure no harm comes to him," Jason said.

"Right," Dent said. He walked over and stood next to Cody and asked, "Why me?"

"I watched you. I watched you fight. You're the man for the job," Jason told him.

The Admiral got up and said that he would have half of his forces ready to leave within three hours and left Jason and his group to continue their planning.

Gizmo picked up his rifle and was now looking at the same green area Jason had spotted in the mountains earlier. "Braz," he said. "Do you guys like camping?"

"I'm not sure what that is. But I might try it if you wish," he answered.

Once the Admiral left, they all sat at the table without much talking at first. Even Braz pulled up a chair and sat with them. They took turns looking through the scopes up at the mountains and searched the small green spot for some sign of life.

"I've never been camping," Hilliard finally said, breaking the silence.

"Seems like forever since I've been. What's it been, Jason?" Gizmo asked.

"Yah. Long time. What, two or three days now?" and they all started laughing. "Should'a loaded my R.V. on that contraption. There's plenty of room."

"Do you think we brought beer?" Eric asked.

"You can't have any. You're driving the transport. Remember? But man, that sounds good right about now. Drink a couple for us when you get home," Jason said.

They continued that way, before going over the plan for the return to Earth, information to relay to the General, and instructions to return if Earth had been destroyed or there was any danger to Cody. They had all agreed that this would become the new Earth if the worst had happened.

"Either way," Jason ended the outing, "We are here for good. Mankind, I mean. We're going to settle this planet. This place is now ours."

"Jason Brand. You own much more than this planet; far more," Braz said.

"You know, I'm not sure these invaders are native to this place. I think they are more like a test-tube race. What about you Giz?" Jason asked.

"Probably right. I think we should get up on that hill and look around," Gizmo said. "I doubt there would be any caves that haven't been dug out, but you never know what we'll find. Maybe something left of the old population, if there was one."

"You up for a little hike, Braz?" Jason asked.

Chapter Twenty

Eric arrived with the two Invader transports in low orbit around Earth. The two ships filled with shuttles had been swept for surveillance and half of the Admirals forces and equipment had been sent back to Earth with them.

The transports were spotted on the ground by the Ruby Ridge base and that sent it into a flurry to defend against another Invader attack. Even the General armed himself and came out to the lookout post.

Each transport had twenty-six hundred and forty shuttles, and Eric had all fifty-two hundred and eighty of them take off from the bays, except two, and they all began flying in a confused pattern. He had to obscure the location of the villagers in case they were being followed or watched

The General watched as they came closer and closer. It was obvious that this was not an invasion; he had watched recordings enough to know their pattern. This was not it.

After giving orders for all to hold their fire, he went to the landing bay where a single shuttle eventually pulled in and landed. Every man and woman cheered as the shuttle door opened and a man in uniform stepped out.

"Greetings from Admiral Harding, General," the man stood and saluted.

"Welcome home," the General saluted back. "Damn good to see you, soldier."

"Colonel Eric Runningsprings sends his regards as well, General. He should be the next to land."

Eric left the transport helm to another pilot and made his way to the shuttle. He stepped through the entrance and surveyed the occupants one more time. There were weapons, supplies, medicine, soldiers, and of course, Dent protecting the most precious cargo, Cody.

Dent had Cody practically pinned up against the bulkhead with his massive body. Eric walked by and said, "Wait 'til you meet the Gunny. I think you two will get along," and continued toward the cockpit, thinking that Cody was in good hands.

He pulled the shuttle out and did a couple of figure eights amongst the other shuttles while slowly descending toward Ruby Ridge, dodging this way and that to avoid being tracked.

To anyone below or anyone watching from above, it would look like a confused hive of bees flying without pattern. This is what was wanted. It was easy for tight maneuvers with these shuttles. The invaders had huge hands and movements were gross. But with the much smaller hands of Humans, they could make smaller and tighter maneuvers.

Eric pulled his shuttle directly under another and they flew their agreed upon route to the location of the villagers. There he would land in a spot that would keep him fairly well hidden, and the other shuttle would continue on. Once unloaded, another swarm would come again, and he would join them, blending in unnoticed again.

This is the spot the relay was kept that powered the transport to the Invader planet. It was what was powering the transports they had just arrived in. If this spot were in jeopardy, the Admiral, Jason and Gizmo, and the rest of the human force may never return and would be without contact forever.

Eric opened the shuttle door and Dent stood and walked over to it. Peering out, the first thing that caught his eye was the barrel of an RPG pointed at him. Not seeming phased by this, he directed the rest of the men out and onto the ground.

From behind the RPG, the Gunny stepped around a bush and walked toward them. Eric bounced to the ground and the Gunny let out a smile and called to him.

"Colonel. You're alive!" and started running.

"Gunny. Isn't that a kick? How are you?" Eric called back.

It was only then, when it was certain that all was clear, that Dent called Cody to the opening. As soon as he appeared, people of the village began coming out from behind trees and shrubs and rocks and ran toward him.

They were mobbed like celebrities and Dent was very ill-at-ease over the advancements toward Cody. Eventually Hellen, Singingbird, made it through the crowd and was allowed to approach. She exchanged embraces with Eric and then walked over to Cody.

"My boy," she said in tears and she hugged him and gave him a big kiss on the cheek. "I missed you so much," and she stood back and looked at him.

"My lord. You look terrible. Don't they have food in outer space? Look how skinny you are. Didn't they feed you this whole time?" she asked with a look of shock.

Cody had never known the correct response to these remarks. There may be no correct response. It was a remark like she had made to him since he was a child any time she had not seen him for a while. It was a remark that somehow always ended in him eating Hellen's corn soup, whether he was hungry or not. This time, he was, and as soon as the words came out of her mouth, as if on cue, his stomach began growling.

Dent stood patiently and surveyed the area during the greetings. Men, well hidden until now, were beginning to give their positions away as the excitement drew their heads up for a better look.

Positions were spotted, easily defended positions, hard to get to, and well hidden. He was about to take notice of a spot that he would have set up, and then saw a barrel of a large caliber gun sticking out. "Humph," he grunted.

Hellen heard it and looked at him.

"This is my friend, Mr. Dent," Cody told her. "He is here to help us."

"Well. I don't know if we need any help, but he sure looks like he could handle a good meal too," and she took them both by the hand. "Come. I have corn soup from yesterday. It's always better the next day, you know."

They were led to a waterfall with a ledge behind it about twenty feet up. Behind that was a cave, obscured by the fall, where the Indian village had set up their living quarters.

Eric looked around at all the items he brought them earlier and took a mental inventory as Hellen scooped out a bowl for each of them and handed it out.

"Ammo," Eric said as he noticed a pile of empty boxes. "We brought some."

"Good. We spent some on a wave of Walkers," the Gunny said.

"Really? They got this far? Where is the nearest base besides the one we know?" Eric asked.

"We are not sure. But they were here. Surprised us too. They may have just chased some animals up here," the Gunny told him. "It was just that one wave."

"You set up the defenses?" Dent asked.

"Yes," the Gunny answered after taking a healthy swallow of hominy.

"It looks good. Well set up. You must be the Gunny I've been hearing about," Dent said.

"Stonefish," he said as he stood up to shake hands.

"Gunny. This is Private Dent. And don't let the private title fool you," Eric said. "Jason sent him to…well, for Cody. Him and the men outside. Cody has some work to do and he is his…" he looked at Hellen and could not bring himself to say he was his protection. It would cause her to worry and wonder why he would need it.

The Gunny got it and stood up again to save him from his predicament and said, "Good to meet you private. I'll give you the ten-cent tour whenever you're ready and we can talk."

A lieutenant that Eric brought with the rest of the men rushed in and ran up to Dent. He stumbled on his words, not knowing how to start because he outranked Dent. Dent was a Private, he was a Lieutenant. He was confused and didn't quite know how to address him and started, "Si...umm, Mr. Dent. We have the shuttle unloaded and the men are waiting for your instructions."

Dent finished swallowing his corn soup and stood. "Thank you, Lieutenant. Tell them to take a knee. I'll be right out," he said as smooth and easily as can be.

Both Eric and the Gunny saw the ease with which he handled the authority and more, how he commanded authority, making the lieutenant feel comfortable with taking orders from him. The Gunny looked at Eric and nodded toward Dent.

"I know. I know," Eric said. "There is a story here, I know. This aint no Private. Are you Dent?"

"Am now, Colonel," he replied. "Gunny, ready when you are," and walked up to Hellen and held her by the hand, "Madame. That was some of the best soup I believe I have ever had. You must make some man very happy."

The men outside stood in formation and snapped to when Dent walked up with the Gunny and Eric. Dent walked through and picked out ten of them and sent them inside with orders to stay with Cody and not let him leave their sight.

"I don't care if he has to take a crap," he said. "You will be there holding a roll of paper for him. And you mind your manners and you watch your damned language around the kid and the lady, gentlemen, I mean it."

As they were heading away toward the cave, Eric and the Gunny heard one of them say, "Do you know who that is? No shit, you won't believe it." But they got too far away to hear what the man was saying.

Eric raised an eyebrow at the Gunny and they walked over to Dent, both about to question him about whom he was. Before they could get a word out, Dent cut them off.

"Gunny. If you don't mind, I'd like to get the gear stowed and your weapons loaded up and supplied. Jump in if I miss anything, but right now, we're way too visible. I'd like to get this shuttle out of here. We're drawing attention to the kid," and then he started issuing orders for the placement of ammo.

To the Gunny's surprise, he named and sent men with ammo to every hidden location in the hills surrounding them. Then he began placing larger weapons in areas the Gunny would have liked to have manned, but just didn't have the weapons. The surprising thing was that he pointed directly at the locations.

Then he had the remaining supplies carried inside the cave. He told one of them to put some light past where they would see Cody and Hellen, and back in the dark around a corner, they would find an area to stash the supplies. They were then to set up defenses at the cave entrance.

He had the remaining men man the defenses the Gunny had set up with Invader weapons and replace the villagers who were posted there with directions they would be on a four-on four-off watch and to spread the word, there was incoming.

The Gunny was impressed. Dent had never been there before, but knew every location he had placed. He had never been inside the cave, but knew about the cavern. Again, it was time for questions. Eric and the Gunny walked up and were about to ask, when Dent cut them off again.

"Colonel. You'd better get out of here. We are going to see action here in about fifteen minutes. I don't want you giving our location away with that shuttle," he said.

"What? What do you mean? How do you know?" Eric asked.

"Don't worry. I know," and he turned to the Gunny. "Let's get up in that hill there," and pointed back above the entrance to the cave. As he started running, he turned back to Eric and yelled in a commanding voice, "Get moving, Colonel."

Eric jumped into his shuttle and called the swarm of shuttles to fly over and cover his departure. As he fired off toward the base, he thought that, yah, the choice Jason made, to use Dent, was definitely a good one.

Chapter Twenty One

Dent and the Gunny were crouched about thirty feet above the cave entrance to the side of the waterfall. From there, they could see the fall pool into a small lake, and follow a small stream running out from it toward the valley before it dropped again over a cliff.

That was where Dent directed their attention now, at the spot that it dropped. The sun was about to go down as three mountain goats jumped up over the top onto a flat area and ran toward them.

"Goats?" the Gunny said. "We're hiding from goats?"

"Watch," Dent said, pointing toward the edge.

Three Walkers jumped up after them. Then three more. Then more. The goats were running as fast as they could, bringing several hundred of them directly toward the villagers. They caught up about half way across the grassy area and pounced on them.

One of the goats, the male, turned to confront the Walkers and instantly had his head torn off while the others were strewn about in pieces and then devoured. They were about a thousand yards away when it was all over.

They howled and growled and slashed at each other and then darted in different directions, searching for something else to move that they could chase and kill.

"Let's see if more are coming," the Gunny whispered.

"Yah. Or see if they will move off," Dent said.

They sat and watched the monsters tear and slash at each other. The noise they made drew even more up the cliff, until the racket was deafening.

"We could start firing," the Gunny said, "but that could bring even more, until eventually, they would find their way into the cave. The last time they came, there weren't so many. We picked them off as they came over the edge."

They were speaking loudly now so they could be heard. "I used to have lookouts over the edge there on either side, but their positions put them at too much risk," the Gunny continued as the herd grew even larger.

"Well. Nobody is getting back here as long as they are there. But I still don't like it," Dent said. "We can take 'em out. We have the invader weapons. But we will have, what, thousands of dead Walkers to dispose of. We are supposed to be hidden."

They both sat for a while longer considering their options. They could call Eric and have him fly over, but that would also give their location away. What they needed was for them to leave.

"Is there another base around here or something? There must be, right?" he asked the Gunny.

"Not that I know of. But who knows where they came from. There might be," he answered. Then he looked at him and asked, "How did you know?"

"Know what?" Dent asked.

"That they were coming," said the Gunny.

"Oh, that. I saw them from up above," he answered.

They stayed there and watched the strange creations of Dr. Bradley in the open viciously slashing at each other and pouncing on the waving grass or anything else that moved. "From up above. You're not talking about up above in the shuttle, are you?" the Gunny asked.

Just then, a rabbit darted from under a brush. The nearest Walkers saw it and instantly gave chase. Within seconds, the entire herd was giving chase. It ran all the way to the cliff edge and disappeared, with the herd of Walkers going down after it.

After waiting another twenty minutes to see if the Walkers would come back, Dent said, "Let's go see how Cody is doing. We have to get communications up to Jason and the Admiral."

Dent stood with the Gunny watching as Cody fiddled with some electronics. Ranger Jenkins came over and struck up a conversation. "You think we'll be getting out of here soon?" he asked.

The Gunny bent forward to look around Dent and said, "I think pretty soon. When Cody is done with this. He's got to get some of these gadgets working to send back to Jason so they can bring some more transports back. Then he has to try and get some communication up."

"He's gonna bring transports here? How many?" Jenkins asked.

"Well. I think twenty to start. But we are going to have a lot of them as time goes by. A lot. In fact, maybe all of them," Dent said. Then he held out his hand to introduce himself. "My name is Dent."

"Jenkins," he said, shaking his hand. "Good to meet you."

Hellen walked up to them and was standing, listening while watching Cody with his hands deep in a mass of wiring. She was wearing her usual Indian attire, a colorful dress with her hair tied in the back. Dent glanced over at her briefly and then continued to watch Cody.

"Mr. Dent," she said. "Mr. Jenkins was the Ranger at Ruby Lake you know. He was with the bunch that captured the first Evil Walkers ever, him and Eric and of course the Gunny...or um, I mean Mr. Stonefish. Did you know that Jason and Gizmo was there? And Bo, too.

My but I miss that dog. Never thought I would. By my Lord, I surely do miss that dog. What a good soul, that Bo."

Dent looked back and forth at the Gunny and Jenkins in surprise. "You guys actually caught some of those things? That, I can barely imagine."

"Well," Jenkins said. "I was only there. The Gunny here along with Eric and Gizmo and his men, they actually caught them."

"Humph. That must have been something. Those things are pretty nasty," Dent said.

"Don't let him fool you, Mr. Dent," Hellen said. "Ranger Jenkins stood up to them as tall as any man could. The Gunny, I mean Mr. Stonefish as well. They were all there. The way it was meant. The way it was supposed to be."

Dent stood there watching and thinking, "The way it was supposed to be. The way it was meant. I wonder what she means by that."

"Cody," Hellen called. "We have to eat now."

Cody had his head deep in his project and was about to protest, but realized how fruitless it would be. Hellen called, and he would go, even if he was in the middle of such minor things as saving the world. He'd learned long ago that she always does something for a reason and does it at some time for a reason. He had long since stopped arguing, and put down his soldiering iron and stepped away from behind his bench, and smiled at her, ready to give her his full attention.

He walked up to her and wrapped his arms around her and said, "It's so good to be back with you."

"Oh, come now," she stepped away and quickly wiped her eyes. "If you start that, you'll have me in tears. No time for such nonsense. We all have some things to discuss over a good meal." Then she lost control and grabbed him and gave him a hug back.

At the table, the Gunny was scooping out a large spoonful of mashed potatoes when he asked, "So, Mr. Dent. Just curious. When we were outside. When you said you saw the Walkers from up above. You weren't talking about when you were in the shuttle, were you? Not up above from in the shuttle, right?"

"No," he answered.

The Gunny grabbed some corn and started shoveling it onto his plate. He looked over at Hellen and gave her a nod. Hellen remained silent. She just reached for the bread and handed it over to Dent.

"Thank you, Ma'am," he said.

He was still thinking about the comment from Hellen; about how it was supposed to be and how it was meant to be. He looked over at the equipment Cody was working on and wondered if that was the way it was supposed to be and the way it was meant to be and if he was supposed to be here or meant to be here.

Cody's eyes darted back and forth between the two men, swallowed some mashed potatoes and asked, "So...you saw the Walkers coming from up above, but not from the shuttle. So...what, where did you see them from?"

Hellen reached over and patted him on the hand with a big smile. He looked at her and knew this conversation was supposed to occur. It was somehow for his benefit. He was being led, they were all being led. He was supposed to hear this. The spirits were talking to Hellen. Cody put his fork down and looked at Dent.

"From above," Dent said. "Just from above."

"But not from the shuttle and not from the transport," the Gunny said.

"Right. Not from there," he answered, feeling a little uncomfortable from the attention.

Cody's face lit up. He sat forward in his seat and grabbed his fork back up, shoveled a few mouthfuls in at once and chewed. After he finally swallowed, he said, "Damn! I read about things like that! The government did some tests on that."

"You watch your language at the table, young man," Hellen scolded. "Just because you are important, doesn't mean you have to act like it and curse at the dinner table."

"Sorry Hellen. Sorry. Please excuse me everyone: my language. Please excuse me," he said.

Dent and the Gunny leaned back in their chairs and snickered.

"And don't you two encourage it," she said to them.

"NO, ma'am," Dent said, shaking his head. "No, no, no."

The Gunny was about to reach over for a slice of bread, looked at Dent and said, "I've heard about it too. What am I about to reach for?"

"Bread," Dent said without hesitation.

"You're right. It was bread," he said, and grabbed a slice.

"Damn! You are one of those guys," Cody erupted.

"Cody!" Hellen raised her voice. "Don't you ever think you are too big or too important for me to tan your hide. I will not hear such language coming from you and I won't tell you again."

"No, ma'am. Yes, ma'am. I'm sorry. It's just that it's exciting to meet someone like, like Mr. Dent," he said.

"There is never any excuse for bad manners. Especially in front of me. You would think you were in the field playing Lacrosse with hoodlums or something," she said. "Next thing you know, you'll be drinking whiskey and ruining your health. You are too smart to go down that path, Cody. You have too much to do. And we didn't raise you to be some lazy drunken hoodlum."

"Yes, ma'am," he said, embarrassed now.

Dent sat and knew what was coming. It was the same with anyone who discovered some of the things he did in the past. There was about to be a torrent of questions about the secret program nearly every government on Earth had and knew about. The Russians called it Remote Influence. The Americans called it Remote Viewing.

Depending on the intelligence and depth of understanding of the persons asking the questions, it could be very uncomfortable for him. Cody was very intelligent. In fact, for a kid to even know about the subject was remarkable. The Gunny seemed to already be familiar with it as well, probably from his time in the military. Hellen, well, she was Hellen, and apparently she knows more than she is ever going to tell.

"That's right," he said. "I was in the program."

"I just have a couple of questions, Mr. Dent. Do you mind if we talk about it now? Or maybe we should eat first," Cody asked, looking at Hellen to check his manners.

"Me too," the Gunny said. "Do you mind?"

"No. Shoot."

"Well. When you say you saw them. How did you see them? I mean, did you actually go and see them? I mean, you knew they were coming. Did you go in your mind to see, or did you actually…go?" the Gunny asked.

"Usually I just actually go. Some people call it astral travelling, some people call it different things. But I usually just go," he said.

"So you actually, what, left your body and floated out to see them?" the Gunny asked.

"Right," he said, and reached for a plate of desert.

"Where did you go?" The Gunny continued.

"I just went up above us and looked. We trained and practiced it for years," he said.

Cody was sitting, riveted, and had to jump in. "So you floated up above and saw them. But Mr. Dent. They weren't there. They didn't arrive for another, what, half an hour or forty-five minutes? Mr. Dent, how could you have floated up and seen them? They weren't there when you floated up," he pointed out.

Dent pushed his plate forward and dropped his fork onto it. He settled back in his chair and looked at Cody. He thought how not many people would have caught that discrepancy. They usually are stuck in their own unreality of being able to leave their bodies, a talent he has introduced to so many people. They usually can't think beyond that.

"You're a smart guy, Cody. That is a good and relevant question," he said. "You know, I'm not sure how much you know about the subject, but some people look at things right now. Some people can see that, but can also see what happened in the past. But some people can also see what is in the future."

"You mean actually go and look. Like go into the future?" Cody asked.

Dent nodded and picked up his cup of coffee. This is where, no matter how smart or open to new ideas a person is, the conversation usually dies. It is too unreal for most people, although it is routinely done, or used to be done before the invasion. It is easier to dismiss it all as something make-believe. This is what he expected now.

He watched Cody push his plate forward as well and pick up a glass of juice Hellen poured for him. He watched his mind turning as he thought about it. He watched a smile come to his face and his eyes start to look around. He had made a decision or came to a conclusion.

"Hellen," Cody said. "Thank you for the meal. I really liked it. Every time you cook something, it feels so special. Like you did it for me. I don't think I ever thank you enough."

"Oh, Cody. I've been cooking for you since you were a baby. It is special. It's special every time. It is made with love, my boy. That's what makes it so special," she said. "But thank you for saying. Now all of you get out of here and get back to work before I start blubbering again."

She got up and started to shoo them all from the table so she could clean up. Cody strolled over to his project with Dent and the Gunny.

"Mr. Dent," he said. "I believe I have done what you described. On occasion, at least. But I have done that: left the body. I know it. I read a couple of books on it. Maybe, if we have time, you could teach me…you know. Maybe you could teach me how to do it like you do."

"It would be my great honor, Cody."

Chapter Twenty Two

Eric was with the General getting a personal debriefing. The attack had been described in intricate detail, going over the orbiting defenses and progressing to the capture and disabling of the Invader base holding the Quantum Capacitors and Relays.

"And that is about when the transports began arriving?" the General asked.

"That's when they started arriving. Once we put the satellites out and were on the surface. When we threatened the base, that's when they started showing up," Eric said.

"I wonder what happened...to the transports I mean. What do you think happened to transports if they were mid-leap to the Invader planet when Colonel Brand pulled the plug?" he asked.

"You know, I wondered that myself," Eric said. "I just don't know. I know that, when we pulled the capacitors, everything they owned died. All power went out. So they could be trapped in the leap or they could just be, well, stuck where they were. The leap, according to Jason, is instant. But I guess there is no such thing as an absolute. That's what Jason and Gizmo were saying; there is no such thing as absolutes."

"What do you mean? No such thing as absolutes," the General asked.

"Well, everything is moving. Even rocks and boulders have motion on a molecular level. So nothing is perfectly still. They're not absolutely still. So there is no such thing as absolutes. They are also decaying, being eroded. That's one example they gave. So, as far as time and the transporters jumping, it is instant, but there is no such thing as absolutes, so it wouldn't be absolutely instant," Eric explained.

"No such thing as absolutes. I guess so," the General mumbled. "We have some smart people here. But Brand and Crozley, they are each one of a kind. Physicists and damn good soldiers to boot."

"I know, General. Talented men, those two. No way would we have done this without them," Eric told him.

"We have scientists that survived; some physicists and quantum physicists. But none of them are trained soldiers. None of them would have been able to do what you described," the General said.

"Hell, General. I don't think I could have, training or not. And none of them, as good a scientist as they might be, none of them figured out this invader power source. That was Jason. Jason and Gizmo," Eric added. "But they seem to think that Cody is going to be important too, and for some reason, maybe even more important."

"Why do you suppose that is? He's just a kid," he asked.

"Maybe it's because he is just a kid. He keeps up with the Scientists pretty well. He keeps up with Jason and Gizmo too. Maybe they're thinking long term. Like another thirty or forty, even sixty years. Maybe they are thinking that with what the kid knows now, Jason and Gizmo will be dead and gone, and he'll still be learning and developing new things," Eric said.

"Maybe. Probably. We're in the space age now; the real space age. No turning back from that. The only way is forward. What kind of formal schooling has he had?" the General asked.

"None. He just had high school on the reservation like everyone else. Pretty poor quality, actually," Eric told him. "But he was always smarter than the other kids; always fixing things and taking things apart. He was always trying to figure something out. Nothing like some of the paint huffers we had."

"I don't like him being out of the base. But I think that, if we are going to be hit, maybe we should keep him hidden. Then, if what you are saying is true, and I believe it is, there may be attempts to gain the Invader power source he's been working on," the General said. "That must be protected at all cost."

"So, we'll just leave him there, for now anyway?" Eric asked.

"Until we get a shield put up like they had on that dome. Then we move him here," the General told him. "I have someone being interrogated who may have an idea of who is behind the Invader plan here. Bradley. I just think he's too nuts to know it, but he may know the link."

"Cody should have about half of the capacitors ready in the next day. I can deliver them and we can have twenty more transporters here. That'll be good protection. I can be there and back in no time," Eric said.

"Right. In no time. But not absolutely no time, right?" the General emphasized.

"Right. Not absolutely no time. Jason really wanted me to make that point," Eric answered.

"Let me put a plan together. Other than that, you're right. Let's get as many transporters as we can here and set up some defenses with them," the General said.

Chapter Twenty Three

Jason and Deri were alone in his quarters discussing her planet. "I have no ship to get back to see if we even survived," she was saying.

"Don't worry. No matter what happened, you can come with us. All of you can. The worst that will happen is you stay and live with us," Jason said.

"But it's not the same," she said, lying with her head on his chest. "It won't be our home."

"I know. But until we know what happened, you are welcome with us. You know that, right?" he said. "And when we are ready, we can take a transport and see what happened to your planet."

"If the Invaders didn't get off, that means there are millions of them stranded at my home. They'll be killing everything. I can't imagine it. Jason, we have to do something," she said. "And what about all the other species that aren't as advanced as we are? All those other people, it's a horrible thought, what would be happening to them. We have to help them."

"We'll figure it out. We have to do it for everyone, too. Don't worry. I'll go with you and we'll find out together," he said.

Bo was busy exploring on the level below. The visitors, the diplomats, the Ambassadors, and the remainder of races from the far reaches of space brought so many gifts that an entire empty deck had been assigned as the receiving area.

Jason walked through it one time, amazed at all the items, but having no idea what most of them were. But Bo was there following the familiar trail of scent he left and was exploring the many odd odors from every civilization that had arrived.

The items were placed on shelves along rows starting at the front of the transport. It was an unimaginable and overwhelming display of wealth that stretched for almost the full length of the craft. Jason walked through, spending an hour looking it over, examining the different objects. Deri tried to explain some of it to him, but so much of it, she hadn't seen either and did not know the purpose.

The receiving room for the guests had been expanded due to additional arrivals and Jason had the next meeting planned with an Invader captured and caged in preparation for his audience.

Jason stood at the head of a long table once again, thanking them for all the gifts and telling them he would open a museum to place them in and asked for an explanation of the cultural significance of each piece before he addressed the issue of the Invader weapons.

"As for your requests for the Invader technology, I have a question for each of you. I want you to look around the room and think carefully before you answer. Look at the people and races among us here and answer this question: Which of you wishes the destruction of any of these races? Just stand up and point to them now."

He waited for them to look about the room uneasily and continued after none had spoken up or pointed. "Of course," he said. "I don't believe any of you would go and annihilate another race, would you? And think about it, do any of you have any concerns that any of the beings here would come and annihilate you? Just get up and point. Look, now is the time to say it," and again waited for any of them to answer who might want to.

"Believe me when I say that I understand. I do understand why you would want this Invader power. But I want you to understand my decision and why I made that decision. I also want you to understand that this is no reflection on your intentions or honor or your morality. None at all.

"But amongst all of you here, only two have asked me to use this technology to go and save their planets; to save the people of your planets and to go and save others on other planets. Even though this…" and he pulled back the covering on the cage exposing the captive Invader. "This is right now slaughtering defenseless populations across the universe. Some of them, your own people."

Walking across the front of the cage, eying the Invader, he continued. "These creatures enjoy killing. They can't be negotiated with and they can't be reasoned with. They won't stop and they won't give up. The only thing you can do with them is kill them, and until you kill them, they will be stranded wherever they might be on your planets, and they will be killing your own people.

"We are compiling a list of civilizations from the Invader databases. We are going to start with the ones at most risk of extinction and we will all go and save them. Some of you have weapons that you can use against them. Since we shut down the Invader weaponry and power two days ago, you have been able to defend yourselves.

"Other races will not be so fortunate. They will be being chased down on their own planet surfaces and they will be killed. Tomorrow, I will have a complete list of those races. We have an historic moment here. I cannot believe that ever in the history of this universe has there been a coalition like yourselves, come together for the aide of each other and to conquer a common enemy. Thousands of races and species. You all should be honored to be a part of it. I know we are.

"Once we have gone and saved these planets, and I mean all of us, starting with the weakest, I will make it a law that you are allowed to freely inhabit your own home planets again. That will be my gift to you.

"And there is another thing. I have not been deaf to your plea. Each planet we go to will likely have an invader transport. There will be thousands of them. We will use them to communicate and move between this Coalition of Planets who is sitting here right now. If ever, ever, ever, any of us are threatened again, you will have this Invader technology and weaponry to defend yourselves.

"For this, I will have only small demands of each of you at times. Any questions?" and Jason looked around for anyone to respond and then pulled out a weapon Deri had provided. "This is the only enemy we have here," he told them. He raised the weapon and shot the Invader in the head, ending the meeting.

Chapter Twenty Four

"Well," the Admiral said. "I hope the General agrees with our decision and our plan."

"Me too," Jason said. "Then again, I hope he's still alive. Earth might be one of the first planets on that list we're making."

"No. We will never put Earth on that list. I never want any of them to know how vulnerable we were," said the Admiral. "Still are, for that matter. Any one of those species you were just speaking to could conquer the Earth; even the weakest of them."

"There are still the two transporters that Eric brought home. He's pretty good at tactics. If there were any problems, he could deal with it. And he knew to come right back if Earth was wiped out. Then, there is the General," Jason said.

"And if the transports here go dead, we'll know they have been hit," the Admiral added.

"Right. But I kept Dr. Hilliard here. If Eric and his men get taken out, we can start from scratch here. Program everything from here again, from scratch. Use this sun for power. The only problem then is, well, every dead transport around the universe could then be alive again," and Jason added, "So we jump in what we have and get the hell out of here before they arrive."

"Let's hope Eric and Cody do the mission," the Admiral said.

"Yah," Jason said. "Let's hope. In the meanwhile, I think we're putting on a good show, don't you Admiral?"

Chapter Twenty Five

Bo came to the end of a row and sniffed a crystal and metallic object before moving around to the next aisle where she stopped, looking straight back toward the entrance. There was a movement by the opening that she sensed, and her ears pointed straight forward toward it, and her hair stood up.

She stayed there, frozen like that, waiting for a sound or a motion, waiting for any sense to detect something. The opening being far away and there being no immediate danger, she went back to her chores, sniffing the items on the shelves.

She continued this, going in and out of the isles, until she heard the scraping of metal about half way from the entrance to where she was. Again she stopped and listened, and then ran to the center of the aisle to look and she froze.

There was something there and she knew it. Whatever was there also knew Bo was there, and they were hiding. Bo knew things about hiding. She knew two things about hiding. Bo knew things don't hide without reason. They were either food for Bo, or Bo was food for them. In her mind, those were the only two reasons for hiding, and since they were moving toward her, she knew that she was the target.

In her mind, she was the intended meal. But whatever this was, it did not know Bo, and she accepted the challenge. She had faced down bear and she had faced down mountain lions. She had dispensed with packs of coyotes and wolves. There was no threat she would not face. She did not know fear. No, she would face this enemy stalking her now.

That is how the game started. It was a game of stealth where one side would try not to be detected and Bo had to find them. It was a game she had played many times. The contest was now started. Who would move first and give their position away?

Her senses were already heightened from exploring all the items on the shelf; all the smells, all the shapes. There were smells she had already associated with some of the visitors in the great room. Now her many other senses were put on alert as well, and she sensed one of the strongest there is for a dog, and that was fear.

Who would move first, that was the next part of the contest, and these contests are always done in parts. They already knew she was there, and most likely knew exactly where, but if she could make them move, she would have the advantage. She was fast, and she knew it, and she had no fear.

She would use their fear against them. Like a rabbit, she would make them bolt. They would move and she would see and hear them. She would sense the difference in air volume. She would track the motion and she would hunt them down like a rabbit.

She could move without being heard. Her soft pads on her paws would muffle any sound. She could breathe without being heard. Most other animals have no control of that. They panic. They breathe too hard and give themselves away.

She stood in the dark, perfectly still and perfectly silent, watching and waiting to capitalize on their mistake. A breath, a motion, a sound, is all it will take. Her steel-grey eyes cutting through the darkness, waiting for the inevitable.

It was one thing she was good at, waiting. Her ears standing up straight and pointing directly ahead, tiny hollow hairs ready to detect the slightest air movement. Her nostrils flared and filled with every scent at once.

Even the hair standing straight up on her back would detect the slightest motion, a change in air pressure. Her paws, with pads so sensitive that she could track with them, sensed every person and thing that had recently passed underneath.

She stood, frozen, and took it all in at once. It was a three-dimensional perceptual capture of this small part of the universe, a still photograph of sorts, and if any part of it changed, she would know. She knew she was being hunted. She was being stalked. She was being threatened. She was in danger. She lived for this, and she would turn this around.

She sensed a slight movement. Something turned its head slightly. Maybe only an inch or two, but it changed, and that was enough to give her the general area it was in.

Now she would use her secret weapon. It was a weapon she was so skilled in using that it came natural to her. She had used it on nearly every chase she was involved in. She used it to detect hiding animals for years, forcing them to flee in terror. She would direct sound waves in the area, like a shotgun, and make them bolt like a rabbit.

She let out three loud barks, directing the waves to the area she had detected the motion. It worked, and the predator was now the prey. It moved from the top of the shelf to another aisle.

It panicked, and panic is the enemy.

Bo raced to the aisle, her paws sliding on the smooth surface as she turned the corner, and raced toward the terrified enemy scrambling to escape up the next shelf. She charged, baring her teeth, leaping through the air, snapping at her enemy, catching its boot.

It stayed there, terrified and petrified, looking below at Bo fiercely growling and barking and gnashing her teeth. She could sense the fear. She could hear the breathing as she jumped at it and caught its leg. She could hear the heart pounding and feel it beating under her teeth as she clamped down.

She let go and walked over to the boot that she pulled off and smelled it, burning the scent into her memory, when she sensed the second one moving toward her. She went toward the motion, creeping carefully and cautiously toward it, hunting it, until an object was pushed from the shelf toward her.

She caught the motion of something move and she sprang forward. Quickly turning back to what would have certainly crushed her as it crashed to the ground, walked over to it and smelled it. Then she lifted her nose into the air and got a whiff, comparing the two.

She started backing up, growling and baring her teeth as she went when another object came crashing toward her. She dodged it by jumping through the shelf to the next aisle and turned and barked.

She sprang to the corner she had just turned and caught the bootless alien climbing down the other side, jumped toward him and dragged him to the ground, shaking his leg under her teeth as it screamed.

She caught the movement of the second alien again as it hurled another object toward her. She dodged it and went after him, chasing him up a shelf as well. She ran from one row of shelves to the other, barking and gnashing her teeth at them until she heard a third one moving farther away and she again went silent.

It was creeping slowly through one of the aisles when she caught a sense of the motion. She could feel the intensity of it. She could feel it was out to kill her. She could also feel that this one was different than the others. It was more of a threat. Stealthier, and more experienced, it crept toward her.

She felt it change direction down the aisle, and then she lost track of its movement. Bo crouched down and slowly crept toward the area, one paw cautiously in front of the other down the dark aisle, slowly, slowly moving to the place she last heard it, smelling all around the area and getting familiar with its scent.

She crept to the end of the aisles, getting to a spot where she could watch both of the two that she had captured and got down on the ground and waited. She stayed that way, lying, poised and ready to spring. Her ears were up and pointing, one toward the two aliens she knew the location of, and the other scanning from row to row.

She stayed, waiting, for the good part of an hour. The two aliens she caught would try to move, and she would growl and make an advance towards them with her teeth showing, and they would cower back to their position. Then she would move back and get back down with her legs under her, ready to spring into action.

There was a slight movement down an aisle and she went to it and looked around the corner down the long row of gifts. She heard a somewhat familiar noise. It was not quite the same as the noise Jason made when he pulled his weapon, but it was similar and it meant danger. The sound it made was not the same when it fired either, but the impact was nearly the same as it hit an object a few inches from her.

She backed up and crouched down as she went slowly and silently down the other aisle to come up behind it, reaching the end and turning back up the other side; she smelled the ground and, catching no scent, went over to the next.

Bo heard a shuffle and let out a growl and then moved quietly in that direction, moving up this aisle now, the one with the alien she had dragged to the ground, when a sight she recognized caught her attention; a form of an arm with a weapon.

Jason taught her to jump for the gun arm and hold it and shake it until it was dropped; to drag it down to the ground and keep shaking it until the weapon was released. She charged, leaping off the back of her downed alien and caught the arm between her teeth as it was coming around the corner, bones crunching under her powerful jaws.

The alien let out a scream as it was dragged to the ground and dropped the weapon. She stood, guarding the gun as she was taught and growling into the face of the intruder, teeth gleaming and saliva dripping into its face.

It slowly backed away while the other got up onto its feet and started hobbling toward the exit with the help of the second, slowly and cautiously at first, and then limping as fast as it could. The other looked back, watching them abandon him to the beast, and continued to cautiously creep backward on all fours. Then he slowly got up and started moving toward the exit, gaining speed as he went and bolted through the exit behind them, Bo barking and growling as they left.

Bo settled down and stood there watching the exit, ears pointing in their direction, then back inside again, waiting for them to come back and continue the game. She looked all round the chamber and checked for more smells or any other sense of a challenge. Then she took a good long smell of every part of the weapon and walked over to where the other intruder had been dragged to the ground by the leg.

There, she smelled around the area on the ground, up the shelf, onto the other side of the shelf and all around it. She followed the scent all the way from where they entered, to where they attacked her, and then all the way back to the exit again. These were smells she would not now forget and she burned them into her memory as well.

Happy with herself that she had done the gun trick that Jason had taught her, she contentedly bounced toward the exit herself now to find him and get her reward, stopping briefly for one last sniff around the opening.

Chapter Twenty Six

The Admiral had nearly every available shuttle manned and operated, scouring the surface and any structures for technology. At the same time, the remaining Invaders kept coming and attacking. The coalition forces were assigned to mop-up duty, routing out and getting rid of remaining nests of Invaders.

Time and time again, though everyone involved was warned against it, they would try to give the Invaders an opportunity to surrender; an opportunity to live in peace; an opportunity to coexist. Time and time again, the Invaders would kill them when they could.

In the beginning, many coalition forces were lost by them attempting to be benevolent, until it became painfully obvious that what Jason had said was the truth, that there was no reasoning with them, there was no talking to them, and there was no negotiating.

He described it as similar to a religion they had back on Earth. No matter how you tried, you couldn't stop them from killing you, even if they appeared to give up and even if they claimed they were peaceful. The only thing you could do was to kill them, because that is what they will eventually do to you and everyone else.

They were now tasked with the horrible job of exterminating an entire race – the Invaders. It was not that they wanted to do it; it was that the Invaders wanted to exterminate them. Jason referred to it as practice and explained how a religious group on Earth would expand and eventually force the good to do the bad, never changing throughout its history, getting stronger and expanding further, exterminating populations as they crept forward, then being cut back when mankind saw it faced another dark ages or faced extinction, then expanding again, over and over. The good would be forced to become murderers and butchers like them for their own survival, or become extinct.

Most of the coalition members were going to have to go to each other's planets and do the same thing, clear their own planets of these unthinking and murdering monsters. It was either that or be exterminated themselves.

The coalition forces were scouring the surface, and shuttles full of humans were pulling into the landing bay after capturing some Invader technology, when the entire planet went on alert. A transport had appeared in low orbit and the entire coalition sprang into action.

"Easy down there! Easy! Everybody hold your fire," Eric's voice came over the radio. "It's just me, guys."

"Welcome back, Colonel," the Admiral called to him.

"Thank you, Sir. I have come bearing gifts, Admiral. Some presents for you, Jason, and Gizmo," Eric said. "I'm leaving the transport here and I'll bring a shuttle down in a few minutes."

The Admiral and Eric were soon meeting in the chartroom along with Jason, Gizmo, and Bo. The room had been swept with the device Braz had provided and security was posted outside the room. Eric was now briefing them on the new plan sent by the General.

"Gentleman, now, to protect the Earth. That's the priority. Cody devised a method of extending the electromagnetic field of the transports around the space defenses here. We can transport the satellites directly home and set them up in orbit there. As soon as the transports jump, the field is extended around the stations, and they will jump with them as if they were part of it," Eric said.

"Smart kid. Smart idea," said the Admiral. "Protect the Earth. At the same time though, leave this place vulnerable."

"Right. In the meanwhile, I brought back twenty capacitors to fit the dead ships with. Another twenty will come as soon as Cody can get them to you. Nineteen of the ships will return home and one will go to Jason and Gizmo.

"I guess your mission was approved, Jason. Once I leave, the next time any of us see you, will be back on Earth," Eric told him. "The general has allotted you five-thousand men."

"When will we have communication to Earth?" the Admiral asked.

"We expect it to be functioning before we leave. In the meanwhile, we can jump back and forth as much as we want. It'll take a day or two to prepare the stations, and the General wanted you to express his appreciation to Deri and her crew and told you to tell her that he is looking forward to meeting her."

"Well, that's that then," the Admiral said as he stood up. "But before you leave, let me just say…well, hell of a job all of you so far, and good luck on your mission, you two."

"Admiral Harding," Eric said. "This is for you, straight from the General," and handed him a folder with Top Secret printed across it. They left him as he sat and opened the file.

Jason and Gizmo were standing with Bo at the end of the fantail, discussing their new mission and looking up at the mountains through their scopes when Eric strolled up with Deri and Braz.

"I have a game for you two," Jason said. "It's called heads or tails." He found a coin he had and showed it to them. "You see, there is a head on one side and not the other."

"But there is no tail," Braz said.

"Right. You just pretend there is a tail," Jason answered.

"So can we pretend there is a head, too? Then why do we even use that. We could just pretend to have that object," Deri said.

"Right. Okay then. So, let's pick another one. It's called rock, paper, scissors," and he explained how it went. "Alright. You ready? You are going to play each other."

"What are we playing for? What is the object?" Braz asked.

"It's a surprise. But you will like it," Jason answered. "Okay. Best out of five. Ready? Start."

They all watched as Braz won three straight rounds and they all cheered and laughed. It was the first time anyone had really heard Braz, Deri, or anyone else really laugh since they had been there.

Deri was smiling and said, "I want to do it again. It was fun."

"Let's do it later for something else," Jason said. "Okay Braz. We go to your home first. Then Deri, we go to yours."

"That's what it was for?" Braz asked. "To see what planet we go to first?"

"Yup, and you won," Gizmo said.

"No. I didn't," Braz explained. "This is a game of chance for you. But for me, it wasn't. I could tell what she was going to do before she did it. It is just something we do."

"What do you mean? How do you tell?" Gizmo asked, looking over at Jason and both stepping closer.

"We can see," he replied.

"What, you mean see what they are thinking?" Jason asked.

"No. No. We can see what is going to happen," he said.

"Okay. So pick another game," Deri demanded.

"No, Deri. We should go to your home first," Braz said.

"But why?" she asked.

"Because it's right," Braz answered. "Whatever is left of my home will still be there if we take a little more time. Your people are visible and more at risk. Mine cannot be easily seen. We should go to your home first, although I appreciate the opportunity your game of risk offered me, Jason Brand. I understand. It was an attempt at being fair."

"When do we leave?" Deri asked.

"Any time within the next two days," Jason replied. "When the rest pull out, we'll go at the same time. Make it look like we are all headed to the same place."

They all stood at the back facing the mountains. Jason lifted his rifle to focus his scope on the small green area he'd spotted earlier and said, "We should go up there, Giz."

Gizmo lifted his own rifle and scanned the area. "Yup. Might be some life up there. Check it out, Eric," and he handed his rifle over.

Eric put the scope up to his eye and looked the area over. Then he dropped it lower to see the access to it. There was a cliff to climb up to get to it and water ran through the small valley coming down from the mountains. He thought about how similar it was to the spot he chose back on Earth for the villagers.

"You know, if I were going to hide from the Invaders, that's where I would go," Jason said. "Some place like that."

"You think we should check it out now?" Gizmo asked.

"Yah. I want to get up there before we leave," Jason answered.

Chapter Twenty Seven

"They tried to drown me," Dr. Bradley thought to himself. "They tried three times to drown me with that stupid bag over my head."

Bradley was back in a cell after another series of water boarding during his interrogation earlier that day. He was sitting, chained to a chair at an uncomfortable incline, unable to rest or to balance his head in any natural position as the muscles in his neck and back screamed from the burning strain.

He tried to sit up straighter to balance the weight, but the chair was designed to make it impossible. Sitting too far back to let his head flop into any comfortable angle, he squirmed with his neck and back muscles in spasm.

"Fools," he thought. "This is the worst chair I have ever been in."

He went over in his mind what they were asking. It was Catskill they were interested in. That's all they asked about. Names, locations, times, over and over they asked. "Then they tried to drown me. They couldn't do it. Three times they tried and couldn't do it," he mused to himself. "I wonder if I'm becoming invincible. They must be terrified of me."

The light was so bright, he could almost see it bore through his skull and into his brain. Closing his eyes did nothing to shut it out. The drugs coursing through his system set every nerve in his body vibrating, alive, and painfully electrified.

He could not remember the last time he slept as the loud music blared toward him. He'd completely lost track of time and could barely even concentrate. He began hallucinating slightly, seeing one of his creations standing in front of him, the Walker.

"Good boy," he said to it. "You came to save me."

He saw the large shadow of a figure walk in front of the lights as the music was turned off, and heard a woman yell, "Wake up!" and felt a hard slap across his face. He focused and saw Dr. Callis, wearing a white smock, hair tied back, exposing a dark satanic tattoo up her neck. She was a large and fearful looking woman, a psychiatrist, tasked with breaking Bradley.

Standing in front of him, she wound up to belt him again as he screamed, "I'm awake! I'm awake!"

The blow landed across his mouth anyway, sending a shock of pain up into his temple. "Wake up!" she commanded again.

"I'm not sleeping!" he cried. "I'm awake. I swear!" he exclaimed as another blow was landed so hard he could hear the bones in his neck make a popping sound.

She stood and watched him quiver in fear before stepping closer to him and staring at him intently. She moved to his side and reached around his neck pulling him closer and rubbed her breast against the side of his head and asked in a sweet tone, "Who were you speaking to, Dr. Bradley?"

"Nobody. It was just...I thought I saw someone, but it was nobody. There is nobody. I swear," he stammered.

She walked around to face him again. "So first you say you saw somebody and then you say it was nobody," and she hit him again even harder. "Tell me the truth! Who were you talking to!" she demanded.

Bradley's lips were numb from the blow as he tried to answer. "I thought I saw sombething, but I guess I was wrong."

She lifted her leg up and put her heel against his shoulder and said, "Now, you wouldn't lie to me, would you Dr. Bradley?"

"No! Neber," he said as his bottom lip was beginning to swell.

Bradley fearfully looked up into her eyes, and then down to her foot and followed up her leg, tracing the black line on her dark stockings up to her skirt, and then further to see a leather corset and, above that, a tattoo of Satan about to have his way with her. In terror, his eyes darted back to Dr. Callis as she watched his reaction with a slight smile.

"You like it, don't you, Bradley," she said as she lowered her heel down to his crotch and shoved. "You do. You like it."

Bradley was at the mercy of the devil. The most evil woman he had ever encountered. She drugged him. She beat him. She tried to drown him. Failing that, she was now torturing him, mocking him, demoralizing him.

"No. I mean yes. No. I mean no. I don't," he stumbled, not knowing what to say or which way to answer to keep from being belted again.

It didn't matter, try as he might, she put her leg down on the ground and wound up for another blow. "You will tell me the TRUTH!" and landed one across the other side of his face.

She lifted her stiletto heel up to his crotch again and put more pressure this time. "What's this, Bradley?" she said, moving her foot up and down as if she were pressing on a gas pedal. "What is that? You do like it, don't you, you naughty little boy," and she walked away.

Bradley sat and caught his breath watching her walk, a large and butch looking beast, an Amazon, he thought, and looked down to where she had placed her foot. To his surprise, he had an erection. It had been so long since he had felt that, as much as he tried, he could not recall the last time that had happened. Perhaps, Bradley thought, as far back as College with his Psych teacher.

"You evil woman!" He called after her.

He froze and gave a slight panicked whimper before his breathing stopped when she paused at the door, looked back at him and smiled, "Oh, Dr. Bradley," she said. "You have no idea." Then she walked out.

As soon as the door shut solid, the music was again blaring into his mind. He started breathing again, going over his plan. He had to get free. He had to continue his work. He was so close to success, so close to conquering the world. Yet, here he was, chained and brutalized by this horrid woman.

"Hairless monkeys," he thought. "They are all hairless monkeys. But her, she's a hairless orangutan. A hairless ape. NO! A hairless gorilla!" and he wiggled a little and pulled on his restraints.

"My creations will be successful. I will take over the world. We will rid this Earth of those pesky hairless monkeys once and for all," he thought, while sitting and steaming at his mistreatment.

"Is this crazy? When did I start to lose my mind?" he thought. "No. It is strategy. It's not crazy. If I were crazy, I could not even ask if I were. It would be crazy to think I'm crazy.

"No. Crazy people don't question if they are crazy or not, do they? That's what that book said. Written by that madman. But he was right about that. This I am sure of. Since I cannot think I am crazy if I am crazy, I cannot be crazy.

"I will complete my plan. I will take over the world. I have as much right as anyone else to do it. Those people. Those hairless monkeys who want to destroy my creations. Those fools."

"Fools!" he blurted out.

Again he froze and gasped as the door opened and the music was shut off. He was about to yell out that he was not talking to anyone, thinking that Dr. Callis was coming back, when two men came in and released him from the chair.

They marched into a room with shower heads and stripped him before standing back. The water came out freezing cold and Bradley's screams echoed off the tile walls down the corridor where Dr. Callis was listening.

He was then covered in a white powder that stung his skin and burned his eyes, and marched through a dryer. Naked and cold, he was brought to a nearby room and strapped to a gurney. The two men left him there looking around wild eyed and panting.

The walls were bare and bleak except for one light, and there was a small table and cabinet next to him. He began eying the objects on the table. It was medical equipment, but odd looking ones, strange and unfamiliar to him.

He looked at one with what appeared to be a strap that would go around your head like a harness you would put on a horse or to muzzle a dog, perhaps, but it had a strange object attached to it.

His fear mounted at the strange shapes and threatening equipment he was seeing. There was a machine on top of the cabinet he was looking at. He squinted and tried to make out the logo it had. It had paddle-like devices attached and, at first, he thought it might be a defibulator. But his heart began pounding as he made out the words under the logo, "Electro Convulsive Therapy".

Just as it registered what it was, Dr. Callis walked through the door. His heart started pounding as she slammed the door shut and walked up beside him, looking down into his eyes with a smile.

"No!" he cried out.

"Yes," she answered as she took hold of the harness and put it over his head. The strange object at the end was put into his mouth, and he tried to spit it out. "Now, now, Dr. Bradley. You don't want to break your teeth, do you?" as she inserted the guard back in and drew the straps tight.

Bradley lay there naked, strapped to the bed and unable to move, his panicked breathing restricted by the mouthpiece; he was only able to breathe through his nose. Feeling like he was not getting enough oxygen, cheeks bellowing, he struggled and struggled against the straps while Callis prepared the equipment.

She turned and watched him fight for air for a moment and then her face lit up. "Oh, I have such a good idea for you. But you'll have to wait until next time," and she took out some cream and applied it to his temples.

"You know, Dr. Bradley. This doesn't have to be so bad," and she attached the leads from the ECT machine. "We might even find a way to enjoy it. Wouldn't that be better?"

Bradley looked at her and furiously shook his head in agreement. She then reached over and turned a dial on the equipment and stood back away from the gurney. Then she reached over and set a timer, and pressed a button.

A shock was sent through Bradley's brain. His toes curled and his breathing stopped as he convulsed. All the while, Callis was yelling, "You can tell me everything! You must answer my questions! You will tell me everything!"

His head felt like it was about to explode by the time the timer went off. His cheeks were ballooning as he tried to catch his breath, and spittle was flying out around the mouth guard.

"There. Now that wasn't so bad, was it?" she asked.

Bradley violently shook his head from side to side; his eyes bulged as she reached and turned another dial and set the timer once more. He tried to yell out, "NO!" when it started again.

"I'm your friend," she said as he began convulsing once again. "You love me. You can tell me anything. You must tell me everything. You can trust me," she repeated over and over, ending it off with, "You won't be able to remember this. You can't remember. Forget! Forget!" Just as the current died.

Again, Bradley's chest was heaving to get oxygen, his eyes were running, his vision blurred, his jaws were sore from clenching the mouth guard, and spit was running down his face. Just as he was regaining his bearings, he noticed Callis was on top of him, straddling him, and moving up and down.

"You like it, don't you Doctor?" she said.

All Bradley could do was to make a high pitched squealing noise as he realized the electrodes had been removed from his temples and were now attached to his testicles. He squealed.

"I want to feel it. Will you do it? I want to feel electricity inside me. I want to feel it coming through and into me," and she reached over and turned the setting and hit the timer.

They both instantly were thrown into convulsions and Callis screamed and pitched and Bradley squealed as she writhed on top of him until the timer went off and she collapsed, out of breath and out of energy.

Eventually, she began to move again. Bradley had passed out under the trauma and lack of oxygen from the weight on his chest. She slowly got off and pulled her skirt down, smoothing the front and looked back over at him. She closed her eyes and shivered, her massive body rippling once again from pleasure just from thinking about what had happened.

Then she lifted her hand, wound up, and slapped him hard across his mouth and screamed, "Wake up!"

Bradley was jolted awake and looked directly into her eyes.

"Now," she said, pulling off the strap for the mouth guard and coiling the leads back up, "Let's go have a little chat, shall we?" And she called the guards back in.

They put him in an orange jumper and lead him, slightly bent over, down a long corridor. As they were walking down to the interrogation room, Callis said, "Wait till you see what I have in store for tomorrow."

Bradley looked at her and thought, "Wait till you see what I have in store for you. Wait until I am done with you, you hairless monkey. No, you hairless gorilla - in heat," and continued to devise his plan. "In another two or three days, I will be free, and you, you will be at my mercy and the mercy of my creations.

"They want to know about Catskill? I can tell them about Catskill. I can tell them all about it," he thought. "But some of it, well, it will be so interesting that they will have to take a look. Yes, they will, and they will have to have me to show them where things are."

Chapter Twenty Eight

Caged!

How did this happen? Jason was standing in the back of a dark metal cage. Nearly pitch black, he tried to focus on the surroundings and find a way out. It happened so fast that there was no time to react. Jason slapped a patch on his uniform and called into it. "Gizmo," and waited for a response. "Admiral," he called a moment later. Then he called Braz and Deri, followed by Gizmo again.

They all went up on the side of the mountain with the creek running through to check for indigenous life, and before they could react, he had been captured.

They took a shuttle and made a circle around the flat area, looking for hidden Invaders or any other dangers. When it looked safe, they landed and stepped out into the green vegetation beside the creek.

"Fish," Gizmo said, looking down into the water.

They all came to look, Jason, Braz, and Deri. It was as interested in them as they were in it, and came close to the shore, lifting one eye out of the water and scanning the observers before casually swimming off.

"No predators up here, I guess. It's not afraid," Gizmo said.

Other than the Invaders, this spot had the only life any of them had seen on the planet since they arrived. The water came up through the rocks deep in the mountain and emptied into the valley, evaporating over the cliff before it reached the bottom. But up here, it was cool and clear.

Jason bent down and scooped some water up in his hand and tasted it and spit it out. "Clean water," he said. "Look at these plants."

They wandered around the field, exploring the life, the fish, a few bugs, the vegetation and noticed some holes for rodents. Bo ran off after a small animal, chasing it down a hole.

Jason called her back. "Better leave that alone, girl. Might be the only one left," and he absentmindedly rubbed her behind the ears while he looked around.

Eventually, they made their way over and stood on the cliff edge and looked out across the plain below. Off in the distance was the dome, huge, ugly, and un-natural and out of place. A gorge off to side of it dropped several hundred feet.

"I bet there was water here. That gorge was probably filled with it. I wonder where it all went," Jason mused.

After some time, they started hauling out some containers to sit on and began heating up packs of MREs.

Gizmo sat, looked around, and said, "Nice."

"This is camping?" Braz asked.

"Sort of. It's like camping, but normally we'd set up something to sleep as well. Maybe spend a few days and just relax," Jason said.

"The shuttle isn't good enough to sleep in?" Deri asked.

"We usually have a tent. It's a small fabric enclosure that you can sleep in. Really, it's just enough to keep the rain and bugs off you. It's almost like sleeping outside. Then, when it is really nice, we do sleep outside on the ground in a thing called a sleeping bag. I guess you have to get used to it," Gizmo told her.

A few minutes of silence went by and Gizmo asked, "So Braz. That game you just played, Rock Paper Scissors. You say you can tell what the other person is going to do before they do it?"

"Yah, Braz. Explain that. Do you actually see it? Or is it some kind of a sense you get?" Jason asked.

"Both," he answered.

They all sat prodding Braz to make himself more visible and more invisible while they tried to hide things from him; how many fingers they would hold up, what they were about to pull out of a pouch, things like that. Of course, he had to play round after round of Deri's new favorite game, Rock Paper Scissors.

Some time went by and they had eaten and were sitting quietly when Jason said, "So, Giz, what about this twenty-one year old virgin?"

"Oh, right. Right. The story," he said.

"Yah, the fantasy story," Jason added.

"Well, it's not really appropriate for mixed company. Know what I mean, Jason?" Gizmo warned.

Deri was checking the translator for what he meant by that. "So, you mean it isn't fit for females to hear? Come on Gizmo. I want to hear a story. Tell it to us," she said, turning around and lying flat on a container with her head in Jason's lap and letting the sun warm her face with a big smile.

Gizmo silently considered it for a while and said, "Okay. So there was this guy, Jim. And it was his birthday. He was twenty-one and he was still a virgin."

"There is some significance to that which I don't understand," Braz said.

"I think that perhaps it is odd that at that age, he is still a virgin. Is that it?" Deri asked.

"Yes. For some, it is. Some try to remain a virgin until they are married. But in his case, he wasn't trying to do that," Gizmo explained.

"So he failed to not be a virgin. I don't get it. Why didn't he mate?" Braz asked.

"Well, I'll tell the story and it might explain itself as I go," Gizmo said. "And by the way, this story is made up and is meant for humor."

"Oh!" Both Deri and Braz exclaimed.

"So his being a virgin is part of the humor," Braz said.

"Exactly," Gizmo said. "He has absolutely no experience and doesn't know what to expect or what he is doing."

Jason was laughing at the whole exchange. "This is going to be the longest joke in history," he said, making himself more comfortable and relaxed.

Braz and Deri did the same, settling down and getting comfortable, looking forward to being told a good story.

"So Jim meets his friend Mike, and he's all depressed. Mike notices this and asks him, what's up? Why are you so depressed?

"Jim tells him it's his birthday and that he just turned twenty-one.

"Well Mike tells him 'Happy Birthday', says he should be happy and celebrating, and asks him why that is so depressing, and Jim tells him it's because he is still a virgin.

"Whoa,' Mike says, and asks him about it. Well, Jim tells him that he is a little shy. He has a problem approaching girls. He says, 'Mike, I'm not like you. I can't do that like you do. I get too embarrassed.'

"Mike listens for a while and tells him, 'Jim, I've known you all my life. You are probably my best friend. I didn't know that about you. For your birthday, you just come over tonight to my place, and I will have a girl waiting for you and you can lose your virginity.'

"Awe," Deri said. "That's nice of him. I like this story."

"Right," Gizmo said. "So Jim is all like, really? You'd do that for me? Mike, you are without a doubt my best friend. So they arrange the time for Jim to come to Mike's house. Problem is, Mike spent the entire day looking for a girl for Jim and couldn't find one that was willing to do this. Jim was so excited and grateful and looking forward to this, and Mike just couldn't find anybody.

"Finally, in desperation, he buys a blow-up doll," Gizmo said.

"Wait. A what?" Both Braz and Deri asked.

Jason chuckled as Gizmo now had to explain what that was and what it was for, reminding them that this is just for humor, and wasn't a real story. They both laughed and settled back in for the rest of the story.

"So there is Mike, standing outside his house that night as Jim drives up and meets him in the driveway. He explains to Jim that the girl upstairs is shy just like him, maybe even more, so she probably won't talk very much," Gizmo said.

"Ooh," Deri said. "Because it is a doll. He's doing what you call playing a trick on him."

"Okay. This is a funny story," Braz said. "So then what happened?"

"Well, Mike had the doll all set up in the upstairs bedroom close to the window. He tells Jim that he left the lights off, so as not to cause the girl any embarrassment or anything and that he should just leave them off.

"So Jim thanks him again, telling him he is the best friend anybody could ever have, and goes upstairs to meet this girl and lose his virginity."

"Okay," Braz said. "That's pretty good."

"Yah. Tell us another story," Deri said.

"Wait. I'm not done. The story isn't over," Gizmo told them.

Jason covered his eyes with one hand and shook his head. Braz and Deri were both sitting up now listening for the rest.

"So Jim is up there for the longest time. Mike is down waiting outside wondering what is going on because it is taking so long. All kinds of things were running through his mind. He couldn't figure out what could possibly be happening, all kinds of crazy scenarios were going through his mind, including that Jim might have found out it was a doll.

"So he is standing there looking up at the stairway when Jim slowly walks out the door, white as a ghost, in total shock, with a look of horror on his face. Mike looks at him and says, 'Jim, you okay?'

"Jim looks at him and him and says, 'Mike. That chick was really weird'"

Deri and Braz were both laughing now, and Jason was laughing, partly because it was funny, but mostly because they were laughing so hard.

"That was a good story. Tell us another one," Braz said.

"Yes. Tell us another," Deri asked as she squirmed in excitement.

"Well, this one isn't done yet," Gizmo continued. "So he says that that chick was really weird, and Mike tells him that he told her she was shy. But Mike's mind is going wild wanting to know what happened. So Jim starts to explain.

"You know, she didn't say one word the whole time. And Mike tells him, 'Well yah, I told you she was shy'. Well yah, he says, but this is crazy. I asked if she wanted the light on, and she didn't answer, so I figured she would be too self conscious or something. I don't know.

"So Mike goes, 'Yah, yah, so what happened?'

"Well, after it was pretty clear that she wasn't interested in small talk, I decided to just kiss her. So I did. She didn't seem to mind, in fact, seemed to kind of like it, so then I did it again. Then I kissed her neck. I think that made her kind of excited.

"Then I went down to her shoulder. Then I went down and kissed her breast. It was the weirdest thing. Well Mike, I kept doing that until I bit her nipple, and as soon as I did that, she cuts a fart and jumps out the window."

Jason was laughing. Deri and Braz looked at each other with bewilderment, which made him laugh even more. Then they started talking about it, which made him laugh harder and made Gizmo laugh too.

"Why did she cut a fart?" Deri asked.

"She is a doll. Why would she do that?" Braz asked. Then it hit him. "Ooh! She's made of rubber. He bit her."

It hit Deri too. "Oh, she's rubber!" And started laughing, putting her lips together and making a raspberry sound and flinging her hand through the air. "Pffft. Out the window!" she cried with roars of laughter.

They all were laughing now, with both Deri and Braz making raspberry sounds now and then, causing Gizmo and Jason to laugh even harder.

"Poor Jim," Deri finally said.

They sat like that, far up on the mountain side, away from the war and the worries, telling stories and describing their planets and what life was like and what the similarities were until eventually they fell back into silence and just sat looking around.

"Camping. I can see how that might be enjoyable. It is so quiet. You can gather your thoughts in peace," Braz said and started to wander off across the stream.

He made his way to the side of the far cliff with Bo following along, bouncing in and out of bushes and tall grass. He watched her jump up into the air through some tall vegetation like a spring, making her way toward him. There at the wall of the cliff, Braz crouched down and looked into a cave partially covered by brush.

Jason was sitting with the rest, glancing now and then in their direction, keeping an eye on his dog. Braz glanced toward them, making sure they saw where he was, and watched both Jason and Gizmo pull up their weapons and look at the cave entrance through their scopes.

Jason and Gizmo stood up to walk over and Deri followed, while Braz instinctively reached for his weapon, giving it a little tug slightly out of the holster and re-seating it, making sure it would clear easily if he needed it.

"I'm gonna grab a light. I'll be right there," Jason said as he sprinted toward the shuttle door.

Bo was looking into the cave now with him, but gave no alarm or sign of danger. Braz crouched slightly and shone a light inside as Deri and Gizmo made their way toward him. He poked his head partly inside, holding Bo from rushing in, and pulled himself back out to tell the rest that he was going to go in, but when he turned, Jason was gone.

He looked around the plateau for him and called out. He had vanished. He called to Bo and ran toward where they had been sitting and called again. Looking around where they had been seated, he saw the MREs now strewn about and Jason's weapon lying on the ground.

Then he rushed into the shuttle to check there. He was gone without a trace. He came out and called again, looking at Bo to see her ears straight up, looking and listening toward the mouth of the creek.

"They could not see me. That is probably why I was not taken." Braz said. "And they had no interest in Jason's beast. You two were probably too far away."

He'd seen Jason with Bo before and knew Jason had commands that his beast understood and would follow. The dog's senses were much better than his, much like the beasts they once had on his home planet, and he wanted her help. He tried several of his most familiar commands and Bo just looked at him.

"We need to find Jason," he finally spoke in frustration. She reacted to the word "Jason".

"Jason, Bo. Find Jason," Gizmo said to her.

Bo looked around and let out an excited squeal, and began sniffing the area and following an animal trail toward the mouth of the creek. Off to the side was a smaller trail, and Bo jumped toward it with her nose down, leading them to a large stone weighing many tons, and that is where it ended. She stopped and scratched at the bottom of the stone and gave a yelp.

They looked around for a way in behind it. Gizmo could see footprints lead right up to it as if they walked through the stone and he tried to get an idea of how many there may have been. They being too scuffed over now, he abandoned that and again tried to find a way in past the barrier.

He tried calling several times, waiting for a response, watching Bo cock her head to the side and look at the bottom of the stone. It was, in fact, a blast door, much like they had on Earth, but concealed to look like stone. He pulled out an Invader weapon and began blasting at it and around the bottom of it. After some time, they gave up on finding a way into the entrance there and turned back toward the cave and darted toward it, Bo following along.

"Admiral," Gizmo called into his uniform while Deri was calling and mobilizing her people. "Jason is missing."

"Dammit! What do you mean?" the Admiral barked.

As Gizmo explained what happened and told him about the cave, Braz pulled his weapon with one hand and held his light with the other and slid into the cave with the rest following. Within a short distance, they were headed downward in what appeared to be a well-travelled tunnel.

Chapter Twenty Nine

Jason heard someone approach and waited at the cage door. A short, thin humanoid appeared and asked, "Are you the new keepers?"

Jason answered him with, "Open this door."

The small person walked away, appearing again with three others. "Are you us or are you the new keepers?" One of them asked again with a confused look.

Jason thought about that before answering this time. Keepers. On this planet covered with Invaders. What kind of keepers would they be? It was obvious he was not one of them, so he answered, "Keepers."

"Please excuse us for holding you. It's just that we weren't sure. You didn't look like either. We thought you might have been one of us. We will have three put to death instantly. You are arriving after the others have left. That has never happened before. It is not usual to be without keepers," he explained as he nervously fumbled for the right key. "For that, we will have twenty five punished however you see fit for whatever we have done to cause this," he answered while opening the door.

He stood and looked at Jason and said, "You look different than the other keepers. Bigger."

"When did the other keepers leave?" Jason asked.

"There were noises from the forbidden areas. That is when they left. We have never been without keepers. It was a very confusing time for us. We sent someone out to look and he reported explosions and destruction. We can have him immediately put to death for this violation if you wish," one of them answered.

"The machines stopped," one of them began speaking again. "We will have everybody line up for whatever punishment you would like to impose. One crop has been lost so far and can be prepared for recycling. But all the machines stopped."

"There will be no punishment and no deaths today," Jason told them, and then asked, "How many of you are there?"

What appeared to be their leader answered, "We have maintained our complement of one million. The breeders were well monitored by the keepers before you. But now the machines have stopped. We have never had the machines stop."

"I'd like to be shown the machines," Jason said.

"Of course, and after that, we can show you to your chambers and begin your learning," he said.

"Learning? What learning?" Jason asked. "And where are the people I was with?"

"The ones you were with are out of our reach. This is very unusual. Normally, the keepers have always been brought directly for learning. We have never had this occur. The machines not working, and also a period without keepers. Now, a keeper that has not been learned. We have never had this before. It is all so confusing," he said.

Jason was led into the facility by the four men. As they passed an entrance, one of them said, "This is your control room."

Jason opened it and walked inside. The others quickly turned their heads away hiding their eyes with their hands and looked toward the ground so as not to be able to see the room interior.

He looked around at the strange equipment and spied a capacitor. Finding a container, he pulled it and stuffed it in, took another look around and came back out.

"You asked if I were a keeper or if I were one of you. What did you mean by that; by one of you?" Jason asked.

"The others. They are us. We are tasked with capturing them when possible and providing learning for them," the leader answered.

"Capture them? Why would you capture them?" Jason asked.

They all turned and looked at him quizzically, and then their eyes began to dart back and forth at each other. Fear began to grow in their faces, terror, and two of them looked as if they were about to bolt.

"Wait. Wait," Jason said. "Just answer the question. No harm will come to you."

"It is as it has always been. There are some who have not submitted. They are us. It is for their protection. They have always been. So we capture and save them when we can," the leader said. "Is that the correct answer?"

"The people I was with; where are they?" Jason asked.

"They are on their way to the others. They are beyond our reach if they have been taken," he answered.

"Where are your weapons?" Jason asked.

"The keepers provide us with this," he held out an object and showed it to him. "It is used for capturing the others. It disables the person it is pointed at while we take him for learning. It is what was used on you, for which we would be more than happy to put any number to death that you would see fit."

"That's all? What about the keepers? Did they have weapons?" he asked.

"Oh, yes. They most assuredly did. But when the machines stopped, their weapons did not seem to function. Nor will our weapons work much longer. The backup batteries and capacitors are nearly drained," the leader said.

"I need to see the people I was with. I need my weapons. Let's get back outside, I have weapons there," Jason said.

"The blast doors have been closed. Without the machines working, we have no power left to open them. We drained them going out to get you. I will proceed with my punishment," and the leader turned to one of the men he was with who instantly began beating him.

"Stop that! What are you doing?" Jason demanded.

"I am sorry," one of them said. He reached over and grabbed a piece of pipe while the leader got on his knees, he lifted it and was about to bring it down and crush his skull.

"Stop that!" Jason yelled out, reaching for the pipe and taking it. "There will be no more punishment unless I specifically ask for it. Got it?"

"Yes," they all said with their eyes to the ground.

"Is it possible, if we direct all power to the doors, the batteries can open the blast doors?" Jason asked.

"No. There is barely power for the lights we are using. Most of the facility is in darkness, and the remaining lights will fail soon. But you are here. We will have power and food again," the leader told him. "That is, after our proper punishment."

Jason walked over to a railing and looked down into a vast chamber. In the dim lighting, as his eyes focused, he began to see eyes looking back. There were eyes staring up at him as far as he could focus. He began to make out the shape of heads spread out as far as he could see. They all just stood silently looking up at him.

He bent over the railing to get a closer look at the ones nearest him and watched as one of them fell to the ground. Looking closer, he saw two others nearby who had collapsed. "What's wrong with them?" he asked.

As he turned to look at the leader, one of the others called down and pointed to the fallen man. "He has expired," the leader said.

"Expired? You mean he's dead?" Jason asked.

"Yes. He is dead. He has expired," he said.

Jason looked around to see the man still pointing. He looked over the railing again to see several people now beating on the person. "What are they doing? Stop that!" he yelled.

They instantly stopped and began punishing each other. "HALT!" he yelled. "That's enough!"

"As of now and from now on, there will be no more punishments unless I specifically command it. As of now and from now on, there will be no more executions unless I specifically command it. As of now and from now on, you will not harm or injure another unless I specifically command it. Do you understand?" He called into the cavern.

Throughout the base, in one thundering and deafening sound, every single person called back in unison. It wasn't an understanding of what he was saying. There was no understanding or agreement. It was a robotic response; simply an acknowledgement of having received yet another instruction. He looked back over the railing to see the eyes still staring up at him as another person collapsed.

"What's wrong with them? Why are they falling?" Jason asked.

"Our punishment has been most effective, Sir. They have been without food and water since the noise started and the machines stopped. Perhaps they have learned their lesson, whatever that lesson might have been. We all have. Whatever it is we may have done, I am certain we will not do it again," the leader said.

"Are you people crazy? Tell them to eat. Tell them to drink water," Jason yelled.

The small group again began looking back and forth at each other, shuffling on their feet, the terror growing in their faces, until one of them couldn't take any more, got down on his knees and screamed out, "Just kill me!"

"The machines stopped," the leader said. "But now that you are here, we can resume our responsibilities."

"So you can't eat without the machines?" Jason asked.

"That is correct. I forgot that you hadn't received your learning. I'm not sure the learning device will work without the machines running, but we can try it," he replied.

"I think I'm going to skip that." Jason decided he had done enough learning. He had all the learning he needed, for now. This entire race of people was at his mercy. They had been at the mercy of the keepers before him.

He looked over the edge of the railing again to see another person drop. He needed to get to Gizmo, Bo, Braz, and Deri, but these people were dying as he was standing there. Hopefully, Gizmo and the rest still had weapons and could defend themselves, and Braz could remain unseen. "Okay. Let's get them some food and water. Then I want to get the hell out of here and get the people I was with," he said.

Braz was up front with Bo when the wall came down behind them, blocking their exit. Gizmo called Bo back and he and Deri each crouched behind a boulder on either side of the tunnel and took aim. Braz slipped back and joined them, bracing for an assault.

"Braz," Gizmo whispered. "Did you see anyone?"

"Yes. They were coming up the tunnel. We are far outnumbered," He said.

"Can you get up there and see what kind of weapons they have and see how many there are?" Gizmo asked.

Braz got up and moved forward unseen. A moment later, he returned and said, "There are perhaps thousands that I could see. I suspect there are even more of them deeper in the cavern. They are armed, but I could not tell what type of weapons they are using. I've never seen them before."

"There is no way out!" A voice came from in front of them. "You can give up now and you will be fairly treated!"

They waited for a minute, and the voice came again. "You have no way out. Come forward peacefully and you will be fairly treated. This is your last chance."

Deri and Gizmo could see them taking up positions in front of them. In this enclosed area, with the invader weapons Gizmo had, and the energy weapons Deri and Braz had, they could hold out and pick anyone off as they came up the tunnel toward them. But if Gizmo and the rest tried to move forward, they could be picked off just as easily.

Gizmo answered, "You are cut off. We have you trapped. You have no escape except back inside. You are the one with no way out." He fired a shot at a boulder above two of the people who were aiming at them.

"The next shot will not be so kind. All we want is our friend. Hand him over and we will let you live," Gizmo called.

There was a pause before the voice came back. "We have nobody and have taken nobody from you. If you are speaking of the man taken from outside, we have no control over that."

"I'm coming forward. I'm coming forward to speak to you. If you shoot, I will kill every single one of you. That, I promise," Gizmo said.

Gizmo waited for a reply. During the silence, he told Deri to stay where she was with Bo and told Braz to follow him, not so close that he could be shot if shooting started, but since he was invisible, he could disarm any nearby threat.

"Alright. We will speak," the voice came back. "I'm coming forward."

Gizmo got up and walked toward the voice, stopping half way between Deri and the people in front of him and waited there.

"I want Jason. Where is he?" Gizmo said as the man approached.

"We have no Jason, nor anyone else. But if he was the man who arrived in the vehicle with you, we know who does," the man said. He looked Gizmo up and down and studied his weapon. "You must be the ones who brought down the base, right?"

"Right," Gizmo said.

The man lowered his weapon and swung it around to his back and held out his hand. "We have been waiting generations for this. We are the Population, and I am the Chief. My name is Wilf."

"I am Colonel Crozley," Gizmo said. "So, who took Jason and how do we get him back."

"We were about to launch an assault on the people who took him. This is the first time in our recorded history here that the dome has been captured. It is an opportunity that we will not miss," Wilf said.

"We tried blasting the entrance. How will you get in?" Gizmo asked.

"We have tunnels. We have been waiting for this day to breach the facility. Generations before us have worked for this day. I've prepared for it all my life. The day the Population will liberate our brothers," Wilf said.

"How many are you?" Gizmo asked.

"Near one million. One quarter of us will breach. The rest will run supply and logistics," Wilf answered.

"I want to see your plan. I don't want my friend getting killed by accident, and we have weapons," Gizmo said pointing to Wilf's rifle. "I think we will do much better with ours than what you have there."

Wilf looked over at the rock Gizmo brought down with a single shot and agreed. Gizmo told him to wait a moment while he went back and spoke to Deri, telling her to remain there with Bo and telling Braz to follow along unnoticed. By now, back up consisting of both the Newcomers and the Humans sent by the Admiral would be arriving.

He had the blockade cleared so he could get outside and muster the forces, bringing a dozen each of Humans and Newcomers to back up Deri, leaving a relay to the outside for communication.

Wilf and Gizmo were going over the maps of the facility and the plans for the invasion. Wilf described the series of tunnels they would squeeze as many people as they could into, and they would pour out the other side like ants.

"Wilf. This is a garbage plan," Gizmo said. "You're going to get yourselves slaughtered. You say there are Invaders in there? You will be picked off and wiped out as you come out of these tunnels."

"There is no other way in," Wilf argued. "And we are going in, whether you come or not. We are going in. Those are our people in there.

We have never had an opportunity like this and may never have one again."

"Do you know what kind of weapons they have?" Gizmo asked.

"No. We know they have stun devices. The invaders have Invader weapons. The keepers do as well," Wilf answered.

"Do you know what kind of defenses they have?" He asked.

"No," Wilf answered.

"Do you know what kind of assault capabilities they have, what kind of combat training they have? Do you know anything about the enemy at all?" Gizmo asked in frustration.

"No. Except this: Besides the monsters that you call Invaders, they are not our enemy. Not strictly speaking. They may be hostile, they may fight, they may resist, but they are not our enemy. They are our own people. They catch some of us now and then, and we capture some of them now and then. It's always been this way.

"But now that the Invader machines don't work, we must strike. Get them out and destroy the machinery beyond repair before they can be started again. Against their weapons, we have never had a chance," Wilf said.

"Alright. Well let's figure out a way to do it without getting everyone killed. Show me all the tunnels you plan to use again," Gizmo said, pointing to the map.

Gizmo devised a plan to create a series of diversions at several tunnel entrances, and while there was a distraction, move as many men into position through the other entrances as possible. The first part of the plan was to get a few people into the facility ahead of time and be ready to set off explosions to drive everyone away from where they would enter.

Once the area was cleared, the initial wave could go in and set up defenses to protect the rest of the wave coming through, and then they could push forward from there. But push forward to what, and accomplish what once they were inside, that was now the question. What were the objectives? How do they get back out once they accomplish them, and how do they get back out if they are overrun?

Wilf realized that they had really not considered all of this. He had never been in combat, nor had any of his people. He had never considered the finality of it all. He had no experience in these things Colonel Crozley was pointing out, the placement of men, covering fire while moving forward, advancing and taking positions and setting up defenses to hold those positions. Supply lines, medics, food and water, the list of items went on and on. A million people were in there and who knows how many invaders.

What would they do once they were inside? Talk? Kill? Capture?

Gizmo took a break and went outside to speak with the Admiral through his uniform patch.

After listening to Gizmo's description of the facilities and his plans for the breach, he gave his conclusion. "Colonel Crozley, you have to get someone in there and get some eyes on intelligence. You could go in and run into a swarm of Invaders. We can't blast our way in, it'll bring the facility down and we could end up losing Jason and everyone else."

"Right, Admiral. So I'm sending in Braz and his people. They can get in and out unseen. There are a million people in there that Wilf has ready to move. But they're retarded or something. A few dozen of our guys will be more effective than Wilf's entire force. They'll be in the way more than anything, but we will bring some along and use the rest for back up if we need them. They're pretty motivated, but completely untrained."

"Camping. Unbelievable," the Admiral scoffed. "What were you two thinking? If you two weren't so damned famous, I'd have you swabbing my decks. Get in there and get Jason. I want to see you two as soon as you get out of there, and don't get yourselves killed! And next time you two want to go on a picnic, don't," he grumbled and signed off.

Chapter Thirty

Jason was shown to the food processing plants. "Don't you have any food storage?" He asked after seeing that they were dead.

"Storage? No. No storage. This is what the Keepers provided for us. It has always been that way," the leader told him.

"What about emergencies? Don't you have something for emergencies?" he asked.

"Emergencies?" He said. "Is this an emergency?"

"Yes it's an emergency. What do you have for emergencies?" Jason asked.

"We have never had an emergency. The keepers have always…It's just always been this way when the keepers…We've, we've never had an emergency," he explained.

"Okay, look. What about exits? An escape plan or an evacuation plan? What about those?" He asked.

The leader shook his head.

"Look. What if there was a catastrophe or a fire? Or what if you had to get everyone to safety? Where would you go?" He asked, to which the leader just stood with a confused look on his face.

"Well. Fire your Union Rep," Jason finally told him. "You MUST have some way out. You MUST have some way to get out of here."

"We have never been out. We cannot get out without the blast doors open. But there are some small accesses to the others. We have to use them when our complement gets too low. Like now, with so many expirations, the breeders will not be able to make up for the loss. We were preparing to send some capture teams," He told him.

"The others, they have food and water? Where do they get it?" Jason asked.

They stood and spoke about the supplies, the others, the accesses and tunnels to the others. Jason noticed that every person there had been standing and found they were not allowed to sit. He announced through the facility that everybody was to sit and stay where they were to conserve their energy.

"Do you have plans for the facilities The Others are in? A floor plan or drawings?" Jason asked.

"Yes. We have a layout in a meeting room. We keep them with the weapons." he answered.

"Weapons! What weapons?" Jason asked.

"When we capture The Others, they often have weapons. Would you like to see them?" he asked.

"What is this? A joke? Yes, I'd like to see them," Jason said.

"Please excuse my ignorance. When you asked about weapons earlier, I thought you were referring to our weapons or the keeper's weapons," he said.

Jason was shown to a chamber where the drawings were kept and plans were made for capture teams to be sent out. Along the back wall were weapons; many thousands of them. There was enough to equip an entire army.

"Where did you get them all?" Jason asked.

"When we capture. Often they have one. We store them in here. We have always done it," He said.

Jason picked one up and aimed it, pulled the trigger and it fired.

"How many people know how to use these?" he asked.

"The ones we have taken them from are the ones who knew how to use them. I'm not sure they would still be able to do it after their learning. Should I call for a few of the most recent captives?" he asked.

They arranged to have some of the captured Others brought in while Jason and the leader went over the floor plans for the facilities occupied by The Others. There were a series of tunnels that was used to enter and capture them, Jason was now devising a plan to invade the facility and take it over one section at a time, cutting off supply and re-enforcement routes, and containing and holding one section after the other.

With the weapons he saw stored there, he would have an entire army to do it with. The trick would be to get enough people through the tunnels and into position to protect the rest coming through. The other side had weapons, and appears to know how to use them.

Four of the recently captured Others were lead into the room and brought to Jason.

"Grab your weapons," he told them.

The men hesitantly moved toward the weapons and stopped.

"Pick up your weapons," Jason ordered them again.

One of the men reached toward it and passed out. The other three held onto their heads and yelled, "I can't! It hurts! I can't!"

"That is what I was talking about. After the learning, I wasn't sure they would be able to do it," the leader said.

"So, learning…it's mind control. There is really no learning to it," Jason said. "You realize that with all these weapons and people, you could have defeated the Invaders and set yourselves free?"

"Free? But we are free. It is The Others who are not free. We save them," the leader said.

Jason picked the man off the floor, sat him at the table, and started to revive him. As he came to, Jason asked, "What happened?"

"My head. I thought it was going to explode. My chest and back were on fire. I couldn't concentrate," he said.

"So…tell me. How did this happen?" Jason asked.

"I don't know. I have never felt it before," he replied.

Jason picked the riffle up and placed it in front of him, looked him in the eye, and said, "Reach for the weapon."

"I can't. It hurts. I can't," he cried.

"Look at me. Concentrate. Prepare for this. It is all in your mind. You aren't really in pain. It's in your mind. Reach for the weapon and tell me everything you feel while you do it," Jason told him. "Force yourself. Make yourself do it. Tell me everything you feel while you do it."

The man sat and caught his breath. He began focusing on the weapon. He winced from the pain, but continued to concentrate. "I feel like I'm going to pass out," he said.

"That's okay. We'll catch you if you do. Just tell me what you are going through. Tell me everything," Jason told him. "How did it start?"

He reached for the weapon again. The other three were watching as their faces contorted in pain. "It's like something screaming at me. No. I can't! It hurts! I can't!"

"What do you mean? Do you mean something is screaming that you can't? Is that what you mean?" Jason asked.

The man opened his eyes and looked at Jason. "Yes. That's it. Something screaming. It isn't me. Something is screaming it," and he let the weapon go. "I can't. It hurts. I can't."

"It doesn't hurt. It is all in your mind. You only think it hurts. It is all in your mind. Reach for that weapon," Jason told him again. "Tell me everything while you do it. Close your eyes and try to tell me what you are seeing."

He reached for it again, this time with a little more ease. He squinted his eyes and grimaced from pain. "I see it. I was captured. I was brought to the learning machine and strapped in. I can see it just like it happened. The pain. It gave me pain. Burning on the chest. My back is on fire. My head feels like it will explode."

"Good," Jason said. "Then what? Tell me the rest. What happened?"

"Loud noises. Yelling. Pain. Electrical. It is telling me, I can't. It hurts. I can't. That's what it is saying. Pictures of weapons. The pain goes with it at the same time. Pictures flashing. The gun. Saying I can't. I can't. Telling me I can't remember. GET OUT! It yelled," he said.

The man opened his eyes and looked at Jason. "That is what happened," he picked up the gun and looked at it. "All I had to do was remember, and then I saw it. Now I know."

He checked the breach and saw it was loaded. Looked around and spotted the leader and pointed at him. "You! You did that. You put me in there."

Jason wasn't quite sure what to do. He had the shortest debate with himself he's probably ever had: whether to let him shoot or not. He lifted his hand and pulled the barrel down. "What's your name?"

"Jakes," he said.

"Jakes. Well Jakes. Lots of time to right yourself later. Let's get the rest of your guys up and running."

The other three sat in the chair without being told. "We want to know what happened, too," one of them said.

Jakes started. "Remember when you were captured," he told them. "Start there. Remember where you were taken. To the room and strapped in. Remember that," and they all started to grimace in pain.

"The pain is not real. It is only in your mind. They put it there. I know it seems like you are feeling it, but it's not real. You have to remember all of it. Just go through it in your mind from beginning to end," he explained.

He walked over and grabbed three weapons and placed them in front of them. "Here. Maybe this will help."

"Ahh!" the first one cried. "It hurts! I can't! It hurts!"

"That's right. Remember that. Remember it screaming in your head. Remember it all," Jakes said.

"I do. I do. I remember. I remember. I see it. I see it all," he opened his eyes and looked at jakes. "I saw it, Jakes. I saw it. The whole thing, just like it was happening right now. It was stuck there. The pain. Just like it was happening right now." he said. "What a relief. I feel so much better."

The other two soon were the same. Opening their eyes in surprise and eyeing the leader picking up their weapons as if to shoot him.

"Jakes. Men. You have to do this with everyone you know. Get them to remember. Get them in here and get them able to function again. We're getting the hell out of here," Jason said.

Then he turned to the leader. "You go and start rounding them up. Everybody you've captured. Bring them here."

"I will go right away," he said.

"Who here has been on a capture team?" Jason asked.

Two of the men answered. He picked the one with the most trips to the other side to go over the maps and floor plans with him and sent the other to go and bring any member of a capture team to meet there. Jason was going to use them as scouts.

Jakes and the other three men began salvaging, getting more to recall the capture and the mind control. Now they had eight. They did the same, and it grew to sixteen. They did the same and they had thirty-two. Within two hours, doubling every time, it would expand to a sizable army. Jason would have his army functioning, and he would invade the other side.

He stood at the table with the capture teams going over the floor plans, devising the strategy to invade and occupy the other side, looking over now and then to see the weapons stash grow smaller and smaller.

They all walked back to the main chamber where Jason slapped the patch on his uniform and floated up to the control room as everyone gasped. He grabbed the capacitor and was shown to the access they would use to capture the others, took two people from the capture team, and disappeared into the mouth of the tunnel.

They crawled quietly toward The Others until there was enough room to stand, and then Jason picked up the pace. One of them warned him about noise, and how any sound they made was transmitted to the other side through the opening like an amplifier. It was how the tunnel remained secret.

Jason sent for the first wave to follow. There would be four tunnels used, and those four would cut off all ability to move inside the facility, and leave one wave to move forward to the outside.

Within a short time, they were at the mouth. Jason looked through a grate to see people walking back and forth. "How do you get through without being seen?" he asked.

One of them went to the grate and opened it and stepped into the corridor. The people walking around looked and just continued with what they were doing. Jason and the other stepped through while more watched.

Jason checked his crude weapon and loosened the snap on his knife, and prepared for an attack. It was an attack that never happened.

The four groups passed messages through the tunnels when they were in place. All were in position. Without a single shot, all movement within the facility was shut down. All access was blocked by positions Jason had them ready to defend.

"What's going on?" He asked. "What now?"

"Now we take them," one of capture team said.

"Take them? But they know you're here. How do you take them?" Jason asked.

"With the devices," he said, holding up the stun device.

"But they know you're here! Look at the tunnel. They can see it. What the hell is going on?" Jason exclaimed.

"The tunnel is a secret," the man told him.

"A secret? A secret? It's a secret that everyone knows?" Jason looked at him in shock. "How long have they known?"

"It has always been a secret. We sneak through and take some of them quite often," he said.

"And they know?" Jason asked angrily. "You guys are nuts. Show me the exit."

"I have only seen it once, it is in this direction. The door was open, and I looked outside. I have been properly punished, but I can see more punishment seems to be in order," he said.

Jason followed them along another corridor on a slight grade upward until they came to a large room off to the side. The men crouched down and slipped past the entry so as not to be seen, giving hand signals to each other and waited for Jason on the other side.

Jason ignored their attempts at stealth and walked to the middle of the entrance to see Gizmo pouring over charts and plans with Wilf.

As he walked in, he could hear Gizmo's frustration with the man. "Okay, so now we've secured the facility. The positions are taken, the defenses are up, and we've captured your people. Now what? What do you do with them? They have just been overrun and taken captive. What are you going to do with them now?"

Wilf stood with a blank stare and shook his head. "I'm not sure. We free them."

"Free them to what? Wilf! Think about it. They've been capturing you guys for as long as you know. You've been capturing them. They must have some idea that what they are doing is right. The same with you. What were you thinking? That you were all gonna hug and magically be friends?"

Jason walked up beside Gizmo and looked over the charts. It was a Gizmo plan. "The man is smart. No doubt about that. This is a damned good plan," he thought. He had different challenges than Jason. The base is more open. It required a different tactic.

Then he spoke. "Why do you have a position here?" He said with his finger on a spot.

Gizmo was so frustrated that it didn't even register to him that Jason was standing there no longer needing to be rescued. As if he'd been there all along, he said, "It's to hold the dang...Jason!" He cried out when it hit him. He reached out and gave him a pat on the shoulder. "Where you been, pal?"

"I've been in this base. You want to get these people out of there? Give them hamburgers. Food and water. They're dropping like flies in there. We have to move quickly," he told him.

"Jason, this is Wilf. He is the Chief here," Gizmo told him.

Wilf opened his mouth to speak, but before he could say anything, Jason asked, "How much food and water do you have?"

"We have some stored up, maybe enough for another day. Since the dome was captured, the supplies have been cut," Wilf told him.

"So you get your food and water from the same place as the facility?" Jason asked.

Wilf stood and looked at him and furled his eyebrows in confusion. "We have always gotten it from the same place. It's always been like that," he said.

The two men in the capture team gathered the nerve to step inside the room as Jason said, "Wilf, come with us."

Wilf looked at the capture team, slumped his shoulders, and hung his head and said, "Agh. Captured," with a sigh.

Jason shook his head and said, "Come on Giz, let's get out of here," then he looked at Wilf and said, "Move it!"

Jason sent word for everyone to stand down and that the operation had been a success. They all walked toward the exit, meeting Deri who was still holding her position along the way. "Deri. Good to see you. Let's get out of here," was all the greeting he gave as they stepped out into the open.

Bo was lying on the ground by the shuttle patiently waiting as Braz went over the last minute plans with his people before going into the facility. She spotted Jason and let out a yelp, bouncing up and running toward him. Jason got down on one knee and wrapped an arm around her neck and gave a little squeeze.

"How ya doin', girl?" and he let her lick his face.

Braz walked up and said, "Jason Brand. It is good to see no harm had come to you. We were concerned."

"Good to see you Braz. No. No harm," he turned and looked at Wilf standing with the capture team and said, "These guys are all freaking idiots."

He slapped his patch and said, "Admiral."

"Colonel Brand. Report," he grumbled back.

Jason explained what had happened, described what he had seen of the facility, and asked for Dr. Hilliard to be sent right away with a charged capacitor. Once all the equipment was secured, and they knew it was safe, they would open the blast doors and get the people inside food, water, and medical attention.

While they waited for the shuttle with Dr. Hilliard to arrive, Jason and the others pulled out some MREs and began to eat.

"Jason Brand," Braz said. "I've reconsidered, and I don't think I like camping as much as I thought."

Chapter Thirty One

"Dr Hilliard," Jason greeted him as he stepped out of the shuttle holding a satchel with the capacitor. "Wait until you see this. All the Invader technology you could ever think of asking about. It's all in there. We just have to make sure everything is shut down and start firing things up one thing at a time. The first thing is to open the blast doors and get everyone out of there."

Jason, Gizmo, Bo, Deri, Braz and Dr. Hilliard headed back into the tunnel, capacitor ready to be placed in the control room, and each carrying a light. They came through the entrance where the leader was standing, still waiting, exactly as he was when Jason left.

"Control room," he said to him.

As they walked along, Jason started to talk to Gizmo in a low voice. "They don't do anything unless they are told. Won't even feed themselves. They would all just stand in one spot until they drop dead unless someone came along and told them what to do."

"The people on the other side are just as bad. Maybe a little better," Gizmo said. "But they're all idiots or something."

"This was all set up. They were both set up. One side here, pretty much as slaves, trying to rescue the others, the Population. The other side, the Population, pretending that they are trying to free this side. They both got fed by the same people. I guess it kept them occupied. Gave them a purpose or something," Jason said.

"I wonder how long they've been here doing this," Gizmo said. "Wilf said it's been generations. Did these guys give you that crap too? That it's always been like this?"

They made sure once more that no equipment would start before putting the capacitor in place. The blast doors were opened and the Admirals forces converged into the midst of a surprised and confused people.

As the forces went through and secured the facility, the leader showed them how he had seen the earlier keepers turn on the feeding equipment. As soon as the equipment was switched on making a familiar sound, the entire base all at once gave a deafening moan of relief.

That fired up, the inhabitants were given food and water and those who could walk were ushered outside where they squinted in the daylight, and cowered from the open sky, afraid of everything. At one point, a gust of wind blew, causing a rush toward the open blast doors to get back inside to safety.

"Look at them. I don't know whether to feel pity or revulsion," Deri said.

"I would think pity," Jason answered. "This is all they have known all their lives and for as long as their history is known to them. We are an unknown to them. We think we may be liberators. But to them, we must look like demons that are threatening to destroy their way of lives."

A call came from one of the scouting teams, "Colonel Brand. I think you should see this, Sir," he said, giving the location in the facility.

They all pulled out the maps that had been distributed to see where it was. "What is there?" Jason asked the leader, pointing at the spot.

"This is where the crops are grown. There is one ready for the last stage. We lost one crop already. But now that the machines are running, we can salvage this one," he said.

They had buggies and Hummers brought in to get to the distant parts of the facility, and they all piled in. As they got deeper inside, the driver slowed and they looked in amazement at the equipment. There was an incomplete transporter being built, all sixteen miles of it, deep inside the mountain. They continued along to see where the weapons were manufactured.

As they rolled up to the spot the call came from, the driver slammed on the brakes and they all sat stunned, looking at miles of incubators, all filled with growing invaders, from the floor to the top of the cave that reached some three hundred feet high.

"Over here, Colonel," a Marine called out as he ran up to them. "You're not going to believe this."

They all proceeded behind the Marine and came around a corner to see men with their weapons pointed, grenade launchers, Invader weapons, and men with .50 calibers manned on top of the Hummer, all poised and ready. Jason whipped his weapon up as he approached, and the rest did the same.

"Invaders," the man said, pointing at about two hundred of them sitting inside a containment area.

"What is this? You actually grow these things, don't you?" Jason asked the leader.

"These are waiting for the aggression process. Please excuse us. They are quite unfinished right now. There was nothing we could do. Whatever punishment you deem fit will begin as soon as you say. We lost the last crop because the aggression process was incomplete. The machines stopped in the middle and they began killing each other," he said.

"I thought they were talking about food, when he said they lost the last crop," Gizmo said.

"No. Not food. These are the technicians and the Pilots. The rest are in behind here," and he began walking toward another branch in the cave.

They stopped again and looked into a huge cavern as deep as their eyes could see. "This is the full crop," he said.

"How many are there?" Jason asked.

The leader was briefly puzzled when he looked at him to answer, "Excuse me, I forgot, you have not been learned. This is a very confusing time for us. This is a full complement for one transport. As soon as they are finished their aggression learning, they will enter their transport and leave."

"Seventeen million of them," Deri gasped.

"Please forgive me. I have never counted them. I will be sure to submit for punishment for this oversight. If you wish, I will start counting now," he said.

"No. That's alright. Don't bother," Jason told him.

"Very well. I will have someone else start counting so I can be properly punished," the leader said.

"There will be no punishment unless I specifically say it. Remember? No punishment. And no executions," Jason admonished.

"Oh, yes. Please excuse me. I will have myself..." and he trailed off, looking very ill-at-ease.

"Why would you make these things?" Jason asked.

"They are the protectors. They are the heroes. They are the fighters. They protect us from the enemy," he answered.

Jason turned to face him, looked into his eyes, and asked, "And who is the enemy?"

"It's who they fight. They always have. It is the way it's always been. They fight and protect us," he answered.

"But you don't know who they fight, exactly, do you?" Jason asked.

"Sure. They protect us from the enemy," he said.

"And that's how slavery starts," Gizmo said. "Protection. You need us to protect you, and all you have to do is this. It's for your own good. Good thing we had gun rights in America, because the next thing you know, presto! You're a slave."

"And an idiot. But you're being protected," Jason added. "A protected idiot."

"So this is the next crop. Seventeen million in a crop," Hilliard mumbled. "How many crops do you have in the making?"

"We always have three. It is coordinated with the making of the transporters," the leader said. "It has always been this way."

"And these ones in here. You say they haven't been through the aggression process. What are they like when they haven't been through the aggression process?" Hilliard asked.

"These you see here are simple minded. They are not informed and have had little learning. The pilots and technicians, they have an understanding of the systems they use. They know of their science. They have to be able to navigate and repair. So they have been put through learning for such things," the leader told them.

"So, you're saying that if we let them out right now, they would be among us and not kill anyone?" Hilliard continued the questioning.

"No. Not without their proper learning. They would be without purpose, however. They would have no drive. Other than to eat, not much would be of interest to them," he said. "And they don't need to eat very often."

"No sex?" Hilliard continued.

"No. They are incubated. They have no reproductive drive or capabilities," he answered.

"You know," Hilliard said to Jason. "Let's talk."

Jason told the leader to stay while the group walked down a corridor.

"I think maybe we can use these things, if they have no aggression. They know their science. I would like to see what it is that makes them aggressive as well. But we can use them, if they know their science."

"Dr., I was hoping that any science you might want to know, you could learn from the equipment they have here. Didn't expect to see this…crop," Jason said.

"We have a whole army there at our disposal if we need it, if we can get them to…if we can find a way to motivate them. We don't want the aggression. A little aggression, maybe. Then again, Maybe Dr. Hilliard can look at the process they use and tweak it a little," Gizmo said.

"We can do something about this later. Right now, let's get back with Admiral Harding and let him know what we have and let the General know. Maybe bring one of them with us. Question him and see how useful they might be. Maybe do some tests on him. See how cooperative they are," Jason said.

"Right. And if they are no good, like that idiot leader says; it's just another crop failure," Gizmo added.

On the way back, they stopped and looked at more equipment. They were going over the food processing equipment with the leader when Dr. Hilliard began opening vats and took a whiff.

146

"This is not good. This goes into the food. It is a drug. Keeps everybody docile," he told them, then reached down and turned a valve. "That was part of their problem. No wonder."

They continued along to the breeding area. Braz stayed outside with Jason and Gizmo while Deri and the doctor went inside. A few moments later Hilliard appeared back at the door and threw up, leaning against the wall.

Deri came out a second behind him and bent over with her hands on her knees trying to catch her breath. "Oh, my God. You won't believe it. I don't think I'll ever have sex again," she exclaimed.

Chapter Thirty One

The Newcomers worked non-stop in order to prepare the stations for transport and get back to their homes with Jason and Gizmo. They were divided in half. One half to go with Deri and Jason to their home planet, and the other to go with Eric to Earth and train the humans in tactics and moves for space battles, hand to hand combat without gravity, and the use of the gravity suits they had.

In return, Jason was taking the other half of the Newcomers, along with five thousand Humans to fight and clear out any Invaders on her home planet, and then move on to help Braz with his. This was the agreement the General had made.

A War Room was set up on Admiral Harding's transporter to plan and execute the clearing of Invaders from the various planets with representatives from each species in the Armada taking a part.

Jason had his transport loaded and was making last-minute preparations. He was sitting at the helm with Gizmo discussing different scenarios and planning for what they might encounter. The greatest worry was if Earth was hit and they lost power, stranding them in space somewhere, so they were certain to have what they needed to reconstruct an entire set of equipment.

Earth was covered, with Cody there and Dent protecting him. If they were hit, Cody could reassemble his equipment and recharge the capacitors with the earth's sun. Admiral Harding was covered with Dr. Hilliard being able to piece together a relay and capacitor if needed and recharge his capacitors as well by the sun there.

Jason and Gizmo were at greatest risk and would have to figure out a way to charge their own capacitors and place a relay floating in space or on another planet near whatever star they were closest to. They could use the sun of either Braz' or Deri's planets if they were close enough, but if the power went out mid-leap, they could end up light years from the nearest star.

They were looking over the maps of where the two planets they were heading to were located. They were far apart in different galaxies, but travel was instant in the quantum world. It was the possibility of being stranded if the Earth relay were hit that had everyone worried.

Sitting and looking at the star maps, amazed at the detail they could get and the volume of area the Invaders had conquered and mapped, Jason touched on Deri's planet and looked over their solar system. Then he moved it in toward the planet itself and looked at the moon and its bases.

"They'll probably be destroyed. What do you think?" he said.

"Might be. We should go to the moon first and check it out," Gizmo answered.

"Yah, I think you're right," Jason said, and then touched on Braz' planet. They looked over that system as well and zoomed onto the moons and looked over the terrain.

Eric walked in for a last minute visit before they all headed out. "You guys ready?" he asked.

"I think so. Can't think of anything else we need. How about you?" Gizmo asked.

"I think it's all set up. Can't wait to get those satellites and defenses up over the Earth," he said. "You know, I was talking to Deri. They had a Scorched Earth policy, the same as we did. There might not be much left on her planet. Just, you know, thought I'd mention it."

"Figured they would. She never brought it up, but it's good to know. How 'bout Braz? Did you talk to him?" Jason asked.

"I did. They had a different plan," Eric said.

"We spoke to him a little bit about it. What did you find out?" Gizmo asked.

"Well, he was supposed to get on board and figure out the Invader technology, but you did it for him. His people would just melt into the background and wait it all out," Eric said.

"Yah. That's what he told us. They will launch attacks and disrupt them as much as they could until he returned or until someone showed up," Jason said.

"Can you imagine?" Eric asked. "It would be like being on a planet of ghosts for the Invaders. They would have to be pretty freaked out."

"True. But Braz still had cities and still got bombarded like everyone else. Who knows how many of his people are left. They couldn't all head for the hills. No time to react that fast. Could they?" Gizmo asked.

"I guess we'll know soon enough," Jason said. "These invaders, they sure tore it up, didn't they? Bad critters. But whoever is behind them is worse."

"That's who we have to nail. We have to find them. Then, Jason, you can call the Armada back together and we all go and hit them," Gizmo said.

"That little worm Ambassador. I think he's our best lead. I don't think he knows we're onto his patches yet," Eric said.

"I want to talk Braz and some of his people into coming back to Earth with us. He's a handy guy to have around," Jason said. "They can get in and out and move around without being noticed. Plus, he's a pretty smart guy. They have to know that whoever is behind these Invaders, they have to have the next evolution ready."

"You mean the next evolution as in, worse than the invaders?" Eric asked.

"Worse than the Invaders and worse technology. It's what any military or even any company does. They develop something and put it out. But they keep on developing until the first level is figured out by their competition. Then they release the next generation. They could have ten or twenty levels of technology worse than the Invaders and what they had," Gizmo explained.

"Well. I guess we just have to find them and put them out of business," Eric said. "Remember that guy, that doctor you guys pointed out back on Earth, Bradley? Well the General has him being interrogated. I don't know, but somehow he thinks Bradley might have some answers for us."

"Frankenstein zombie-making freak," Gizmo muttered. "But that's another lead, maybe. But I don't get why Catskill Pharmaceuticals would be involved in the invasion and destruction of our own planet."

"Me either. It doesn't make sense," Jason said. "But the whole thing doesn't make sense. For example, why the Invaders would go around killing off races and exterminating species they could just as easily have formed alliances with."

"And then, why would they steer Catskill to develop the Walkers and the gas? It makes no sense. Maybe Bradley is just a dead end," Eric said.

"What about this? Run this past the General when you get back, too," Jason said. "How about this," and he sat for a moment putting the thought together. "It's a given now that these Invaders didn't make this technology. They don't have the brains or the dexterity for it."

"Right," Gizmo said.

"So they had to get someone to do it. The Invaders were developed. A test-tube race. We know that now. Then, whoever made them would have to either make the initial technology themselves, all the weapons and such, or they would have to have another race do it. Probably a conquered race," Jason said.

"Right. Like slaves. They would have enslaved another race to make their stuff. A race with smaller fingers. Like humans. Smart enough to do it, but not developed enough to have figured it out yet. Not evolved enough," Gizmo said.

"Right. Right. So then it makes sense. Right? It makes sense why they would allow the development of the Walkers too," Jason added.

"Okay. Now you lost me. Why would they do that? Why would they help develop the Walkers?" Eric asked.

"Simple. They never did want the Invaders to live and inhabit the Earth. They had to make a weapon to clear them out. Maybe that's it. Sure, they wanted the human's near extermination. They wanted them living in underground bunkers. They could know about the scorched Earth policy. We couldn't leave the caves for...maybe millions of years," Jason explained.

"Right," added Gizmo. "We would be slaves for the bastards. They would be the only contact with the outside world. And we really have nothing in the way of space travel. We couldn't leave. Eventually we would run out of food and resources. The surface would have been nuked. The planet virtually dead. The human race would be at their mercy for even the basics like food and water."

"But why would they want us to be able to kill off the invaders? Why would they help develop the Walkers? I'm still not getting that part," Eric asked.

"I'm not sure. They don't give the Invaders the technology. They hardly let them carry weapons. They are only there to use it. They don't trust them. So they wouldn't want the Invaders on the planet that was making equipment after the invasion was over. They would want them cleared off," Jason said.

"So why us? Why would they need us?" Eric asked.

"I don't know. Maybe the other race was dying off. You met them. They're idiots. Or maybe they just can't do what we can do. For sure, they are stupid beyond reason. I'm sure they didn't start out that way. That takes generations to accomplish," Jason said.

"But there are other races, like Deri or Braz' species. They are more advanced than we are. They could work with their technology better. Better than us, anyway," Eric said.

"True," Gizmo answered. "But they don't want that, do they? They want slaves; ignorant slaves that will follow orders and not think too much. Smart enough to do what they want, but dumb enough not to be able to figure things out."

"Right. They would probably cull the remaining population. Weed out anyone with any kind of talent. Anyone educated. Our leaders would do almost anything to be able to continue the survival of mankind. So they would most likely agree to have us make their equipment for them. Even just for food. It wouldn't seem like slavery in the beginning. Just a...just a business deal," Jason said.

"Shit. A fluking business deal. Damned politicians probably set it up. Slaves, the whole human race. It's just a business deal," Eric said, shaking his head. "Oh, man. It makes sense. It all makes sense now. The gas. The damn gas. That's why the gas. To keep everyone drugged. So, Bradley may be our best connection after all."

"That Frankenstein, zombie-making piece of garbage," Gizmo said.

Deri and Braz walked in and announced that they were all loaded and ready. Eric said his goodbyes and left to get into his transport. Technology from around the planet had been gathered and stored, filling one entire sixteen mile deck. The work on the satellites had been completed and it was time to go.

"Admiral," Jason announced into his uniform.

"Colonel," Admiral Harding came back. "Looks like you're all set. Good luck, men."

"Good luck to you, Admiral. We'll see you soon," Jason replied. Then he looked down at Bo and said, "You ready, girl? We're going on a trip."

Bo looked excitedly at the screen as if it were the windshield of the R.V. and gave a little squeal. They watched as the first five transports left to arrive ahead of the rest and provide protection in high orbit around Earth, and then waited for the satellites to blink out of sight to arrive in low orbit attached to the three other transports.

Then Jason brought up Deri's planet, touched the screen, and they were gone. In the same blink it took them to arrive, it came to him. He looked over at Gizmo and said, "Giz. It just hit me. I think I just figured it out. I think I know how to find who is behind all this Invader business. I think I know why it's Earth that they picked."

"Why?" Gizmo asked.

"Because someone else has something worse than the Invaders, and they're coming," he said.

"You think?" Gizmo asked.

"Let's wrap this up. We have to get back to Earth, and then back to the Admiral. I really wish our communication was up, because I think we're in deep shit," Jason added.

Chapter Thirty Two

Eric didn't even get out of the shuttle for the trip, since it was near instant. He waited for the bay doors to re-open and lifted the shuttle down toward Ruby Ridge where the General was waiting and watching for the arrivals.

He pulled the shuttle into the cave and stepped out into the middle of a briefing. Four large marker boards were set up and names were scrolled on three of them in columns. The General was standing to the side while another man was going over the names with a pointer.

"First Infantry," he called, followed by cheers and whistles. "Looks like you got the high score this week," followed by more celebration.

"Who got him?" the General asked, laughing as a man stood up. He pointed at him and said, "Good job, son," and turned it back to the man in the front.

He came over when he saw Eric and returned salutes. "What's this, General?"

"Oh, just a little contest. It's a zombie hunt," he told him. "You see that blank board on the left? Well that's for whomever we find alive as far as elected officials. Politicians of any sort."

"And the others?" Eric asked.

"The first one over, well, it's a board for elected officials that are zombies that we put down. The next is for famous people. Actors and actresses and such, we ran across pockets of them. It's for fun, you know. Gotta have a little of that now and then.

"Then we started I.D.ing some famous criminals, so we had another board set up. Most of them, we found in Chicago and New York. Some in California," the General said.

"You mean the criminals or the politicians?" Eric asked with a chuckle.

"Same thing. Right now, they are having a debate. It's a contest. They found a politician and wanted him put on the criminal board. Let's listen." he said.

"Alright," the man at the board said, laughing with everyone else. "Alright. So this is the Governor of New York. That is the highest yet, so he gets the prize for the week. Sure, he is an elected official. But some here say he is a criminal. We put Pascal from Chicago on the politician side, so should we change that too? It's your game; your contest, so you decide on the rules. So let's hear the debate."

A man stood up and walked toward the front and picked up the microphone. "Alright, well, nobody is debating that he was the Governor, it's whether he was a criminal or not that is the question. Look. Before he was the Gov., he was in an office of attorneys for these appraisal management companies and banker scum. You know.

"No big deal, right? Except that he was an attorney. And you all know why attorneys wear neckties, right? It's to hold the foreskin back," and he waited until the laughing died down and said, "But then he passes a law once he is Governor that makes the Appraisal Management companies run all the private appraisers. Then they start paying them squat. Then, they start cutting into the Real Estate Agents and the Mortgage Brokers fees.

"Pretty soon, the whole real Estate industry is shut down and run by the real criminals, the bankers and such, the people he said he was trying to protect everyone from. That is one third of the entire economy of the country - gone.

"He said it was to keep the industry honest," and the crowd laughed. "So he put the real criminals in charge of the only ones who kept them honest, to protect them from, you know, undue influence, is what he said. What a joke.

"Think about it. When Real Estate shuts down, the lumber companies shut down, the truckers, the plumbers, the electricians, the Hardware Stores, on and on the dominos fall, down to the guy who pounds the for sale sign on the lawn. This guy single handedly put millions and millions of people out of work so he and his thug banker pals could make some free money. So I vote for the criminal board. How about it?"

The crowd started chanting, "CRIMINAL, CRIMINAL, CRIMINAL!" until the man in charge walked up and tried to take over again, but before he could start, the guy added, "This dickhead crippled the entire country. And then, here's the kicker: Turns out, I think it was his nephew or something, who owned some of these companies."

Again, the crowd started cheering, "CRIMINAL, CRIMINAL, CRIMINAL!"

"Alright, alright. I tend to agree," the man said, taking back the microphone. "Either way, the contest goes to Ist Infantry this week. Would the shooter please come forward and claim your award and give a few words," he said.

The room went wild as a man walked to the front. Some laughed and cheered, some jeered and booed, and they all tossed paper cups and wrappers at him.

"Well. There I am," he started once he reached the microphone. "I seez a man with a nice suit on up New York way. Looked to me like a thug. Bit of a Nancy boy, but a thug. As I gets a closer look, damn, I thought it was him. Sure nuff, it was, too. I looks at 'im and sez to my buddy, 'Hey, is that the Governor of New York?' And there he was and that's how we found 'im, getting down and eatin' off the ass end of a dead dog." The room exploded in laughter again.

"So my buddy sez to me I better make sure he's a zombie before I shoots 'im. So I looks at my buddy and sez, you really think he'd be eatin' that butt-end like that if he weren't no zombie? I mean, he's Italian, where's the damn marinara sauce?" And there was another roar of laughter.

"So we watches for a bit, then I sez, hell, I'll just go down and ask 'im. So we gets down off the roof and I walks up and whistles like this," and he put his fingers in his mouth and gave a sharp whistle for demonstration. "And dang, if this wasn't the confusing part. He starts runnin' at us, me an' my buddy. But he's got a pistol in his side. I kin see it.

"So I'm thinkin', that sombitch candy ass doesn't allow guns in his state. Maybe it aint him. But he's a comin' and he's a fast one. And he's a yellin' too. So I puts a couple in 'im 'bout center mass. And he keeps on acomin'! Then my buddy hits 'im with a couple, but he's a runnin'' and a yellin' and keeps on a comin', even faster now. That's when I remembers. Oh, right, ya gotta git 'em in the brain.

"So we're standin' there watchin' 'im runnin' at us, and it's awkward and kinda comical, in a homosexual zombie gangster kind of way. My buddy sez we should git out a there, but me, I waits. I waits 'til he gits right up nice an' close and, BAM, gets him right b'tween the eyes. 'Take that you gun-totin Sodomite gangster zombie!' I screams. Dropped 'im deader 'an that dog he was a chawin' the ass end off of."

The man got a little bit serious before continuing and said. "So keep this in mind. They move faster'n a cheetah, and you gotta get 'em in the brain. Otherwise, you're lunch. No tenderizer. No seasonin'. And NO DAMN MARINARA!" and he left the stage while everyone rolled laughing again.

"Alright," the General said to Eric with a chuckle. "Let's get you debriefed and onto your next assignment."

Eric had tears in his eyes from laughing. "Oh, man. I can't imagine there's another place in the universe like this. I love the Earth. It's good to be back, General."

Chapter Thirty Three

Bradley could hear the cheering through the walls. At first, he wasn't sure if they were talking about him. He could swear they said his name, he just couldn't hear what they were talking about. The walls muffled the voices, but he thought he could hear them clearly when there was a loud outburst of laughter and cheering.

But in his head, he could hear it. "Bradley," followed by laughter. "Bradley," and more noises. "Bradley, Bradley, Bradley!" He swore he heard them cheering.

"And it's well they should be cheering," he thought. "After what I just told them about Catskill Pharmaceuticals, they should be cheering for me. Especially after I told them how I changed the DNA splicing protocol without Catskill's knowledge and produced the Walkers. I single handedly saved the world."

Then he thought, "Are they laughing at me?" he turned his head quickly and said out loud as he could have sworn he heard his name again. "No. They wouldn't," and then paused, "Are they? Those bastards!" and listened some more, sure this time sure he was hearing voices from the ventilation.

"No," he thought. "No way would they do that," as his thoughts wandered back to his interrogation. "If they are, I will make them suffer."

The best part, he thought, was telling them he knows what the file looks like, but would have to show them himself. It was a maze of tunnels and labs and rooms and offices on several levels both above and below ground. Only he could recognize the single file out of tens and possibly even hundreds of thousands of them, and they had reorganized.

He had an itch in his crotch and squirmed to get some relief, but his chains made it impossible. He looked around the room and noticed what an improvement it was. Finally, he was getting some respect. There was no ECT machine, and he was not strapped to that stupid chair. There was only a gas mask.

The General was sitting at his desk with Eric when a report was brought to him. It was a Base Report, going over the boring details of supplies and health and moral. On the top was a medical report that he leaned over to look at. He noticed the word "Infestation" circled in red near the top and read the report. The last thing they needed in an enclosed base was an infestation.

"Crabs!" he said to his Aide. "What the hell." `

"Not a big problem, General. We have the medics checking everyone. Should have the whole base gone through in a few days," he said.

"Alright, well keep me informed," he told him and looked back at Eric.

"Crabs," he said, shaking his head.

"It happens, I guess," Eric said.

"So. This Ambassador. He is the one who arrived earlier. Up on the transport. He's the one you're talking about?" the General asked.

"Yes, Sir. I think so. The grey. Do you have him on a video so we can make sure it's the same one?" he asked.

The General had his Aide get him a video on the laptop and pulled it around so they both could look.

"That looks like the same one. Same type. He said he was an Ambassador," Eric said.

"Alright. And tell me, how sure are you that he doesn't know you found the patches you're talking about?" The General asked.

"Fairly certain. It was one of the main things Jason and the Admiral insisted on, that we keep that between us and not let on. They wanted to find a way to exploit it," Eric said.

"We have to. We have to find out who is behind the Invaders," and he sat back in his chair, thinking.

Eric watched as the General considered one thing, then another. He'd gotten used to it. The General would ponder one thing, and his eyebrows would raise, then another, and his eyebrow would lower. He sat and imagined the General considering one action, then an aspect of that one thing, then the result, then another with its result, raising and lowering his eyebrows all the while.

"Jason said that, when he gets back, he wants to draw them out and find their location. Then, I think he will send the entire Armada out and take them down," Eric told him.

"Well, that is a good idea, but I think that we will need better weapons. I can't see them losing the Invader weaponry to us or anyone else, and then not having something better on the shelf and ready to go. And the smartest person we have here to figure something out is a kid, Cody," said the General.

Eric sat and twiddled his thumbs and asked, "So, what have you found out through Bradley?"

"Callis is going to start interrogation again any minute. She got some good Intel. Turns out there was a guiding hand involved in all this; the development of the Walkers and the gas. Maybe even your grey," he said pointing back at the screen. "She wanted a little more time with him before we move on the information he provides. Just in case."

"Anything good so far?" Eric asked.

"We have a location and a list of names. Catskill Mountains, most likely deep underground. I guess that brings us to your next assignment," he said.

"I'm ready, General. What did you have in mind?" Eric asked.

"Two things. I want you to take your shuttles from your transports and clear the surface of any Walkers. We have to re-take and occupy the surface. To do that, we need to make it safe. So you set up the operation how you think it'll work best and let me know. It'll be good training for the pilots, too. Maybe even work up some ground forces and set up tactics for them. Good training.

"Next, I want you to go through the library. Get every map and every drawing and blueprint of that facility in the Catskills. You're going, so get to know every inch of it," the General said. "And look, this is no reflection on you, but I'm sending Jason and Gizmo with you as soon as they get back."

"No, not at all, General. I understand. These guys are, well, they're scientists. I wouldn't know what the hell I would even be looking for," Eric told him.

"So I want you to be ready to go in the next day or two, maybe three. They should be back by then," the General said.

Chapter Thirty Four

Bradley was falling into a semi-dream state in his cell. Today, if all went according to plan, he would get back to work. He would be freed from his bonds and be back in his laboratory and continue testing and research. Already, he had been allowed to sleep. There was no longer any loud music and there were no bright lights. It was all going his way, little by little.

Today, he would tell them all how close he was to a solution for the Walkers; that he and Emily had nearly discovered the combination to rid the Earth of them without making it uninhabitable for humans. He would tell them how unfortunate it was that she had her accident so near to the solution.

Down the hallway, Callis and a nurse were preparing for Bradley's next treatment.

"What will this actually do?" The nurse, scowling behind her, was asking Dr. Callis.

It was a male nurse assigned to Callis because of his size in case more muscle was needed for Bradley. He was running through his head who it might have been that he may have gotten crabs from and came to the conclusion that the only possibility was Callis, the only female he had been in recent contact with. She had somehow tricked him into it, possibly even slipped something into his coffee.

He racked his brain trying to imagine what might have gotten into him to be involved with such a hideous creature, huge, unkempt, and entirely unappealing. "It must have been drugs. It's the only way. The cow slipped something into my coffee," he thought, trying to run back in his memory to when it could have happened.

"Carbogen?" she answered, interrupting his thoughts. "Oh. It will make a person convulse and struggle for air, but it also produces a narcotic effect. It tricks the person into thinking they are suffocating and dying, but it's just the high level of carbon dioxide that does it. They are actually getting enough oxygen to survive it, well, most of the time."

"I don't understand. You are going to make this guy feel like he is dying and suffocating? I don't get why you would do that to someone," she said.

"There are some studies that showed miraculous changes in a person" and she picked up a paper out of the file on it. "Like this guy. Look what he wrote."

He took the paper and read aloud. "After the second breath came an onrush of color, first a predominant sheet of beautiful rosy-red, following which came successive sheets of brilliant color and design, some geometric, some fanciful and graceful. Then the colors separated; my soul drawing apart from the physical being, was drawn upward seemingly to leave the earth and to go upward where it reached a greater Spirit with whom there was a communion, producing a remarkable, new relaxation and deep security."

When he finished, Callis said, "That was after his first treatment."

"Sounds like an out-of-body experience. Is that what you want?" he asked.

"No. We all know that is just delusion. It's hogwash. But what could happen is it could make him more susceptible and open to further treatment, and maybe a little more manageable," Callis said.

"So what happened to the guy?" he asked.

"Well, since he was now obviously delusional on top of everything else, he was lobotomized. A short time later, he apparently committed suicide. Some people you just can't help," she said.

The nurse stood up straight and turned toward the wall with his mouth open in shock, unable to imagine the torment the man went through before finally committing suicide to escape it, and he was unable to face this person who was about to use it on someone else.

"Don't you think that this is, maybe, a little dangerous?" he managed to ask.

She took a confrontational air and stood up and looked at him. "What? You are a trained psychiatrist now? A few days working with me and you're the expert all of a sudden?"

"No. No. I don't mean it that way. I meant..." and he was cut off.

"I know what you meant. I have a task to perform. I have to get Bradley to talk. Is that something you can do? Are you a trained interrogator?" she pushed.

"Well no, but..." and he was cut off again.

"So don't question my work. Bradley, humph, don't worry about Bradley. I doubt he will live for too long. Once he is done with this, once we're done with him, I think he will be put down like a sick animal," she said.

He was about to ask if she had tried just asking him for what she was trying to find out, but decided to keep his mouth shut. There was going to be no gain from any further talking about it. He lifted the container of compressed gas and put it on the cart and said, "There you go. Have a ball."

Callis stood up again and said, "You think I'm pushing this down the hallway? That's what you're here for. Move it!" and she opened the door and stood to the side.

He grudgingly pushed the cart out and down the hall toward Bradley's cell. Coming up to the guards outside, he saw them look at Callis with disgust, while one of them scratched himself. The nurse was rudely dismissed by her and started walking back down the hall when he heard her telling one of the guards to push the cart in for her, at which she was told to do it herself, in the most unkindly words. He didn't quite get the physics involved, but it ended with the cart being somehow parked up her behind.

Chapter Thirty Five

Dent sent word that Cody was ready to bring his equipment and set up at the base and asked that Dr. Stanford assist him. Eric went personally to retrieve him and the rest of the villagers and personnel he'd left to defend the area.

They were met in the bay by Dr. Stanford, and Cody immediately began speaking to him. "I know why we can't get communication up to Jason and the Admiral. It was directed through the dome shield. Once the shield is working, we will have direct communication again."

"Good, Cody. So how do we do that? What do you need from me?" Stanford asked.

They stopped and both looked up into the air when they were interrupted by an announcement through the speaker system that had been running twenty-four hours a day since the invasion.

It was a soothing female's voice saying, "As a reminder, under the new Bill of Rights, you have the right to your freedom of thought and to your own opinion. However, opinions must be voiced to the proper terminals, located at recording stations at the entrance to berthing areas. Remember, lethal force will be used for violations."

"God I hate that," Stanford said. "Every twenty minutes it comes on with another right that is not a right at all."

"Wow. You have freedom of thought?" Cody said. "How lucky. When can we get out of here, Mr. Dent? We can set this up back at the waterfall. At least we can complain without the threat of lethal force. All we have to watch out for is our language around Hellen."

Dent noticed several people looking and listening and pulled his weapon across his chest, considering that Cody had just expressed an opinion, and said, "I don't care what you're thinking, one move and you are gonna lose that freedom of thought right now."

Stanford snickered. "Yah! I like this guy. But don't worry; the General cancelled it all as soon as you guys showed back up. We're back on the real Bill of Rights and he's working on putting a Constitutional Government back in force. We just can't turn the dang recording off. It was designed by Catskill Pharma; piped in from someplace we haven't found yet."

"Cody. How long will it take you to set up the shield?" Eric asked.

"With help from Dr. Stanford, maybe a day or two. Then we have to test it," he said.

"Alright. When you're done, I brought a whole ship full of gadgets for you two to look through that we scavenged from the Invader planet. Maybe you and Dr. Stanford can go through it and see what you can make of it," Eric said.

Four days went by without word from Jason. Cody and Dr. Stanford had experienced setback after setback on setting up the shield and decided to look through Eric's transport for possible equipment they could use and try to fit them in with Cody's configuration.

Nothing that they tried on the shield was working and worry was growing about Jason and Gizmo. Eric and the General came down several times to check on their progress, and more scientists were assigned to see if they could come up with something. The most they could get was a momentary field being generated; just a blink.

The frustration had grown to the point that three of the scientists had gotten into an argument and came to blows when Jason finally came on the radio through his suit.

"Eric!" He called. "Need to meet with you and the General right away."

A shuttle pulled into the bay a few minutes later where Cody had the shield equipment set up, the door flew open, and both Jason and Gizmo came flying out at dead run, rifles on their backs and Bo sprinting along beside them.

He glanced at the equipment as he ran by and yelled out, "Got that thing up, Cody?"

"No! I can only get it to appear briefly, and then it blanks out," Cody called back.

Jason was at the double doors, waiting for the guards to open and pass him through, when he turned and asked, "Did you synchronize it with the waves from the sun?" and the doors opened and he bolted through without waiting for an answer.

Cody and Stanford looked at each other and Cody slapped his hand to his forehead. "Of course," he said. "The waves will cancel each other out. We're using the sun for power. We have to get them in proper sync. That's why it won't stay up," and he looked back at the door and said, "How does he do that?"

Jason, Eric, and Gizmo were soon in the Generals' office going over the coming threat. Jason was explaining, "So that's when it dawned on me, we were putting the cart before the horse. We didn't figure out the Invader power source for years after we found them. All throughout most of a century, this has been being planned. The Walkers were developed and the gas was developed, way before Gizmo and I figured out their power source."

"Right. So it's not us they are worried about. Why would they? We're practically cave men to them. It is someone else. They, whoever this someone else is, either have a better system or they figured out the Invader power themselves. We're guessing that they are on their way and they have a better system or better technology," Gizmo said.

"Either way, we have to prepare for more advanced weapons. Whoever is behind the Invaders will have to up their game too, because the threat to them is already more advanced," Jason said.

"So, you're thinking that whoever is coming will have superior weaponry, then the Invaders will have superior weaponry to fight that, and we're going to be in the middle," the General said.

"If we can contact the new threat, maybe they won't be as malevolent as whoever developed the invaders. We would just have to find them. Maybe we can work with them. Any ideas?" Eric asked.

"I do. So happens, I have some resources at my disposal," Jason said.

"Yes," the General agreed. "I understand you acquired a little Real Estate in your travels."

"He actually owns all the people, too. I guess that's the law. You beat 'em, you own 'em. There are literally thousands of planets that were conquered, and there were more in the middle of being invaded," Gizmo told him.

"Yah. That's right. But none of them had defenses against the Invaders. But maybe collectively…" Eric trailed off.

"No," the General cut in. "Collectively, they had all been defeated. Collectively, they couldn't even take out one planet of them. Collectively they couldn't figure out the power source. That was you guys. No, I doubt they would be much help technologically. But there is a way they can be useful. Collectively, they could gather intelligence."

"How is that going, by the way?" Jason asked.

"We think we may find some answers deep in the mountains at Catskill Pharmaceuticals. You two will be going there shortly with Eric and whatever resources you need. I'm thinking we will at least find a link, some trail," the General told them.

"I think we have another trail to follow too," Jason said. "I think we have possibly a very good one. But we have to get with the Admiral for that."

"What do you have in mind, Colonel?" the General asked.

"Well. If I am right, if they were really just going to conquer Earth and then get the Invaders killed off or just pull them out and not actually occupied by them, then there would be others like us. If they have ten or fifteen or even twenty generations above what they are using now, as far as technology, then there should be that many conquered planets without the Invaders actually occupying it," Jason told him.

"Right. Right," Gizmo said. "And each one would be making or developing something; some more advance weapons. They could even have something like the Walkers on the surface."

"Probably each one would be pretty much uninhabitable, so there wouldn't be much interest in anyone else inhabiting or taking it over. It could lead us to whoever is actually behind the Invaders," Eric said.

"And the first planet to start with is ours, starting with Catskill. The others on the other planets will be deep down in bunkers like that, developing new weapons. Catskill Pharma, that'll be our practice run," Jason added.

"What are you thinking in terms of time for the new threat to appear?" the General asked.

"I'm thinking that we had about two years of supplies here. They would have come and offered you a lifeline just before you ran out. Maybe let you starve a little. Get good and desperate before offering you a deal, food and water for... slavery. Then, maybe anywhere from a few months to a year to get everyone in production; tool up and such. So let's say two years minimum. Max, I could only guess. Not long after that," Jason said.

"I don't think they would set up manufacturing here if this were going to be where the battle was. Not at the front," the General pointed out. "So we'll be behind the lines. But, that doesn't mean it won't be here in a short time after it all starts. This planet would be one of my first targets if I were at war. I'd be looking really hard for it."

"Yup. When it happened, we would have been the highest valued target, for sure. That is, if we had been subjected and were making their equipment. Now, who knows? It's anyone's guess," Jason said.

"Two years, plus or minus. Two years to find it, figure it out, and then to make it or make something better. At the same time, find the new threat and figure out what they have. Find a way to defend against it and improve on their weapons. That's not a lot of time, Gentlemen, considering we have the entire universe to search for them. We'd better get moving," the General said. Then he asked, "So was your mission successful?"

"Sort of, General," Gizmo told him.

"Yah, sure it was successful. It's just that we have an added bonus, if you look at it that way," Jason added.

"Sort of? What bonus?" the General asked.

"Well. Sir. Uhm. We did clear out Braz' planet. That went about how we thought it would. We brought him and a couple hundred of his people back with us," Jason hedged.

"And?" the General asked.

"Well, Deri and her planet was a bit of a problem. We cleared the Invaders out, but their planet is no longer able to support life. It's their version of the Scorched Earth policy. It'll take about two hundred years before they can inhabit the surface. Longer to get their agriculture going again and support their population," Jason told him.

"And?" the General demanded.

"Basically they would be extinct without our help," Gizmo told him.

"And?" the General prodded.

"And we brought some of them back with us," Gizmo said.

"How many?" he asked.

"Twenty seven," Jason said.

"Well, bring them in. I'd like to meet them. We'll make them comfortable," the General said.

"No. Uhm, that's twenty-seven million," Gizmo said meekly.

He sat down again and thumped his fingers on his desk and asked, "So, what were you thinking?"

"Really, we couldn't leave them there. There are more, too. We just didn't bring them all. But we have to relocate them," Jason said.

"That is more people than we have left alive on Earth. Advanced race, more technologically advanced than we are. You know what that means don't you?" he asked.

"Yes Sir, General. It means we would end up pretty much extinct if we allowed them here," Jason said.

"If they are an advanced race," Gizmo added.

"Right. If they're an advanced race," Jason agreed.

"Are you suggesting they aren't?" the General asked.

"Well. Here's the thing. They have some advanced things. They had light travel and space travel and better weaponry. That gave them an advantage over us and maybe makes them appear to be an advanced race. The advances they made were all developed due to their having that one thing, light travel, and that put them in space. So they developed weapons and tactics for space," Jason explained.

"Sounds like an advanced society to me. More advanced than we have gotten yet," the General commented.

"Two weeks ago, yes. They were more advanced than we. Now, I'm not sure. We now have the best weapons and defenses in the known universe, that is, that we know of. We also know how to make it work. We travel in the quantum realm. They hadn't thought in quantum terms.

They do light travel. It's practically stone aged in comparison," Jason said.

"They are more advanced," the General said after thinking about it briefly. "There is no arguing it. Just because one or two people figure out the Invader power source doesn't make us, our entire species, magically more advanced over two or three weeks. That takes evolution. Our job is to protect mankind now, and there are precious few of them left. We can't let them live here. I don't care how desperate they are. Understand?"

"Yes sir, General," they answered.

"Whatever we're going to do, we have to be humane and considerate. We'll consider them our allies. You brought them here. You figure it out. Let me know what your solution is by morning," he ordered.

"Yes sir, General," Jason and Gizmo answered.

"Are they comfortable up there?" he asked.

"Cramped sir. We really packed them in," Jason said.

"Bring them to Nellis. Let them stretch their legs. Set up tents. Did you bring any officials with you?"

"Yes, General. We brought several dignitaries," Jason said.

"Bring whatever dignitaries you have and I'll meet with them," and he ordered his aide to make arrangements for food and quarters.

Chapter Thirty Six

Jason and Gizmo came out of the library. They had finished going over last minute planning with Deri and Braz and their crew, and they were about to head out to enter Catskill with them. The blueprints had been downloaded on mobile devices with key locations and checkpoints marked.

They entered the landing bay where Cody and Stanford had been working nonstop with their team of scientists to get the shield up and were now demonstrating it to the General. Bradley managed to get himself included in the mission and was standing to the side as a crowd gathered around Cody and his equipment.

"It's working," Cody told Jason as he walked up. "We just have to test it."

They all looked out toward the entrance where they could see the energy shield glimmering. Every now and then, a few lights would flare up. "Those are bugs. I hope this is more than just a really good bug zapper," Cody said. Then a bird flew by and was disintegrated.

"OH!" everybody exclaimed at the same time.

"Well. I guess that much works. But can people get in and out?" Jason asked.

"We've been afraid to try it," Cody said. "The human body puts out a radio wave that we fed into the shield, but we haven't...we just, well, we're afraid to try it. What can I say? Take a look, I'll show you what we've done."

Jason and Gizmo walked over to the equipment, and while Cody and Stanford were explaining the frequencies, Bradley, who hadn't seen daylight in weeks, absentmindedly walked toward the light.

It was the thought of being vaporized by the shield that had everyone's attention now, including the guards, which allowed Bradley to continue to wander out into the sunlight. He kept going further and further as the frequencies were checked again and again.

He felt the warmth of the sunlight on his face and thought about his vision of him standing in the sun with his creations, his Walkers, surrounding him as they would their god with his arms stretched out, standing atop a hill. It was a vision he was certain he would realize any time now. He felt a slight wisp of fresh air on his face and moved farther out to get more sun. He was enjoying the warmth, the sight of the blue sky, and the soft fresh wind on his skin.

As he stepped further out, he was amazed at how soothing and warm the sun was, which drew him out even further. Still unnoticed, he continued, right into the shield. He continued until it was too warm. It became uncomfortably warm and acutely warm.

As he turned to come back out of the sun, one of the guards yelled out, "What the..." causing the crowd to turn just as every crab on his body burst into flames, causing smoke to rise from the crotch of his pants. He walked back in, not even noticing. All he noticed was that everyone was looking at him, as well, he thought as he stood smoldering, they should be, for he was the most important man in the world.

The General and Eric looked at each other and chuckled. "Dr. Bradley," the General called. "You look like you need more sun. Go out for another minute or two."

He ordered two guards to follow and told them not to walk into the shield, but to let him into it. If all was okay, they could follow.

Bradley, in his drugged state, obediently followed the General's commands and spun about, walking zombie-like toward the sun once more. They watched as the shield washed over his entire body and he was completely immersed in the field before the General called him back.

"Alright. Who else wants to try it?" the General asked.

"I'll go," Cody said.

"No. Not you," the General answered.

Jason and Gizmo both said in unison, "I'll try it."

"Hell no!" the General responded emphatically. "You two," he said to two of the guards. "Feeling lucky today?"

"Every day, General," one of them said and they both marched into the shield and walked all the way through. They turned and waited for the General to call them back in and said, "Didn't feel a thing."

"What about Deri and Braz?" the General asked.

Before they could respond, both had ordered one of their men through the shield. They instantly complied, not wanting to be shown up by the Earth soldiers, and passed in and out without so much as a sparkle.

"How?" the General asked.

"They are pretty much like us. We took DNA samples, and well, they are us. Don't know why. Same radio frequencies too, same DNA," Stanford answered.

"Good job Cody. You too, Dr. Stanford. Times aburnin'," Jason said. "We have to go," and he pulled a few sheets of paper out of his shirt and handed them to Cody. "Let's go over this with Dr. Stanford a little bit before we leave. It's important. I want you two to start working on this."

They were well into asking questions and getting explanations from Jason when they were interrupted by the General. "Can you get me in touch with Admiral Harding now?"

"I should be able to do that, now that the shield is up. Should be less than an hour," Cody said.

"Good. Get going Jason. I'll brief the Admiral and tell him to expect you by tomorrow," the General said.

They loaded into the shuttle and were gone.

Chapter Thirty Seven

Bradley sat against the bulkhead of the shuttle as they approached Catskill. He felt an odd euphoria that accompanies the dying of brain cells from electroshock and wondered why everyone doesn't try it. Soon, that euphoria would turn to depression; to forgetfulness, and then, often, to dementia and even suicide. But for now, between the drugs and the shock, he had never felt better, that is, that he could recall.

The base was set up much like Ruby Ridge. There would be a main entrance into which they would fly and land the shuttle. Beyond that would be the blast doors containing the Evil Walkers, and to the side would be doors leading to offices and living quarters. There would be only variations based on the natural formation of the cave. Since Catskill Pharmaceuticals had done all the designing of all bases, including Ruby Ridge, they already would have some familiarity with it.

The main differences would be that behind those blast doors would be unleashed Walkers, millions of them, and behind the doors to the living areas, would be people, many of them as well. But they would have been gassed by the drug company's concoction, and turned into mad and unthinking monsters by Bradley's design of the gas valves. They would be zombies.

Their plan was to get into the offices and laboratories where there would be only a limited number of skilled workers, rather than hordes of mindless charging zombies in the civilian living areas. They would avoid the general population. There was also hope that some laboratories would have their own filtered air systems, and some of the scientists might still be in there and still be safe.

The mission members were going over the maps on the way to the Catskill Mountains when Jason started speaking with Deri and Braz. "So, our science and your science – let's compare," he said.

"Alright. Let's," they both answered.

"I'm thinking about gravity and the strength of gravity. Our science on it is that the amount of gravitational pull depends on the mass of the object. The more mass, the more pull," he said.

Braz and Deri both agreed that that would be their conclusions as well.

"So how does that explain your gravity suits? How does that inverted square root equation work with that?" Jason asked.

Braz was about to speak, but Deri cut him off. "Jason. I'm just surprised you even ask. I know you know, you just haven't done it; figured it out," she said.

"Well. I have been a little busy," Jason told her. "Saving the universe and such."

"I'll tell you what. If you haven't figured it out by the next time we get a chance to sit down, you can play Rock Paper Scissors with me to get the answer," she said.

"But wait…" he tried to protest.

"Nope. Rock Paper Scissors. That's it," she said with a playful smile at Braz.

"It's only fair, I think," Braz joined in the game. An instant of silence went by and then he added, "Besides, I don't think this is about the gravity suit, is it?"

"No. Actually it's not. I have an idea," Jason said.

"We have a planet we thought you might be able to borrow," Gizmo told them.

"A planet? You have a spare planet?" Deri exclaimed. "Why haven't you been living on it?"

"Well, that's the thing. Gravity. It looks like it used to have life, but I don't think you could really inhabit it right now," he said.

"Well, what's wrong with it?" she asked.

"It used to have water, surface water. It probably even had life at one time, maybe like us. Some people think that that is where we came from. But something happened. The air is really thin now and all the water vanished from the surface. But I have an idea," Jason told them.

"Gravity," Deri said.

"Yes gravity. More than that, mass, which would make gravity; increase it. We have a planet that revolves in the opposite direction of all the other planets in our system. It is surrounded by chunks of ice and rock. I have a theory that we captured that planet long ago when we passed through another system about sixty-five million years ago. The planet is huge and would have had much more gravity than this planet, Mars.

"So it could have pulled water, the atmosphere, and even loose chunks of rock from the surface. Losing all that mass would have given it less gravity. Now, it won't even keep a decent air cover. And the captured planet has giant rings of ice and rock floating around it now, billions or probably even trillions of tons of it," Jason said.

"So we were thinking we could bring them back to Mars, now that we have these transports. We could bring them back and deposit them in the empty rivers and canyons that used to have water. It would add mass and gain gravity again and it would generate an atmosphere again, and in a short time, you could live on it," Gizmo said.

"Yes. You are right. That could be done," Braz said.

"Then, your people would have a home until your planet is back in shape to live on. Might be a little cold at first, but it'll warm up." Jason said.

Deri was looking hurt. "You don't want us living with you?" she asked.

"I would like nothing more," Jason responded, rubbing her knee. "But it's about History. Our History. It'll be better for both of us, believe me. I will explain it all to you, but later."

Eric was pulling into the landing area and called into the back, "Blast doors are intact. The double doors are all sealed."

They all came forward to look. Eric circled inside the landing area one time checking for dangers or threats and put the shuttle down near the main double doors. "In case we need to get back in really quick," he said.

They compared what they were looking at to what was on their mobile devices and it matched except for a few differences. Once they had their orientation right, Jason said, "Equipment check," and everyone looked their weapons and ammo over once more.

The first item on their mission was to turn the gas off. The tanks would be right there in the landing area, and above that would be the observation area surrounded by protective glass. Bradley was looking up toward that when the shuttle door opened.

Bo was first to bounce out and began sniffing around. The others stepped out, followed by Bradley. A bird was nesting in the bay and decided to fly off, causing Bo to bark. The echoing bark started a rustling noise behind the blast doors and soon the Walkers were thrashing and screeching and howling behind them. This alerted the zombies behind the double doors who started to screech and howl as well.

"Well," Jason said. "Kinda what we expected, right?"

Bradley was standing well behind them, still looking up at the observation room. He turned to them when Jason spoke, and in his dazed state, finally realized who he was with. "It is that horrible man, that Jason Brand, and that other one, Goncho or something. What a stupid name." he thought. "Good. They'll both soon be dead, and I hope it's painful. Fools. Hairless monkeys."

He looked around the landing area and saw what he was searching for; the control panel and the gas valves. One of those switches would allow him to get into the observation room. There, he would find that shiny and smooth red button, the same as the one he had caressed before

179

the invasion; the one that will release his creations upon them. But it wouldn't be right away. It had to be properly planned and properly timed.

Jason sent two men over to shut the valves on the gas canisters and was setting up to breach the double doors while Bradley watched.

Bradley ran it over in his mind again. All was going perfectly and as planned until that horrible man showed up. "That Jason Brand. People listen to him. And they do what he says. Why? They should consult with me first. I am the expert," he thought. "Him and that Gecho. Stupid name. They are nothing but hairless monkeys. I hope their death is extremely painful. They are all nothing but fools," he thought.

Without any control he burst out, "Fools!" sending the sound echoing through the empty chamber.

They all turned and faced him. Quickly, he had to think of something to say. He stood like a deer in the headlights, trying to come up with something. In his drugged state, he was having difficulty thinking but finally, it came. "Let me look. You don't want to accidentally gas the clean rooms."

Over by the canisters, there was an electric panel. One of those switches would release the magnetic locks on the double doors. That would release the people from behind those doors. "Zombies," he thought. "That's what that man called them. Silly name calling, that's all. Fools. Especially that horrible man, that Jason Brand and that other one, Gonad. What a stupid name."

His plan came to him as he walked toward the canisters. "I just have to watch myself and not say what I am thinking. I must take care. I wouldn't want anyone to think I was crazy."

Unlocking those doors would distract them long enough for him to get into the observation room and beyond. They would be busy fighting off the charging madness. From the observation room, he could do whatever he wanted, and what he wanted was to release his creations from behind the blast doors. Release the Walkers.

He paused as an announcement came over the speaker system. It was the same comforting female voice as the Ruby Ridge announcer and every other base Catskill Pharmaceuticals had set up. "As a reminder, under the new Bill of Rights, you have the right to work under safe conditions and be free from bodily harm, unless otherwise requested by a Government Official. Remember, lethal force will be used for non-compliance."

Jason and Gizmo both got that funny feeling something bad was about to happen. "Watch him!" Jason yelled to the man closest to

Bradley. They both got down on a knee and held their weapons at the ready.

Bradley was reaching for the valves, when he was stopped. "What are you doing?" the man asked.

Bradley stopped mid reach, turned to look at Jason and the rest and explained, "First, I have to turn the valves off so no more gas comes through. Then I have to throw the circuit to shut the pumps off, so the lines will stop being purged into the base. Then, in a short while, we can go in," Bradley calmly told him.

The vast room echoed and carried the sound causing the zombies to clamor and claw at the double doors. The man watching Bradley looked back at Jason for approval.

"What do you think?" Jason asked Gizmo.

"I don't trust him. He's gonna do something," he answered.

"You're one of the only other races I know that can do that." Braz said.

"What?" Gizmo asked.

"You know what's going to happen ahead of time. You know what he is thinking," he said.

"I can't say I know what he is thinking, but I have a strong feeling that he is thinking something bad," Jason said.

"Right. That's how it starts. Next you can know what it is. It's development. Have you always been able to do that?" he asked.

"Most of us have premonitions or precognitions, some more than others. Eric here, he's got a good gig going. He has spirits that talk to him; his ancestors," Jason quietly told him.

"Fascinating," Braz said. "I'd like to speak to you about these things sometime, Eric."

"Later Braz. Right now, what is Bradley thinking?" he asked.

"I believe he is intending to throw a switch. That will cause us some difficulty. The man has been damaged, so his thinking is muddled. He has much talking in his head," Braz said. "But it doesn't really work like that anyway. I can tell actions. Like with the Rock Paper Scissors game, it's intentions. I can tell the decision ahead of time. I can see what they will end up doing. With un-muddled thoughts, we can perceive more. With very clear thinking, we can have actual conversations."

Jason thought about what the consequences could be if Bradley threw the wrong switch. He looked back at the double doors with the zombies behind them, then at the blast doors containing the Evil Walkers.

There were two things he could do. One, he could let the Walkers out. Two, he could let the zombies out. He needed to get inside where the zombies were anyway. He would need to clear them out. So there was a fifty percent chance of him being helpful.

On the other hand, if he released the Walkers, they would be overrun within seconds. It was too high a risk, so he walked over to the panel and opened it, then looked over the valves and started turning them, shutting off the supply of gas. Then he went back to the panel.

"Gizmo!" he called. "Take a look at this."

They looked over the panel and tried to decipher the codes. Jason had a finger on a breaker labeled "M.L.". "What do you think? Magnetic Lock, 'M.L.', you think that's what it stands for?"

"Bradley. Is this it?" Gizmo asked.

"Yes. That will power the double doors," he answered, thinking that as soon as they threw that switch, they would be charged by zombies. That's when he would make his move. He was getting a chill up his spine at the thought of escaping. He was smiling to himself as he thought how easy it was to outsmart that horrible man, Jason Brand.

Then he started thinking about his revenge. How he would make them suffer. How he would get back to Ruby Ridge and find that hairless gorilla, Callis, and make her pay. As Jason called out for everyone to be ready, he thought how, soon, the future of Earth would all be in his hands once again and he would show them no mercy.

Then, without control, he blurted out, "Yes. No mercy!"

This caused Jason to pause before throwing the switch. "Bo! Heel," he called, bringing her to his side. Then he threw it. They heard the inner workings of the latch on the huge doors clank, and the doors flew open. The long corridor was filled with them.

It was the sight of them that made them all hesitate. They were men in uniform, everything from private on up. They were their own kind, men they would fight with and fight for; men who would fight and die for them. Braz, Deri, and their crews held back from firing as they charged forward. They all knew that it was Jason's own people they were about to mow down, and it would be an unthinkable disrespect to be the first to fire.

They charged half way across the floor to them before Jason finally yelled, "FIRE!" and began shooting. All of them opened up and they began to fall and kept falling until the dead bodies were piled up and more zombies were crawling up over them. As they would come over the top, their heads would appear making it a better target, and making the pile grow even taller.

The noise from the weapons drove the Walkers wild behind the blast doors and their howls and screeching drowned out the howls from the zombies. That's when Bradley made his move. When they were all firing as fast as they could possibly pull their triggers, Bradley moved toward the stairway to the observation area and went up and into it.

It was set up exactly the same as it was in Ruby Ridge. It was his command center, his home, and he knew every inch. From there, he could control everything. He hit a button and the magnetic lock snapped on his door, locking him behind a near impenetrable wall of thick glass and metal. He then went to a computer terminal and, just in case, began purging the air inside the private accommodations set up for Catskill Pharmaceutical staff, where more controls and over-rides were installed.

He then walked toward the observation area in the back and punched a code into a monitor, opening the secret entrance he had left off all plans, and then disappeared into the facility, thinking about how the workers who installed that door had come to such a tragic end, and end he orchestrated, and had become a tasty meal for his creations.

He turned and punched another key code, the panel slid shut, and he was free at last.

Chapter Thirty Eight

It took no time at all for Cody and Stanford to get communications up once the shield was working. He was now setting up the General's link to Admiral Harding as well as the rest of the transports. The Newcomers had made a set of uniforms for the General and were outfitting and training people to fight in low and zero gravity.

As planets were cleared of the Invaders, transports had become available and ready to be taken back to Earth. On each planet, the Admiral had a contingent of his men sent to take possession of the transports and guard and keep secret the capacitors.

There were thousands of planets, and sending enough of his men to occupy and retain possession of the transports was beginning to take a toll on his own ability to occupy and defend the Invader planet. As each planet was cleared, only a handful of his men would return with the capacitors to be reprogrammed back on Earth and be sent again to the next target, while the rest stayed with the transport, waiting for someone to return with a recharged capacitor.

The General dispatched a transport with another five thousand men to Harding to help maintain and fortify the Invader planet security, and to start bringing back the capacitors. On Earth, a project was set up to go to the cleared planets and return the men along with the transports.

The General turned to the problem of feeding the few million human survivors after their stores ran out. The Admiral and he were discussing this now.

"We can gather whatever farming equipment is lying around and get them going, there's lots of land to do farming. We just don't have a whole lot of farmers. And the fact is, all I know about farming I learned by planting flowers in the yard for the Misses," he was saying.

"Well, General. You got one up on me. I've never even done that," the Admiral confessed.

"We have some civilian population left here. Some of them were botanists, I suppose. We can start assigning work duties. I guess it'll be safe enough for that once Eric's men have cleared out the Walkers. And there will be some survivors off the base and spread around the country here and there. They will mostly be farmers and preppers out there," the General was musing.

"And then there are all the planets we are going to. We could start setting up trade with some of them," Harding said.

"Trade what? We have nothing. We don't have manufacturing capability on earth any longer. Every city has been leveled. Not a lot we can trade."

"Well. We do have something," the Admiral said. "Security. We have the transports. We can impose a tax on them to keep their planets secure. Can't do that for free forever."

The General thought about that for a while and said, "No. I'm just not going to go there. The Governments here tried that with the terrorist racket. Imposing laws to keep them safe, taxing the hell out of them, scaring and controlling them. Pay and comply for your Security. Bull. Didn't work. It's just another form of slavery. I don't want the Human Race to be some new overlord or just another oppressor or tax collector. No, I don't think I want to go that route."

The Admiral paused and considered that. After a time he answered, "No. You're right. Even though it isn't a made up or manufactured threat, we would end up being as hated as any government that did that."

"Worse. We would be alien oppressors, too. Alien tax collectors. We'd be hated and despised throughout the entire universe. No. I wouldn't go that route. We have a chance to do it right, so I think we should. Here's the real problem, Admiral. You and I, we're warriors. That's how we think. That's why we need a civilian government," the General said.

"Right. So then, they can screw up, and we have to come in to fix it anyway," Harding joked.

"Exactly," the General laughed. "But they can set up some sort of deal until we become self supporting again."

"Remember the North American Indians, trading beads for gold and furs? Remember the islams, trading baubles and trinkets for people in Africa during the slave trade. These other people, the other races, they have some pretty advanced stuff. They could show us something that is pretty useless to them, and we could end up trading something valuable," Harding said.

"True. And if we leave it up to the politicians - Hell, they could screw up a wet dream." he said.

"So what's your plan?" Harding asked.

"Well. I guess I'll start assigning work details. Start with setting up food and water. Get irrigation and such happening. One year of no crops or crop failure, and we're done," the General said. "Maybe two, if we scavenge all stores and warehouses around the planet."

"We do have space travel now. And Jason is now pretty important in the Universe. He is the ruler, in fact. I think they expect him to rule. So he could rule they give us food in a pinch," Harding said.

"Who's to say that these other planets aren't in worse shape than us?" the General said. "No, we should row our own canoes. By the way, speaking of our future, you have what, seventy thousand women with you? How many are pregnant?"

"Thousands," he said. "How about there?"

"About half the civilian population are women and ten percent in the military. We have an explosion of pregnancies reported and more every day," the General said.

"Good. We may survive after all," Harding replied.

Chapter Thirty Nine

Deri saw the grim look on Jason's face as he was looking down at the uniformed pile of dead bodies. She turned to Gizmo and saw the same look. "I'm so sorry. That must have been very hard for you," she said.

Jason took a deep breath and straightened a name tag and looked at it for a moment. "They were dead two weeks ago. It's just official now."

Although he gave a hardened and harsh reply, she could see his eyes beginning to tear up. She looked at Braz who nodded and looked silently at the ground. Eric and Gizmo were off to the side deep in reflection.

"That's no way for good men to go," Jason finally said. He looked at Gizmo and Eric and then the rest of the team. There were none that weren't feeling the same way; guilt for what they had done; shame; sadness for the loss of their comrades.

He looked around at the faces of the soldiers they had and saw the horror on their faces. "These people died two weeks ago. What we did here was a kindness. I know it's hard. But they are already dead. And they were about to kill you.

"That's no way for good men to go," he repeated louder. "And we're gonna find the bastards responsible. That's why we're here. We're gonna find them, and dammit, we're gonna track 'em down and then, we're gonna give them some payback."

Just then, another zombie came screaming down the corridor toward the sound. Jason pulled up his weapon and dropped him. "So I don't want any of you to hesitate. There is no reason to feel bad about it. These things no longer have feelings. If you want to have feelings about it, have the right feelings. Have them for the bastards responsible. Meanwhile, you see one, you drop him. He's no longer even human."

They all began snapping out of their shock, their focus coming back, checking their weapons and reloading magazines. "If they did it to us, they've done it to others, and they'll do it again, too. So our mission is to find out who these critters are and put an end to them. We're going to succeed at that mission, dammit!"

He was speaking for his own benefit now as well as for the others. He was feeling his own determination building and could see the rest becoming more focused.

"Bradley, you sick son-of-a-bitch, get up here. Bradley! BRADLEY!" he called.

The crew looked around, but of course there was no Bradley. "Find him!" Jason yelled, sending everyone scurrying about the landing area. "Eric. Get in the shuttle and look outside in case he bolted out there, take a spotter with you."

Jason stood fuming while he watched the crew scurry around the landing area. It was open and nearly empty with only a few places that would conceal somebody. Jason looked down at Bo and called her over to the last place he had seen Bradley standing by the gas canisters. He bent down and pointed at the ground where Bradley stood and said, "Track, Bo. Track. Go get 'im."

She instantly went to that spot and took a good sniff. Then she smelled to the sides and went around in a circle. She first followed the trail back to where Bradley stepped out of the shuttle, then back to the starting point. Then she went from side to side and started heading toward the stairway to the observation deck, where she stopped and looked back at Jason and gave a bark to let him know she found the trail.

She waited for Jason to come, then went up the stairs ahead of him. Once at the top, she smelled around the landing, put her front paws on the door, looked back at Jason again, and gave her signal.

"Son of a..." Jason said walking toward the door to check, knowing Bradley had gone inside and locked them out, but fruitlessly giving it a yank anyway. Eric was pulling back in with the shuttle and stepped out to the deck.

Jason swung an Invader weapon off his back, gave a nod toward the door, stood back and fired at the locking mechanism and gave it a kick. The door flew open and several men rushed to the top of the stairs, ready to enter.

The observation area was enclosed in bullet-proof glass, so Jason had already seen that Bradley was not there. He walked in behind Bo and followed her to the back, where he had her stop. There, he had the area cleared before allowing her to move forward around the corner. They walked over to the rear observation area and looked over the edge into the room where testing on the Walkers had been done.

Bo was sniffing around in circles and pacing back and forth. She would walk up to the end of the room, turn and come back again, then sniffed her way to the end of the room again. At one point, she got up on her hind legs and sniffed a computer terminal, then got back down and sniffed to the wall again, turned to Jason, and gave her bark.

She had done her job, now it was his turn. Where did he go? That was the question. Jason raised the weapon and shot at the wall panel, exposing plate metal that would take far more force than he had to break through.

He looked over the edge and saw a door in the testing area. It was the same setup that Bradley had at Ruby Ridge, the same setup where he had tossed Emily to her death, fed to the Walkers because she had found the combination of chemicals to kill his creations without rendering the Earth uninhabitable.

"Rope," Jason called.

The men with him looked amongst each other and one of them said "Didn't bring any, Colonel."

"No rope? Why didn't we bring any rope?" he asked.

"What are you going to do? Restrain your beast?" Braz asked.

"No. I want to check that door," he said.

"Use your uniform. Remember. The gravity upgrades," Deri said.

"Oh, yah. Well. I haven't used it yet. Been kind of busy," he said.

Almost before he finished the sentence, two of his men took a jump toward the edge, one of them saying, "Gotcha covered, Colonel," and screamed, "Yeeehaa!" on the way down, the other yelling, "Man, I love these."

One of the men stood to the side of the door with his rifle ready and gave the other a nod. The door was quickly opened and even more quickly slammed shut when they saw the instant charge of Walkers toward it. "Whoa! Don't think he went out there, Colonel," one of them called up.

The man who opened the door kicked off and flew back up to the observation area, the other seeing him, kicked off even harder to try and beat him to the top.

"What next, Colonel?" one of them asked.

Jason looked around the area again, checking for any other possible escape route or hiding place that Bradley may have had access. He knocked his weapon against the walls and listened to any difference in the sound. Knowing there was a way out, but finding none, he answered, "Next? We do the mission."

Bradley had already made it to the suite of the man who would have been in charge of Catskill Pharmaceuticals. In fact, by the time Jason and his group were finished defending themselves from the initial rush of Zombies, he had showered and changed, putting on a shirt and clip-on tie and a clean smock, and was now sitting in front of the monitors watching every move they made, filing pens neatly into his shirt pocket.

He realized that his focus was a little off. His plans were nearing completion and he needed to think clearly now, especially now. He walked over and reached into a cabinet and pulled out bottle after bottle of drugs and placed them in front of himself on the desk. Looking them over, he picked one up and muttered, "This will give me an edge," then swallowed a handful.

"Fools!" he called out to the monitor as he watched them move from the observation area and prepare to enter the corridor.

From his new living quarters, he had control of the entire facility. He could watch every move through every room and corridor, open or lock every door. He could stop or release and direct the zombies to them, and, when he was ready, he could release the Walkers.

He would orchestrate their capture; get them good and trapped, and when they called for help, they would send the transport over. That's when he would release the Walkers, load them on the transport, and unleash them on the remaining Human forces holding out at Ruby Ridge. All threats to his plan would then have been eliminated and he would, at last, rule the world.

"That fat-assed Callis. She will pay," he said to himself. "That rapist gorilla."

Jason had ten of his men stay behind, five inside the observation room and five just outside, with directions to capture Bradley if they could. That left him thirty men.

He then stopped at the shuttle and placed two men right at the inside and eight more in positions on the outside, four on each side, including Eric, leaving instructions to lift off if they were going to be overrun. That left him twenty.

"Eric. Would like to bring you along, but you gotta stay here with the shuttle and direct us. Lift off if the men are in danger," he said.

Bradley watched them take up positions to enter the double doors and begin piling in, switched cameras and followed their progress toward another set of double doors and watched them take up positions there.

"What are we looking for now that Bradley is gone?" one of them asked.

"Not sure. But we have to find it. You were all chosen for a reason. Some of you know manufacturing. So if you see something that looks odd, call out. Some of you are computer techs. So if you've never seen something, call out. You medical and electronics people, same thing. Basically all of us do that. If we see something out of place, call out," he said.

"And Deri and Braz, if you see something that you DO recognize, you should tell us. Anything familiar, no matter how small," Gizmo added.

"Jason," Deri said. "The next hallway, use your suit. You should get some practice with it," and gave him instructions on basic movements.

Jason counted down from three and the doors were opened. He pressed a patch and floated toward the end of the hall, Gizmo and the rest following.

Bradley watched in horror as Jason held his hand up and counted down with his fingers and then floated down the corridor. "Magic?" He said under his breath. "What is this? He can fly?"

"Oh my God. I knew it!" He yelled out loud, jumping back from the screen to the back wall. "He's some kind of witch!"

"No wonder they listen to him, he has them under a spell!" he thought as he tried to squeeze into the crack behind a bookcase in terror. He froze there, eyes glued, watching the screen, his heart racing and every shortened and panicked breath making a low screaming sound.

Jason ordered two men to stay at each end of the corridor using hand signals. They instantly complied, running up to the spot he pointed at and got on one knee and froze, one looking in each direction. Now he had sixteen men.

Bradley slowly caught his breath and gathered the courage to approach the screen once more. His heart was still pounding over the new revelation. "I need to be cool and calm, especially now. Now that I know he's a witch," and started shuffling through the bottles of drugs in front of him. "This should do it," he muttered to himself as he swallowed another handful of pills.

He sat and looked in amazement at Jason's men. "Oh, my god. They're frozen. They're petrified. He turned them into statues. What kind of a monster is this Jason Brand?"

Then he switched cameras to the men in the observation area, then to the shuttle. They were all frozen in spot. "None of them can move. What powers this man has," he thought. "I was right about him," and switched the camera back on Jason.

He watched as he was setting up to go through another set of doors. He called Bo over beside him and said something to her. "It must be some kind of demon dog," he said out loud.

"It is a demon dog," a voice came from behind him.

Bradley was so full of drugs and was so used to hearing voices now, he paid no attention. He continued to watch as they came to a door and lined up to clear the room, then watched in astonishment as they entered, half of them floating through the air, and the demon dog frozen like a statue until Jason came out and said something to her, releasing her from her spell.

"I'll have to be very careful with that one," he said.

The voice came from behind him again. "Yes. You should. It has already injured two of us."

193

This time Bradley spun around and saw three familiar faces. "You! How did you get in here?" he asked.

"We helped you in the design. Don't you remember, Dr. Bradley?" one of them answered.

They came around toward the front of the desk, one limping, and one with a bandaged arm. "We had an encounter with that demon beast back at the base on one of the transports. It is very capable and very dangerous. Together with that Brand fellow and Crozley, they are too much of a risk."

"So what are you doing here? What do you want?" Bradley asked.

"We want to kill them. We came here to do that. You're going to help. We want you to set a trap, and we'll kill them and be done with them once and for all. After that, there are some items we have to deliver from one of your testing facilities."

Chapter Forty

They laid the trap. Jason would be lead through the corridors to a Research and Development room. Once he entered, Bradley would cut off his retreat by flooding the corridor behind them with zombies. He could only move forward and the three visitors would have him where they wanted. They would be there, waiting.

"Then," Bradley thought, "I will deal with these three aliens as well. Another snack for my creatures."

Jason stopped and placed four more in position, making sure they all had a view of each other all the way to the shuttle. Now he had twelve.

They moved forward to a side door and breached it for clearing. There was a group of zombies inside that charged at them and were put down.

"These look like technicians," Gizmo said. "Let's look around."

There were computers and files, and microscopes and test tubes. They went through every drawer and every cabinet. Jason looked into the microscopes to see what they were working on and called over one of his men. "You know what this is?"

The man peered into the eye piece and said, "Looks like some cell I've never seen. Maybe we should grab all the slides and tubes and get it back to the base."

"Right. You four. Box it up and head for the shuttle, and grab the hard drives, everything, take it," Jason ordered.

Now he was down to eight men, including himself and Gizmo.

He came out and asked Deri to post her remaining two people to cover the flank and they pressed on leaving six, saying, "Just yell 'Contact' and everyone will come running," he explained to them. "You all hear that? You guys stay with the shuttle and the guys up top, hold your position there in the observation room," he said into his radio. "The rest, you come for support. We can clear our way back to the shuttle if we get stampeded."

Jason was on one knee beside Gizmo and Bo, looking down the darkening corridor. "What do you think? Getting a little thinned out, huh?"

"Yup. Getting a little thinned out," Gizmo quietly agreed. "Let's say we run into what we ran into back there, that many zombies. We start shooting. They'll be funneled in the corridor and dam up. I think we'll be okay."

"Is this that premonition you were mentioning?" Braz asked.

"Yah. How about you? You getting the tingles?" Jason asked.

"I guess you could call it that. Something is ahead. Something planned. I don't think those men we shot were capable of planning. They were too damaged," Braz answered.

"Good point. So, it's something else. Maybe it's some of those live scientists in a lab," Gizmo said.

Deri checked her floor plan on the mobile device and said, "There is a research facility through those doors. There could be a clean room. Maybe they're in there."

Bradley bounced up and down in excitement watching them move toward their certain death on his monitor. His hands were sweating and trembling. Every muscle in his body tensed. "Oh boy," he said to himself. "This is it. I've got to settle down," and looked through the bottles in front of him, opening one and swallowing a handful.

They approached the double doors and stopped. Jason checked on everyone's position behind him and reached for the handle. Opening the door a crack, a small draft came through, sending Bo into alert.

She quickly stepped forward, almost getting her head inside, and let out a low growl, her hair stood on end around her neck and down her back, and she stopped, standing and growling at the familiar scent from the transport. The enemy was inside, the ones who attacked her, and now she knew.

Jason and Gizmo looked at each other and nodded. Bo was telling them something was there. And Bo was always right. It wasn't a matter of maybe something is there or there might be something there. Something was there. She did her job, and now it was up to them to do theirs.

Bradley watched Jason look down at her and give her a pat on the head before they all vanished through the opening. He watched as the door started to close behind them and seemed to pause and have a hitch in its swing as Braz and his men followed. "I'll have to get maintenance to look at that. Oh right. There is no maintenance," he thought.

"Let's see your witchcraft and magic work on aliens," he mumbled as he switched cameras and started squealing with laughter.

Jason and Gizmo took up positions right inside the door. Deri was behind Jason, and Braz and his men were with Gizmo. Bo continued making a fuss, wanting to charge forward, with a constant low growl.

"Easy, girl," Jason said to her, reaching out and stroking her neck.

Bradley could see the three visitors already set up for the ambush. They were in perfect position, well hidden and up high, able to fire down from three different angles, and they had a diversion: Zombies. Any moment, he thought, he would be rid of this menace, this horrible man, Jason Brand.

Jason looked around and got a good idea of the layout of the long room and where any likely dangers might be. He decided on a little more planning before moving forward and wanted to issue instructions. He reached back for the door to pull everyone back out and found it had been locked behind them.

He looked back toward the far end of the room and saw another set of double doors. He crept around a counter and saw there were three zombies mulling about near the end. The last thing Jason wanted was to make noise and draw a stampede through those doors.

"Braz," he called in a near whisper. "I want to know if they can see you."

Braz stepped forward and walked toward them waving his arms and came back.

"Okay Braz. I want you and your guys to go high and start crossing the room. We'll have to use knives. No gunshots until we know what's on the other side of those doors. Remember, the brain. You have to get the brain," Jason said.

"Right. When you're ready," Braz said.

"We're going to wait for you to get part way. Then we'll draw their attention; make 'em come at us. You'll be behind them then and can take 'em out from behind," Jason said.

"Everyone set?" he asked. Deri and Gizmo pulled their knives and gave him a nod and he said, "Go."

The three aliens were already taking aim down the center aisle, waiting for them to start moving forward. Two of them were shaking from fear, not just because of their past encounter with Bo, but now they were about to kill the most important man they had ever seen, perhaps the most important person who had ever lived, a man who now owned a large part of the known universe and all its inhabitants.

Braz and his men lifted up and floated toward the double doors. When Jason saw they were about half way, he stepped out with Deri and Gizmo and whistled.

It all happened at once. The three assassins gave Bradley the sign to cut off their retreat, releasing a herd of zombies into the corridor behind them. The three zombies inside turned at the whistle and saw Jason and instantly charged. As they charged, Jason heard "Contact!" being yelled into the radio and gunfire erupting in the corridor behind them. That's when Bo bolted forward.

They all had their knives out, ready to plant them in the Zombies' skulls in case Braz was not able to get them in time, and they would quietly dispense with the menaces. Bo charged toward the zombies and jumped, sailing right through them, and kept going toward the back of the room.

She jumped onto a table and leapt toward a file cabinet. Braz turned and saw what she was going after and spotted the assassins. He quickly ordered his men to disarm them instead of taking out the zombies. As Bo sailed past, the zombies turned to follow her. That's when Jason and Gizmo sprang forward and planted their blades into two of their heads.

Bradley watched in horror as Bo took down one of the assassins, tearing at his arm with her powerful jaws, and watched in terror as the other two seemed to be picked up by some invisible force, disarmed, and thrown to the ground. Just as the last zombie was about to pounce on one of them, unseen by Bradley, Braz drove his blade into it.

He fell back into his chair with his hands on his mouth and said, "Fools! This witch is more powerful than they thought," and turned off the screen, unable to watch any more, fumbling for the bottles in front of him.

Jason walked up to the three aliens lying on the ground, listening to the gunfire echoing down the corridor getting more and more muffled. He looked down at them and said, "Giz. We were looking for clues, and I think we hit the jackpot."

"No kidding. Look at them, will ya," he said.

Bo came limping toward them, her leg grazed when she wrestled the weapon out of the leader's hands. Jason checked her over, putting his hand on her leg, and she let out a squeal.

Jason helped her jump up on a desk and looked her over. "Poor doggie," he said, wrapping his arm around her neck and giving her a squeeze and a rub under her chin. He looked around the lab, found sterilized knives and scalpels, shaved around the wound, cleaned it and pulled a bandage out for it.

When he was done caring for Bo, he had all three of the assassins stripped and placed on their knees. Zip ties were found in a cabinet for their hands, and bags for dirty rags were brought over to put over their heads.

"Which one of you shot my dog?" Jason demanded. He waited for a reply and demanded again, only louder, "Who shot her?"

Shaking in fear, one nodded at the leader. Jason placed the bags over the heads of the other two and pulled the draw strings tight. Then, he called Bo over to his side and stood her face-to-face with the leader. He gave her a command; a word he had made up so that no one else would know the meaning of it and nobody could likely guess it. It was for their protection as well. It was his and her secret, sure that no other person would be able to use it, because this was an order to guard this thing, and if it moved, to kill it.

To the alien, she appeared to instantly double in size as her fur stood up and she bared her teeth, moved forward, and roared ferociously into his face, looking straight into his eyes. Every time the alien so much as twitched, she would increase the volume and intensity. Jason pulled the bag over its head, pulled the drawstring tight, and left them in that position while he contacted the rest of the team.

Bradley was pacing feverishly back and forth behind the desk. "FOOLS!" he ranted. "Complete and utter fools! These aliens were no good!" He cried, flapping and flailing his arms in the air. "They can't fight a witch with normal, regular aliens. Why didn't they send me some magical aliens? Fools!"

He gathered the courage to turn the screen back on and watched the demon dog snarling at its prisoner. Then he switched to the corridor and saw that Jason was completely cut off from the rest of his team. The pile of dead bodies had reached top to bottom creating a dam in the corridor, and behind that, there were hundreds more thrashing about.

If Jason attempted to get through, he could send in so many from the civilian population that he would be overrun. Magic or no, with only the three of them that he could see, they would not be able to kill them fast enough.

"Perfect," he said. "I didn't need those three aliens after all. All they did was waste my time. Useless."

Bradley switched back to Jason and Gizmo and watched them for a moment, then switched to the room on the other side of the double doors. Then he switched to the area outside that. There was the majority of the civilian population mulling about, held out only by another double door.

He started switching the magnetic lock on and off, drawing their attention to the clanking sound of the inner workings, drawing them toward the noise. Soon, there was a charge toward the door. He left it unlocked and watched them fill the room. Then he switched to the corridor and did the same to fill that even more.

Jason was now trapped. It was only a matter of time before he would call for a transport for help, and Bradley had much preparation to do.

Chapter Forty One

Bradley could barely contain his excitement. He started imagining the mighty Jason Brand being ripped to shreds and devoured, and contemplated which side he would try to get through. Not wanting to miss his painful end, he flipped from camera to camera.

Finally, when the transport arrived, all Bradley had to do was unlock the doors on either side, and he would be dead. "Good," he said to himself. "I hope their death is painful. Him and that Gumbo. What a stupid name."

The piped announcement interrupted his thoughts and announced, "As a reminder, under the new Bill of Rights, you have the right to the pursuit of happiness. All pursuits must be preapproved and properly scheduled before hand. Lethal force will be used for violations."

"HAPPINESS!" Bradley scoffed. "There will be no such thing. Especially for that horrible man, that Jason Brand," and he shut off the recording through all the bases entirely.

Bradley walked deeper into the executive quarters and opened a sliding door exposing what Catskill Pharmaceuticals had as their private research and control quarters. He walked to a cabinet and opened it, pulled out two pods and stuffed them under his arms.

He brought them to a table, checked the batteries in each, and replaced them with fresh ones. "This will call my creations to the transport. Then, all I have to do is take them to the Ruby Ridge base, and it's all over. The people in the transport will be instantly overrun, and shortly after that, the people in the base and my plan will be one final and glorious step to being complete."

Bradley started looking deep into the circuitry and lost himself in the wiring. His mind traced the wires from the power source along the side into the circuit board, stopping and staring at the light shining on a loop of wire. Then he followed the circuit board, tracing the lines to the strange alien objects they powered.

It looked so much like a city to him; a small, small city. The metal circuits were like roads and highways. The microchips reminded him of large buildings and warehouses set amongst them.

He followed beyond that, lost in the details and intricacies, touching the various parts as he went along, until he got to the emitter. He thought about how it imitated the brain waves of his creations, called them toward the pod or sent them running from it. He thought about how it was so easy for them to duplicate brain waves, these aliens, and how he could have done it for people too.

That snapped him out of it. His paranoia took over, and he thought, "What if they did that? How would I ever know? It imitates the brain wave, so you would think it is your own impulse."

He closed them back up, stuffed them back under his arm and walked into the executive suite setting them on the desk. He checked one more time to make sure Jason and his people were still trapped, and then turned the monitor to the landing bay.

"The transport won't fit in there, but it will land just outside," he thought. "But how do I get out there past those people?"

He searched the different video feeds for a way to get out past the guards when it came to him. "They're frozen stiff. Petrified! They are harmless statues! Under the spell of that witch. I can just walk right past them," and he turned the cameras on them again. Sure enough, there they were, frozen in position. "That Jason Brand actually helped me!" he thought, and started squealing with laughter.

Chapter Forty Two

Jason and Gizmo were going through the pouches and possessions of the three assassins, laying them out on a counter in the dimly lit research lab. They would pause and hold an object up to inspect it, and Braz or Deri would call out, "Tracker device" or "Jamming device" and they would label it with a post-it sticker.

They were killing time by going through the entire research lab inch by inch for any other technology they might find and were now waiting for the General to send backup, front-end loaders to clear away the dead bodies, a transporter, and more men to gather up the assassins and their space craft as well as take any other items they found.

"I think I'm gonna go and get my R.V. and load it up on the transport," Jason mused as they went through the items.

Gizmo chuckled, "So, a transporter isn't a big enough camper for you? It's only sixteen miles. I guess you might run out of room and squeeze into that, what, twenty-four footer?"

"It's not the same," he answered while they continued looking at items.

Eric and the rest of the crew were listening on the radio to the banter as well. "Do you have any idea what kind of R.V.s would be just laying around that you could pick up?" he said.

"Yah," another chimed in. "You could grab one of those busses, you know, marble floor, Jacuzzi, the whole nine yards. I saw some, they're just sitting around."

"Maybe," Jason answered, continuing going through the alien items. He was looking over a strange looking item, turning it over and over in his hands. "But I have things in mine, and it's set up right."

He held the item up for Braz and Deri to see and neither had a comment. "Let's see," Braz eventually said, holding out his hand.

He and Deri looked at it closely and Braz began rolling it over and over as well. "No idea," he said to Deri. "You?"

"None," she said, holding her hand out. She took it and felt the weight of it and said, "Not completely solid," and after another minute said, "No idea."

"Let me see," Gizmo said.

He grabbed it and started looking. Jason caught Braz and Deri's attention and nodded toward him and said with some sense of pride in his friend, "Watch."

He rolled it over a few times like the others had, and then he walked over to a microscope and pulled the bottom off. He set up some light to bounce off the top and up through the lens and peered into it, rolling it over and over.

"Amazing," he said, and continued looking. "Just amazing."

Jason came over and looked through it. "Kind of like what we saw in the pod, similar kind of circuitry, but so much smaller. It's similar to some of the systems on the shuttles and transports too, but way more complex. What do you think?"

"A multiplier. It's a power multiplier. That's one thing it'll do. But there is something else. I'm not sure," and looked up at Jason. "What do I think, my friend? This could be a small sample of the next generation," Gizmo said.

Jason found a piece of grid paper and drew a circle on it. "I'm going to make a map. Look at this," and he started to draw a crude diagram of the item on the grid. Then he put numbers going up along the side and letters going along the bottom. "Okay, now look at the area of twelve "G" and tell me what you think that is."

Gizmo came over and looked at it for a while until he was interrupted by Braz, who stared down into the microscope, followed by Deri. "Not a clue," they both said.

Gizmo nudged his way back to the microscope and continued silently looking. Jason watched him make a couple of notes on his drawing and pick the item back up, taking the drawing, and wrapping it up in it. He gave the slightest glance at Jason, and then shoved it all into his pocket. "Well. I want to look at it later. Let's get moving."

They've been working together for too long for Jason not to know what he was thinking from that glance. He didn't want to discuss it in front of anyone, and even though Deri and Braz were entirely trustworthy, it is something that just isn't done, even with your own people. Secrets are kept secret, and the more people who knew the secret, even trusted people, the less likely it will remain secret.

Jason lifted into the air and started floating around, practicing using the new addition to his uniform. He circled the counter where they were all laying out the items, and tried to keep his focus on one spot while his feet swung in a circle.

"I wonder what else they have on their ship," he said, now walking on the ceiling.

He kicked off one of the walls toward the end of the room and practiced stopping mid-flight, then kicking off again to another wall. He came to the center of the room and stopped, looking down at Bo still snarling at the prisoners and stopped to give her a break, floating down and standing next to her.

He put his hand on her head and released her from her duty and pulled the hood off one of the trembling assassins and stood him up. "How did you get to this room?" he asked.

"The same as you did," he said.

He put him back on his knees and called Bo over. The assassin thought of the tales that had grown of the mighty Bo that had been spreading throughout the universe, able to take out entire mobs of Invaders by herself, defending Jason from charging monsters, and his own encounter with her back on the Invader planet proved them all to be true.

Bo didn't kill them and didn't eat them when she easily could have, and it was decided that it was only to let them go and tell of their unfortunate encounter as a warning to any others who would be so foolish as to try to harm either of them. To prove it even further, there he was himself, never having felt more foolish than now.

He also knew about the Human's design and making of the Walkers, an animal that would kill and devour anything that moved, stronger, faster, more vicious and ruthless than any Invader. It was a natural conclusion that Bo was even worse, for she was Jason's protector, and he was the single most powerful being to have ever existed.

There he was now, face to face once again with the mighty Bo, trembling, certain he was about to die, when Jason commanded Bo. She again snarled ferociously into his face, and he instantly passed out.

Jason skipped the leader and walked over to the other assassin on the end and pulled off its hood. It looked, trembling, barely able to breathe at the sight of his comrade lying on the floor, certain he had been killed.

"Through the back!" he called out as quickly as he could, not even waiting for the question.

"The back, where?" Jason demanded.

"Through those doors. There's a way to get in. From the Pharmaceutical offices," He said frantically and began explaining the facility.

Jason looked at his mobile device and pulled the hood back over its head. He walked over to the counter out of earshot and said to the others, "I'm not seeing it, are you?"

They all looked through their mobile devices and came up with nothing. Eric had been listening and told them he hadn't seen anything the assassin described in the blueprints at the library either.

Bradley was having another mood swing, feeling a little disappointment as he fondled the remote controls for the pods. He looked at the palm of his hand, at the Made in China brand, and considered how he had been deprived of displaying it properly. He had either been in chains or in handcuffs almost entirely since it had happened.

He felt the texture of the new controls and ran his fingers over the buttons. The smooth, almost velvet feel of the buttons gave him comfort. Then, he looked at them closer and tried to match up the Made-In-China stamp with the scar that was branded into his hand.

Bradley turned to the viewing monitors and flipped a switch. It showed a base, much like all the rest would be, blast doors opened, zombies mulling around, and his creations running freely. He switched to different continents and saw the same.

"My plan is succeeding," he said to himself. Then he switched it to Ruby Ridge, the last threat to his complete success; the final significant population of mankind; the last force to be reckoned with. "Yes. I will rid the Earth of these hairless monkeys and I will rule the world."

He searched through the halls and corridors and rooms until he found Dr. Callis. "Gorilla Rapist," he said to the screen. "I have such exquisite plans for you."

He turned to the landing bay and watched as men began loading into a transport on the outside. It was time for him to place the pods that would call his creations into that transport. Then, he would go back up to his control room, and when the time was right, press the big red button he had lovingly caressed so many times before, opening the blast doors, and he would release his Walkers.

As he walked, his wild mood swings continued, and now he was barely able to contain his excitement, he made his way back toward the frozen soldiers in the observation deck, a pod under each arm, one to call the Walkers, and one he would keep under his arm to keep them from attacking him. He had butterflies in his stomach, his entire spine was tingling, and his toes were almost curling. He stopped to punch in the key to the secret passage, trembling with elation; he fumbled the code three times before he was finally able to get the panel to open.

The door slid to and he stepped through it, turning to close the entrance he thought, "Who am I keeping it a secret from? They will all be dead soon," and continued walking out and past the soldiers toward the landing area, deep in debate with himself over if he had gone mad or not. After all, it was his last chance to check before his total success. A reality check was in order.

Concluding once again that his plan was sound and rational, he continued as the men watched in amazement while he strolled casually by without as much as glancing at them, a strange looking object under each arm.

"Colonel Brand. We have Bradley," one of them called as he pointed to three other men to follow.

Eric looked up and saw what he was carrying. "Pods," he said. "Two of them."

They watched him stroll without a care toward the entrance when Eric ordered them to bring him to the shuttle. Two of them grabbed an arm each and the third took the pods. They turned him about and steered him toward the shuttle.

"Wait," Bradley yelled. "You can't do that. You're statues!"

Bradley protested all the way back about how unfair they were being until he was standing in front of Eric. "Where'd you get the pods?" Eric asked.

"You can't do this. It's not fair! You're frozen. Statues can't do this. It's…it's cheating!" He objected.

Eric shook his head and said, "Cuff him."

"Wait! Wait! I have something to show you! It's important! You have to see it!" Bradley frantically screamed, wrestling to loosen the grip on his arms.

Eric stood back and pointed his weapon at him. "Okay, let's see it," he said.

Bradley shot his arm up into the air to show him his Made-In-China brand. Then he turned to the others standing around watching and did the same, desperately hoping this would somehow make a difference.

Eric shook his head and said, "Cuff him and keep him inside," pointing to the shuttle. "And hog tie him or something this time."

Chapter Forty Three

"Well," Jason said. "We're going to continue the mission."

He assessed his resources. They could carry one of the assassins, maybe two, but not all three and Bo as well. They would have to carry them to float over and past the zombies in the large room beyond the double doors. He walked over and patted Bo on the head, reached into her back-pack and gave her some food. He let her lap up some water from a pan and threw the rest onto the unconscious assassin, shocking him back to life.

"What did you do to me?" he cried as he realized he had been unconscious. Anything at all could have been done. They could have put something in him. They could have used hypnotic commands. They could now have him completely under their control. The worst thing was he would not know it. He ran through his mind all the things they could have done to him in the short time he was out, all things he would do, all the things he had done to others, and knew he was now ruined.

"You did something to me, didn't you? I should never work around drug companies, you're all monsters!"

Jason stared down at the alien, considering his comments and set him on his knees again. Then he called Bo over and gave her a command. She came up, silently and slowly, crouching slightly, and stared at the assassin without a blink. "Look into her eyes," Jason told the assassin. "Look deeeep into her eyes."

"Oh, no. Nooooo!" it wailed and shut its eyes as tight as it could.

Jason waited a few seconds and pulled the bag back over its head as it began sobbing.

Jason walked over to the other two who had been hooded and blind to everything that had happened, only hearing the screams of terror and now the pained whimpering from their comrade, imagining the horrors he was suffering. Jason gave them a slight knock on their heads with the butt of his weapon and said, "And if you two so much as move or make a sound, the same will happen to you, except worse."

The assassins would be a wealth of information. As far as Jason and Gizmo's mission, to find clues to who would be behind the plan to enslave Earth, they were the most valuable find so far.

Gizmo watched Jason as he tried to work out a problem in his mind. Who would continue the mission and who would stay? That would be the question now. The logical choice was to leave Bo with the assassins and leave two people with them. They would have to remain there until the corridor was cleared and they could be extracted. What Jason was mulling over as he walked back out of the assassin's earshot, was who to leave behind

"I'll stay," Gizmo said, not wanting Bo to be with strangers.

"No Giz. I'll need you," Jason said. "I appreciate it though, buddy."

It would have to be either Deri, staying with one of Braz's people, or it would be two of Braz's people that stayed with Bo.

"Rock Paper Scissors time," Jason said.

Deri sprang forward with a big smile, holding her fist in front of her, excited to try the game again. Braz took a step forward as well, knowing that Jason knew he could tell the move before it happened, and quizzically said, "Really?"

"Not you, Braz. I'll play your spot. You cheat," Jason said jokingly. "Okay, Deri. Best out of five."

They went through four sets and Deri won three of them. "You won," Jason congratulated her as she laughed and bounced up and down.

After she calmed down, she asked, "Okay. So what did I win?"

The game was to decide who would stay. But Jason couldn't do it. He thought of Bo already being injured and being there without him. Then he thought of Deri staying and them possibly being overrun. He would lose both at once. And although she was a good fighter, she was still a woman, and as repulsive as a sickened society may have made it seem, he still thought it was the job of men to protect them.

But it was something more than that. Much more. It hit him, what it was that made him change the rules of the game. It was love. He wouldn't lose her and he would let no harm come to her. He would protect her and keep her out of harm's way, with his life, if necessary, almost the same as Bo protected him.

No, he was in love, so he lied. He cheated at the game, mid-play, and said, "You come with Gizmo and me."

Then he turned to Braz and said, "Braz, you come with us. Your guys will stay with Bo and guard the prisoners."

Braz knew exactly what happened. Rarely had anything been so strongly and clearly perceived by him. After he had issued orders to his men, he walked back to Jason and joked, "And you say I cheat. Jason Brand. You are a good man."

And now they were four.

Chapter Forty Four

Jason went to the far wall and used Deri's weapon to punch a small hole through the thick concrete up near the ceiling. No sooner had he done it, than zombies were instantly clamoring on top of each other to get to it.

"Well. Not going that way," he said.

Then he lifted a tile off the suspended ceiling and looked up into it. "Here," he said. "I think we can do this."

The drop ceiling was suspended by wire, which was attached to anchors driven into the rock above it. It left about three feet in most places and they could lie flat and hover through it to get close to where they needed to be. This would be the back entrance to the private Catskill Pharmaceutical suites where the assassins came through.

He came back down and grabbed some duct tape and put it over the hole. "Spare the duct tape; spoil the job, as Red Green always says."

"Who is Red Green?" Deri asked.

"Red Green? A genious. He's one of the most brilliant men that ever lived. Can build anything, fix anything. You ever see him, Gizmo?" Jason asked.

"On Youtube. Who hasn't? Brilliant. Him and Trailer Park Boys. Anyone who's got any sense has seen 'em," Gizmo said.

"Red would be able to figure out this alien stuff, no problem. And Ricky and the boys, they would mess them up real good," Jason added.

"Geniuses. All of them," Gizmo said and started laughing. "Strategists beyond the comprehension of the mere mortal mind."

"Maybe they are alive. Have you tried to find them? You should try to find them if they are this brilliant," Deri said.

"We should. Definitely. When we get back, we'll show you recordings of some of their work. I think you'll be impressed," Gizmo told her.

They were up above the ceiling, floating toward the back entrance. Deri explained how it's done in tight quarters. The person in front moves forward, the rest grab a foot of the person in front of them, and they all float along like a train.

Jason and Gizmo were recalling various episodes of Trailer Park Boys as they progressed and, when they got to where they had to punch through, were laughing at the episode where they hid their hash by paving the driveway with it.

The entire crew was still listening through their suits. One of them said, "Oh, man. I really thought they were going to do it that time," and another one added, "Then Ricky sets the house on fire," and they all started laughing again.

Eric cut it all off. "Cut the chatter," he ordered. "Jason, the transport is here. It'll take an hour or two to get through to Bo and the others, and we're sending a team through the back way. Found where Bradley went. There is whole other part of the facility where you are going."

Jason responded, "Roger that, Eric. Tell them not to accidently shoot Braz's men."

"Roger that. Dent is heading up the team. I guess the General sprung him now that the base has a shield up," Eric told him.

Jason didn't like hearing that. Cody was too important. He considered it for a moment and asked, "He's still got security, right?"

"He's still got security. We're getting a little thinned out on personnel with all the transport retrieval going on. Don't forget, Jason, you and Gizmo are pretty dammed important too. And Dent is a talented man. Once the General heard that assassins were sent for you, well, that was the deciding factor," Eric told him.

Jason didn't answer. He kicked at some duct work and looked down through the air register and saw an empty corridor. "Okay guys," he said as he removed the register and went down through it.

They made their way to the end of the corridor where it came to a "T" and looked at both directions. "What do you think?" Gizmo asked. "That way goes at an upward angle. That would be my choice."

Jason agreed and they followed it. After a while they stopped and turned around and said, "This is way too long. No way we're still in the base," looking back in the direction they came.

"Yah, but where are we? You think there's another entrance? We've come this far, I say we keep going. See what's up there," Gizmo said.

"Right," Jason answered. "They built this for a reason. Dent will clear the other section. Then, we can look through it. Why do you think he sent Dent and not someone else?"

The corridor took a long bend, and as they came around, they could see electric vehicles, one turned over, one upright, with bodies on the other side. Gizmo examined them and said, "Look, Jason. This is Secret Service. Looks like this guy got attacked. These other two, shot multiple times. Probably killed him before he realized it takes a head shot. Couldn't have lived with that damage. That means someone else shot these ones, and that means there might be people alive here."

A desk was sitting about fifty feet up the corridor and Jason went to it. "Look," he said pointing up. "The Vent. Clean air. They got gassed back there. Turned. Went crazy. Maybe the others got away."

They continued up the incline of the corridor and saw a set of doors with more dead. One side was propped open by a leg, and they took up positions on either side. Jason carefully moved the door with the barrel of his gun and peered in.

"More Secret Service," he said in a whisper, and entered the corridor. "Look. It's the dang President."

They rolled a body off him and looked him over. "Looks like they were trying to protect him still, but he was a zombie. I guess someone finally put him down."

"So, what the hell, Jason. The Government, they gotta be in on this. Some of them, anyway," Gizmo said.

Jason didn't answer at first; he just stood and looked down at him. "Well, not him," then he pressed his uniform and said, "General."

"Colonel. Something to report?" The General answered after a short pause.

"Found the President, General. He's dead. Looks like there might be some survivors up ahead. There was a stand here with Secret Service," Jason told him.

"Roger that, Colonel. Keep me informed," he answered and clicked off.

"He must be busy," Gizmo said in response to the short conversation.

"I bet he is," Jason replied. "Let's move." Further ahead there was a barricade and another door with more dead bodies in front. "They set up a barricade. Must be people up ahead."

They looked over the bodies and Gizmo said, "Head shots, all of them. They learned. Gotta be Secret Service that did that. That's some good shooting."

"This place didn't get gassed. Otherwise they couldn't have used the guns," Jason said as they prepared to go through the door. "Ready? On three, two, one," and shoved the door open.

As their eyes adjusted to the dark hallway, the first thing they could see was more dead bodies. The second was the charge of zombies coming toward them. The dim light beyond the charge framed their heads, silhouetted against the background as they came rushing.

The four of them rocked back on one leg to steady their aim and fired until nothing was moving, then waited to see if more would come when a figure appeared from around a corner at the far end of the hall, and quickly disappeared again. They waited a little longer and the figure did the same, came around the corner and ducked back.

Then it stuck its head out and a flashlight pointed toward them. "Hmm. Zombies don't use flashlights," Gizmo said.

"YOU!" Jason yelled. "Show yourself."

"I'm normal! I'm normal! Don't shoot. I'm normal," a voice came down the dark corridor.

They rushed forward to the corner to see one of the kitchen crew standing with a cleaver in one hand and a flashlight in the other. "We heard the shooting. Thank god you're here. We're all back here in the kitchen."

He swung the door open and four people replaced a barricade behind them when they entered. "The rest are all in here," the man said, opening the walk-in freezer. Inside there were a dozen more kitchen staff who all rushed forward at the sight of a familiar uniform.

"It was crazy," the man said as he began to describe how people went mad and started entering the building. "We didn't know who was…who was right and who wasn't. We just blocked the door and listened to people screaming and people shooting."

He looked around at Jason, Gizmo, and Deri and, not seeing Braz asked, "So where are the rest? When can we leave?"

"We're it for a little while longer," Jason told him. "You've been here for a while. Looks safe. You're gonna have to stay here until more of us show up. Won't be much longer now. Someone will come back for you."

The kitchen staff was questioned about the facility; who hired them, how long they'd been there, and what they knew of the layout and floor plan. None had ever been to the upper floors, but there is always talk in the kitchen from the other staff. It was a large mansion, set against the mountainside with sprawling grounds and both service and guest quarters.

The staff was shocked to know there was an underground base so nearby, but relieved not to have been in it at the wrong time. They were hired to care for politicians and their visitors and told of seeing the president and several other high-level officials, but had no idea of who would be left alive, or perhaps more important, who would be left that was normal.

Security and a large safe room were located on the second floor. This, they found out when one of them would come down to eat mid-rats, midnight rations, and strike up conversations. It would be zombie proof, terrorist proof, and angry mob proof, with someone constantly there watching the camera feed and monitors.

If there were survivors, they could hold up there for some time. That's where Jason was now heading. It was not so much the politicians that had his interest, that was the least of his concern, it was what they knew; that was what he intended to learn.

They were creeping up a stairway to the second floor when they encountered the first zombie. Deri took him out before it got to the first landing. The shot alerted more and they came charging, from both upstairs and down, with them in the middle.

They came from up top first, and they rushed toward Jason's group, rounding the banister and heading toward them. Then the bottom floor stampeded toward the sound of howling and gunfire, rounding the railing and coming up from there.

As Jason and Gizmo took out the first wave at the top of the stair, the inertia of the dead carried them forward, falling down on them and swamping them. They dodged and shoved the falling bodies away, trying to get off the next shot as the herd pressed closer and closer. Deri and Braz, unable to help, were frantically covering the charge from below.

The Zombies kept coming at them from above, pressing nearer and nearer, closer and closer, until they could no longer even maneuver their rifles for a clear head shot, so Jason dropped it and pulled his side arm. Firing now at near point blank, with his forearm under the neck of a dead zombie to keep it as a barrier, that gave Gizmo enough room to pull his, shoving against a dead zombie falling at him, holding it up as a barrier, he unloaded into the nearest heads.

Two Zombies tried to leap across to the stairs, jumping over the banister and falling to the floor below. They started up behind them, broken limbs and all, climbing over the dead bodies Deri and Braz had accumulated as they put down the last of the charge from below. Braz quickly took care of them and came to catch up with the rest as Deri helped with the remainder from above.

It was quiet now, and Jason looked some of the dead over, reached down and pulled an ear piece and radio set off one of the Secret Service and spoke into it. "This is Colonel Brand. Is anyone receiving?"

He waited and repeated it. Someone came on, "Agent Forester here. Damn good to hear from you, Colonel."

"I bet. What's your twenty?" he asked.

"Second floor, Northeast corner," he answered.

"In the safe room?" Jason asked.

"No. Didn't make it in. The Vice President did. That prick. Locked us all out. How do I say it…he's nuts!" Forester said.

"Nuts, as in Zombie nuts, or just Politician nuts?" Jason asked.

"Politician nuts. He's been gradually getting worse over the last year. We've all been covering for him. But he really lost it recently," he said.

"How many of you are there?" Jason asked.

"I'm here by myself in a suite. There were three others who were on the radio until the batteries went out. Mine's about to die too. These things, Zombies you call them; they're no good with doorknobs. Can't seem to use them. So as long as they stayed inside, my guys may be safe," he said.

"Suite? Describe the suite," Jason said.

"The whole place is a system of suites: kitchens, bedrooms, studies, and the whole thing, even butlers and servants quarters in some. Hell, each one is bigger than my house. There's twenty of them. Then there's a main kitchen downstairs. The entrance to each one is pretty secure. But who knows if they're open or not. I couldn't get out to check all of them. I got pinned in here," he said.

"Roger that, Forester. Hang tight. We'll be knocking on your door soon enough," Jason said.

"That's good news. I'm down to my last can of peaches. I have four rounds left and ran out of toilet paper two days ago," he said.

"The important things, huh? Save your batteries and listen for us," Jason said. "Out."

Chapter Forty Five

Braz was off to the side staring over the banister to the floor below. Jason asked, "You okay, Braz?"

"Sure. I am good," he replied.

Jason reached down and pulled the pistol out of the dead Secret Service man's holster and found three magazines. "Never even had a chance to use them. They'll all be using .40 cal. If we get to them, we'll have some decent reinforcement," he said, holding up a magazine. "Let's look the rest over."

Braz hadn't moved from his spot. Jason walked over while reloading and looked down to where he was staring and asked, "What is it?"

"Oh, well it's really nothing. I was just thinking. We had a similar problem you are having many generations ago," he said.

Jason was shocked. "Zombies? You had that problem?" he asked.

"No. Not zombies. Well, in a way," he began to explain. "We had drug companies, much like yours appear to be. They began defining natural reactions as illnesses. For example, if you had a family member who died. They would say you were suffering from what you would call depression, and they would drug it. But it was natural for a person to feel some unhappiness after such a thing. So it deprived the person of a part of their life and classified them as mentally ill."

"Yah. People here fall for that," Jason said. "I can see them, maybe if they were happy after someone died, maybe if they weren't a little depressed...I can see that as um, well, unusual. Well maybe then something was wrong."

"It got even worse. People that are, how would you say it, capable of much more than what they were doing, or at least felt that way, they would naturally get frustrated by feeling a lack of accomplishment. This would normally drive them to do more and accomplish more; to change their lives and their world along with it, or leave the environment they were living in and being stifled in for a better one.

"But these drug companies classified it as a mental disorder, these feelings of frustration and anxiety and wanting to improve, and gave them drugs, so entire generations were lost, wasted without drive and without accomplishment. A normal or usual dissatisfaction with unacceptable circumstances was classified as a mental illness.

"Eventually, even happiness was considered abnormal and was drugged. The Rulers found it as a way to control the population. It nearly destroyed us. Things that you would rightly be angered over were given a medical name and drugged, so these things were never fixed as part of society.

"We ended up being so controlled and so drugged, that it became a Governing System in itself, and any attempt to free ourselves from it was dealt with by more drugs. It continued until our culture had been so degraded that we could no longer think, feel, or act without the approval of a drug company sponsor. On my home, they even had unqualified persons classifying made up mental illnesses and issuing drugs at our learning institutes."

"Sounds about like how it was heading here. You'll have to tell me how you got yourselves out of it," Jason said.

"Right. Later. Let's get your people and do our mission," Braz said.

Gizmo and Deri came up holding magazines with ammo and more pistols. Gizmo said, "I think we're ready."

"So Braz, how long did it take to get back to normal?" Deri asked.

"We have never returned to normal. Not really. It was determined later that it suppressed a section of our normal evolution and that there would be no catching up with that. That time had passed and it was gone forever. But it took generations of parents having offspring, and them having offspring and on and on. The parents were without drive, without the natural instinct to change or achieve and better things.

"So that impulse did not get passed on and ingrained into their offspring for that generation, nor the next, nor many more afterwards. Even the drive to reproduce was waning. It has been centuries now. We are slowly coming back to life; real life. Small things are being noticed. Our children are beginning to get into tussles with each other at the learning institutes.

"Small things like that, we consider them normal and a good sign. They will learn how to deal with people. They will learn how not to upset each other, how to negotiate, and how to live with other people. It is much better than drugging them into a complacent stupor.

"I wonder if we might not have developed technology above the Invaders had all that not happened," he said. "Think of the countless lives that could have been saved; entire civilizations, world after world. All for the profit of drug companies and using them as a Governing System."

They were creeping slowly and quietly down the hallway to the first suite. Jason reached for the handle and pressed down. "It's unlocked," he whispered. "Ready? We'll go inside, close the door behind us so we don't get mobbed from behind, clear it out, and move on to the next one."

He pushed the door slowly and entered, the rest following, closing the door without a sound. They moved up on either side of the entrance and looked around the open living area. Jason motioned to follow him to the first closed door. He opened it and they went in, clearing it, checking closets and under a bed first.

He pointed and whispered, "Bathroom," and they all quietly got in position outside the door. He started to open it, and there was a rush inside toward the motion, banging the door shut again and repeatedly flailing itself against it.

They all found it humorous. "No good with doorknobs. Leave him," Jason said.

The next room, they entered the same way and cleared it, then the next throughout the suite. They continued back into the corridor to the next suite and to another door. Jason was about to press the handle when Eric came through, giving them all a start.

"Dent is headed your way," he said.

"Roger that," Jason replied and reached for the door again, slowly opened it, and they all filed in. They went through the first room as before, leaving the bathroom for last.

"Let's knock this time, really lightly," Gizmo whispered.

Jason nodded at the door and pulled his weapon up. Gizmo got down low and lightly knocked. They heard a muffled scream from inside.

"Someone in there?" Gizmo whispered as loud as he could.

"Who is that? Are you one of them?" a woman answered.

"Them can't talk, can they? So, no," Gizmo answered.

A woman opened the door a crack and saw the uniforms, flung the door open wide and said, "Oh, thank God. What the hell took you so long? Do you have any idea how long we've been here? I want all of your names, right now!"

"Anyone else in there with you, ma'am?" Jason asked.

"Two others. A Secret Service man was here, but left for help and didn't return. That bastard Forester. I'm gonna kick his ass when I get hold of him. And don't call me Ma'am. Call me Senator," she said.

"Close the door, Senator, and stay inside. Help is on the way." Jason said.

The Senator fussed and complained as Jason pulled the door closed and tried to get her to stay quiet. With far too much noise, she eventually allowed it to shut when the commotion caused a violent movement with crashing and thumping in the next room.

"What an asshole," Gizmo chuckled to Jason. "You better give her your name, Dexter Morris. You're in big trouble now. She's going to report you to your superior."

"I HEARD THAT!" she bellowed. "And I want yours too!"

The screaming caused a rush at the outside door that shut her up, scratching and clawing at it with the now familiar howl of zombies. They waited quietly until it died down and they seemed to have moved off.

Jason opened it a crack and peered into the hallway. "Looks clear, but we know they're out there," and looked around at the other three, "Next room."

They filed out quietly and prepared to enter the next room when the Senator threw a tantrum, coming out of the bathroom and flinging the bedroom door open wide, screaming, "I am a United States Senator, and I demand that I be rescued and taken to safety now!"

Faster than Jason and his small crew could react, she was mobbed by more than a dozen zombies. They whipped their weapons around and dropped as many as they could as fast as they could, but four of them reached her and shoved their way into the bedroom, feasting on her flesh.

Jason and Gizmo ran back to the opening and put the rest down, pulling them off the Senator, only to find her dead.

"Well," Gizmo said as he looked down at her. "We know how to clear these suites now."

"Yup," Jason said. "Now, if only we had more Senators."

Deri and Braz lost control, finding it to be so hilarious that they couldn't stop laughing and soon Jason and Gizmo Joined in.

When they quieted down, Jason said, "Let's clear the other rooms and take five," and moved through the rest of the suite quickly and then into the living room where they all sat. Jason looked around and put his feet up on the table and sat back. Gizmo relaxed for a bit, then got up and checked the kitchen and then came around to the wet bar.

"Beer!" He called. "Hell yah," and he tossed one to each of the others.

Jason popped the top and took a pull, looked around and said, "Nice digs."

"Only the best, right? As long as we're paying for it," Gizmo said.

Just then, they were startled by the other two people that had been in with the Senator peering meekly around the corner. They all reacted by pulling their weapons up and pointing at them. They stood without a sound, suits in tatters, filthy, unshaven and generally disheveled looking.

"You should stay in the bathroom until more people come for you," he said. But then, he couldn't resist and added, "Wait. We could use a couple of Senators. You wouldn't happen to be Senators, would you?"

They both instantly turned and sprinted back across the hallway to the bathroom without a word, slamming the door shut and locking it. Deri and Braz were taking a sip of their beer when they realized the significance of what had just happened and both sent up a geyser into the air and out through their noses. It shimmered like fizzling mercury, running down Braz' uniform.

They were on their way to the next suite and ready to open the door when Dent came on the radio. He had found his way to the basement corridors and had taken a wrong turn, landing him in a civilian area that he had to fight through. He was now with the kitchen crew and should be joining up any minute, taking the back stairwell.

They entered the next suite and listened for motion, looking around the entrance and living area. Creeping slowly toward the hallway, they saw an open door at the end and the flash of someone moving inside.

"Giz, watch," Jason whispered as the person flashed by the open doorway again.

"Was that Nancy What's-her name?" Gizmo asked. "It looked like it."

The four of them stayed crouched in the hallway watching, not wanting to make a sound and be overrun.

"Is she a Zombie? I can't tell," Jason whispered.

"Me either. Let's get a better look; see if there are more in there," Gizmo suggested. They moved forward and stopped, staying still, watching her cross the entrance over and over. "Shit, I can't tell. Is she a zombie?"

"She always looked like a zombie to me anyway. And now she's been what, two or three weeks without a facelift? Hard to tell," Jason said.

The four of them sat and watched as she went across the doorway and back several more times and at last came to a stop right in the opening. She stood and put her head down and stared, focusing into space.

Not wanting to alert any more that might be in there, and not knowing if there were any, and not being sure she was actually a zombie, Jason called Braz over and said, "Go to the end of the hall and see how many more are in there."

Just as he said that, a shot rang out from behind them and she dropped. They all spun to see Dent. "Humph. That was What's-her name," he said.

Jason and Gizmo looked at each other and chuckled when four more Zombies rushed at them and were put down before they could lift their weapons. There were two more suites to clear before getting to the secured area, and they sent Dent and his men to clear one while Jason and Gizmo took the other.

Jason opened the door once again and they quietly entered. There sat Forester, sitting at the table, finishing off his last can of peaches. He watched them enter and set his pistol down. "Oh, man! It's good to see someone. Come on in. Close the door," he said. "Haven't seen anyone in a while. Haven't spoken to anyone in days."

Jason had his guys check the rooms just in case while he walked over to the table, pulled out an MRE, and tossed it down. The man nearly dove for it.

"Never seen anyone go for one of them before. Not like that." He chuckled.

"I'm so damned hungry, I was thinking of hunting down and skinning a zombie," he said as the package heated up. "You find any of my guys?"

"No. Not...not alive. Sorry. But we haven't been through all the rooms yet. Did run into a Senator that told us she was really looking forward to meeting you again though," Jason said.

"Was she fat, stupid, and arrogant?" he asked.

"Yah. That's the one. Good idea putting them in the bathrooms. Kept them alive," Jason told him.

"Oh boy. I couldn't wait to get away from her. I'd rather be eaten by zombies. So where is she?" Forester asked.

"Well, after she was brought here to be safe and after you kept her here safe and then left her in a place that was safe and we came to rescue her and make sure she was safe, she Darwinized herself," Jason told him.

"Darwin's a mother. It's tuff," he said with a snort as he began eating the Meal Ready to Eat. "Umm. I think it's chicken or something." He said, holding up the package to read the contents.

Gizmo came in with Braz and Deri, placed three magazines on the table beside him and said, "Forties, right?"

He stopped shoving food in his mouth and grabbed them, dropping his near-empty magazine and slapping in a full one, checking to make sure he had one in the breach and sat back down. "Thanks. My men. We have to get them. I know they're alive. Pretty sure, anyway."

"We'll get 'em. Don't worry," Jason said as gunfire erupted from down the hall.

Forester jumped up with his gun in hand. "Don't worry, relax," Gizmo told him. "Zombies can't shoot."

Dent burst through the door a minute later with three Secret Service men in tow. "You! You live!" they called as they saw Forester. "You kept us alive man! You kept us going."

They all paused to watch the happy reunion when Dent walked over to Jason and said, "Colonel. I guess I'm your body guard."

Jason watched as Gizmo almost laughed at that and went behind the wet bar. He searched around and saw empty bottles in the trash and said, "Forester, you dog. You didn't save a beer for us?"

"Ah! Sorry about that. What manners, right? Don't worry. I'm definitely buying you guys a round," he said.

Gizmo was surprised when he looked back up to find himself surrounded by men. "You too, Colonel Crozley," Dent said.

They rolled their eyes at each other and Jason said, "Alright Dent. Just don't get in our way or get yourself killed."

Dent leaned back and raised his brow and said, "Don't you worry about that, Colonel. I pull my weight."

"That you do, Mr. Dent. That you do," Jason said.

"Well, what do you all say to getting your guy?" Jason said to Forester.

The Secret Service men all stepped forward, unshaven, malnourished, dehydrated, and dirty, ready to do their duty. Jason looked them over and saw there was no way he could have kept them from participating, nor would he try. "No whining, no complaining, and ready to go. These guys are badass. Damn good shots too," he thought, trying to think of how he was going to use them best.

"I have to warn you, he's not right in the head," Forester said. "But, yah, we have to get him."

The men pulled out their pistols and pointed at the handles to show they had no ammo. Deri and Jason handed them all magazines and they loaded up and were ready to go.

"Explain the set up," Jason said to Forester.

"It's a hell of a bunker. Right at the end of the hallway." Forester started. "Solid steel, two feet of concrete and rebar, around that, steel again. Video and sound feed. Air filtration system and food storage. He's locked himself in and, short of an explosion, or hours of cutting, we aren't getting in there."

"Who are you talking about?" Dent asked.

"Benson, the Vice President," Forester said.

"Benson! Hang on," Dent growled. He pointing at two of his men, "You and you," and walked out the door.

The whole bunch went to the hall and watched. Dent walked up to the video outside the bunker and yelled, "Benson, you sick son-of-a-bitch. You get out here right now, because if you make me come in there and get you, you know what I'm gonna do to you!"

A minute later, the lock snapped and Benson appeared.

"Get your ass over here," Dent demanded, pointing to a spot on the ground and waited until he came meekly to it, leaned over and said in a low voice, "I should just shoot you, you know that, don't you," and then ordered his men to take him.

They each grabbed an arm and marched him like a marionette toward Jason and the Secret Service men.

"Men, thank heavens you are okay. We have to secure the President," Benson said in a frantic attempt to gain authority.

"Shut yer pie hole, Benson," Dent said to him.

Benson stood shivering, looking like he had been on a two-week binge, and smelling even worse. The Secret Service men all looked to Forester after having their Vice President spoken to in a manner they had never seen or heard before. To make it worse, since the President was now dead, this man was now the Commander In Chief.

Dent was checking on his teams, one for each floor to clear the building. They were reporting the floors cleared, people rescued, and zombie casualties. After he was sure that the entire building was safe, he said into the radio, "Alright, targets secured, we're moving them now. On your toes everyone."

Forester and his men stepped toward the new President when Dent said, "Not him," and, to the astonishment of Forester, told two men to cuff and bag Benson. Then he ordered more to surround and hold Gizmo, he Grabbed Jason by the arm as more soldiers raced up the stairs toward them and said, "Ready, Colonels?"

Jason stepped back out of his grip and walked over to the men holding Gizmo and said, "Get your hands off him," and turned to Dent. "Let's understand each other right now. We need shootin' room. I know you know what I mean."

"Colonel," Dent said politely with an open palm, "After you, Sir." Although he said the words "After You", there was another thirty men in front of them while he was right at his side, and another thirty following right behind.

As they headed toward the exit, Gizmo stepped quickly forward a few paces until he and Jason were side-by-side. "Nice place," Gizmo said. "Maybe we should move in. Lots of room. My wife would like it."

"Maybe. I did kind of like it. After things settle down a little, we should look it over again," Jason said.

It was the typical small talk Gizmo started before jumping into something more serious. "Plus it has a whole other base."

"Right. Nice one too. Bigger," Jason said beginning to smile because he knew something was coming; something he missed, and he was about to get his nose rubbed in it.

"Yah. All we have to do is clean up a bit. You know, get the zombie goo off the furniture, and move right in. Right?" Gizmo asked.

"Well, obviously we'd get your wife to do that. It's only, what, eighty-thousand square feet," he joked. Jason was waiting for it. It was something he'd missed and Gizmo was about to rub his nose in it for sure. They had done this for years with each other, through caves and bunkers in Iraq, through factories and mines in America; they had always challenged each other this way. It was tradition.

"Right. Right. Plus the guest and servants quarters. Yah, you know her, one afternoon, varooom, it's done. But there's something different about this place. What's the one thing different about this base than any other base?" Gizmo asked.

"You mean aside from the huge and really nice mansion that we're gonna live in, maybe?" he asked.

"Yah. Besides that," he said.

Jason pondered that for a while as they continued toward the exit. He thought he must have really missed something big and obvious. It just wasn't coming to him. "Okay, and besides the research labs and the Pharmaceutical research and living areas? And besides a dead president and mentally deficient politicians and all those things?" Jason said.

"Yah, yah. All that, besides all those minor things," Gizmo said.

"Alright. Give me a hint," Jason laughed.

"Bad neighbors," he said.

"Bad neighbors? You mean the zombies and the Walkers. They all have those," Jason said.

"Really? They all have them? How many bases still have Walkers behind the blast doors?" Gizmo asked.

Jason stopped, forcing the rest of the procession to do the same, and they all turned and watched him press a patch on his uniform. "Eric," he called into it.

"Jason. Got your dog here with me. You're heading out, right?" he asked.

"Eric. You've been clearing out the Walkers. How many bases around the planet still had the blast doors sealed?" he asked.

"None," Eric replied. "They were all opened."

"Alright. I'll be right out," he said and clicked off.

They started walking again and Jason said, "Good one, Giz. Damn good. The only one with the blast doors still shut. The only one with Walkers still in it, and the only one we can't go all the way into. That was a good one my friend."

"What do you suppose is in there?" Gizmo said.

"Can't wait to find out," Jason replied. "But here's an interesting question. Ruby Ridge, those doors didn't open either. Remember, Eric had to blast through them."

"Good point. Fifty miles of cave in there, and we've never been through them," Gizmo said.

"Yah. The Walkers came out, and we just assumed that Bradley…" Jason trailed off.

"A valid assumption at the time, I think. But still an assumption," Gizmo said as they finally walked out of the building. "Well, in our defense, we have been a little busy. I mean, with all this saving the universe, being heroes, and ruling galaxies, and such, who's got the time?" Gizmo said.

"Yup. I guess play time is over, right? Time to get to work?" Jason said.

They looked up at the sky to see the sun beginning to be blocked by the many Transports sitting in space. "Yah, enough of this foolery. We have to quit screwin' around," Gizmo told him.

"Really. Lazing about in our fancy mansion, drinking beer. Look, the General had to send Dent and practically the whole United States Army to get us and drag us out, just to get us to go back to work," Jason replied.

"Where did we go wrong? We better get our act together. Look what slackers we've become," Gizmo said.

"Embarrassing. Total slackers," he replied.

Chapter Forty Six

The General was sitting with his aide. He had just ended another meeting with the Newcomers and caught the radio traffic from where Jason entered the first corridor and was sitting on the edge of his seat as they took the mansion.

"Find out if we have a…what was that name? The one Gizmo used. Dexter something. Marsh was it?" he asked his aide.

"Morris, General. Dexter Morris," he replied.

"See if he exists. If those were Senators in that bathroom, he's going to be in a world of trouble," the General said.

"Maybe we should send him off to Harding for a while," the aide suggested.

"Good thinking," he said. "Get him ready. It's Jason and Gizmo's next stop."

The aide issued orders and sent men scurrying to locate a Dexter Morris, if there was one. They continued listening, and aside from getting entertained by the conversation that Jason and Gizmo just had, the idea that something may be deep inside his own base made his hair stand on end.

He rushed down to the landing bay and looked at the gaping hole Eric had blown in the blast doors. The only defense from what might come out of there now was yellow caution tape.

The shuttle carrying Jason and Gizmo was pulling in and landing. Jason and Gizmo went immediately to see the progress Cody had made. Eric stepped from the helm, and before he could even say the usual greetings, the General said, "Colonel. I want six shuttles right here, weapons pointed at that hole and manned twenty four seven. Get some mortars pointed in there, every damned thing we have. Get some sensors, motion sensors deep inside. Mines. You get me, Colonel? I want it buttoned up. Then I want a scouting team in there. Not Jason or Crozley and not you."

"Yes Sir, General," he answered turning and yelling, "Gunny!"

"General. I'd like to introduce you to someone very handy," Eric said as the Gunny ran up.

Jason and Gizmo were looking over the equipment Cody and Stanford had been putting together. "You guys. This is magic. Just magic," Jason told them as he was reaching to flick off a small ball of solder that had fallen.

"We figure it has something to do with waves. Some kind of wave converter, right?" Cody asked.

"Exactly. But before we try it, I have to make sure of a couple of things. Like if it's going to destroy the base or not - just minor things." He joked.

Stanford was standing beside Cody, proud of their accomplishment. "It seems like there is something missing. The part that actually captures and holds the wave just long enough. That has to be pretty complex."

"That's right," Jason said looking at Gizmo, making sure he had his attention. "It's not like we're going to find someone walking around with it in their pocket or something."

Gizmo went closer to the device as Jason continued speaking and put his hand into his pocket and felt the item they had found on the assassins at the research lab. He then rolled a chair over and sat down and began going over each part.

Jason said, "Cody, Dr. Stanford. How about a break? We need to go over a few things in the library with Braz before we make any decisions. Do you mind, Braz?"

"Me? No. I don't mind. It escapes me how, but if I can help, of course I will," he said.

"You guys go," Gizmo said. "I'll catch up in a little while."

Just then, the shield was shut down and the transport was maneuvering to the opening of the base. The bay doors were sliding open revealing the assassin's craft. Gizmo and Jason looked at it and then at each other. They would have to go through it. They should go through it now, but they had something else to do now.

Then the assassins were marched out. They needed to be interrogated. And they needed to do that as well. They needed to do it now. Then came Bradley, who they should question now.

They needed to go through two bases as well, all now. They needed to finish the project in front of Gizmo now, they needed to find the source of the Invaders now, and the new threat now, and they were supposed to be on the Invader planet with Admiral Harding now. They needed to do everything now.

Then the Secret Service men walked out with the crazy new Commander In Chief; the new President concealed with a bag over his head. He should question him now as well.

They were followed by the people rescued at the mansion. They would be politicians. The last thing, the least important thing he could imagine, is to waste a minute listening to politicians blowing air about themselves now.

They had visiting dignitaries to speak with, the planet Mars to make habitable, the millions of Newcomers at Nellis and millions more still underground on Deri's planet. There were food issues for planet after planet. But most important was the survival of mankind and the protection of the Earth. That had to be dealt with, and now.

Time was a pressing problem. To anyone else, that would be the end of any thought about it, there just isn't enough time. But not to Jason. That's not how he thought. Jason knew there was enough time. There was plenty of time.

The problem, the real problem with time, is that it was all happening now. Access was the problem. All the time they've ever really had access to was NOW only. Time was always happening at the same time, now. It was everywhere, but it was all happening now. That was the real problem to be solved.

But time just might be the solution too. That's what Jason was thinking after his conversations with Braz. There was lots of time. It was endless. It was endless all the way in the past and endless all the way into the future.

Time is by far one of the most common and abundant things throughout the universe. It is everywhere and it is always, including now. So what he was going to do was have a polite chat with Braz, Cody, and Stanford, and he was going to do it, now.

He reached down and pulled the backpack off Bo and said to the others, "Let's go," looking back at Gizmo getting back to work.

"Slacker," Gizmo and Jason both jokingly called to each other as they walked away.

As he headed toward the double doors, Jason watched the General on the floor as the Gunny began taking over placement of defenses. The General watched as the men came out of the transport, the prisoners, the boxes of intelligence, and then the politicians.

It was a flurry of activity with the General standing in the midst of it all. He caught the look on the General's face when he saw Jason about to go through the doors, almost separation anxiety.

He saw the look on his face at seeing the politicians step out, and saw the hours and hours drained from him that he would have to spend holding their hands and listening to them, wasting his precious time while the very existence of mankind was at stake.

"Yup. That's the problem. Plenty of time. Time is everywhere and always, but it's all happening at once and everywhere, now," he thought.

Chapter Forty Seven

"I have this idea. Not sure how to phrase it, because we've never done it before," Jason started, with Braz, Cody, and Stanford sitting in front of him in the library. "So if any of you have any questions or something to add, just jump in. It came to me when we were talking to Braz about his seeing the future.

"Quantum Physics. In Quantum Physics, everything is a wave. Everything. Before that, everything that was…was a thing, a particle. And time was just a name given to a perception of movement of particles, like the sun and moon. It was a name given to perception and sensation, without it being defined as a real thing.

"Einstein comes along and pretty much redefines it all and proves that it is actually a thing," He stopped and thumped his fingers on the table, wondering the best way to voice what he was about to say.

"You know, when we talk about things, is there any 'thing' that we haven't been able to change? Think about it. Is there a thing that we haven't been able to manipulate and change? Rocks. Electricity. Metals. Chemicals. Liquids and Solids, you name it. I can't think of a single thing that is a thing that we haven't been able to change or manipulate or alter in some way. Can you?" he asked.

"Well no, but time? Is that what you're thinking?" Stanford started. "All those things you are talking about are able to be touched held and molded. These are things that you can melt and cut and burn and combine with other things. Time, I'm not so sure, Jason."

"Well," Jason said. "Neither am I sure, Doctor. But that's what I'd like to discuss. I have some of the smartest people I know in front of me, and I was thinking we could explore the possibility of it together. We have to. We are in danger again, not just the Earth, but everyone. We figured it out before with the Invader power source. This time, well, it may be more difficult."

Eric and Gizmo both entered the room and were taking a seat at the table when the General came in behind with an Aide running in to catch up and join them all.

"Politicians. They're going to eat up every minute of my time," the General said.

"Hell, General. We can't have that. We need you. In fact, no. We'd be screwed. We have too much to do," Eric said. "Hell, General, you're the only General there is left."

"Can we send them campaigning or something? That'll keep 'em out of your hair," Gizmo said. "Plus, we need to interrogate them all. Assholes."

"Not enough. And these ones, once they find out the President is incapacitated, they'll all be clamoring for the spot. It'll be like pulling a wallet out in a Tijuana whore house," he said.

"I got it," Jason said. "Let's brief them on all the planets we own. Send them to campaign there. We'll give them translators. Better yet, not give them translators. Send them to spread their ideas across the universe."

"Oh yah," Gizmo exclaimed. "Send them to new worlds where the population is grazing animals, rodents and lizards, cave people, you know, strange fish and things like that. Keep them out of the way for a good while, until we're ready for them."

"Not bad," the General said. "By the time they get back, we'll have our elections organized and done anyway."

Braz spoke up. "Jason Brand. If they are similar to the ones we encountered earlier, they must not be allowed to interfere. I don't mean to be rude, and I know it is not my place to say, but that was the most childish behavior. One of them had even gotten herself killed."

The group sat, brainstorming the near treasonous and ridiculous plot, but not as treasonous as allowing mankind to be wiped out or enslaved in an attempt to placate the same group who allowed and governed the world into the circumstance in which they found themselves.

"I think it is too good not to do," Jason said. "We can find tons of planets with life like that. Just think, tell them that there is a dictator ruling the universe, and they could change it all to a democracy and govern billions and billions, no, trillions and trillions of them as their Representatives. Even though I'm the dictator."

"Some kind of hogwash like that, they would eat it up," the General said.

"Jason Brand. You are too well thought of in the universe as the ruler. If word got out that they were doing such things, I don't believe they would survive long. Maybe I could offer you a couple of my people as guides. We know many, many planets like you describe. The inhabitants would have no developed language and word would not spread," Braz said.

"These guys were in that mansion. We don't know why. Until we find out, let's keep 'em out of the way. I say let's vote. After all, this is still a Republic," Jason chuckled. "Thumbs up or thumbs down?"

The vote was unanimous, the campaign message was devised. The message would be, "The Earth had been all but destroyed, but because of the structure of our Republic, mankind had emerged victorious, saving all across the universe from a horrible death, and would offer its method of governance, ensuring freedom to all." A nicely printed "Vote For Me" sign would be left in the middle of a pasture with odd looking animals or barren wastelands with lizard-like creatures.

"Braz. Thank you," the general told him and ordered his Aide to make arrangements.

Jason continued the conversation on time. "Look, I know it's a stretch. A big stretch. But I have to tell you something, if we don't stretch, I don't think we are going to be around long. So stretch everybody. Stretch big."

"I wish to retract my earlier statement, Jason," Stanford said, taking off his glasses and setting them down in front of him. "We can control time already. To a degree, we have already done it. Been doing it for years.

"We can speed it up or slow it down with proximity to gravity. It's been being done since we discovered the time differences in our GPS satellites. As they were further away from the gravity source, the more the timers in the satellites and on the ground went out of sync."

"Right. Okay. So now, let's stretch, let's go on from there. So, Doctor, you're right. Never thought about that. But you're right. It's already a fact that time changes with gravity. So it can be changed. But let's go a step farther. Braz here can tell the future, not way into the future, I don't think, but he can tell. Right Braz?" Jason asked.

Before he could answer, the General stated, "We've done experiments with that sort of thing; remote viewing and such. It works, it's somewhat dependable, but I wouldn't want our survival hanging on it."

"You ever play Rock Paper Scissors, General?" Jason asked.

"Sure. Who hasn't?" he said.

"How many times in a row would a person have to win before it would be considered dependable?" Jason asked.

"Ten. Twenty. I don't know, a hundred. Depends on what's at stake," the General said.

Braz and the General played ten games, Braz winning every one. The General demanded another fifteen, which he also won. Then he made Cody play twenty straight, and won every time as well. Then he had Dr. Stanford play until he told him to stop.

"That's pretty impressive," the General said. "But Jason, when the enemy comes, what are we going to do, challenge them to a game of Rock Paper Scissors?"

Everyone had a good laugh, including Jason. "No, sir. But here is what I am thinking: Is it possible to perceive something, provided you are not deluded, and I'm not talking about imagination, is it possible to actually perceive something that doesn't exist?"

They were all sent into silent contemplation by that. Each of them knew what Jason was leading to by that question. Each of them knew that an answer was the same as a commitment.

They could not answer. They had a choice: Lie or agree. Eventually, one by one, they turned and looked to Stanford for an answer. After long and deep consideration, he looked up to see everyone staring at him and said, "No Jason. No you can't. It would be impossible."

"Right. Right. And since Braz has proven that he can see the future in that game, he is seeing something that will happen in the future, therefore, he is perceiving it, and therefore, the future exists. Right now, our future exists. We exist, all of us, in the future. We're already there," Jason continued.

"You've all had premonitions. You have a perception that something is going to happen in the future. Therefore, that future or at least something of that future must exist for it to be perceived," he said.

Gizmo had the advantage over the rest and remained silent until now. He had seen the device Jason had Cody and Stanford make, and had a pretty good idea of what it would do. He also knew the possible dangers and spoke up. "So you want to catch the wave."

"Exactly," Jason said.

"What…what's that mean?" the General asked.

"You are going to catch the damn wave," said Dr. Stanford. "I see it. The wave converter. Interesting. Not a bad idea."

"It's Quantum Physics, General. It postulates everything is a wave. Since time is proven to be a thing, it is a wave. We catch it right, and we can slip on it. Surf the wave, so to speak. Brilliant concept." Cody said.

"So what's the plan? Are you gonna go back before the invasion?" he asked.

"If I can. That would be great to do that, and we should work on it, but no. No General. We're going to go into the future. But not me. Not just one person. Look at Braz and his people. He is constantly seeing the future, in the future, and perceiving the future.

"I watched him while he played that game, and you can't see him. He vanishes more when he looks in the future. I want to make Earth like that," Jason said. "Make it disappear."

"Well now. That is a stretch. Go on," the General said.

"Braz, when you make yourself more visible, and then completely invisible, how do you do it?" Jason asked.

"It's been so long. We're taught when we are young. I haven't really dissected it or analyzed it." Braz concentrated, becoming more visible and then vanishing over and over. "When we become visible, we concentrate on the present. The surroundings, but not just that, it's something about the surroundings, it's... You're right, Jason. It's like the vibration of it. It's the wave. You are absolutely correct."

"And you think you can do this, Jason?" the General asked.

"I think we have to try. We've already found things the assassins had with them that were far above the Invaders technologically; just one little item. This item could multiply our power tremendously. Something is coming. We have to prepare.

"We have three[1] of the Invader stations floating above Earth. Tremendous power goes through them. The power of the sun goes through them. It's an enormous amount of energy.

"We have the dome shield around the base, again, tremendous power and energy. We can generate the wave through those and blanket the entire Earth. That's what I was thinking. I'm pretty sure we can do that."

"And we won't be a target for their weapons, because we won't be there. Well, that's not exactly right either. We'll be there, just at another time," Gizmo added.

The General sat thumping his fingers on the table as his eyebrows raised and lowered. He was thinking how unreal it was that Jason was talking about slipping in time, but then, he did figure out the Invader power source.

He reminded himself that he was wearing a new uniform as well; one that he could float in and fly in. It was anti-gravity. One that has an attachment for different atmospheres and filters poisons.

They all sat and watched the General, his eyebrows would rise as he pondered one thing, and then furl as he pondered another, on and on.

Then there were the transports, an entire fleet of them, floating above him and all around the base. There were aliens, good ones and bad, right there in his base. Then he looked toward Braz and thought, "I just played Rock Paper Scissors with an invisible man. Why would time travel seem so unreal?"

His Aide walked back in with some papers and was carrying the General's clipboard, setting it down in front of him. The Aide had developed a habit the General had come to appreciate. He would set the clipboard down, and if he wanted to draw the General's attention to something, he would discretely tap on some part of it.

"Found Dexter Morris," he said.

It was his schedule for the day that he tapped now. The general looked at it and scanned down the long list of things he would be required to do; the meetings, more meetings, duties, and then even more meetings.

As always, the General had notes that he would write along the side as the day progressed. Things he had to do, things he should do, things he would like to do, and things that he needed more information on, to decide on whether to do or not.

He looked at that list now.

1. Dame's rank back, Morris to Gen.
2. Include Newcomers 'til Mars ready. Give option stay/leave.
3. Call Harding.
4. Tell Jason not to forget his keys.
5. Enjoy contest.
6. Trust Braz.
7. Reach out to Jason/Gizmo.

They were things he had been strongly considering, except for the keys and trusting Braz, but for the life of him, he could not understand the reaching out line, nor could he remember writing it or even seeing the day's list.

"When did you give this to me?" he asked.

"General, I thought I was late, but it must have been earlier, Sir. Those are your notes," the Aide told him.

"Jason," The General said, "Do you have your keys on you?"

"Keys?" Jason rustled through his pockets and said, "No. Must be in my quarters. Why, General?"

"Well, don't forget them," he said and turned to his Aide, "Has the contest started?"

"Just about to begin, General," the Aide replied. "You want them to wait for you to kick it off, Sir."

"Yes. We're coming right now," and he stood up. "Let's go, gentlemen."

Jason stood up and said, "General, you mind if we skip the meeting and go over this some more?"

"No, Colonel. We have to be there. All of us. Let's go," he said.

Chapter Forty Eight

The General was an intense man; a dynamic man. It was what made him a General and what Jason, Gizmo, and Eric had come to appreciate about him. Decide and do; that was his way. But he had an added energy as he made his way to the meeting. Even his Aide was breathing heavily trying to keep up the pace.

He burst through the double doors like a freight train and the entire room jumped to attention. He didn't even bother to walk from the entrance, but slapped his suit and floated toward the podium.

"Where's Morris?" He said to his Aide floating along with him.

The Aide pointed him out and was told to pull him aside while the General had a short conversation with him.

"As you were," he said once he reached the podium, drawing everyone back to their seats. He looked at the contest boards and walked over to the one board with only one name on it underlined, Benson, the new President. Under that were four more names, the rescued politicians. Tapping on it, he called out, "Mr. Dent."

Dent stood up and the General pointed at him and said, "He's won the contest this week, without a doubt. His unit, well, I haven't assigned him to one yet. So he's the high man this week."

The crowd cheered for him. Dent gave a quick wave and sat back down. Jason saw that the General was actually happy, even excited. At the front of the meeting were chairs set up for the newly rescued politicians who sat, arms crossed, looking at the General in silent contemptuous judgment.

"Come on up here, Mr. Dent," the General told him, and as had become the custom, showers of wrapping paper and empty paper cups were tossed at him on the way, followed by both jeers and cheers.

The General was actually laughing now, and when Dent stepped up to the podium, he said, "Been good to have you around again, my friend," and shook his hand.

"For those of you who don't know him, well he has a story, and maybe he will tell it one day. But let me just say, he is the best damn General that this army has ever had. Busted to private, and continued to serve," and walked back over to the board and tapped on it, "By this man right here, the very man he saved earlier today."

"So, all past, he decided that it was, in fact, an error and miscarriage of Justice. He is hereby restored in Rank with all benefits, and all three hard-earned and much-deserved stars," followed by more applause.

"General," he said to Dent, shaking his hand again, "It's good to have you back."

"Thank you, General. I know you stood up for me. Thank you," Dent said away from the microphone.

"Next, another bit of business. Dexter Morris!" he called and he pointed to Morris and said, "Come on up here son."

Morris, confused and looking overwhelmed, walked toward the podium, watching the soldiers picking up the empty cups and wrapping paper off the floor, re-arming themselves, and began up the center aisle under another shower of tossed trash.

"Name sounds familiar," Jason said. "Do we know him?"

"I think so. Don't remember him though," Gizmo answered.

"Look," Jason said, pointing at the Senators at the front.

The newly rescued politicians all turned and scowled at Morris as he made his way. "Ooh. He's in deep shit," Gizmo said.

The General shook his hand and said, "Just keep your damn mouth shut, Morris. Just play along."

The General walked back to the microphone and said, "You may have noticed more names on that board. We now have the beginnings of a civilian Government, and it's all due to this man, Dexter Morris."

The General began describing acts of bravery, courage, and sacrifice while he was swarmed by zombies, and when he was done, you would think that Dexter Morris had single handedly cleared out the mansion and rescued these politicians as well as all the troops involved.

Dexter stood at the side, listening, as the General went on and on, having never set foot in the mansion and not even knowing where the Catskill Mountains were. The General ended the fabrication with his promotion to General.

Dent had made his way to the rear of the meeting. Now standing with Jason and Gizmo listening, he said, "Smart move. A throw away. Poor kid."

The General ended and shook his hand. "Thank you, General," Morris said.

"I doubt you'll be thanking me by the end of the day, son," the General said. "Just play along, we'll take care of you."

Chapter Forty Nine

"Well," Jason said to Gizmo, as they sat working on the new device, "How's your day going, I mean generally speaking?"

"Very well, thank you for asking," he said back. "And, generally, how's yours?"

"Well, generally, I think that I have a lot of general things to do," Jason said.

Morris had just walked in and was standing beside them listening to their banter. It had taken no time at all for the politicians to demand that Morris be punished. He barely had time to change uniforms and meet with them all in the General's office to get busted down to Lieutenant. Still, it was a promotion, with only a small price to pay.

After feeling a bit of guilt over putting Dexter Morris on the hot seat, they began to see the humor in it when the General explained how it was them that caused it all back in the mansion. Morris was now assigned to them and Jason and Gizmo were ribbing him about it.

Jason sent Cody and Dr. Stanford to do some more work on his helmet once they found they were getting in each other's way. There were just too many hands and heads trying to get into the same space.

"What we can do in the micro, we can do in the macro," Jason mused as he placed one last resistor into a circuit and sat back.

"Yup," Gizmo said. "Generally, I think it's ready."

Gizmo and he were about to power up the wave converter and do a test. If they could make it work on something small, micro, then they could make it work on something big, macro. They were looking it over one last time when Morris held out two envelopes.

"What's this?" Gizmo asked, looking up at them.

"I don't know. Maybe you should ask the Lieutenant. That is, if he generally knows," Jason said.

Gizmo looked back up and said, "Lieutenant. Can I help you with something?"

"No, Colonel. I mean yes. It's the...how did you..." he stammered. "It's the envelopes, Colonel. We just met up..." and stopped mid sentence and passed an envelope to each of them.

"Can I ask? How did you get here before me?" he asked.

Jason took the envelopes and asked, "What are these?"

"We just met. Remember? You told me to give this to you the next time I saw you and to come here. Somehow, you got here before..," then he stopped and said. "I don't understand, Colonel."

Jason and Gizmo each looked at the envelopes and told him to take a seat at a counter a short distance away. "Curiouser and curiouser," Gizmo said.

"This is my handwriting," Jason told him.

"Mine too," Gizmo said. "You know, it's too bad Morris isn't a General any more. Remember? We had a General's Aide once. It was great. Now we have a Morris. I guess that's okay, but a General's Aide, Morris will have to really work hard to beat that."

They both opened their envelopes and looked at the papers inside. "It's my handwriting," Jason said. "It says:

1. Test equipment before you leave.
2. Yes, what happens in the micro can happen in the macro.
3. Take Cody and Eric to village for book.
4. Don't forget your keys.
5. Help Giz get guy out of shed.
6. Tell Deri to stay.
7. Go to cave.
8. Bring back RV.

That…is…too weird."

"Yah? Well, try this:

1. Go to village.
2. Tell wife you want kids.
3. Watch yourself at the shed.
4. Get suits at cave.
5. Gadget in pocket works.
6. Find more (in cave).
7. Tell Jason bring rifle, you and Eric too.

This is too much," Gizmo said after reading off the list.

After a couple of minutes of thinking about it, Jason said, "Well? What did we expect to happen? Nothing?"

"So what. We went back in time and gave ourselves a note?" Gizmo said. "No, wait. We had to go forward to know about the shed. Then, must have come back and met our Morris and gave him the notes. I wonder how far we can go," Gizmo said.

"I wonder why we didn't just give the envelopes to ourselves. Or even just go do the list ourselves, for that matter," Jason pondered.

The General was walking up behind them, having just gotten off the comm with Admiral Harding. He had a feeling something was up when he read his notes to himself earlier, notes he couldn't remember writing.

He knew Jason and Gizmo were onto something when Harding thanked him for sending Jason and Gizmo earlier and started going on about how much they'd accomplished since they'd been there and that it was almost impossible.

Now, he was trying to decipher what he meant by reaching out to Jason and Gizmo. Did they need help? Did he need help himself? What would he reach out to them about?

As he got closer, he heard Jason say, "Okay. On and off really fast once," and then watched as they both vanished and reappeared.

"It worked! Damn it men, I saw it! It worked, you vanished!" He yelled.

"Okay. Let's try it again, a bit longer," Gizmo said. "Ready?"

Again they disappeared, and in another short while, were back. Morris jumped to his feet, astounded, and the General walked up beside them and stood with his hands on his head in near disbelief.

"Okay," Gizmo said. "Let's try it backwards," and Jason turned a dial. "Ready?"

That's when it occurred to the General what his note meant. He reached out and touched Jason as they flipped the circuits to life, and there he was, in the past, watching himself go through the double doors, off to have a game of Rock Paper Scissors with Braz and talk about time travel.

His aide was left behind to catch up with him later, as is usual - left behind to carry out some duties and meet up back at the library. The General's clipboard was lying on a nearby table. "Just a minute, you two," he said to Jason and Gizmo, and he ran to his Aide, took his clipboard off the table, scribbled some notes, and came back. "Okay," he said.

Jason turned the dial back and watched Morris leap to his feet again.

"Okay! Okay! Time!" Jason called out with his hand making a time-out sign. "We need to talk, General."

They walked over to a table and sat without another word until Gizmo pulled out the note he had written himself and handed it to the General. "I made myself a list. I told myself I have to go to the village."

Jason pulled his out and said, "Me too. I wanted to go help Harding. Can you hold him off a bit longer?"

"Gentlemen. I just spoke with Harding. You're already there. Been there for a while. In fact, from the way he was talking, there may be more than one of yourselves with him," he said.

"What am I doing?" Jason asked.

"You're doing what you would be doing if it were you, and in fact, it is you," he said.

Jason wrestled with the concept and said, "Somehow, it feels uncomfortable."

"Don't worry. Look, I just wrote myself a note that I'm going to read hours ago. It was me, making a decision that I would make, doing what I would do. Not another me or a different me. It was me. The same as it is you with Harding," the General said. "And you obviously sent yourself there."

"So we can ride the wave backward and forward. I wonder how far back," Gizmo said.

The general got on his radio and checked with a reconnaissance flight he knew was out, asking them to look down and describe what they were seeing. "Well, it's what used to be Detroit, General. Just a big blotch right now," and continued on describing what he was observing.

"Not far enough back to change the invasion," the General said. "I'm sure you would have done that by now. But you did vanish. You did reappear. And we have all effected the past, and therefore the future. In fact, I don't know how, but in the present, you are in more than one place. So was I. I would say your little experiment has potential," the General said.

He then looked at the two notes they'd left themselves and added, "You should do this list. If you had time to do it yourselves, you would have done it already," and furled his eyebrows, adding, "What the hell. You know what I mean."

Cody was walking across the floor toward them with a big smile on his face. "Okay, I'm ready," he called as Eric came through the double doors with Bo.

Jason and Gizmo looked down at the list at "Go to the Village" and they both excused themselves saying they had one thing to do before they left.

Gizmo went to see his wife, and Jason went to see Deri.

Chapter Fifty

They told Eric to land in the same spot he did when he rescued the villagers. It seemed like it was years ago, but it was less than three weeks. Commenting on it, Gizmo said, "Goes to show, it's not the miles, it's how rough the road was."

Jason and Gizmo were going to go down the path to make sure the compound was clear and then call for them. They walked toward the razor wire fence that once held the Villagers captive, as Eric, Cody, and Morris sat on the familiar rock overlooking the village and watched Bo following along, leaping in and out of the brush behind them, happy to be in the open once again.

They were both silent and brooding as they went along the desert path until Jason suggested they pause and take a seat on a flat rock. Jason finally spoke up. "I'm not sure how to feel about this, Gizmo. I hate myself, every one of me. I've seen Deri one time today for about ten seconds, and already I've boinked her four times earlier. She thinks I'm an animal; a sex machine."

"You think you have it bad. I knocked up my wife while we were away. I'm gonna shoot me when I see myself," Gizmo replied laughing.

"Hell, I'm probably banging Deri right now," Jason said as he began tossing pebbles at the fence. "This is something."

"Assholes, all of us," Gizmo said and they both started laughing.

"Here's a question. Where do they get the time?" Jason said. "I've been too busy to fart."

"I know, right? We're totally being used by ourselves. Sending ourselves messages and lists of things to do. It's bull," Gizmo said. "Hey, we must have told ourselves to do that, knowing we were too busy."

"You think we're doing ourselves a favor? So, we're all assholes and our own personal stud service. Horned dog assholes, that's what we are. Every one of us," Jason picked up another handful of pebbles and plinked one at the fence.

They continued sitting and both started plinking stones at the fence. Finally Gizmo asked, "How many of us do you think there are?"

"At least four, judging by what Deri had to say, plus you and I. That's just here at the base. Don't know how many are with Admiral Harding. Maybe some in other places too. We're very unpredictable, you know?" Jason said.

"Maybe we should make more wives and more Deris," Gizmo suggested.

"Hmm," Jason made a noise as he considered that.

"You know, I spoke to one of me today. Just briefly," Gizmo told him.

"What did you say?" he asked.

"Well, we were both kind of on the run. So I told me I would meet up later. I guess we are going to all have to get together and plan. We're sure getting a lot done," Gizmo said.

Just then there was a loud vibration sound and they looked up toward the sky where they thought the defense stations would be. The radio came on and the General said, "Jason, Gizmo. I am sitting in space in a transport just past the moon's orbit, and I just watched the planet and the moon go away. Your idea is a success. No radar signature, nothing," he said.

Jason was about to answer when a torrent of comments from the various Jasons and Gizmos started. He waited for the cacophony to subside, and said, "Good news, General. You should launch a shuttle to watch from a distance, then slowly enter the Earth's gravity. The defense stations should put you in sync with the time wave and the Earth's gravity will start to grab you, and the Earth should become visible to you." he said.

There was a pause while they waited and he came back on, "Dead on, Jason. Congratulations all of you. See you all below," and he clicked off.

"Congratulations, Gizmo and all the other Gizmos. Wow. The General in a transport. He's a busy guy," Jason said.

They both looked at each other and got the same idea at the same time, reaching for their hand-held radios. "Let me. Let me," Gizmo said.

Jason stood and watched as he raised the General on the radio, and after he was asked if he had something to report and asked why he wasn't using his uniform patch, said, "So General, you know that shutter the transport does when you come out of a leap?"

"Colonel. I'll have to take your word for it. I've never ridden in one. What about it," he said.

"Oh, well never mind then, General. Sorry to waste your time," he said, and they both clicked off.

"Yah!" Gizmo said. "He couldn't resist. I wonder how many of him there are."

"So now, I guess you and I are in a different time. We just surfed the wave," Jason commented.

"I guess so. The whole Earth did it. That is…pretty dang impressive, Jason." Gizmo said.

"I'm glad the communication still worked. I thought it probably would." Jason said.

Gizmo slapped his patch and called for the Admiral to do a communications check. "How?" he asked Jason after a brief conversation with the Admiral. "We are in a different time."

"It's the scary entanglement Einstein talked about. You know, particles still having an effect on each other even when they are separated. It's how the Capacitors work. It would be particularly entangled with the Hydrogen Bond. Hydrogen has always been around and will probably always be around," he said.

"Right. Right. So time wouldn't matter. And the Quantum Relays and Capacitors are filled with hydrogen." Gizmo added.

"Yup. Filled with hydrogen. Always there, always will be, so time is inconsequential, they remain entangled," Jason added.

"Smart man, Jason. Smart man." Gizmo patted him on the back.

"Well, Einstein was. It's not like I planned it or anything. It's just the way it is. I'm glad, though," Jason said.

Jason picked up a larger stone and tossed it toward the fence, making a louder sound and skipping through it, bouncing along the ground inside the compound. A growl came from between a building and a zombie appeared and chased it, pouncing on it and trying to bite it.

"They must be hungry by now," Jason said.

"Yup. Catskill Pharmaceutical zombies," Gizmo said, and then he muttered, "What kind of animals would do that to people?"

"My opinion, Pal, the kind of animals that think people are nothing but animals. Drug companies are all the same. Not just here it turns out, but even on other planets, like Braz's planet," Jason said.

Jason put his invader weapon away and whipped his rifle around. "Wonder why I told myself to bring my rifle," he said as he pulled the cover off the scope and started looking through it.

Gizmo pulled his rifle out, one that was given him by a Newcomer, and started looking through that as well. "I see two," he said. Jason didn't respond, and they both continued searching. "No, no. There's one over in the corner. See him?"

"You know, I would miss being a Colonel," he said looking up at Morris, thinking about a promotion the General discussed with them earlier. "I'm not sure I'm gonna like being a General," Gizmo said after a while.

"I know. I wonder why he would do that to us," Jason said. "A Colonel, well, you have a bit of freedom and just enough authority. A

General? Meetings and more meetings. Politicians and dignitaries. I'm with you Giz. What did we ever do to him?"

"I guess I could get myself busted. Complain that I cheated on myself and knocked up my own wife," Gizmo said.

That made Jason laugh. "Good thinking. I like it," he said.

"Why would I tell myself to bring my rifle?" Jason asked again.

"Don't know. Did you bring your keys?" Gizmo asked.

"Shit. Shit. Didn't even look for them," he said as he instinctively reached into his pocket. "After all that, I forgot my damned keys. It's alright. I have an extra set behind the generator."

They both trained their scopes on his camper and checked all around it. "Check it out," Gizmo said. "The side door."

He looked through the scope at it, and there were his keys, dangling in the door. "What the..." he said. "Why would I do that? Tell myself to not forget my keys when they are already there? I must have brought them here. But why would I do that and then tell myself that?"

"Well, Jason. It was our first try at time travel. We'll have to tell ourselves to be more upfront with ourselves. More explicit," Gizmo said. "Besides, you were probably in a hurry. You know, had to run off and bang Deri."

"I'm an assholes," Jason said.

"Well, let's clear it out," Gizmo said.

Jason got down on one leg, put his elbow on his knee and looked through his scope. "At the end, the guy with the suit. Left eye or right, call it."

Gizmo focused his scope on it and said, "Right."

The rifle fired and Gizmo watched the round instantly explode out the back of its head. "My turn. Monkey suit to the right. Call it."

"Left," he called and watched it fall and start kicking. Two more ran out from behind a building and jumped on it. "Well, I guess they have been eating," he said.

They both started firing as more began to appear into the open yard, howling at the gunshots and pouncing on the thrashing newly dead.

The man in the shed was quietly watching. For almost three weeks he had been up there waiting for his opportunity. He lived off the dwindling supplies left at Hellen's store, climbing over the roof and down through the swamp cooler vent he kicked off.

He sat looking, ever since being trapped inside when he found the Gunny's hiding spot and was cut off when the explosions began releasing the gas into the compound he had set up; high enough that the gas wouldn't reach him. It was one last experiment, an experiment gone wrong. It was an experiment to pit one half of the Villagers against the other. One half zombies, one half normal, all trapped behind the razor wire to see which would survive.

He would crawl up there and watch patiently for the only opportunity he had found to escape. It was the keys dangling out of Jason's camper door. He waited for the time when he could rush in and drive away, crashing through the cage he had built, and put some miles between him and the zombies.

He had no idea who was shooting, but he could see they were good. A shot would ring out, a zombie would drop. He didn't know who they were, but the fact that they were there at all meant that the invasion had a complication, and he would have to fix that. He'd been out of touch with the world since that day. The only thing he knew was that explosions rumbled across the Earth and shook the ground while he remained trapped like a rat inside his own experiment.

So there sat Jerry Styles, the man tasked with setting up and documenting the experiment on actual human beings, an entire village of them. He was a man of no conscience, no morals, and no restraint, hired for these traits by Catskill Pharmaceuticals, waiting for his coming opportunity to be released upon the world once again.

He watched as they were thinned out, dropping one after another, counting down the number he knew there were. Soon, the shooters would come around the side buildings and through his cage into the compound, and when they do, he would be in the camper and gone.

He prepared to climb down, swinging over and hanging from the rafter, to be ready to drop to the ground at the right time. The motion rattled the metal ductwork and a zombie came through the garage sized double doors, heading toward the sound. Styles slowly and quietly pulled himself back up and picked up an empty soda can, tossing it into a dark corner.

The zombie chased after the sound to the corner and stayed there, still and silent, waiting in the dark for the next noise or motion to draw it to attack again.

Jason and Gizmo scanned the compound through their scopes for any more signs of activity. "Okay," Gizmo said. "Looks clear. You remember? There's supposed to be someone in the shed you have to help me with."

"Of course I remember. Why wouldn't I remember?" Jason said.

"Well, you know, you forgot your keys," Gizmo answered.

"What do you mean, Giz? They're right there in the door," he replied. "You know, I bet they've been there since Catskill tried to kidnap us. Those assholes. I just have to remember to remember them now."

"Can't really not remember, since we're taking the camper back on a transport later. Why do you think you told yourself to remember them?" Gizmo asked.

Jason just shook his head, told Bo to stay, and said, "Let's get the guy in the shed."

Styles crept up past the vent in the roof and was quietly heading along a joist toward a piece of equipment to jump down on and make a run for the camper.

Jason and Gizmo checked the first shed. It was the War Room that Eric had set up; now empty except for accumulated filth. They came out and made their way to the next.

"He's got to be in here. No other sheds," Gizmo said.

Jason looked in and crossed the opening to the other side while Gizmo crouched down and looked in. They nodded and entered, both clearing to each corner, then walking to the center of the opening and stepped deeper into the shed.

"Well," Jason said, and let out a shrill whistle.

The zombie came barreling out of the dark at them, howling and screeching. That's when Styles dropped down onto the equipment. Jason and Gizmo looked at each other as it charged and just shrugged. Gizmo waited, lifted his weapon, and pulled the trigger. That's when Styles slipped out the door.

They walked over to the zombie and looked. "Why would I need your help with that?" Gizmo asked.

"I don't know. Let's get it out in the light and take a look at him. Maybe I'm supposed to help you drag him out and search his pockets," Jason said.

They each grabbed a leg and started pulling, and that was when they heard Styles start the motor and heard the wheels spinning in the dirt as they ran back into the light, and watched Jason's R.V. crash through the razor wire and head toward Ruby Lake in a cloud of dust.

"Don't say it," Jason said. "I should have grabbed my keys," and looked around and yelled, "Hey, the Runners, their new Fords."

Jason called Bo and she sprang toward them as they both sprinted across the lot for the fleet and checked the door on the first Edge, opened it, and saw the keys dangling in the ignition. They jumped in and were giving chase.

Eric was running to the shuttle with Cody and Morris following close behind and jumped to the helm. "Jason!" he yelled.

Jason was about to answer when he let off the accelerator. He slapped the patch on his uniform and said, "Okay guys. Let's think about this. Who the hell is this guy and where is he going with my camper? Eric, we'll fall back while you follow him."

"It's not adding up," Gizmo said. "I didn't need help in the shed, but because Jason was there, the guy got away. If he would have stayed outside, Jason would have nailed him."

"And I'm not supposed to forget my keys. At the base, I couldn't forget them, I didn't have them. I didn't forget them back at the village either. Just didn't get to the RV," Jason said. "Nothing to do with forgetting."

"Okay guys. He's headed down the road toward the lake. I got him. Let's see where he's going. Since he isn't part of the village, we know he's part of Catskill," Eric said.

Cody asked to hear exactly what the messages were. Gizmo read them off while Jason continued up the dirt road.

1. Test equipment before you leave.
2. Yes, what happens in the micro can happen in the macro.
3. Take Cody and Eric to village for book.
4. Don't forget your keys.
5. Help Giz get guy out of shed.
6. Tell Deri to stay.
8. Go to cave.
9. Bring back RV.

1. Go to village.
2. Tell wife you want kids.
7. Watch yourself at the shed.
8. Get suits at cave.
9. Gadget in pocket works.
10. Find more (in cave).
11. Tell Jason bring gun, you and Eric too.

Cody said, "You might be reading too much into this. It didn't say Gizmo needed help with the zombie. It said help him get the guy out of the shed. Looks like he's out of the shed to me. Now you're supposed to go to the cave, and it looks like that is where he is probably heading. As far as forgetting your keys, there's plenty of time for you to forget them, I mean not forget them."

Jason and Gizmo went through the list again as they bounced up the dirt road. "He's right," Gizmo said.

"Smart kid. Wish we had more of him," Jason commented. "You know, I'm thinking of that mansion. We must be confusing the hell out of people at the base. Maybe we should move in."

"I'm not bringing my wife to that bunch of..." he trailed off and then said, "Yah. We should set up our operations there. But I don't think I want to bring my wife."

To their surprise, Dent came on the radio and said, "Jason. Mansion's all set."

Jason slammed on the brakes and said, "Roger that."

They sat thinking about what just happened, Jason with his hands glued to the steering wheel staring out the windshield, Gizmo with his hands on the two lists they sent themselves and staring at them.

Eric came through the radio and said, "He pulled off and headed toward the cave."

"Roger that, Eric," they both said.

"Okay, Gizmo. I think I'm getting it," Jason said still half buried in thought. "I think I'm getting it. Yup, I'm getting it. This is good. I'm really getting it."

"They are us. They are totally us. They would do exactly what we would do," Gizmo said.

"Completely. And what would be the most important things for you to do right now?" he asked and started driving again.

"First, get my defenses up. Then, get my offensive capabilities up," Gizmo said. "How about you?"

"Definitely. Those would be my first actions. Then, I would scour the universe to see what's coming our way. Find out everything about them, weapons and defenses and such," Jason said.

"Maybe they are not even bad. I mean maybe they aren't even our enemy," Gizmo said. "Maybe they are only enemies to the Invaders."

"Maybe. But I have a bad feeling that's not the case," Jason said.

"I'd set up a whole section of you and I to go back in time and see if we could stop the invasion, wouldn't you?" Gizmo asked.

Jason punched the radio in the SUV to see if they did that and magically the invasion hadn't occurred and the world was back to normal, but all that came through was static. "Maybe we can't go that far back yet."

They were following along the tire tracks of the RV now, coming up over the rise where they captured their first Walkers, and saw the camper sitting not far from the cave.

"Let's see what this guy is up to," Jason said.

Bo bounced out as soon as the door was opened and started sniffing around. Jason pulled a fresh magazine and put it with the others in his pouch and started scanning the area.

They walked up to the old campsite and stood behind the rock and started looking through their scopes into the entrance of the cave. "So pretty much anything we can think of that we don't have time to do, we can make another of ourselves to do. We go back a little bit in time, come back to where we are, time has already moved ahead, even if it's only a few seconds, and we double. Like the General did earlier."

"Looks like. He got in and interacted, wrote some things down. He could have stayed right then. There would have been two of them. Right?" Jason said.

"Right?" Gizmo answered.

"You think the guy left my keys in the ignition?" Jason asked.

Jason had Bo stay with Gizmo while he went over to his camper and grabbed his keys, looked around quickly, locked the doors, and came out. He came back over to the rock, stopping briefly to check the stream.

"Dead fish still," he said, taking one last look through his scope and pointing at the cave, "Let's do this. We've got a lot of things to do."

They went along the side of the cliff face to the entrance and peaked into it from the side. Eric had his men set dynamite earlier, bringing the roof down and closing it up to be sure no more Walkers would get out.

"I don't see anything," Gizmo said.

"Me either. It's completely closed," Jason replied and moved in.

They tried to get as far back as they could, climbing up on rocks and trying to climb over rocks, eventually concluding there was just no way in. Their minds were racing as they attempted to get through. The things they would do when they were not limited by time, the experiments and tests, the investigating and scouting. They began listing them out as they were climbing over some rocks to get back out the entrance.

The two things they were discussing now were how far into the future they could get, and how far back they could get. If they could get far enough back, they could go to before the invasion and stop it. Right now, they only moved the Earth seconds into the future, making it invisible.

If they could go far enough into the future, they would know when the new invasion would be and find out what weapons they would have and, hopefully, how they could defend themselves from it.

They walked to the entrance and turned around, looking back into the cave. "We're supposed to get into this somehow. Get some more of those gadgets," Gizmo muttered in frustration.

"Where did that car-thieving Catskill douche nozzle go?" Jason asked. "We have to get in there. Wait. I got it! There's an air shaft!"

They rushed back to the camper and put Bo onto the scent and followed her as she crossed the trail back and forth up past the cave entrance to the top of the hill and watched as she followed the trail through the tall grass. There was a rock pile up ahead of them and, although they knew that would be it, they allowed Bo to lead them there, patting her on the head when she turned to signal with her bark that she had found it.

Another shuttle pulled up and landed close to Eric, and two people jumped out. Jason looked through his scope and said, "Look. It's us."

They watched as they took Cody and flew off. Then Eric lifted his shuttle and flew toward them and landed, hopping out with his rifle, Morris right behind.

"That was weird. It was you guys. I guess you were in a hurry and wanted Cody back with his books," Eric said.

"Did they say anything?" Gizmo asked.

"Yah, they did. They said to tell you they called you slackers," Eric chuckled.

They were descending deeper into the airshaft, still listing out the many things they would need to find out, experiment on, research, and all the things they would want Cody, Dr. Stanford, and even Dr. Hilliard to start doing.

About half way through the shaft they came to the conclusion that there was no way to do everything they needed to with all the transports they would be using and with the limited people they had available, there just were not enough human beings left, especially technical ones.

Jason stopped and slapped the patch on his uniform and said, "General."

He was instantly on and said, "Something to report Mr. Brand?"

"We're on our way into the back end of the cave. Have you considered what we spoke about, I mean concerning Deri and her people?"

"Jason, we're practically deserted up here. You've got us spread all over the universe. I started using the Newcomers already," he said. "I sent Deri to get the rest of her people and bring them. Jason, I think that invasion we were talking about may come earlier than we thought."

"Roger that, General. Have you sent scouts into the cave yet?" Jason asked.

"The scouts went as deep as they could until they hit another set of blast doors. Dent and Braz are about to blow it," the General told him.

"Sir, maybe you could hold off on that. We're about to enter the backside. There are some things we need to retrieve and there is a person of interest I'd like to capture. I'd rather not get blown up while we're doing that," Jason said.

"Get in and out of there. You guys are starting to get frantic up here. Admiral Harding found two of those planets you were looking for and there are scouts he sent out that went missing," the General told him.

"Roger that, General," and they both clicked off.

"Okay guys. Things are heating up," Jason said to Eric, Gizmo, and Morris. "Let's not get careless. We'll get in there and get this guy and whatever else he has."

They started heading deeper. The shaft took a steeper angle and they found themselves holding the side of the walls to keep from slipping through. As they descended, the light from the opening faded until they were enveloped in complete darkness.

"Why didn't we tell ourselves to bring a flashlight or night vision? Infra red might help right about now, at least to find that guy," Gizmo said.

Jason pulled out a light that Deri had given him like they used at the Invader dome. "I have three lights. We'll wait until we get to the opening. Then I'll toss one in. Otherwise, we're sitting ducks up here with a light," he whispered.

The shaft leveled off and in another twenty feet they found the opening. Jason felt around for Bo and held her. He tried to see if the man was using a flashlight or if there was any point of light at all beyond the opening, but it was pitch black.

"How does the guy see?" he whispered.

They sat and listened for sound. There was a shuffling noise, but the acoustics in the cave made it impossible to determine what direction it was coming from.

"Okay," Jason said. "Here goes. Heads down," and he flicked the light on and tossed it away from them as quickly as he could.

As it sailed across the cavern, gunfire erupted, knocking it flying in another direction and then hitting it again, putting it out completely, giving them just long enough to see their way down and see what direction the shooter was in.

"Good shooting, don't you think?" Eric whispered as they all pulled back into the mouth of the opening.

"Damned good," Gizmo said. "Let's be careful."

They arranged the order they would climb down and feel their way in through the dark to some counters once the shuffling noise started up again. Jason went first, and then lifted Bo down, and silently made his way behind a counter. Once he was in position, Gizmo followed, Eric and Morris went last feeling their way along in the dark.

Jason estimated the center of the room, switched the light on and tossed it while remaining hidden. The firing started instantly again. As soon as he tried to get up and get a shot off, bullets started impacting around him. Eric and Gizmo tried to give him cover and were instantly pinned down as well, and then the light was extinguished with a single shot.

"Shit," Gizmo whispered. "This guy is good."

"Did you get a look?" Jason asked.

Neither of them got a look at the shooter and were again crouching in total darkness. They could hear a shuffling noise start again and knew the general area now. Jason told Bo to stay, moved further forward around the counter to the next aisle, slapped his patch and whispered, "My last light. Get ready to take your shot."

Before he could turn it on and throw it, there was another barrage impacting the counter around him. Eric and Gizmo saw the muzzle flashes and shot just to the left and right of it until they too received fire, forcing them behind cover until it stopped.

"Ready?" Jason whispered again.

Eric and Gizmo got their weapons up and ready to point in the general direction of the shooting. Jason started the count. "On three, two, one," and sent the light sailing past the center of the room.

As soon as Jason popped up with his weapon, he saw a figure climbing up and into the shaft. Eric and Gizmo got one shot off each, and Jason kept the mouth of the airshaft in his sights when he saw the arm come back around holding the weapon.

He put it in the cross hairs, fired, and hit it, sending the weapon to the ground. The man looked out at them, turned, and fled. As he turned, Jason could see he was carrying a container of the gadgets they were there to get.

Jason ran, calling for Bo and yelling, "And that's why I brought my rifle."

They lifted Bo into the shaft and each climbed up, giving chase. By the time they made it up and out of the entrance, the man had made it half way to the camper. Jason sent Bo after him and ran as fast as he could to catch up.

He watched as the man got to the camper and tried the side door, then he ran to the front, then he checked his pockets for keys. Then it was too late, and Bo brought him to the ground where he was held until Jason and the rest caught up.

Standing, bent over with their hands on their legs catching their breath, Gizmo panted, "Well then. All things considered, I guess those were okay instructions after all."

Jason pulled some rope out of his camper and tied the man up, set him down on his knees, and went and got the HAZWOPPER suits. Then he called the General.

"I think we should get inside and open the blast doors from there. We have to get back in and see what else is in that cave and it would be better if we didn't blow it all up," he said.

The radio was silent. Jason waited for him to come back on; strolled a few feet to the man they'd captured, and addressed him. "You're Catskill, right?"

The man didn't respond, he just looked up at him and smiled an evil and treacherous smile.

"These things, where did you guys get them?" he asked, nudging the container with his foot.

Again, the man didn't answer, but just grinned. He looked over at the gadgets, gave Jason a contemptuous glance, and then stared at the ground.

Jason considered the man's position. He had been at the village since just before the invasion. He may not know about it. He may not know how close they came to extinction. But he does know something. He knows what those gadgets are and he knew about the cave.

He was about to tell him that mankind was near extinction. That the invasion had wiped out almost all of them, and for the sake of the species, he should cooperate. It was that look that changed his mind. He would be giving him information he might welcome. He might enjoy hearing it.

"Play the man, not the puck," Jason thought.

"You see that shuttle over there?" Jason said. "It's ours now. All the transporters, we own them. The Invaders...dead. We killed them. All of them. We rule the universe. Us. The invasion failed and your people failed."

Jason got down on one knee and looked him in the eye and said, "You want to be part of the winning team, pal? You better start talking, 'cuz you got nothin' and you got nobody left."

He could tell that rattled him when he looked over and noticed the shuttle for the first time and thought what Jason just said could be true. He was even more rattled when the transport appeared to lift Jason's RV and realized that what he had said could likely be true. But when men stepped out of it with weapons, humans, he slumped his shoulders in defeat, realizing it was, in fact, true.

Jason watched the reaction as a group of men approached. He could hear orders being issued, and soldiers rushing about. He could hear the men approaching behind him and watched his captive's response, his eyes widened looking like he was in terror.

Two men walked around behind the prisoner and pulled a bag over his head and one of them said, "Sir," and pointed.

Jason stood up and both he and Gizmo turned around and saw two others walking toward them. He took the remaining rope and locked it back in the RV's storage and leaned against the door as they came closer.

Gizmo called him again and pointed to the back of the transport. His Camper was already inside. The same camper he was leaning on. He moved away from the door and looked at the men coming toward him and in a few seconds, Jason and Gizmo were standing face to face with themselves.

There was an instant flood into his mind, all of their history, all of their experience, everything they knew, Jason and Gizmo now also knew in a rush of new memories. It was now their memory and their experience.

He recalled how they took the prisoner to the base in the transport for interrogation, jumped into a shuttle, and flew toward the landing bay. As they passed through the shield, he burst into flames and was disintegrated. They both understood that they had sent themselves back to correct this error. This man they thought was a traitor to his own kind was really an alien who's DNA was so different that he could not pass through the shield.

They also knew that this one act created two sets of themselves who could now move about in time as well, creating more and more sets that could freely move about. There they were, standing in front of him, operating freely with their own decision processes based on their own knowledge; knowledge that passed in a timeless flood to both sets when in proximity.

"I have something for you," the new arrival said. But Jason already knew what it was. He knew what he was going to say and what he was going to do. It was a pin that he would wear; both he and Gizmo would have one. It was to demark the original.

They were going to bring the prisoner back down into the cave and find out everything about it. Jason did not know what they would find because it had not happened yet. He did have a funny feeling that as soon as he arrived at the base, he was going to know.

Gizmo's mind was racing. He wanted to do a test. Just how independent are they? Just how original are they? Are they complete carbon copies that would do exactly the same thing? It needed a test. It was the only thing he could think of; the only test that came to mind; the only test he could think of that would be completely random.

It was Rock Paper Scissors.

He held up his hand and said, "Best out of ten."

The other Gizmo said, "Good idea. Let's see."

The two Jasons watched them play round after round with one winning, then the other. Then one won two sets. Overall, they were indeed different, separate, and individual. They were making their own decisions and living an entirely different life.

After the game, there was really nothing to say to each other. They already knew what the other knew. So Jason said, "Well Gizmo. Looks like we got things to do. Time to go," and started walking at a quick pace toward the shuttle with Eric and their Morris beside them and added, "I don't see what Deri saw in him."

.

Chapter Fifty One

Dent was assembling a group of men when they pulled into the landing bay at Ruby Ridge. Off to the right was another Dent, the original, with a pin on his shoulder to show it, the same as Jason and Gizmo. The second Dent and his men were assembling around another Wave Converter, ready to go somewhere in time.

There was another group standing in a half circle with Cody in the center. The General was there talking and issuing instructions. He paid little attention to Jason and Gizmo as they walked over, he just briefly glanced at them and called Dent over and waited.

"We think this is yours, General Dent," he said, looking down.

Dent stared for a moment and reached down to his lower pocket and felt around, pulling something out. "Check the pocket," he said.

There was a slight hesitation before a man moved toward it. Jason and Gizmo came around to get a better view. It was a leg, bloodied, with its foot dangling from a piece of flesh. The man reached in and pulled out a Zippo lighter and looked at the emblem. "Seals," he said, and clicked it open, giving it a flick.

Dent clicked his open and did the same, giving it a flick and holding it up. It was the same, and that meant that Dent and his men had just died.

Dent walked over to the Gunny and spoke to him. The Gunny flew into action, sending men into an explosion of activity. Within minutes, Dent's lightly-armed Scout Team had been transformed into a full-on Assault Unit.

The two Dent didn't need to speak. Information was passed instantly between them. They just nodded at each other before the group blinked away.

"How many times we face death, Jason, thinking it is certain? How many times have we done that?" Dent mused.

"And yet, here we are," Jason said.

"Here we are. There is always some hope that it won't come, a refusal to accept it. You fight against it; deny its very existence. You keep fighting and denying it, raging against it, until you're through it and somehow you do get through it. But you always know it's there," Dent said.

Just then Jason noticed himself standing there. He instantly knew what Dent was talking about, because this Jason had witnessed it and the information transferred to him as if he had been there himself. This was the third team being sent. The other two never returned.

They could be gone for two minutes or two years. It didn't matter. If they lived, this is the time they would return to. If they didn't come back, they didn't live.

"You're a brave man, Mr. Dent," Jason said.

"You as well, Sir," he returned. "You as well."

Jason and Gizmo wandered across the bay floor to gather their thoughts, walking toward the quietest area they could find. There was a Cody and a Stanford in front of two large boards with a grease pencil in their hands.

One board had a picture of waves, smooth and rounded, with four peaks and three valleys and a line drawn vertically into one valley. Underneath it was equations, line after line, scrawled and wiped out and written over again and again as they feverishly tried to come to a solution.

The General and Dent came over with the original Cody; each of them turning several times as they crossed the floor, looking back anxiously and hoping for the arrival of Dent and his party.

"We got stuck. We can't move forward or backward more than fourteen days. We just can't for some reason," Cody said as Jason got to the board.

"We think that we are sliding on this wave, surfing it," Cody explained, running his finger from the crest of the wave to the bottom. "But when we try to slide up the other side, well, we can't do it. It's like a barrier. We're thinking that we may need to alter our converter frequency for some reason once we actually get there to that time." he ended with his finger on the spot with the line through it.

"And you can't go backward any more than that either, right?" Jason said.

"Exactly," Stanford said. "We get in that trough on either side and can't move either way."

There was a loud rush of movement back at the inverter. They all turned and looked, hoping to see Dent. To their horror, it was Gizmo with Jason draped across his shoulder, both covered in blood. "The shield failed! They killed him! Jason is dead!" He yelled. "He's gone! Bo is gone! We're all gone, the base, everything!" and he collapsed, dead.

Everybody in the bay rushed toward them. Jason and Gizmo pushed their way through the crowd as someone rolled them over. Both were dead from injuries, and worse, they were both wearing their pins. It was them, really them, back from the end of humanity.

Jason straightened up and rubbed his chin as he stared down. "Well that don't look pretty, does it Giz?"

"No, my friend. Can't say I like the looks of that," Gizmo answered. He turned around to the board, and then looked back at themselves lying there dead. "Think maybe we're doing something wrong?"

"Can't get much more wrong than dead," Jason answered. "Let's see what the hell we're screwin' up," and they began walking slowly back toward the board, calling for Cody to follow.

They were about half way to the board when Jason started. It was one thing that Gizmo enjoyed about working together all these years. When things were too real and too serious, he had a way of yanking him in the right direction and getting his mind working again, and things were getting serious now; deadly serious.

"You know, I don't know why we would think it's us that screwed up. I mean really, we just got here. It's those other Jasons and Gizmos that screwed up," he said.

Anyone else would have thought that it was a ridiculous statement, but Jason and Gizmo had worked together too long not to know that this is how it starts. Gizmo smiled, mostly because of the ridiculous timing, but also because he knew that out of this would come something they could use.

"Yah, I think you might be right. And look at that. We're the ones who have to pay for it. All dead and everything," Gizmo said, trying to figure out what he missed that Jason was about to rub his nose in.

"What slackers, right?" Jason said.

"Total slackers. The whole bunch of them," Gizmo agreed, the smile getting bigger.

He could hardly bear it. They had just witnessed their own dead bodies and their existence was about to end. But tradition is tradition, and their tradition dictates that if the other person doesn't figure something out, they have to get their noses rubbed in it. It's what kept them sharp all these years, and more importantly, it's a tradition that helped keep them alive.

Although they had just seen their own deaths, this was not the first time they faced the threat of their own end and neither of them saw this as a reason to dispense with tradition.

"Yah, lazing around writing us notes, telling us to do things, go here, go there, go left, go right, do this, do that," Jason said. "Do you think they wrote us a note to go get ourselves killed?"

They were getting closer to the board. Time was running out. He had to figure this out before they got there and they both knew it. He looked and saw Jason smirking. He knew he was practically telling him the answer. He just wasn't getting it.

"Hint," Gizmo said.

Jason timed it well. The General and Cody were following behind them listening, with Dent catching up, and must have thought they had lost their minds.

"Well. You notice the directions didn't say go North or South. They didn't say go up or down or backward or forward," and waited for Gizmo to get it. In the last few steps he said, "All in all, it was positively negative," coming to a stop at the board and turning to Gizmo.

Gizmo slapped his hands on his head and said, "Ah! The dual terminals! Why didn't I think of that?"

"Cody," Jason said. "I don't want you wasting your time on this any longer. We can't go forward more than fourteen days because we won't exist in fourteen days."

"I don't know, Jason. Why can't we go back in time then? We exist then. We should be able to go back farther, right?" Stanford asked.

"I don't think so, Doctor. I don't think so. Not the way we're doing it at least," Jason told him. "Gizmo will explain."

"It's the dual terminal nature of the universe. In electricity, there's Negative and Positive. On the planet there's a North Pole and a South Pole. Same thing with magnets. Can't have one without the other. You can't have a backward without a forward. There is two of everything, opposites; heat and no heat, light-dark, up-down, vacuum and mass. You can't have the opposite of something that doesn't exist. You can't have one terminal only," Gizmo explained.

"So we have fourteen days," the General said. "We can go back fourteen, but tomorrow, you're saying we can only go back thirteen. Is that how it works?"

"Exactly. So that means we have fourteen days in either direction today. If we can go back fourteen days, we may be able to educate and begin new from there; we might be able to send those people back more days. There would be fourteen days until now, and another fourteen until...until the end. Maybe," Jason said.

"Right," Stanford said. "Can't have the opposite of something that doesn't exist. So these are like two ends of a pole getting shorter and shorter. No matter how short it is, we will always be in the center. Even if there is only a week, a day, or even a minute left. Even with one second or even a fraction of it, we will always be in the center. Man, we have so much to do and dwindling time."

"On our side, we can use this Wave Converter like a copy machine. You and Cody should start printing yourselves off and getting to work," Jason said.

"Yah. For sure. We can maybe leapfrog back that way," Gizmo said. "Hell, let's bring Cody's wave converter to him and Dr. Stanford fourteen days ago. Give him a head start, maybe he can come up with something better."

"I think we should. I think we should send whatever technology we have back as far as we can. Then we can develop it from that point. It'll buy us some time, but I think we need to concentrate on a few more things as well.

"First, we are moving in time when we use this equipment, but we're not moving in space. We are leaving and arriving in the same space. It happens to be the space where we're being killed in," Jason said.

"Of course," Cody said. "We need to put it on our transporters and move it away to see what it is that is killing us," he looked around to see one of himself nod and start working on it.

Jason and Gizmo turned to see some medics arrive to carry their bodies away. "When did we go?" Jason asked.

"Wait. They had pins. Did we go through with pins?" Gizmo asked, and before there was an answer yelled for the medics to stop. "Did you send us...did we go through with pins?" he asked again.

"No. Not that I know of. No, you just got them, didn't you?" Cody answered, throwing his arms up and shaking his head in confusion.

"So, when did we go? Why come here, to this time? Let's take a closer look," Jason said.

Their dead bodies were laid out on a table in the landing bay and they were about to go through the morbid task of examining themselves. Not being doctors of medicine, they could only assume the damage was caused by explosions. They had been through and seen enough of that before.

Going over Gizmo's body first, they looked down at the mangled mess and started by straightening the torn clothing. On the leg, a box was uncovered, held by a Velcro strap with a bloodied label saying "minus day 7" written in Cody's handwriting.

"It's the countdown," Jason mumbled to Gizmo. "Day seven. They came back as far as they could in time with this."

"So the battle started at least a week before the actual end," Gizmo mused.

They took it off and opened the box and looked at the workings inside. "Gizmo, look. The circuits, the circuit design, way better."

"Personal Time Wave Converter. Good stuff," he said.

"Must have improved on it; sent it back to ourselves. Let's get Cody to take a look and send him back as far as we can. Improve it more," Jason suggested and called Cody to look.

Jason looked over at his own body. "Looks like I had one too. Let's keep one, send the other back. Make a bunch of them."

"I think that was the intention. Last chance to do it, maybe - bringing those," Gizmo said as they continued looking.

"You want to go through your pockets? You know, in case there's a crack pipe or something embarrassing?" Jason asked.

Cody was looking through the box and said, "Looks like an automatic return built in. It's already dialed to the max. Dead or alive, it just drops the wearer back as far as it can."

"Good addition. Cody, you've gotta get your guys working on this stuff. That's the plan, remember. We send it back and you improve it. We take it back and they improve it. We're gonna run out of time," Jason said.

The General and Dent were standing nearby listening and watching. Dent spoke up. "What were you yelling about the shield before you died?"

"I wasn't real close, didn't get the transfer. I thought I heard that the shield went down. If the shield went down, that means we weren't surfing the wave. We were sitting ducks. Visible and no shield," Gizmo said.

"And if the shields went down, our defense satellites went with them. Maybe even all our transporters and weapons," Jason added. "We're making the same mistake the Invaders made: too dependent on their technology; too sure of themselves."

"Fortunately, it's a mistake we can prevent," the General said. "You just haven't had time to fix it. Get on it Jason."

Jason and Gizmo took their pins off, laid them on the table and walked toward the Wave Converter. Gizmo set the dial, and they both turned to see themselves taking their pins off and laying them on the table and stepped out of the field.

All four of them paused and looked at each other. "We're us," Gizmo said as the other set turned and put their pins back on.

"What would happen now if they didn't walk through?" Jason pondered.

"But we already did. That's why we're here, right? What would you do next, if you were them, which you are? I mean, besides go see Deri."

"I'd send me to go find the new Invader weapons and defense. I'd also send me to find the new enemy and see what they have," Jason said.

They turned around to see two more sets step away from the Wave Converter. "Totally us," Gizmo said again as they all briefly looked at each other and the knowledge they had of the last minute instantly transferred. Without hesitation, they all sprinted off to do their tasks.

Chapter Fifty Two

Bradley was sitting in a cell again, mulling over the recent events, chained this time by both ankles and wrists to the floor. How did he get in such a condition? That was what he was wondering.

He had it all figured out. His plan was nearly complete. It was just that one little hump to get over before he had his complete success. But again, he was denied.

That one little hump; that last little remaining pocket of mankind is all he needed to do away with. He was so close to his goal, and just as he was about to grasp it, again, it slipped out of his reach. Again, Jason Brand was there to foul up his works.

"That man, that horrible man, that Jason Brand, he is all things evil. He's a witch, a warlock, and who knows what else. He's a man that can fly and can make people freeze like a statue, a fake statue, a statue that only makes you think it's a statue until it's too late," he thought. "And they are, by far, the very worst kind of statue there could possibly be; a moving statue!"

He sat and thought about it, how devious it was; how treacherous and deceitful, to have all these statues walking around. Anybody could be a statue. Even Callis could be a statue; a hairless-gorilla rapist statue. The entire base could be nothing but statues now. How would anyone know the difference? "Jason Brand must be stopped!" he thought. "Him and that Guano. What a stupid name."

He would have to devise a test; a scientific test to determine who or what is a statue, and who or what isn't. There must be a way to tell. He looked around his cell and realized he was in the observation cell the Invader had been kept. He sat, high up on the seat designed for an invader, swinging his legs like a little child, chains dangling down and rattling.

There was a large viewing screen in front of him and he sat and sulked, watching people as they walked by now and then. Two happened to be coming by then and stopped momentarily and looked in at him.

"I don't know about the guy on the left, but the one on the right is definitely a statue. I'm almost sure of it," he thought. "I'll blend in; make them think I'm one of them. I'll make myself look like a statue." He stayed as long as he could in one position without moving or taking a breath until they continued walking.

"It worked. I think it worked," Bradley thought gasping for air once they were out of sight and panted to get oxygen flowing again. "Definitely a statue. Definitely. Just like I thought. The one on the left, absolutely. The one on the right, probably, but I can't be sure," he thought.

A short time later, the men reappeared at the screen wearing smocks and looked in at him again. Bradley froze once more and stared at them, noticing the smocks were inside out. They reached over to the breast of the smock and pulled it over, displaying a Catskill Pharmaceutical logo, and then continued walking.

Bradley raced toward the front, forgetting for that moment he was chained, and was whipped around landing flat on the floor. Just then, Callis opened the solid steel door behind him and pushed a cart through it, leaving the male nurse outside.

"Dr. Bradley," she said looking at him sprawled on the floor. "Boy, you had enough drugs in you to make an elephant hallucinate. You need to pace yourself, Doctor."

He picked himself from the floor and crawled to the seat and dragged himself up onto it. Bradley sat and looked at her, wondering what it must be like for her to be under the spell of a witch. He began to feel pity for her. "I know why you do what you do," he said, looking into her eyes. "I know that you can't control it. I don't blame you for any of those things. It's the monster that made you do it; the demon. You had no control."

Callis stopped and looked at him in surprise. "Nobody has ever said that. I didn't think anyone could possibly know. I didn't think anybody would ever understand."

Bradley watched the two men come back, look in, and turn off the view screen. He must find a way to test Callis and devise a way to release her from her spell. "It's that demon that tells you to do it, impels you to do it. That's what makes you do these things. I found out at the base, there is no one who can fight it, no one. Not even aliens. But perhaps I can find a way."

"I can't believe I'm hearing this. It is. It is a demon. It forces me to do it. I so wanted to tell someone, but I didn't think anyone would understand. Dr. Bradley, I..." and she trailed off.

"I believe I may be able to help you," he said while listening to the scuffle behind the steel door. "I want to kill this demon."

The two men from the corridor burst into the cell, pointing a weapon and were about to kill Callis when Bradley yelled out, "NO! I need her."

They paused and gave a frustrated look and one said, "Fine. We'll take her, but we have to hurry. The shield will only be down for a minute and we have to be in position or we won't get through."

One of the men tried to shove Callis toward the door, barely moving her, and pushed the weapon into her back while the other freed Bradley. They went out to the corridor past the unconscious male nurse, and disappeared.

Chapter Fifty Three

Jason and Gizmo continued going through items they found on their dead bodies. Jason pulled a bloodied piece of paper out of his pocket. It was the same as one he had on him with some additions; one of his drawings he was going to give to Cody and Dr. Stanford. He looked at the two, comparing the parts that weren't covered over with blood and called Cody.

"I wanted to add a few things and give this to you, Cody," Jason said, holding the paper up to the light to see the writing that was covered over with blood, and handed both copies to him. "I guess I didn't get the chance."

Cody looked them over, comparing the two and holding one up to the light. "The helmet," he said. "Looks like you put one of those gadgets on it."

Gizmo took the papers and started looking them over. "You gonna wear this, Jason?" he asked and handed them back to Cody.

"I want Cody to do it. I think Cody should be the one. But one of us has to. We have to make a stretch. A big stretch. A quantum stretch," he said looking back at their dead bodies. "Otherwise, this."

Cody continued looking the papers over while Jason and Gizmo finished looking for any other items they might have had on them. "You done with these drawings?" he asked.

Jason nodded and Cody walked away with them, stopping to speak with Dr. Stanford before they both walked toward the back of the landing bay, stopping to walk through the Time Wave Converter.

"Wonder what happened to Bo," Jason said, calling her over and petting her at the thought of what Gizmo said as he came through the Wave Converter, that she was dead.

Bo began sniffing at Gizmo's body and whining. Then she went around to Jason's body and did the same, sniffing deeper this time with more intensity and whining more. She got up on her hind legs and smelled all around and let out a long mournful howl that echoed through the base.

Then she sniffed around more, burying her nose into the clothing and then let out a vicious growl. Her fur stood up, and she barked, running toward the back of the landing bay, turning, and barking again.

Gizmo and Jason both whipped their rifles up and sprinted after her. She led them back toward the holding cell entrances, sniffing back and forth all the way, following a scent. They followed her into the corridor, saw the unconscious nurse and ran up to the open door.

Jason slapped his patch and said, "General," and waited for him to answer.

"Colonel?" the General responded.

"We have security issues, General. Bradley is gone," he said.

Just then, the base alert was announced as the shield went down and a shuttle flew in with Jerry Styles as a prisoner.

"They knew!" Gizmo cried out into his patch. "They knew the shield would be down so Styles could get through. They're getting out. We have spies!"

Jason brought Bo over to where Bradley was chained and said, "Track, Bo. Track."

She took a good whiff of the scent. It was Bradley's scent, but more than that, there was the same scent she had smelled on Jason and Gizmo's bodies; the same scent that was at the transport where she was attacked. The scent she had burned into her memory.

It was the scent of the enemy. They had escaped.

She bolted out the door with Jason and Gizmo following, stopping briefly to make sure she was going in the right direction when the corridor made a turn, and she ran, full bore down the next corridor, growling and snarling all the way.

Jason and Gizmo were running as fast as they could and could not keep up. Bo turned another corner and vanished from sight.

"Eric. Can you get in a shuttle? These guys are getting out. I want to know where they are going," and he continued running. "General Dent. I think we are heading for the cave. Can you put a team together with some transportation and meet me there?"

They turned the corner to see Bo at another door, spinning in circles, anxious to get through, barking and growling and leaping at the door. Jason and Gizmo prepared to go through, Gizmo got on one knee and pointed his weapon toward the door, Jason whipped it open and they both bolted through.

They were now in Bradley's test area below his observation deck. They opened the door leading to the cave that was once filled with walkers and ran through that as Dent appeared with three vehicles filled with men.

Dent barely stopped to let them jump in, while the other two vehicles continued on, Bo still running ahead, he slowed slightly as Jason called her and reached out and grabbed her as she jumped into the vehicle onto his lap and then to the backseat, and they sped off in chase, deeper into the cave.

Past the Walker's feeding arena, the pneumatic corrals where the cattle were unloaded, along the train tracks they sped, beyond the perimeter of the shield. Behind them, Jason could see more vehicles giving chase. In front, as they turned a bend, they were approaching the blast doors and he could barely see two vehicles pulling through them.

He jumped up top to the .50 cal., and started spraying them with rounds as they tried to close the doors. Under fire, they were forced back to their vehicles, and Jason blasted away, disabling one of them.

The occupants that abandoned trying to close the blast doors now abandoned their vehicle and ran to the lead vehicle, and Jason kept firing, dropping one of them who was slowed down carrying a large object, while the rest piled in and sped off around another bend.

"Grab that!" Jason called to Gizmo as they neared it. It was a duffle bag. Gizmo reached down and snatched it up when Dent slammed on the brakes, and instantly sped off again.

"Eric!" Jason called. "We're headed to the back side of the cave where we found Styles. Are you up there?"

"On my way," he called back.

As they pulled around the bend, they saw the vehicle stopped under the airshaft they had chased Styles through earlier. Dent pulled up and Jason jumped from the top of the Hummer into the tunnel, turned and grabbed Bo as Gizmo passed her up, telling her to track, then he grabbed the duffle bag and started moving up the tunnel with the rest following.

He came out running, looking for Bo. Listening for her bark, he ran toward the sound. Eric was pulling up as Bo snarled, spinning in circles again and barking to let Jason know the trail ended there.

The shuttle landed and they all piled in and took off.

"They went this way," Eric said as he lifted off. "They had a ship here, and they went this way, in that direction. I don't know how fast this shuttle will go. I think we need to jump in a transport if we want to catch them. They really took off."

"Do it," Jason said, and then called, "General."

"Colonel. Did you get them?" The General answered.

"No, General, we're still after them. Have to jump to a transporter. We're gonna have to get everyone out of the base; get 'em to walk through the shield. It's the only way we can tell if they are human or alien. We don't have time to do DNA tests on everyone.

"Spies, General. Spies. Alien spies and saboteurs, that's what we're dealing with. They knew we were gonna have the shield down to let Styles through. But it's not just aliens. Look at Bradley. We could have more like him in the base," Jason told him.

"Keep me informed, Colonel," the General said, and clicked off.

Jason stood, watching Eric at the helm, doing something he had never seen. "What's that?" he asked.

"I'm trying to figure out where they were going," Eric said. "I know the general direction, but over any distance, we could be light years off. Even if I'm off a fraction of a millimeter, even a nanometer, we could be off target by light years over enough distance."

"So, what you're saying is that we're screwed," Jason said.

"Pretty much. But if we can get going in the same direction soon enough, we should be able to actually visually follow them. Light speed, you know, they're pretty slow compared to us in a transport." Eric said.

Jason looked down at the deck. He knew it would be easier to find a needle in a haystack. They are minutes ahead of them, which means that, at light speed, every minute they travelled, they were over eleven-million miles away. The chances of finding them were near impossible, and every second put them 186,000 miles further out of reach.

Gizmo watched. He knew the math. He knew that it was an impossible task. But he also knew they had to do it. He knew that Jason knew that as well.

It was never their job to do something easy. Anyone can do that. No, he and Jason did the hard stuff. That's the way it is and that's the way it's always been.

He watched Jason absentmindedly turn, still looking down, and seeing Bo, he stopped and rubbed her with both hands behind her ears. He looked up and saw who was in the shuttle with them as Eric pulled into the transport landing bay.

His face lit up a little when he realized Dent was there. Then it lit up more when he saw Deri and Braz. His attention was jolted back to Eric when he called him over.

"Jason. You jump at the helm of the transporter. You see this line here?" and pointed to the consol. "Just get it going in this general direction, and I'll be right up. I don't want to lose this trajectory."

Eric made a bumpy landing in his haste, and everybody piled out. Jason bolted toward the helm and instantly had it moving. He judged as near as he could the line Eric pointed out and got the transport to leap instantly to a point he estimated to be four minutes of light travel away.

Then he proceeded at approximately light speed, scanning the area for an object that could be a spaceship, knowing it to be fruitless, but doing it anyway while he waited for Eric to join them. It made him think.

"Hey Giz. What day is it?" he asked.

"Hell, I don't know," Gizmo said.

"We'll. It's a nice day for a drive. Maybe it's Sunday. Where would you want to go if it were?" Jason asked.

"Oh, oh," Gizmo said with a slight chuckle. It was happening again. The challenge. What did he miss? "I'm not sure. But it is a good day for a drive, isn't it? I think we should go some place interesting, don't you? Don't want to be bored, and I really don't want to blow another Sunday. We only have one left, maybe two. So it should be some place interesting."

"Some place interesting. Some place very, very interesting," Jason muttered back.

He watched as Jason pulled up a galaxy on the screen, and then another. He was now flipping back and forth between the two. "Where's Eric?" Jason asked impatiently.

"He's coming," Gizmo replied.

Gizmo had a good idea of what he was getting at before he even started. But to be sure he asked, "So what kind of abandoned planet should we invade?"

"Exactly," Jason said. "Exactly right, Gizmo."

Eric bounced into the bridge and started to point out the most likely direction the ship went, which happened to be toward one of the galaxies Jason was flipping back and forth between.

Gizmo called into his uniform, "Admiral."

"Colonel Crozley?" He answered.

"Those planets the Invaders went to and abandoned, is one of them in Cygnus A?" Gizmo asked.

"One of them is. I can pip you over the location," he said.

"Great, Admiral. Could really use that in a big hurry," Gizmo answered.

They received the location of the planet, Eric drew a straight line from there to the Earth, and Gizmo calculated the distance the ship they were after would have travelled along the line. Eric took the helm and maneuvered to the location, and with some searching, there it was on their screen, heading straight for it.

"This galaxy, it's six-hundred million light years away. They're still going light speed. They have to have some other drive, something other than light speed," Jason said.

Eric placed his two hands on the screen and blew the picture up and they all started looking over its engines.

"Maybe it takes them a few minutes to warm it up. They have to make a jump. The question is, should we take them now or follow them," Jason said.

"Why don't we just blow 'em up? I'm getting tired of that Bradley character," Eric said.

Dent walked in with the duffle bag. "Wait 'till you see this," he said laying it on a table. "And did you know you had Cody and Stanford on this transport?"

"No," Gizmo said. "What are they doing here?"

Just then, Cody and Stanford walked in, followed by Braz and Deri. "We were going to hook up the wave converter to the transporter to see what's killing us, remember?" Stanford said.

"Shit. Of all the transporters to grab," Jason said, and then called the General to let him know he had them.

Dent emptied the bag onto the table and Jason and Gizmo came over to look. "What's this? Is that what they were carrying? That's our stuff. That's our time equipment. Where did they get it?" Gizmo asked.

"Wherever they were going, that's what they were bringing. That and Bradley," Dent said.

"Let's just blow them to hell," Eric said again. "If they jump, they might have other stuff that they stole. We have to stop them."

"Hang on. Hang on," Dent said. "This is the first real opportunity we've had to collect any intelligence on the enemy. So we're not blowing them up," Dent said.

Eric was about to open his mouth, but stopped as he realized along with everyone else that this was now General Dent speaking, not just Dent. He was one of only two humans with that rank, and the General back home gave him that rank for a reason. "Yes sir, General," he said.

"We know where they're going. If they use quantum travel, we can get there as fast as them. The only problem then would be finding them on that planet," Dent said while flipping through the items on the table. "Cody, how close are you to doing your time surfing with the transport?"

"The Wave Converter? It's ready. We just have to test it," Cody said.

"Okay. Jason, get in a shuttle and move off a few, maybe ten or twenty miles and watch. We'll turn it on and off again, you see what happens," Dent said.

"Yes, sir," Jason said and ran toward the launch.

He leapt into the seat with Bo jumping in beside him and Deri coming along to watch, and they lifted out of the landing bay. Eric slowed the transport down to a speed the shuttle could keep up with. "Okay," Jason said. "We're ready."

Back on the transport, the switch was flipped and a puff of smoke rose up when a circuit was fried. Cody and Stanford both had their heads down close to the melted parts looking it over.

"What's the hold up?" Jason eventually called.

"It'll be a few minutes," Cody said. "Roasted a few parts here. We're going to have to rewire a circuit or two."

Jason and Deri sat waiting in the shuttle and were looking over the ship they were following. "Have you ever boarded something like this?" Jason asked Deri.

"Something like it. A similar design. You can enter just in front of the engines. There's a coupling there with an access panel. It's dangerous. All the power goes through it to the engines," she answered.

Jason sat and continued looking at the ship, zooming in on the engines as much as he could. "You think we could get on that thing?" he asked.

"Sure. But it's moving at light speed. No way to do it. We'd have to stop it," she said.

General Dent was listening to the conversation and started looking over the craft with Eric. This ship and its inhabitants was their first real solid lead on the enemy and their possible location. Finding out who they were and what they're capabilities were, that was all he had in mind.

"How's that Wave Converter coming?" he asked.

"It's going to take a little time, General," Dr. Stanford told him. "Some of these circuits got badly burned."

"Gizmo!" Jason called.

Gizmo was already walking into the room and nudged Cody and Dr. Stanford aside. "On it, Jason." After a short time looking it over, he said to Cody and Stanford, "See here? We'll run a loop and bypass this melted mess. Put a diode on it so we don't melt it again and you should have had the capacitor down here. Show me what you brought," and he started snipping wires and soldering while Cody and Stanford brought him the box of electronics, stood back, and watched him work his magic.

While he was doing that, Jason started talking. "You know, General Dent. If we could get someone on board that ship, we could find out what they have. See how badly we've been compromised. Maybe take anything else they've stolen from us. The only problem would be getting them back out of there if they get to that planet before we get them off; you know…if they make a jump."

"They are going too fast. There is no way to get on it at light speed," Deri said.

"It's all relative. Right Giz?" Jason said.

Gizmo paused what he was doing and lifted his head slightly to think about it. "It *is* all relative, isn't it?" he responded.

"Braz. If I could get you on that ship, are you up for it?" Jason asked.

"What are you thinking?" Dent asked.

277

"Yah, Jason. What are you thinking? You'd get killed trying to get on it at that speed," Deri said. "Braz, have you ever done this before? Boarded a ship like that?"

Braz spoke up. "It is all relative, isn't it? And Deri, I have done this, but not at light speed. I think I know what Jason has in mind, and I think we can do it."

"Deri has done it too, just not at light speed. I think we can put a team together and get on that thing. We just have to decide whether to ride it all the way to Cygnus, or just grab what we need and get off. Gizmo and I will come. Right Giz?" Jason asked.

"I'll be done in a minute," he said. "I guess the real question is whether Eric is up to the task."

"Me? Hell yah. I'll come," Eric said.

"No, Eric. I think you are going to have to navigate. But you'll have to navigate through both time and space," Braz said.

"I'm all set. I'm gonna try it now," Gizmo said.

Thirty seconds later, the transporter vanished from sight. "Alright," Jason announced. "You're good. It works," and they flipped the switch back off and he headed the shuttle back toward the shuttle bay.

"So what are you thinking, Jason," Dent asked once he got back on board.

"Okay, look. We can flip the switch and disappear. To them, anyway. If we match their speed almost exactly, we can let them fly right into the landing bay. They won't even see it; won't even know. We will be in the bay waiting. We attach ourselves to it, get inside, and Eric speeds up again," Jason said.

"That's gonna be some maneuvering," Eric said. "I don't know. That's going to take some math. Jason, I don't do math."

"You'll have Cody and Dr. Stanford. They do," Dent said. "We're getting on that thing, or we are going to the planet. One or the other. Maybe even both. I'd rather get on the ship first and see what we're dealing with."

"Math is only going to get you so far, Eric," Jason said. "The rest is going to be judgment. That, you are the best at. You'll have to get in front and match its speed, and then you'll have to drop back just a hair and let it slip into the landing bay. Then it'll be like it was standing still to us."

"Right. We'll grab on and Eric can take off again. If we do it fast enough, they won't even know what happened. But if they happen to be looking out..." Deri trailed off.

"Right. We shut all the lights down. If they look out, it'll just be black," Gizmo said.

"Okay. Good so far, but how do you get back out and back into the transport?" Dent asked. "Do the same thing over?"

"Do the same thing over. How long to go through the ship? Five minutes? Ten? They have to jump. They might jump while we're on it," Jason said.

"At least that, five or ten minutes. But I don't understand why they haven't jumped already. There is no reason for it," Braz said.

"Maybe they're not going to Cygnus. Maybe someone is meeting them," Eric said, looking at the screen. He started to zoom out beyond the craft, out into space, searching for something that would meet them.

"You're right, Eric," Dent said. "They could be meeting someone. That is all the more reason to get going. If we're going to do it, let's do it. We'll keep looking for them while you're over there."

"Jason. What do you think?" Eric asked. "You take everything you can get your hands on and if they look like they have...if they know about your Wave Converter, kill everyone there? We'll leave the ship travelling to where it's going? Let it crash into the bastards?"

"Can't let them find out about our little time secret. Seems like what they were after. We'll have to play it by ear once we get on board. Ready?" Gizmo said. "Because I'm starting to get bored."

"Can't have that. Let's do it." Jason jumped up and started heading toward the landing bay.

Chapter Fifty Four

Bradley sat in the back of a room with his chair against a wall. Through the doorway was another room, where now and then someone would walk by. "Statue!" he would call out to Dr. Callis every time he'd see someone. "Statue!" he would call again.

Callis would look, wondering what he was talking about. He had saved her from death. He was a brilliant doctor who Catskill had used to develop a monster. He somehow knew about the demons in her mind driving her to do the things she does. And he said he needed her.

So she paid attention, looking every time he called out. She knew there was something to it; she just couldn't figure it out. He was still under the effects of too many drugs.

She was standing against a wall with a metal collar around her neck attached to the bulkhead. Unable to move, she would strain to look each time he called out. Her new love, possibly her only real and true love, Dr. Bradley, sitting in a half daze, his mind spinning, seeing something that she was unable to.

The things he had done to her and the things she had done to him, they were experiences she had only dreamed of. The gas, the shock, the convulsions, the screams, the torture, all made her burn with desire now.

"Dr. Bradley," she said. "I'm completely trapped. I'm completely chained. I'm completely at your mercy. You can do whatever you want to me. Do it, Dr., do it now," she panted.

Bradley thought for a moment, walked up to her, lifted his hand and slapped her. "Wake up!" he yelled. Then he did it again, and then again. "You can tell me everything!" he cried out, followed by another slap and another scream, "Wake up!"

The people in the other room rushed to see what the commotion was, and seeing Bradley slapping Callis, they were quickly unimpressed and turned away, back to their business.

Callis felt the sting on her cheeks as Bradley belted her again and again. "Dr. Bradley," she moaned, "Take me now. Take me, you bastard. Take me now. Oh! You are so evil."

"Oh, Dr. Callis," he said. "You have no idea," making her heave and writhe against the wall even more.

In the other room, the three went back to their debate. "I don't care," one of them was saying. "We need more payment for this. We want a bigger cut."

"You aren't getting it," the man in charge said. "Any bigger cut for you means a smaller cut for me. I'll be damned if I'm giving you my money. You'll take what you agreed on, or you can leave right now," and he pointed at the airlock.

"I've been injured!" the man cried. "I've been injured! This job was misrepresented to us! I didn't know all the dangers, and I sure didn't know who was involved."

"He's right," the third man said. "We was never plainly informed. He has been injured. We wasn't told we was going to be tangling with Jason Brand and Gizmo."

"And that beast! Don't forget the beast. We didn't know we were going after them. We need more, and I say we ain't turning anything over until the matter is settled proper to our liking," the other man demanded.

"Well that's something you'll have to take up with Styles then, isn't it. You can take up with Styles the renegotiation of your contract. And you know what that'll get you? Dead! That's what. As for now, you're gonna take what you agreed to, or you're gonna get nothing," the leader said.

The argument went on as Jason and his crew prepared to board the ship. Eric had the transport lined up and everyone braced themselves for the vacuum as the shuttle bay was opened. They watched as the ship's nose began to enter and become visible as the energy field from the transporter began to wrap around the ship, synchronizing it with the transporter's time.

As it nosed closer and closer and deeper and deeper into the landing bay, a deafening noise from the engines set everyone on edge.

"You guys hold on," Deri said. "If you get blasted out with those engines, we'll never find you again in space. Not at this speed."

Just as she said that, the first half of the shuttle bay was sucked empty. Shuttles were sent like paper in a tornado, whirling out the bay doors. Jason grabbed onto what he could and held tight. "Hold it right there Eric!" he yelled over the noise.

Dent was near the front watching as the engines began to appear. A bulk head near the end of the transport started to bend toward it as the powerful engines reached ahead to drive through it whatever mass or energy it could use to propel it at light speed through space.

He struggled his way into a shuttle and jumped at the helm. "Eric. I'm going to use this shuttle. I'm going to use it as a block. We'll let the ship in right up to the engines. Those engines, I think they'll tear us apart if we let it all the way in."

Jason and his crew were pinned where they were. The buffeting of the energy being drawn was brutal. If they let go, there would be no more left of them than electrons scattered in space.

Dent lifted the shuttle off the deck and allowed it to be pulled slowly backwards toward the ship, maneuvering as he went to come into contact at the nose. "Tell me when, Jason," he yelled, hoping he could hear him.

He felt the solid contact of the shuttle and started to pull it back foot by foot and inch by inch, pushing the ship back out of the landing bay, slowing it down slightly, until he heard what he thought was an "Okay" through his uniform, and held it in position.

"Deri. Can you get it open?" Jason yelled at the top of his lungs.

Braz tethered himself and crawled along the side of the ship and tethered himself again to the ship, then let himself fall back toward the opening, whipping up and down as he neared the engines. He caught the opening and grabbed on, giving the latch a hard pull. It opened and he thrashed about to climb through.

He secured the tether inside and the rest of them slid down on it and were grabbed by Braz and vanished through the hatch.

Once inside, they all stood and looked each other over. Holding onto the bulkhead, dizzy from the buffeting, catching their bearings, their clothes shredded from the force.

"Piece of cake," Gizmo said out of breath. Reaching around to be sure his weapon didn't fly off, he pulled it in front of him, and said, "Let's go before they jump."

"You two know the ship; you lead the way," Jason told Braz and Deri.

They crawled through another hatch and were in a corridor where, in a room off to the side, the three aliens were still arguing payment while their ship was left to the autopilot.

Jason crouched down and listened for a moment.

"You didn't have your mind probed, did yah? Well I did. I had it probed by that beast! I was bleeding unconscious for who knows how long. I may never get another job. I've been damaged, I tell yah," one of them was saying.

"You've been damaged, have yah?" and he held up his bandaged arm. "Well what do you call this?"

Jason took a quick peek around the corner. All three of them had their guns out and on the table now, and all three of them wouldn't take their eyes off the other two as they began yelling.

"Braz," Jason whispered. "Go get their weapons."

Braz looked around the corner and slowly crept up to the table, reached for the weapon farthest from him, and slid it toward him, scooping up the other two as he did. The three jumped out of their seats as Jason, Gizmo, and Deri rushed in with their weapons pointed, pushing them against the bulkhead.

Jason heard a noise from the other room and went to the opening to see Bradley, his pants down around his ankles, with Callis in their throws of passion. He saw she was chained and Bradley was unarmed and came back out. "I think I'm going to gouge my eyes out," he said.

"What?" Deri asked.

She walked over with Gizmo and Braz to look. "Holy..." Gizmo exclaimed as Callis started screaming more instructions to Bradley.

Bradley turned at the noise and saw them. "Statues!" He called, and continued.

They came back out and Gizmo said, "Okay. What now?"

"What now?" Dent yelled over their uniforms. "Turn those damned engines off before we get torn apart. That's what now."

"Yes, sir, General Dent," Jason said.

Gizmo looked at Deri and Braz. "You know how to do that, don't you?"

Jason and Gizmo watched the three captives listening as the engines wound down and glancing in terror at each other. "Should we even bother interrogating, or should we just call Bo now?" Gizmo asked, causing one of them to instantly pass out.

Bradley found himself chained once more at the ankles and wrists with Callis beside him. He looked over at a strangely familiar scene. There were the three hooded aliens again quivering on their knees, and there was Bo in front of them snarling.

"DEMON DOG!" he screamed. "DEMON DOG!" making them shake even more violently.

Jason and Gizmo were with Dent on the bridge along with Deri and Braz, talking to the General back on Earth.

"I don't think they'd lie to us, General," Jason was saying. "They're pretty shook up. The only one that's seen them is Styles, and he's there with you. They know there are three of them. Gizmo and I can go with Deri. Braz, they won't be able to see. We can get in there and see what we're up against."

"It's an opportunity we can't pass up," Dent added. "We know nothing about the enemy right now. Not a damned thing, except that in two weeks, we are all going to be dead. Can't fight what we don't know."

Admiral Harding had been included in the call. "I agree. But they are going to want something from you. They were supposed to deliver something. You have to deliver something to them. What will it be?"

"Whew. Good point, Admiral. It'll have to be something convincing, too. They'll catch us on anything that's garbage. Any ideas, you guys?" Jason asked.

Cody and Dr. Stanford were off at the side, listening while fiddling with the new Wave Converter. "How about the helmet?" Cody asked.

"No way. Not that," Jason said.

"What helmet?" Dent asked.

"Just something we've been toying with," Jason said. "It's not ready. Wouldn't give that up anyway."

"Admiral," Gizmo said. "How about if we put you in the game a little more. We tell them that you captured the base there on the invader planet, which they should already know, but we'll tell them as if it is new news. We'll tell them you are developing a new crop. A new crop like they grow the Invaders. But better and smarter, more deadly."

"They might buy it. We found test tubes and cells at Catskill. It could even be what they wanted them for. So, they could think it's true. That part of it anyway. All they know is that we have a new weapon. But it'll put you in the crosshairs there, Admiral," Jason said. "They could come after it."

"We're all in the crosshairs, Colonel," he responded.

"Alright then. It's settled," Dent said. "We'll go back to Earth, pick up the samples. Drop off these aliens for interrogation. Then we'll take off. Jason and his crew will infiltrate as much as he can, we'll stay invisible in the transport, ready to grab them if they're in trouble."

"Right. We'll have to shut the shield down for you to get the aliens through," the General said, and thinking about what he just said, muttered, "The shield. Shut the shield down. I wonder if that's what Gizmo was yelling about earlier."

"Could be. Maybe that's what happened. Maybe that's why we all get killed. We shut the shield down," Dent said.

"Let's bring them back to Catskill. I'll have something set up there. We'll interrogate them there; see what else we can get out of them. What about Bradley?" the General asked.

"Bradley? We should just shoot him out in space. He's gone. His mind is gone," Eric said.

"Maybe. Maybe," Dent commented. "But on the other hand, I don't know if we would have any Intel at all without him. They seem to think he's valuable. Because of him, we have a location and are about to meet face-to-face with the enemy. I say we keep him around a while longer."

"They had that huge doctor captive. What's her name? Callis, I think. Had her chained up by the neck. I don't know. She was yelling and sounded like she was putting up a fuss with Bradley. But she looked like she might have been likin' it, too," Gizmo said.

"Yes, she was. No doubt about it," Deri said.

"Okay. Get back here and I'll have the mission plans ready for you. Dump Callis and Bradley at Catskill with the others and get back to base," the General said, and clicked off.

Jason and Gizmo pulled the transport outside Ruby Ridge and stepped out, taking a moment to look around the outside of the entrance. A van was parked to the side pulling a small green camper. They absentmindedly strolled toward it discussing the results of the interrogation of their new captives. Inside the base was another meeting and they could hear the cheering and laughter.

"Gaynor" Gizmo said, looking at the wheel cover on the back of the van with the name stenciled across it.

Morris finally caught up and was strolling along beside them. "Yup. Gaynor. Don Gaynor. Found him somewhere between Montana and Washington up in the hills. The General wanted me out of his hair while you guys were gone, I guess. Sent me scouting for more survivors."

"He's that Twisted Tunes guy, right?" Gizmo asked.

"I heard him play a couple of times. Once, I think it was in Idaho, he did a Credence tribute. Badassed, I thought. You know, tribute bands, they have to be better than the actual band when they play live, otherwise it's just a bullshit garage band," Jason said. "I think it's a lot of pressure. Gotta be."

"I guess it would be. But we don't know anything about pressure, do we Jason? So we have an actual live celebrity, and he's not even a zombie. And you found him? I suppose it's good to have a Morris around after all, right?" Gizmo said.

"Generally, I agree. Good job Morris. We're gonna have some actual entertainment. So you got to hear him play?" Jason asked.

"Yup. A few songs. I don't think they knew we were there at first. Jeannie, that's his woman, was a little...medicated. I don't think Don sees that well. But we took in a few tunes. Magic, that's what I thought," Morris said.

"So...tell us about it," Jason said.

Morris started to explain. He was flying over the mountains outside of Spokane when he thought he spotted some smoke and circled around for a better look. There they were.

"I pulled up and stepped out. We took a transporter because we thought we would see if we could get some things from Boeing up by

Seattle while we were out. There they were, his woman, Jeannie, cookin' up some grub on the side of the camper, and Don off to the side strumming the guitar and singing something I never heard before.

"After a while I walked up to him and told him we were taking them to the base. I'm not sure he really knew what happened in the world. They were out in the middle of nowhere. But he told me we had to talk to his woman. She made all those kinds of arrangements. Then he goes into his camper and slams the door."

"Hmm. That's kind of funny. So then what?" Gizmo asked.

"Well," Morris continued. "I think he was practicing a new tune or something, because we could hear him screaming. I guess it was a rock tune, because he used words like the "C" word and whore and bitch. Couldn't catch the words in between. Eventually the door flew open and he yelled, 'And your ass is fat' pretty loud. Can't wait until he's done with it. I think it'll be pretty good."

"And you were there at the beginning. That's gotta be exciting for you," Gizmo said.

"Really. You ever watch the Sympathy For The Devil movie? The Stones movie?" Jason asked.

"That was something, watching that song evolve. Sounded like crap in the beginning, and then turns into this masterpiece at the end of the show. But this one Don is working on, I don't think it sounded as bad as that," Morris said.

"So…?" Gizmo prodded.

"So they wouldn't leave without their rig. They wouldn't leave without their camper. Kept saying something about a green room. I don't know. Anyway, here it is," he said, pointing at it. "And now we have a Celebrity and his name is on the board."

"And you are going to get called up to the front again for your award. You're going to be famous too if you don't watch yourself. Funny. Is that why you are out here?" Jason asked.

"Yah, I guess. I was going to get called up again. At least this time I actually did something," he said.

"Well, let's get in there then. It's your fifteen minutes of fame," Jason said and they all turned to go inside.

"I'm Don Gaynor from Seattle," they heard as they walked in. "This is called Tea In a Coffee Town," and he started to play.

They stood still and watched and listened as the room fell silent when he hit the first chord. The stage filled with something that can't be named and the guitar strings jangled and dangled, drawing everyone there into the space, captivating them, and making them each a part of the music just by observing. The notes and the words spilled forward, and the space between the notes drew them in further to fill the void.

"Wouldn't you like to be
Where there's only room for
You and me around, around?
For tea in a coffee town"

The crowd soaked up the highs and lows, not wanting to miss a single vibration of a single note. Jason looked around at the people; at the faces, mouths opened, mouths closed, hands on their laps, drawn desperately into a huge expanse filled entirely by a single man who welcomed and invited them all to join him, like they were long lost friends at last returning from madness to refuge.

"Wouldn't you like to come
Where there's only room for
One more soul around, now?"

The music continued with some guitar lead, not enough to even make it seem so, but just enough to add to the mood, as if a saxophone had just crept in. Deri walked in and stood beside Jason and they wrapped an arm around each other and stood, not needing to say anything. For this brief moment, the war was gone and all that existed was this.

"Wouldn't you like to be
Where there's only room for
You and me around, around.
Tea in this coffee town."

No. For that moment there was no war. There were no decimated races and species clinging and clawing for their existence. There was no threat. For that short period of time, all he could think of was all the beauty there was in the world. Time didn't exist beyond this moment, and it was again worth being in.

"Colonel Brand," the General called into his uniform. "You and Gizmo meet me in the War Room."

"Yes, Sir, General," he said quietly. He looked over at Morris and patted him on the back. "Good job, Morris. Good job." He took Deri and kissed her on the cheek and walked away.

"Time to save mankind, my friend. Time to save mankind. I think it's worth saving," he said to Gizmo as they headed to the double doors.

Chapter Fifty Five

"The Uglies. What a name," Jason said, riding on the transport to meet the enemy.

"I wonder how ugly they actually are. Must be worse than the Invaders," Gizmo said.

"And worse than the ones we are about to meet," Jason said, and then repeated, "The Uglies."

They were on their way to a meeting with an alien named Tarr. A meeting with the ones who created the Invaders, and the ones they all suspected had something worse. Worse weapons, worse monsters than the Invaders, and there was something else even worse. It was what this race was tooling up for. A war with something worse than themselves: The Uglies.

Whatever their actual names were, that is how it translated; The Uglies. It was all that the three spies knew. Bo extracted it from them. Even Styles spilled what he knew. The Uglies, that was all. They were coming and the masters of the Invaders were scrambling after the loss of the Invader planet and their army.

It was likely now that new weapons had been dug out from deep beneath a cavern on some distant slave planet, and Earth was to be subjected and set up next as the new production center for more advanced equipment and weaponry and now, perhaps more importantly, since Jason had destroyed their army, a new test-tube race; the new and improved Invaders.

This Earth and its people were proving to be more troublesome than they had anticipated. There was a man, Jason Brand, and his side-kick, Gizmo, and a beast, Bo, who had caused so much destruction that their very existence was now being threatened. Then there was Dr. Bradley.

Dr. Bradley, whom they guided and steered all this time in the development of the Evil Walkers. This was the new army they had planned on. But Bradley had become unstable and undependable. He was useful while he was testing. He had entire teams of chemists and scientists testing to see what would kill the creatures, and as soon as they found something, they could alter the DNA slightly to make it stronger.

All was going according to plan until Bradley decided to make them aggressive. They already had equipment for that. They could train entire armies for aggression; the kind of aggression they wanted; aggression toward whom they wanted. The same type equipment Jason had found on the Invader planet. The same equipment that turned the Invaders into murdering monsters, feared throughout the universe.

The Walkers, along with the new weapons, would have been unstoppable. Now, The Uglies are coming, and the Walkers are out of control. The Humans have control over their equipment, and the Invader home planet itself had fallen to them. Now they were desperate, and desperation leads to panic.

"I'm going to tell them that Bradley lost his mind. He won't be any use to them and I didn't want him on my ship," Jason said.

"But we have the slides. That should be as good, I hope. This guy, Tarr, he doesn't sound too friendly," Gizmo added.

Dent had a hundred-thousand men assembled in the transport, both Humans and Newcomers. Weapons, artillery, tanks, nukes, and every imaginable contingency was covered. Plus, they had the most powerful of them all, the transporter hooked up to a Wave Converter, which at the first sign of trouble, would blink into existence above them and start blasting, followed by more transporters standing at the ready to show up in the blink of an eye.

"Right now, they are weak," Dent was explaining to a group of men. "We hit them now and destroy them as soon as Colonel Brand and his team are extracted and safe. If we wait, they will have weapons that will destroy us. But first we have to find out about this new threat, The Uglies."

Jason walked past the briefing Dent was giving on the deck of the transporter to the next level and went toward the alien craft they had captured, and his team disappeared inside. Deri and Braz went to the helm and navigated it toward the launch bay door.

"Eric. I'd sure like it if you came along, but I gotta tell you, I feel a lot safer with you driving that transporter," Jason said.

"We all do our part, there, don't we pal? I'm going to pull the gate and let you out. Remember, first sign of trouble, you just say the word, and we'll come in shooting," Eric said.

"Roger that, Colonel," Jason answered. "Roger that."

"We're going to need landing coordinates," Jason was saying as he approached the planet.

"Styles knows where to land. The shield is prepared," the gravelly voice came back.

"Styles has been taken captive," Jason told him, and added, "And before we hand over anything, we're going to talk to Tarr about our payment."

He was playing the part. Mercenaries and pirates, that is who was once on this ship. Thieves, crooks, murderers, and the basest dregs that could be hired were the ones that were now sitting in a cell at Catskill, and why wouldn't this be the case? The people who hired them exterminated race after race without thought or remorse. Of course these would be the people they would use: people with no allegiance to anything but their own wealth.

Jason looked briefly behind him at the location he had the samples hidden. The first item brought up at the mission briefing was that they would likely be boarded, the samples taken, and Jason and his crew killed. Embedding it within a metal piece of fascia was suggested by Braz. It would never be found without melting down the entire ship, destroying the sample with it.

As long as they retained control of the samples, they had at least some control over whether they lived or not. There was very little else they would have control over once they put down. They would be at the mercy of a race that recognizes no other right to life.

That part of the plan proved even more valid as they stepped out of the ship onto the platform and were instantly shot by energy weapons and rendered unconscious as the ship was boarded and searched.

Braz remained silent at the side with his two men, but followed as instructed as they brought the crew to holding chambers until they regained consciousness. It was all as described by Styles of what happened to him on his three other dealings. Once he saw where they were put, he left one of his men there and followed the enemy with the most glitter on his uniform, assuming he would report to whomever was in charge.

He was lead directly to a room where the conquest of the universe had been planned and directed for centuries. It was their War Room, containing maps and timelines with three distinctive features that shot out at him. One was the location of The Uglies, flashing red on a wall sized screen, another was the location of the Earth, and the third was the Invader home planet labeled "Reacquisition".

Braz followed him through that into the Hierarchy Council Chambers, where the man in the uniform took his place next to the head of the table. The man at the head looked at him and asked, "Tarr, did you get what they brought?"

"Their possessions have been taken and the ship is being searched now. We should have it shortly, Overseer," Tarr answered.

"This Earth," the Overseer said, shaking his head. "This Earth and its inhabitants; they are not what we expected. Once we have what we need, it must be destroyed and all mention of it erased. Only once in our history have we experienced such a setback. These beings are threatening our very existence. With the looming offensive of The Uglies, this destructive infestation and their acts could not have been timed in a more deadly manner."

At the end of the table, another of the Council stood and spoke. "Your Eminence, we have been forewarned of the coming of a competing life form."

Tarr and the Overseer both looked down toward the end of the table at Doyl. He sat among the Philosophical Determinants; those who decide how their domination will develop and the result of any actions of the Council before action is taken. These were the planners. They were not warriors like their ruler, the Overseer, and his second in command, Tarr. That fact made them noticeably somewhat less in their eyes.

"Yes, yes. The purpose of our existence from the very beginning. I know. I know," the Overseer stood and began slowly pacing around the long table. "To compete with all other life forms. It has been a contest of survival since our very beginning and we have overcome and crushed all threats.

"But these humans are weak and could only be meant to be slaves or be exterminated, placed here by our creator for our benefit and enjoyment. They are a race of weak and superstitious dullards."

"No, Doyl," Tarr joined in. "It cannot be them. As the Overseer stated, they are a weak and temporary infestation, and that is all. It is The Uglies who are our greatest threat."

"And yet, the Humans now own our weapons and our occupying armies are all but gone. We and a small remnant of our army are what are left. As a competing organism, a weak and temporary infestation, they are accomplishing the unimaginable, worse than enemies of old, more destructive than even the Scorpions we battled so many centuries ago," Doyl retorted.

"The Scorpions were a different matter. They were a brilliant species with great strength. The Scorpions nearly brought us to extinction. The humans are nothing like the Scorpions," Tarr said.

"It wasn't their brilliance that brought about our near demise, nor was it their strength. It was our underestimation of their capabilities," Doyl argued.

Braz sent his companion to plant his explosives around the relays for the shields while he continued to listen to the conversation. After that, he would find the main Quantum Relay for the planet that would transmit power to the Quantum Capacitors for all their defenses and their weapons.

They were inside the shield now, the most protected area of the planet. Somewhere inside this facility would be his target.

"Enough!" the Overseer yelled after the debate went on. "Today will be the end of the Humans. Tarr will personally lead our remaining forces and end their threat. Whether they are the competing life form, as forewarned by our creators, or not, by the end of this day, it will be a moot point."

"Yes, your Eminence," Doyl recoiled.

"And your task now is to undo all that the humans have done. It is a task that will take centuries. You and your Determinants set the path, we will conduct the battles. But we have endless time to accomplish it, don't we?" The Overseer pointed out.

"Yes. Once Tarr is successful on Earth, that point is moot. But we must deal with The Uglies before reclaiming our loss. Any remaining forces we have must meet them first. There will be no time to rebuild and reoccupy across the universe before the conflict. This is the sequence laid out by the Determinants. Once the Humans are dealt with, and then The Uglies, only then do we have endless time," Doyl said.

"We will start incubation of the new breed. They have to be tested and meet every challenge. This is the sample brought by our prisoners. We can begin production again as soon as testing is done and the Invader planet is reacquired. This new breed will be our greatest accomplishment," the Overseer said.

"How long until they are ready?" Doyl asked.

"In five weeks we will have the numbers we need to meet The Uglies. In five weeks we will be able to mount a proper assault," Tarr said.

Chapter Fifty Six

All was going according to plan, Jason thought as he began to regain consciousness. All was going according to plan except the large pounding headache he had. He could tell one of Braz's men were there watching them, so he knew Braz and the other were on their way doing that part of the mission, the most important part. Everything else was show.

He silently waited and watched as Gizmo began to stir, followed by Deri a short time later. The longer they stayed locked up, the greater the chance of success of the mission. As long as they were not being released or killed, Braz was gathering intelligence and secretly sabotaging their defenses.

After their ship was searched, the enemy would come for them. Although their pockets and possessions had been gone through and everything had been taken, when they were unable to find what they were after on the ship, they would come to more thoroughly search Jason, Gizmo, and Deri. If they struggled enough and argued enough and mislead enough and confused them enough, this could add as much as an hour to the success of Braz's mission.

It was Jason that convinced everyone of the plan. In the War Room back on Earth, the two Generals were discussing strategy for the coming war. There was no way that Jason was going to talk them out of sending their troops and having an armada of transports sitting on call, nor was there good reason to do that.

He sat in the War Room back on Earth, in awe at the discussions of past battles where an inferior force was able to defeat another larger and better equipped enemy. Things like the Oblique Battle Order were drawn out and discussed, not only on a battle field, but now in three-dimension, and now, they could even add a fourth-dimension; time.

Battles were discussed, historic battles from Gideon to the last great Cavalry charge of history; that of General Galliffet's Chasseurs d'Afrique, where a single great volley of fire shattered it and sent it scattering.

He was amazed at the wealth of knowledge and tactical aptitude they had, and almost wanted to go to war just to use some of what they were discussing. But when Jason finally spoke, it was of simpler things. It was a simple something that he knew well.

He spoke of hockey, and the whole room turned and listened.

295

One rule that he knew and used is this: You play the man, not the puck. If you play the puck, the other guy will play you, and you will not only lose the puck, but you will lose the game. It is a rule he had used too many times to recall. Play the man, not the puck. Deke him out, make him commit. Then it is too late.

"The Earth is the puck," he explained. "We keep trying to protect the puck and to keep the puck and to hold onto this puck. This is important, we have to do that, but what we should be doing is playing the man who is after it. Then we end up with the puck. Then we end up winning the game. If we don't play the man, he will play us and take the puck, take the Earth.

"They have taken planet after planet and galaxy after galaxy. They have conquered every kind of advanced civilization there is, and there has been no stopping them. I'm betting they know battle plans and tactics pretty well after who knows how many centuries of doing this. I can't imagine a thing they haven't encountered. But I'm bettin' they never played hockey."

That was when he began laying out his plan, a plan to conquer and defeat a superior force, a plan to play the man, not the puck. They would force him down the ice. They've already crossed the center line. They have almost exterminated the entire human race, and they were coming in to score.

They would force him down across the blue line now and make him commit to a play. They will think it is their play, and will be ready to make a charge at the goal. Whoever they were going to meet, he will think it's the smart play, the only play, the brilliant play and the fortunate play, but it would be the Human's play all along. The puck would be gone, and he would be taken out of the game completely.

After centuries of conquering without failure, after every effort thrown against them was crushed, the hope was that their certainty and their arrogance would be their downfall, just like the Invader home planet.

Now he sat, waiting for the enemy to complete the search of the ship. His headache was beginning to lessen and he watched Deri and Gizmo rub their heads. He thought about when the last time he slept might have been, and decided he'd better take advantage of the down time. With their death, a death they had witnessed, coming in thirteen days, he doubted he would get much rest between now and then. Gizmo looked over and had the same thought.

He woke up to the sound of pounding footsteps coming toward him, and three aliens soon stood outside looking at them through the thick glass. The skin looked much like the Invaders, thick, scaled, and reptilian, but they were smaller and they were weaker, still standing feet above Jason. These things were just a smaller version of the Invaders.

It began to make sense, that they were smaller versions of the Invaders. They made the Invaders in their own likeness to conquer the universe and spread their DNA.

"Where is Tarr? I aint talkin' to no one but Tarr," Jason demanded.

"I am Tarr. The items you brought, where are they?" he demanded.

Jason and Gizmo began looking at each other with an expression of puzzlement.

"You have it, don't you?" Jason asked Gizmo.

"No. I thought you had it," he replied.

They both looked at Deri and said, "You?"

"No," Deri said. "I thought you had it. Maybe…you didn't leave it back on Earth, did you?"

"You know, maybe it's on the ship. Why don't you go look there?" Jason told Tarr and got back down closing his eyes and preparing for another nap.

They went away and soon returned, a little angrier, and Tarr demanded, "Where are the items?"

Jason and Gizmo woke back up and noticed one of Braz's men had shown back up and flickered in the corner. Gizmo began searching his pockets and said, "Where's my things? You took my things. Get me my things."

Again they went away. The mission was near completion, they just needed Braz back. Then all they had to do was get out. They returned with a bag containing Gizmos possessions, opened the door and handed it to him.

Gizmo slowly went through each item, inspecting it, turning it over and over while they watched. Then he would take the item and put it in his pocket, or strap it on, or stuff it in a pouch the same way it was before he was knocked unconscious.

"You must have had it," he eventually said to Jason.

Again they went away, returning with two bags, one for Jason and one for Deri. "Enough of this. Give me the items," Tarr demanded.

Jason and Deri did the same thing, taking as much time as they could without much concern about being too obvious. When Jason was done, he looked at Tarr and said, "Oh! I get it now. I bet you thought we were just going to hand it over to you so you could kill us. I bet that's what you were thinking, wasn't it? Well it isn't happening pal. We want our payment and you're getting nothing until we have it and we are far away."

"I will kill your friends," Tarr said.

297

"Friends! Friends! They are no friends of mine. These two would kill me if there was profit for them. These two would kill their own mothers if there were profit in it," Jason said.

"Yah. Do that. Kill one of them. That only means a bigger cut for whoever is left. We already get to split Styles' cut," Gizmo added.

"But you still aren't getting a thing until we are paid and far away. I know your type," Jason sneered. "Styles said you can't be trusted to uphold a contract. And look at him, the scum that he is, but he was right. You can kill every damned one of us. You still won't get it," and he laid back down for another nap.

Tarr shook with anger at the insult and contempt, holding his weapon as if he were going to explode in gun fire. Jason barely gave him a glance and closed his eyes. Tarr marched away again, faster, clomping his feet as he stepped.

They waited again until Braz showed up. "You done?" Jason asked.

"Done," he said. "They are quite angry with you, Jason. Apparently you have foiled their plan to take advantage of Styles. They are going to make you an offer in lieu of paying you now. It will be much more lucrative, but they are sure you will be killed."

"Did you get done what you needed?" he asked.

"Everything is set. Jason, there is a smaller Invader Army preparing to go to Earth. Tarr will personally lead them later in the day," Braz said and sent one of his men to watch over the ship.

They waited until the man with the shiny uniform showed up to make him the offer. Jason had no idea of the amounts he was talking about. It was a denomination he was unfamiliar with and his translator would not quantify. It didn't matter though. He had a feeling their money would not be worth much soon.

"No. No deal," he said once the offer was made. "I've dealt with your kind before. Promises of money in the future instead of being paid now for what's already done. I did the job, now you do yours. Pay me. If you want to make a contract with that other business, that's another contract. You pay and you pay now or you don't get what I got. And there won't be another contract, neither."

"Styles was right. The lowest of garbage and scum, and a lying dog, he is. But he wasn't lying about these people. I agree. They are worse. Don't trust them. No deal," Gizmo said with Deri chiming in to agree.

"Where are the items?" Tarr insisted once more, not entirely sure, but pretty certain he had just been insulted again. "Since we have searched your ship and your possessions, we have to conclude that they are on your bodies. Which of you would like to be dissected first?"

"You really didn't think I was going to do that, did you? Have them on us? Just hand them over? You're worse than Styles, and he's the lowest scum I know. I got 'em. They're safe. As soon as we're paid and as soon as we're far enough away to be safe, I'll send you a pod. They'll be inside. We'll be gone," Jason said.

"I want them before you leave," Tarr said.

"Really? After all this? You shoot us. You jail us. You threaten to kill us. Then you try to squirm out of your contract. Do you really think we're gonna hand anything over to you before we're paid our due? You've proven yourself to be lyin' wretched scum. No wonder Styles deals with you," Gizmo told him.

"And as far as that other bit of business you want us to do, we want double," Jason said.

Now he was certain he had been insulted. Tarr pondered his predicament. True, he had demonstrated himself to be untrustworthy. They called him on it. Usually, at this point, he would just execute them. He had done it for less. But the Overseer wanted what they had. Tarr wanted what they had. If he didn't get it, his entire race was at risk.

But trust and honor among criminals is a myth. For this reason he could only trust these three to do exactly what he would do. He couldn't trust them to send the items once they had been paid and left. He knew he wouldn't.

But they did agree to do the next job, sort of, and that means they wouldn't burn this bridge, that is, if they wanted to be paid for the next. Like Styles, it was riches they were after, and riches were all that mattered to them.

"You say you are sending it in a pod. I'm going with you to make sure. I will come back in the pod with the items. No more negotiating," he said, and stomped away.

Dent and Eric were up above listening the entire time. Three times, they were about to tell Braz to blow the shield and they would make the jump and start blasting to get Jason and his crew out. They sat at the helm and listened now as Tarr walked away and waited for what would happen next.

"Good bluff," Dent said. "Remind me never to play poker with Jason."

"It's hockey. But who has the Puck?" Eric asked. "I think I lost track."

That is what Jason was thinking too. Who has the puck? Who is making the play? Was it him, or was it Tarr? He still has what they want, the cells, but Tarr was making some kind of play. That one thing was certain, a play was being made, and Jason would have to check it.

Braz' man came back and the three were talking amongst themselves in the corner. Now and then they would look at Jason and continue. Eventually, Braz came over and said, "They are loading up the ship with explosives. They will set it off shortly after the pod is launched. It is on a timer, the pod launch is the trigger."

"So they threw another puck on the ice and were putting that in play hoping nobody would notice," Jason thought. "That's something you can only get away with in a game of scrimmage with neighborhood kids, and usually in the dark. It was strictly amateur, and only done when the other side can't see what they were doing and pocket the first puck once the score was made."

Now, the ship was this new puck, and Jason would have to score with it. He considered his mission: To find out who the enemy was and to infiltrate and shut down their defenses, and if they could, launch an immediate attack. The second target was to find out what they could about The Uglies.

Jason walked over and sat beside Deri. "These uniforms we have; how long would we be able to float in space until the transport can get us?" he asked her.

"Maybe twenty minutes," she said. "Without an atmosphere to convert, it would just have the supply it carries. In space, there is nothing to filter and convert to oxygen. When it runs too low, it will start to use your own body mass and feed off that, making oxygen from it for you to breath. You will start losing your toes. At least it'll keep you alive; keep you breathing for a while longer."

Gizmo came over to get in on the conversation and asked, "Can you put that thing on autopilot? The ship? And can you set the pod to launch on a timer?"

"Sure we can," she said.

Jason was watching Braz and his men in the corner, still discussing something among themselves, every now and then looking over at him. "General Dent," Jason called. "Are you and Eric listening to this?"

"We are, Colonel," Dent answered. "How much damage will that ship do if it slammed into the surface, Deri?"

"A lot, General. A lot of damage," she said. "It would be enough to level one of your continents on Earth. The most damage will come from the drives piling in and eating into the surface; much more damage than the impact of the ship. But the ship itself would be like an asteroid hitting if it were going fast enough."

"Like at light speed?" Dent asked.

"Light speed is more than enough," she answered.

"Jason. I'm going to have a talk with the General. I'll get right back to you," Dent said.

"Tell him I'm on board with it. This is a chance we may never get again," Jason said. "We can hit 'em, and then bring our forces in and get whatever they have left for weapons. I know they have to have some pretty good stuff to fight The Uglies with," Jason said.

Chapter Fifty Seven

Jason and his crew were marched at gun point to the landing pad and entered the ship. The alien with the shiny uniform was standing inside waiting for them. Thinking he was the only one with a weapon now, Tarr began issuing orders. "Head the ship toward the items. Once I have it, you will get your pay, and you will take me near enough to the planet to launch the pod. Then, you can be on your way."

"Right," Jason said. "Let's do it then."

Neither he nor Gizmo had any idea of how to run the ship, and Braz couldn't involve himself in it and give himself away. He didn't want it to appear the ship was running itself, so Braz stood to the side, weapon ready.

Deri went to the helm and began punching at lights and buttons on the control consol. Braz walked up next to Jason while Gizmo walked toward the rear, calling to Tarr for a distraction, "I want to see the money before we move one inch," Gizmo said. This allowed Braz time to grab Jason's hand and push the right buttons, and the ship began moving.

"I got it from here," Deri told him in a low voice.

Jason turned to the back where Gizmo was still arguing with Tarr and said, "Yah. Let's see the money."

Tarr pulled some dull colored rectangular objects about a quarter inch thick with dull markings on both sides from a satchel. It was a form of computerized credits that was their form of money, and he and Gizmo both said they wanted to count it before he gets off the ship, without any clue of what they would be counting.

Deri finished programming the ship to enter light speed shortly after the pod was launched and set in the location. The explosives had been set to go off after the pod was a safe distance away. Braz had sabotaged the shields around the planet to go down at the flip of his switch, and General Dent was waiting with his force of transporters and men to enter and overwhelm the remaining planetary forces.

High in orbit were the defense satellites, similar to the ones now protecting the Earth, and Dent was looking them over now. "I want those," he told Eric. "I want those and I want them set up above Harding. We will set up the shield, the dome shield, and we will set those up over the Invader planet. Maybe even put those above the Earth and send the old ones to Admiral Harding."

"Another boarding party. We can do that," Eric said. "It'll be easier with the gravity suits. We'll bring some of Deri's people."

"After they lost the other set of satellites, they must have made improvements. They would be idiots not to be prepared for another assault, so I don't think it'll be easier in that respect, but yah. You're right. It'll be easier with the suits," Dent said.

Eric sat with the defense satellites on the screen, looking them over, enlarging one on the screen and going to the next, and said, "It's only been, what, two weeks? Maybe they haven't had time to make physical changes, but they will probably have more security. Wish we could get in there. Maybe we can send some of Braz's guys first."

"Braz is coming in kind of handy, isn't he?" Dent said. "You know, Colonel, with a little luck, we might survive after all. Deal with these critters, and then The Uglies."

"The Uglies. I don't like the sound of it," Eric said. "Let's hope Braz found out something about them."

Jason was on his ship listening. "The Uglies," he said to Tarr, "What can you tell us about them?"

"You just do your contract. That's all you ever need to know. We'll deal with The Uglies," he said, looking around at Deri and Gizmo. "Now. Do you give me the items, or do I start shooting people? I can start with you."

"That's where you're sending us. You're sending us there – to The Uglies. We need to know what they are," Jason said.

"We've heard rumors about them. Nasty rumors. If that's where we're going, and if you aren't telling us, I want triple. It's hazard pay," Gizmo said.

"Just rumors. Just crazy space talk. You know these people. They get out for too long and start to see things; imagine things in their weak minds. The Uglies, all those stories, they're just hallucinations from space madness," Tarr said.

Jason was thinking about how he would give the rest of his crew time to get off the ship. He would launch the pod himself and then get off the ship through the coupler panel. Shortly after the pod was launched, the explosives on the ship were set to blow up. But before that happened, it was set to slam into the surface of Tarr's planet. Good plan, but they would have to find him floating around out there. He would be a speck floating in space.

Tarr was having other thoughts. Yes, he was thinking the pod, the life raft, would be ejected, and shortly afterward, the ship would blow up. But he was also thinking that, if it were him on that ship, as soon as he was paid, and as soon as the raft was safely away, he would just shoot the pod out of the ether. That's what he would do.

"Alright. Give them to me. The next time I have to ask, someone dies," Tarr warned.

Jason walked over to the fascia and pulled it off, rolled it over a few times and threw it to him. "There's your samples. It's sandwiched between those two pieces of metal."

Tarr caught it and rolled it over, inspecting it. He held it up to the light and looked closer. Then he took a tool out of a pouch and broke it open and looked at the samples.

"Straight from Bradley's lab at Catskill," Jason said.

Tarr shoved it all into his pouch and growled, "Let's go to the pod."

Jason stood at the entrance to the life rafts with Braz. Deri and Gizmo were making their way to the coupler with the two men Braz brought with them, listening to Jason as they stood at the hatch, waiting for him before abandoning their ship.

Jason opened the access to the pod, and Tarr stepped through, turning and reaching out, he grabbed Jason by the collar and pulled him inside, closing the access and ejecting the life raft before Braz could make a move.

"He took Jason! He grabbed him and pulled him inside!" Braz yelled as he ran toward the coupler access. "He's in the pod with Tarr! They launched!"

"Dammit!" Gizmo cried out. "Alright. Everybody out before this thing blows. Come on Braz!"

They all slipped out the access into space, and floated away from the ship. Deri was counting; four, three, two, one, and the ship sped off, climbing instantly to light speed and vanishing toward the planet. They turned to watch for the explosion.

"Eric," Gizmo called. "You tracking the pod?"

"I got it," Eric said. "I'm coming to retrieve you guys first."

Jason was squashed against the door, listening to the radio chatter with Tarr pointing his weapon at him. Barely large enough for three people, the pod was cramped with Tarr taking up most of the room.

"You thought you were going to blow me out of this pod, were you? Shoot the pod, once I was away? You think I'd trust you?" Tarr asked, jabbing him with his weapon and looking proud of himself.

Jason looked out through the portal, watching the planet coming closer and closer. "We had an agreement! What is this? What are you going to do?" he asked.

"What am I going to do? I'm going to drop onto the planet and watch the shield disintegrate you. Then, I'm going to have lunch. Then,

I'm going to invade the Earth. I'm going to destroy it this time," Tarr said.

Just as he said that, a brilliant light filled the pod and Tarr paused his gloating to look out the portal and watch the surface of a large section of his planet turn bright with detonations, frozen at the sight. He watched as transporters appeared over the planet and began bombarding the surface.

Tarr sat back, stunned at first, then shaking with rage, pointed his weapon at Jason, aimed, and repeatedly pulled the trigger. Braz had been successful. He sabotaged the system. The weapons, their ships, their defenses were all fed by the Quantum Relay, the same system they had on the Invader planet, the same system they had used and depended on over and over for centuries. It was the magic combination they had found; the system that allowed them to conquer without challenge.

Jason glanced out the portal to see the Defense Satellites approaching, looked at Tarr, pulled his collar up, and said, "Hey Tarr. Take a deep breath."

He snatched up the samples and punched the button on the hatch with his elbow and was pulled by the vacuum out into space, kicking off the pod to float through the void toward the defense satellite, looking back to see the powerless Tarr watch him drift away from inside the dimly lit pod before closing the hatch.

"Eric. General Dent," he called. "I'm heading for a satellite. I have no weapons, but neither will they. At least they will have air."

Dent was watching and coordinating the attack of the planet, relaying information to Admiral Harding and the General while they were listening to the radio chatter. After ten minutes of bombardment with no retaliation, he said, "I'm pulling everyone back out into orbit. The defenses are down, their systems appear to be down, and there is no counterattack.

"I think they're crippled. I'm pulling our ships back in case any new arrivals show up. They can defend us from space while we land and occupy the surface. I want to get in there and see what resources and technology they have before it's all destroyed."

"Can I make a suggestion," Admiral Harding asked.

"Of course, Admiral," Dent answered.

"If you pull them all back into orbit and a wave comes in to attack, well, maybe you should pull some back even further. Leave some in orbit and pull some of them back further, maybe two-thirds of them," he said.

"Good thinking. Trap them, right? Otherwise we'll be sandwiched," Dent said.

"Exactly. Be in a position to trap them instead. Maybe even take some more weapons and technology," Harding added.

"Mr. Dent. Well done. So far, so good. I believe you made a good call to take the fight to the enemy," the General said. "I can't say I like this hockey idea of Jason's very much, but it did work. Where the hell is he now?"

"Eric is in a shuttle with a team about to retrieve him. Right now, he's floating out in space somewhere toward a satellite and wants to get in one. He has no weapons. But he doesn't have much air either," Dent said.

"What the hell does he think he's gonna do?" the General asked. "Wrestle an Invader?"

"I think he mostly wants to get to air before it runs out. The shuttle should reach him about the time he gets there. They're picking his team up now. This... this...what he is doing, he called it something. On the fly, I think it was," Dent said.

"It's another hockey term. On the fly. You do it on the fly. Kind of means to make it up as you go. Or change something as you go along depending on conditions. You guys never played hockey?" Harding asked.

"Not me. I'm a Southerner," Dent said. "Well anyway, he's sure flying now, isn't he?"

"Let's get him on the radio," the General said.

A few seconds later, they were all on the same channel and in touch with Jason and his crew.

"Colonel Brand," the General called to him.

"General. How are you sir?" he said, making fruitless swimming motions through space. "I guess we can call this a success. They're shut down. I imagine they could have other planets like this one, General. If they do, I don't think they are going to be making the same mistake. I doubt we'll be able to disable their systems like this again."

"Right. No doubt about that. General Dent is going to put boots on the ground and make sure there will be no more offensive capability from them. Then he'll get whatever new technology they have and get it back here for you guys to go over," the General told him.

"Good plan. Good plan. Let's get Cody and Stanford on it. And Dr. Hilliard. He's a smart guy too," Jason said.

"You and Gizmo. That's who needs to go through it," Dent said.

"Shit. I'm only about half way to the defense satellite. How long until they get here? I'm going to be out of air here pretty soon. I think I can feel my toe start to tingle," Jason said.

"Eric is rounding up your team now. Should be there in a few minutes," Dent said.

"I wonder how fast this suit will eat a toe," Jason pondered. "Hey, is the Admiral on?"

"Right here Colonel," he responded.

"Admiral, how is the inventory going? How many transporters have we accounted for versus how many were out?" Jason asked.

"We're missing seventeen. Why do you ask?" the Admiral asked.

"Well, I figured there might be a few of them stuck in a leap. It's not really instant. Not absolutely instant," he said.

"Right," the General joined in. "Eric was mentioning that earlier. No such thing as absolutes."

"That's right. So if we've been to all their planets and we've captured everything there is to capture, the number of missing transports would be the ones stuck in the leap to the Invader Home planet. Seventeen seems like a pretty realistic number," Jason said. "I have a plan. We need to talk about it."

Eric chimed in and announced they had recovered the rest of his crew and were on their way when another voice popped onto the channel. "FIVE WEEKS!" the voice screamed. "FIVE WEEKS!"

"Who is that? Cody?" Jason asked.

"FIVE WEEKS, JASON! FIVE WEEKS!" The voice came again. "We can go forward five weeks!"

"Five weeks!" the General exclaimed. "Hell, we can go back...that's before the invasion. Five weeks! That changes everything. Five weeks! This thing you guys did, it must have set everything back."

"Cody, I could kiss you. Remember, you asked if we were going to save the world? You're doing it Cody. You're doing it!" Jason howled.

"Me! It was you guys. You and Gizmo. It's whatever you guys did," Cody replied. "Five weeks, Jason. We can live another five weeks! We can go back...that's before the invasion!"

The General sat back on Earth listening to more and more enthusiastic chattering on the channel. It would never be allowed normally, but this was one time he would allow this exception. He heard more people enter the conversation, Dr. Hilliard and Dr. Stanford even joined in, and further excitement and celebration arose.

Barely able to be heard over the cacophony, he caught Jason and Gizmo in a short, low voice announcing they were going to switch channels, inviting Eric, and they left the conversation. The General let them. They were going to do what they do best. They were going to figure something out. They were going to put a plan together, and they were going to try to save mankind five weeks from now.

He told Admiral Harding and General Dent to switch channels as well. There he would have his own conversation in private. He had his own plans to make and he ordered Dent to round up Jason and his crew and deliver them to Earth immediately, then he ordered Admiral Harding and Dent each to leave someone in command and get back to Earth. They would need to meet in the War Room.

The war was still coming. What they just did only put off the end of mankind for a short time. They all agreed they would not likely have another easy job of attacking or infiltrating any other Invader planets. That option was gone and their security would be tightened. In five weeks, the end was coming. This just gave them a little more time to figure out something else.

Chapter Fifty Eight

"I want to thank you, Deri, for your help back there on the ship. We couldn't have done that without you. You too Braz. Both of you. Without your help, well…you know what we're facing," Jason was saying.

"It is we who should be giving thanks, Jason Brand. It is a distinct honor to be allowed to participate in your efforts. We would have no hope at all without those efforts. So thank you, and you also, Colonel Crozley, and my thanks to your brave beast as well, Jason Brand," Braz answered.

Deri seemed a little melancholy and Braz would go off now and then and have his private chats with his men, again looking over at Jason briefly, and continuing the conversation in private. A team was set up to go through the data captured by Braz and his men, and another to sift through some of the equipment and devices the ground forces gathered.

Two days had gone by and Jason and Gizmo had their grease pencils out now, diagramming time loops and events and sequences on a large board. Strategies and plans had been drawn up and redrawn over and over in the War Room for the coming confrontation.

The coalition of planets would again be assembled, this time without the Grey Ambassador's knowledge, and conquering the Invader Home Planet would happen before Earths near destruction.

Word was being sent out and another attack was being planned with the same goal for the humans: They had to enter and disable their satellites, and then enter the Dome to disable their power source once more. It would take days for most of the coalition to cross the great distances of space and assemble within striking distance un-noticed by the invaders.

While the coalition was gathering, Jason and a crew were about to head out to do some reconnaissance on The Uglies. Team after team had vanished without a word, teams including other Jasons and Gizmos. Time was running out. The Invaders had little information on them except for the locations they had been through and conquered and limited information on their weaponry.

Bo was lying under the table when Jason sat down and gave her a pat on the head. Gizmo joined him, and they both leaned back in their chairs and looked at the board.

"I don't know," Jason said. "I think it might work."

"Might do that. Might do that," Gizmo said. "Let's run it past the General one last time and see what he thinks."

"Killing all those people. That's what I don't like about it, sacrificing all those people. " Jason said, looking over at Deri and asking, "What's the matter Deri. You seem glum."

"Oh, I'm just sad. It's my planet. You can go back five weeks. I'm happy for you, but our invasion happened before that. If you could have gone just a few more weeks," she said.

"We're not done, Deri. We're not done. You too Braz. We're not done. We'll figure this out. When we do, you and your planets are at the top of the list," Gizmo said.

"Five weeks ago, what were we doing?" Jason asked Gizmo.

"We were crawling through that Catskill Chemicals explosion," Gizmo said.

"Well. No way around it. That's as far back as we can go, so that's where we go. We'll wait until we come out of the facility and go give ourselves the news. Hunt down Cody and Eric. Get things rolling," Jason said.

"And we're going to have to get into Ruby Ridge and speak to the General without being arrested," Gizmo added.

"And without being shot. You know, let's take a transport; go visit Dr. Hilliard up at the moon. Maybe even take Hilliard from here to meet himself. You know, in case there is any convincing needed," Jason suggested.

"Yah. He kind of got a kick out of that, showing us that grey alien video up there and watching us to see how shocked we would be. Wait until we show up in another transport and introduce him to himself from the future," Gizmo snickered.

"I wonder how the General is going to react. Hell, I wonder how we are going to react. I just quit my job, remember? I just handed in my notice. You too, Gizmo. We're not going to be in a very receptive frame of mind. Now we are going to find out that we've stumbled into a position where we have to save mankind and all those other species. Hell of a thing to come to work to," Jason said.

"Yup. Hell of a thing. But then there is that instant transfer of information we'll have on our side," Gizmo added.

Jason pulled off his boot and sock and stared down at his toe and rubbed it. "Giz, I have two issues with this whole thing," Jason said.

"What's that?" Gizmo asked.

"Well, first of all, we know that we defeat the Invaders when we invade their planet," Jason said.

"Right. And you become some kind of ruler of the universe as a bonus," Gizmo added.

"Right. So if we go earlier, if we go before the invasion of the Earth, what if we aren't successful? At least we know we did it this time. What if something happens and we don't succeed the second time?" he asked.

"Okay. Possibility, I suppose. What's the second thing?" Gizmo asked.

"The second thing? What if it all works out and everything is back to normal. Earth is back to normal. The Invaders are defeated and The Uglies are dealt with? I mean, really. What are we going to do, Giz? Are you going to go back to your normal life? Wash your car and punch the clock? I can't. I don't know about you, but I can't," he said.

"Nope. I don't think I could. Not with knowing what we know now. So what do you want to do?" Gizmo asked.

"I don't know. But I can't go back to what I was doing. Go back to normal? Paying bills and working for another Borden? I'd be bored to death. Let's make a plan," Jason said.

"Right. A real retirement plan," Gizmo agreed.

Chapter Fifty Nine

During the last two days, scouts had been sent out to gather information on The Uglies. Now that a map had shown where they were, they were being sent to study their offensive capabilities, their weapons and defenses, and mostly, whether they were an actual threat to anyone but the Invaders.

It was a religious interpretation that drove Tarr and the Invaders. This is what they discovered from their records. It was this that molded them for countless centuries into what they were. It was their religion that proclaimed their singular right to exterminate all other life forms. It was this that gave them license to cleanse the expanse of space of all other life.

They sat in the War Room and read it as it was repeated in the heading or in the body of nearly every document: They had been placed by their creator in the universe to compete with all other life forms. It was their duty and it was their obligation to compete that ensured their continuance.

All other life was an infestation; a competing life form. The universe was theirs. So it was decreed, given them by their creator, and all infestations would be removed as competition.

Now, they may have been defeated entirely. This planet Jason had just conquered was their home and there was no other. Aside from minor outposts whose power for weapons depended on their relay, they could find nothing more of the Invader threat. After the bombardment of the planet, only a fraction of their population remained.

As the records and information were being pored over, it began to appear that for all intents and purposes, the war with them could very well be over, but nobody could be certain. There was still the force Tarr was going to use that day to destroy Earth. That was still missing.

Jason walked into the entrance of Ruby Ridge with Gizmo and Bo. Dent was about to send another party into the future. A transport had been outfitted to see what they could from space. They all stood by as the party blinked out of sight and waited, hoping for an instant return, a return that never came.

General Dent shook his head and looked over at Jason. Something was killing them, and they still had no idea what it was. Transports had been sent out into time, never to return. Team after team was being sent to their near certain death.

Dent came over to speak with them. "We have to figure this out. We have to at least be able to see what it is."

Eric strolled over, looking toward the Wave Converter, hoping for something to return. Braz and Deri joined them when the General walked in.

"General. I guess we're about ready," Jason told him.

"This better work, Colonel. I'm not sending any more people to their death. You are the last ones I'm sending," he said. "This is it."

Jason stood and looked down at Bo, then at Gizmo, and then the rest of the crew about to be sent out with him. This time, they would not be going into the future, and this time, they would not be going into the past.

This time, they knew where The Uglies were. This time, they would take it to them, far away from the Earth.

"It'll work, General," Jason said. "We'll make it work. We have to."

THE END: Ron Howson

Look for other books
By
Ron Howson:

Book One in the Ruby Series
RUBY LAKE

and

Book Three in the Ruby Series
RUBY RISING

www.ingramcontent.com/pod-product-compliance
Lightning Source LLC
Chambersburg PA
CBHW060520180626
46817CB00002B/433